Lori

Praise for the novels of Marjorie Farrell

Red, Red Rose

"Powerful and compelling, this splendid reading experience reverberates with the unforgettable intensity of a classic treasure." —*Romantic Times* (4 stars)

"If you like historical romances, if you like strong and admirable heroines, if you like brave and dashing heroes, if you appreciate writing that can, when appropriate, bring tears to your eyes, then you will like *Red, Red Rose*." —*The Romantic Reader*

Journey of the Heart

"Two beautiful love stories for the price of one. Readers get more than the sum of the parts: the relationships are top-rate and believable, and all the characters are wonderful. Fans of western romance will definitely want to take a *Journey of the Heart*."

—*Painted Rock Reviews*

Sweet Awakening

"Rich in detail and filled with adventure. . . . A delightful love story." —*Rendezvous*

"Original and darkly compelling, *Sweet Awakening* is a powerful historical debut for Marjorie Farrell."

—Mary Jo Putney

"Powerful and utterly satisfying. . . . I couldn't put it down!" —Mary Balogh

"A dazzling transition from Regency romance into historical romance. . . . Ms. Farrell mesmerizes us with her masterful characterization in this wonderfully crafted novel. . . . A treasure indeed for your bookshelf."

—*Romantic Times* (4 stars)

LORDS OF LOVE

Jack of Hearts

Marjorie Farrell

SIGNET
Published by New American Library, a division of
Penguin Putnam Inc., 375 Hudson Street,
New York, New York 10014, U.S.A.
Penguin Books Ltd, 27 Wrights Lane,
London W8 5TZ, England
Penguin Books Australia Ltd, Ringwood,
Victoria, Australia
Penguin Books Canada Ltd, 10 Alcorn Avenue,
Toronto, Ontario, Canada M4V 3B2
Penguin Books (N.Z.) Ltd, 182–190 Wairau Road,
Auckland 10, New Zealand

Penguin Books Ltd, Registered Offices:
Harmondsworth, Middlesex, England

First published by Signet, an imprint of New American Library,
a division of Penguin Putnam Inc.

First Printing, February 2000
10 9 8 7 6 5 4 3 2 1

Chapter One

September 1815

"I can't believe you are set on doing this, Anne."

Anne Heriot completed another entry in her ledger before giving her companion a quizzical look. "And just what is it that strains your credulity, Sarah?"

"You know perfectly well. Your stubborn determination to martyr yourself to your father's wishes."

Anne placed her quill in the inkstand, carefully blotted the account book, and closed it. "I assure you, Sarah," she replied calmly, "I don't have the temperament for martyrdom, as you are well aware, having known me these last ten years. Please, sit down and join me in a cup of tea."

Sarah Wheeler took one of the comfortable wing chairs by the fire, leaving the other for Anne. A pot of tea and a plate of crumpets sat on the table between them.

"Shall you pour, Sarah? My fingers are all ink-stained," Anne complained, holding out her left hand.

They sipped their tea quietly for a few moments, and then Anne broke the silence.

"Do you think I am going to London because of my father?"

"Why else? Surely you don't wish it for yourself?"

"But I do."

"You wish to *sell* yourself to the highest bidder?"

"Ah, I see why you are upset. You have got it backward. I am not selling but buying," Anne replied with a twinkle in her eye.

"How can you joke about it, much less contemplate it? Marriage is not a market transaction. We are not speaking of buying a mill, Anne, but a husband!"

"But that is exactly what marriage is, my dear friend. An exchange. 'Your daughter for my son, and the fact that our estates run together, well, all the better.' "

"But that is only how it is with the nobility."

"Oh, come now, Sarah. Even a farmer's daughter knows that her father is looking out for a good match. It is always a matter of money, whether the dowry be five sheep or five thousand pounds."

"Marriage is a matter of the heart!" protested Sarah.

"Well, that is one of the many ways in which we are different," said Anne with an affectionate smile. "I look at the world practically and you, you see it . . ."

"Through rose-colored spectacles! I think not!"

"Of course not. But you are a romantic, Sarah."

"Anyone is a romantic compared to you!"

Anne laughed. They had argued this point so many times before, but their arguments had usually concerned the fates of fictional maidens, such as Marianne of Miss Austen's *Sense and Sensibility*. "I am afraid my mind will always rule my heart, Sarah, but that doesn't mean I don't have one."

"Of course you have a heart, and a most affectionate one where friends are concerned. So why can't you develop an affection for someone in Yorkshire, someone more . . . appropriate?"

"You mean more appropriate for a wealthy mill owner's daughter than an earl or a marquess?"

"You know I don't mean that. Someone who would care for you for yourself, not for the fortune you would bring him."

"And who might that be? Sir Francis Cooper?"

"No, though his fortune is almost equal to yours. But he . . ."

"Is fifty-seven, gout-ridden, and has such pride in his family name that he would never besmirch it with the dust or lint of trade."

"Perhaps Sir Francis was not the best example," Sarah admitted with a rueful smile. "But what of the squire's son?"

"Adam Wentworth? He is three years younger than I, is horse and hunting mad, and hasn't a thought in his head."

"Your cousin?"

"Second cousin. Joseph? My father gave me a choice, you know. He said if I liked Joseph well enough he would not think of going to London. But I don't! And neither do you, Sarah."

"I confess I never have." Sarah hesitated. "Your father was a reserved man, but I would call Joseph Trantor a harsh one."

"I'm not sure I agree with you, but he reveals even less of himself than Father did." Anne dipped her crumpet into her tea and smiled as she watched the edge of it dissolve. "I suppose if I marry an earl I won't be able to dunk a biscuit or a scone."

"If you marry an earl, you will never know what it is to lose your heart to someone, which is more to the point." Or to find it, Sarah added to herself.

"If I marry an earl or a viscount or a baron or a marquess . . . or even a duke," listed Anne teasingly, "I will have a family and children of my own, and my children will know just where they belong."

"I didn't think you cared that much about rank."

"I don't. But I do know what it is like to fit nowhere, Sarah. I am only the daughter of a manufacturer—but I am as rich as Croesus. And educated way above the others of my class."

"You are likely better educated than most young ladies also!"

"Yes, well, that is the point. I am too smart and

too rich for those of my station and yet only a Cit's daughter to the *ton.*"

"Yet you are willing to submit yourself to a year among them?"

"Only a part of the Little Season, to get the lay of the land, as it were. We will be home for Christmas, and if I am lucky, in the spring I will make my choice."

"But . . ."

" 'But me no buts and uncle me no uncles,' " Anne scolded. "I want children, Sarah, and the only way to have them is to marry. And the only men available to me are those who are high in rank but lacking in funds."

"Well, you may be right, but I don't like it."

"Trust me, Sarah. I am nothing if not a good mathematician. I have weighed the debits and the credits, and I will order my life as neatly as I order my accounts!" Anne fell into broad Yorkshire: "Tha knows I am nothing if not a practical Yorkshire lass!"

They were to leave for London in less than ten days, and Anne was praying she would be spared a farewell visit from Joseph Trantor. Her prayers mustn't have been loud enough, she thought as she watched him ride up to the door two days before her departure.

Joseph handed the reins to one of the footmen and strode up the stairs of Heriot House while Anne watched from her bedroom window. She tried to look at her cousin as a stranger might, to see him dispassionately, as a possible husband. He was of medium height and slender without being unmanly. His face was pleasant enough, although his expression was always shuttered. His hair had begun to thin early, and Anne smiled as she saw the sun shining on his balding head and glinting off his spectacles.

Surely a bald head and spectacles should not determine her feelings about a man, she chided herself. For all she knew, her best candidates in London might be bald and myopic.

No, it was something in Joseph himself, though she couldn't quite put her finger on it. She sighed when one of the maids announced him.

"I will be right down, Mary. Have Peters bring us some sherry and biscuits, please." As Mary turned to leave, Anne reconsidered. "On second thought, never mind." I don't want him staying too long or getting too comfortable, she added to herself.

Joseph was in the morning room, looking out the window.

"Good morning, Joseph. It was kind of you to ride over to wish me a pleasant journey."

As he turned and smiled, Anne realized that one reason she wasn't overly fond of Joseph Trantor was his smile. It was as though someone had pasted it on, for nothing of himself was in it. There was no energy in his face, though she knew he was a most energetic worker.

"Tha must have known I would not let tha leave without wishing tha a comfortable journey, Anne."

"Still, you are a busy man and it is a kindness."

"Th'art still determined on this mad idea then, lass?"

Anne hated it when Joseph called her "lass." It was a common Yorkshire expression, but while she felt cared about when her head shepherd or a shopkeeper used it, with Joseph she felt like protesting that she wasn't his "lass."

"You know it is what Father wanted for me."

"I am not so sure of that. Your father . . ." Joseph leaned forward, and the expression on his face was determined. Anne knew he was going to try and broach the subject she had successfully kept him from raising this past year after her father died.

"How are the mills doing, Joseph?" she interrupted quickly.

He sat back. "All is going well, and as tha could see from the latest figures, our profits are up this last quarter."

"My father chose well when he brought you into the business, Joseph." Anne was glad that at least on this subject she could speak warmly and sincerely.

"It were good of him to do so."

"Nonsense. You were his only relative except for me."

"Aye, and he treated me almost like a son, tha father. I am sure he would have welcomed me as a son-in . . ."

"I noticed that the returns from one of the mills—Shipton, I believe—were a little less, though balanced well by the others," Anne interrupted again, to keep him away from the subject.

Joseph frowned. "Aye, Shipton has been a bit of a problem."

"And why is that? It is one of the oldest. In fact, it is the second mill my father purchased."

"It was also the one most influenced by the followers of General Ludd."

"I was away at school when they marched on William Cartwright's mill, but Father sent me the newspaper account. He said we had nothing to worry about, and indeed, by the time I came home that summer we must have had more soldiers billeted here in Yorkshire than on the Continent! I have never understood the workers' dissatisfaction. They earn as much as thirty shillings a week, and they act as though they are superior to other trades," she added indignantly. "Father was always a fair employer, I know."

"Indeed. But there is a young lad now who seems to think he invented Jacobite rhetoric all by himself. He has been influential in slowing down the work."

Anne frowned. "Perhaps I should delay my trip a week, Joseph, and come and see for myself."

"No, lass, 'tis but one troublemaker. I can take care of him."

"Thank you, Joseph. You've become indispensable over these past ten years. I know how fortunate I am to have you."

"I would be nowt but a small farmer were it not for tha father, Anne."

"Nonsense. I cannot see you being satisfied with anything less than an empire, Joseph, albeit only a cloth-making one," teased Anne.

"I'll be on my way, then. Have a safe trip south and don't stay away too long."

"I will be back before the holidays. I wouldn't miss Christmas in Yorkshire."

After her cousin left, Anne walked over to the window and gazed out. Stretching back behind the house was a small expanse of lawn that ended in a stone wall. Beyond that was rougher ground sprinkled with rocks, and the land rose steadily. Only a few sheep were scattered over the hill, for the rest of the flock were still up on high ground for summer grazing. Her father had insisted on raising sheep, though they certainly had no need of the income. "Just so tha and I don't forget where we came from, lass."

Where her father came from was a small town in the West Riding. His mother, a widow with seven children, had sent him off to a factory in order to help support the family. It was a combination of hard work, a shrewd head for business, and a wise marriage that had gotten him all of this.

Robert Heriot had married above his station, for Anne's mother was the daughter of a wealthy farmer. He had made up his mind to have her when he realized she could bring him a decent dowry, one he invested wisely, but he grew to love his wife very much. He had raised himself from very little, her father, and some of it was due to his choice of mate. It seemed fitting to Anne that she continue her family's rise to success in the same manner.

A frown flitted across her face, however, as she thought of the Shipton mill. She had visited only one of her father's factories, and that was just over in Rawley. He had taken her twice, once when she was twelve, and again at sixteen, just before she went off to school. "Tha should see where t'shillings and pence come from that tha'rt so good at counting, lass," he'd told her. But she hadn't really seen much. Just walked down a long room filled with machines, which were silent in tribute to her presence while the men and women who ran them stood at attention.

They had seemed content. As they should be. Her father paid them fairly, after all, and kept the machines in good repair. Well, she couldn't worry about one rabble-rouser, she decided. She had too much to do in the next few days, and if she worried about Joseph from time to time, it was certainly not his ability to deal with the clothworkers that concerned her.

September continued to be a warm month, and Anne and Sarah's trip to London was a pleasant one. They traveled in easy stages, stopping at the most comfortable inns. The roads were dry and smooth, so they made good time despite their leisurely pace and arrived in the city almost a full day before they had expected to.

Anne's first few days were spent getting the London house in order. Her father had purchased a small town house on the edge of Mayfair years ago for his business trips to London. There was always a skeleton staff in residence, but Anne needed to see to the hiring of extra maids and footmen, as well as check the state of the stables. She had not wanted to drag her elderly groom down from Yorkshire, a decision that she regretted when she discovered that the London groom had resigned.

"He said the pay was good, Miss Heriot," said Mrs. Collins, the housekeeper, "but he was that tired of just sitting around. We have a good stable lad, though, who can take care of things until you find a replacement."

Anne sighed. It was one more thing to deal with, and she preferred putting her energy into the business of finding a husband rather than replacing servants.

"Thank you, Mrs. Collins. Will you inform the employment agency that I will start interviewing for a groom next week. And Mrs. Collins, I will need a footman to accompany me this afternoon."

"Of course, Miss. I'll see if William is free."

Anne was just finishing up her breakfast when Sarah came down.

"I am sorry not to have joined you earlier Anne," she apologized. "You know how long carriage trips tire me, and I didn't sleep well. I am not used to the city noises yet."

"You can have a day of leisure, Sarah. I can't get to shopping till tomorrow. This morning I am interviewing maids, and this afternoon I am off to Smythe and Blaine's. Oh, and I must remember to send Elspeth a note."

"Does Mrs. Aston know why you are in town?"

"Yes, and she is as opposed to my plans as you are," Anne admitted. "But she is eager to introduce me into Society. I think she is hoping that if she brings me to enough dances, I will meet someone and fall in love instantly."

"Well, perhaps you will!" Sarah hesitated. "I know the two of you were good friends at school, but will the daughter of an army officer have entrée into the important households?"

"Her mother was the daughter of an earl. And she has married the eldest son of the earl of Faringdon, after all. She assures me that her husband and father-in-law are very willing to take me under their wings."

"Yet her husband was . . . ah . . . illegitimate, I believe?"

"His father recognized him a few years ago after the death of his heir. Of course, Elspeth and Val have been with the army all this time, but now that the war is finally over, Lord Faringdon is happy to have them in London with him."

As Anne gave her note to a footman later that morning, she realized how much she was looking forward to seeing Elspeth. They had met at school when Anne was sixteen and Elspeth a year older, and each recognized the other as a kindred spirit. Both were outsiders—Anne because of her father and Elspeth because she had been following the drum with her parents since she was five. And both were interested in more than the narrow educational pursuits of the gentlewoman, like watercolor or embroidery. They realized how lucky they were to have discovered each other, and also Miss Tillotson, one of the younger teachers, who encouraged Anne's facility with mathematics and Elspeth's with languages and history.

Anne had loved listening to her friend's stories of India and of the many adventures she and her parents had shared in the army. She envied Elspeth for her interesting life, but even more for her loving family. Anne couldn't imagine what it would be like to have two parents, let alone a father who quite clearly adored his daughter. Her own mother had died when she was three, giving birth to a stillborn son, and her father had withdrawn into himself. Always quiet, he gave most of his time and energy to his business. He had hired an older woman as Anne's nurse, but when it became clear that her charge's intelligence far outshone her own, Mr. Heriot had found Sarah Wheeler to be Anne's governess. Sarah had encouraged Anne in her unorthodox passion for mathematics and had helped to create a stronger bond between father and daughter over the accounts and management of the Heriot business.

Anne knew her father had an affection for her, probably loved her in his own taciturn way, but the only warmth he ever displayed was in his approval of her assistance with business. Elspeth's family had sounded like a fairy tale, and she was determined to create something like that for herself. She would likely not marry for love, she realized early on, but there was no reason she could not have a warm and loving relationship with her children.

Anne set off for Smythe and Blaine early in the afternoon. Mr. Blaine was expecting her, and she was shown into his office immediately.

"Miss Heriot, it is delightful to see you again. Please sit down. Would you like some sherry? A cup of tea?"

"A sip of sherry, Mr. Blaine," replied Anne with a smile.

"Here you are, then," said Blaine, pouring them both a glass and taking a seat across from her. "I was very sad to hear about your father's death, and I apologize again for not making his funeral."

Anne's face clouded over for a minute. "He went very suddenly and unexpectedly, Mr. Blaine, and the weather kept many away. But your letter of condolence was greatly appreciated."

"I meant every word. Your father and I have known . . . knew each other for many years, and it was always a pleasure to see him when he was in town. A fine man, Robert Heriot," said Blaine, shaking his head sadly. "But enough . . . what business brings you to London?"

"An unfinished piece of my father's business. I believe you and he had talked of my marriage," she added matter-of-factly.

Mr. Blaine's eyes widened and his face grew pink. "Why, yes, he had told me of his thoughts in that direction."

Anne's eyes twinkled. "I am a Yorkshire lass, Mr. Blaine, and tha knows we don't beat around the bush in Yorkshire. My father and I had no secrets, I assure you. I am here in London to follow out the plans that were interrupted by his untimely death."

"He told me you were a practical young woman,

Miss Heriot. But I thought you might reconsider your cousin, rather than pursue this course without your father's guidance."

"My father and I were in complete agreement, I assure you. He never planned to choose my husband for me, but to provide me with appropriate choices. I hope you will agree to do the same?"

"Of course, Miss Heriot."

"Thank you," Anne said, giving him her warmest smile. "I am here in London for a part of the Little Season to survey the field, as it were. Once I have narrowed down the choices, I will make my final decision in the spring. Now what I need from you is a list of all the titled gentlemen who are in need of my fortune!"

"That would make a very long list!"

"We will make it shorter by eliminating all the inveterate gamblers, drinkers, and hardened fortune hunters, my dear sir."

Mr. Blaine went to his desk and pulled out a piece of paper from a leather folder. "I started just such a list more than a year ago for your father," he said, handing it to Anne. "But there are some we will have to eliminate. George Brett has married, James Trevor died of a fever, and two others fled to America. And there are a few names I could now add to the list."

"Who is the Baron Leighton?" asked Anne, pointing to an underlined name.

"A good choice, I think. He holds an old title, but the estate is very poor. He is a widower of about thirty-seven, I believe. A pleasant man . . ."

"But you hesitate?"

"He has a daughter, about fifteen years old."

"I like children, Mr. Blaine. That is one of the main reasons I wish to marry, to have a family of my own."

"Then we will put the baron on our preferred list."

"What about Lord Beresford?" Anne pointed to another highlighted name.

"Married the daughter of a steel manufacturer in

Sheffield just last month." Mr. Blaine hesitated and then said, "There are two others not yet on the list."

Anne's eyebrow lifted inquiringly.

"Richard Farrar, the earl of Windham, is a delightful young man. He just came into the title. The late earl made some very hard decisions at the time of Waterloo. Sold all his stocks before final news of the victory came through and then went into the woods and shot himself."

"How sad. So Windham was landed with all his father's debts?"

"Yes. He is, as far as I can tell, a very responsible man with a highly developed sense of honor." Blaine smiled. "And young and handsome to boot, Miss Heriot."

"That is not my primary requirement, but it would certainly sweeten a bargain, wouldn't it," Anne responded with a grin.

"Then there is Jack Belden. Viscount Aldborough. He just inherited his maternal uncle's estate in Suffolk. He recently sold his commission . . ." Mr. Blaine's voice trailed off.

"Is there a problem? I promise you I do not require a husband to be young and handsome."

"Jack Belden is twenty-eight, and though he is not handsome in the way Windham is, his looks seem to appeal to many young ladies."

"Is he a rake, Mr. Blaine? That would not do for me either."

"No, no," Blaine reassured her. "Although it is true that before he joined the army he was known as Jack of Hearts, there seems to be no real harm in him. It is just that he is charming to young women. Evidently, each one is convinced that she and she alone holds his attention. I believe that a few of the more susceptible young ladies had their hearts bruised, but he is careful not to promise anything, from what I understand."

"Let's eliminate him," said Anne. "If there is anything I despise, it is a professional charmer."

"I may have painted him too black, Miss Heriot. And the stories I have heard are all from a few years ago. War changes men."

"Not always for the better."

"No, but Lord Aldborough is not a gambler or drinker or confirmed fortune hunter. In fact, you might regard him as a hero. He was one of Wellington's reconnaissance officers."

"Oh, all right, you may put him down. But I will only consider him if the others prove disappointing in some way."

"Good. Then you have three excellent candidates!"

"Yes," said Anne with a satisfied smile. "Now I must set about meeting them."

"Do you have an entrée into Society, then, Miss Heriot? It would be far better if you make your own choice before I open any preliminary negotiations."

"My old school friend is Mrs. Valentine Aston and has offered to introduce me."

"Aston?"

"She is married to the earl of Faringdon's son."

"Oh, yes. That will do very well for you. You won't get a voucher for Almack's due to Aston's, er . . ."

"Illegitimacy?"

Blaine blushed. "Yes, that is what I meant. But the earl has done a good job of making it clear that he would make Aston his heir if he were able to. Mrs. Aston can introduce you to most of the *ton*, and you will have every chance to meet all three men."

"I am sure there will be gossip about my presence in London, Mr. Blaine. But I do not want you to make any approaches to any of the men before I make my decision."

"Of course not."

Anne got up and held out her hand. "Thank you so much. It will be a pleasure to continue to do business with you, Mr. Blaine."

* * *

After Anne left, Blaine knocked on his partner's door, opening it even before he heard a "Come in."

"What did the Heriot heiress want, George?"

"A husband, to put it as bluntly as she did! She is as forthright as her father and of the same practical bent."

"Vulgar?"

"Not at all," Blaine protested. "Would you expect Robert Heriot's daughter to be? There was not a vulgar bone in the man's body. No, she is a very attractive young lady who knows exactly what she wants. I liked her very much. Any one of her candidates would be a lucky man to have her to wife."

"So you've made a list, have you? Who are they?"

"Windham, Leighton, and Aldborough."

"Well done, George. Any one of those should suit."

"They all meet her criteria, but I would like her to find some happiness in this bargain. I have a few reservations—not that I told her, of course. If she doesn't want a drunkard or a gambler, then they really are her best choices, but . . ."

"To take on Leighton's daughter could be difficult?"

"Exactly."

"And Windham?"

"I stressed his sense of honor. But I did not tell her it led him to break off his engagement with Lady Julia Lovett."

"Was his heart given, do you know?"

"I am not sure, and it has been almost a year."

"And then there's Belden," said Smythe dryly.

"Yes, and then there's Belden," Blaine sighed. "If Miss Heriot is out to buy herself a husband, then some might say we ought to pin a sign on Belden—*Caveat emptor*. Let the buyer beware!"

Chapter Two

"So it is marriage or bankruptcy, Stebbins? My cousins out to beg and me God knows where?"

"I am afraid so, my lord."

Every time someone addressed him as "my lord," Jack Belden almost looked to see who had just walked in the room. He had been Viscount Aldborough for five months now, but five years wouldn't be long enough to get used to it. Damn his uncle for getting pneumonia, and double-damn him for producing only girls.

"I'm not ready to set up my nursery, Stebbins," he complained.

"Even so, my lord . . ." That Jack Belden was not ready to be leg-shackled was no surprise to Joshua Stebbins. His client was notorious for his charm and address, but although he readily bestowed them upon one young lady and then another, he had been very careful never to go so far as to place his own heart or hand in any danger. Word was that before he left for Spain, he had become persona non grata in many a mother's eyes, no matter how their daughters lit up when he entered a ballroom. But then, what could you expect from someone a quarter Spanish? mused Stebbins. Had his mother been Spanish, rather than his grandmother, he might well have qualified for Don Juan. Given his uncle's debts and his reputation, he would never find a bride among the nobility now.

"No sensible father will give me his daughter's hand, no matter what sort of dowry she has."

"Not among the nobility, my lord. But a man in trade . . ."

"A Cit's daughter! I don't want to marry some vulgar offspring of a jumped-up unknown, Stebbins."

"It is the only solution I can see, my lord."

Jack groaned. "Unless I could raise a stake and win at vingt-et-un every night, I suppose you are right."

"Perhaps it does not have to be as bad as you think, my lord. I had dinner with an old friend of mine last night, who acts as a solicitor for the Heriot family."

"Robert Heriot? Isn't he the cloth manufacturer from Yorkshire? He was most generous in supplying Wellington with funds, I believe. If it hadn't been for Rothschild and a few like him and Heriot, the army would have starved!"

"Robert Heriot died last year, my lord. But his daughter, Anne, is in London for the Little Season."

"Looking to buy a husband?"

"I understand that you are on her shopping list," Stebbins announced with a wry grin. "She will have none of your gamesters or drunkards, I hear."

"So Miss Heriot is choosy," Jack said sarcastically.

"Should she just fall all over the first wastrel lord who needs her money, my lord?" Stebbins said sharply.

"Why should she, indeed? You are right, of course, Stebbins. So I'm to feel flattered?"

"I think so, although there are a few others under consideration. At any rate, she will be here for the fall and then back again in the spring. I would recommend that you have yourself presented to her. And I understand that you are most charming with the young ladies, my lord," Stebbins added with subtle irony.

"I haven't felt much in the mood for charming anyone since I have been back, Stebbins. But 'needs must if the devil drives,' as they say. I promise you I will do my best."

"I think Miss Heriot would be very suitable for your needs."

"But will I be suitable for hers? Well, thank you, Stebbins."

"Good day, my lord."

After his man of business left, Jack Belden let himself relax his devil-may-care posture. He sat there on the sofa, his shoulders slumped, staring blindly at the carpet.

How had his life changed so drastically in only a few months? In the spring, he had been Major Jack Belden, newly attached to Wellington's army after three years in the mountains of Spain with Julian Sanchez. He had survived *guerrillero* warfare, as well as the hell of Waterloo, only to return home and find himself embroiled in another sort of battle, one he couldn't seem to win. He had had no time to adjust to the change in circumstances, for his mother's brother had left him a bankrupt estate, his widow, and two daughters to assume responsibility for.

When he came to London, instead of setting himself up in bachelor rooms, he had had to move into the Aldborough town house, which had been uninhabited for more than a year. There were still holland covers on much of the furniture, and Jack had not had the energy or the desire to have them removed. Instead of celebrating Boney's final defeat with his fellow officers, he was involved in an ongoing struggle to find enough money from here or there to hold off the most insistent of his uncle's creditors. His money from selling out of the army was steadily disappearing. And instead of setting out to charm the young ladies or to proposition a willing widow, he was being forced to contemplate marriage with some vulgar chit who most likely spoke such broad Yorkshire he wouldn't even understand her when she proposed to him!

He got up and paced the room restlessly. He had craved activity ever since he had landed back in England. Perhaps it was a blessing that he had been thrust into the business of rescuing his uncle's . . . no, *his* estate, for as depressing as the task had been, it did keep him occupied. He needed to *move* in order to escape the dark mood that threatened him every time he sat down.

There was a small, ornate mirror on the wall of the morning room, and he stopped for a moment to stare at himself in the glass. He had the look of a Spanish grandee or an El Greco saint, with black hair and brown eyes so dark they appeared black. His face was long, which lent him a pensive or melancholy look. It was that look that attracted the young ladies, he knew, as he lifted an eyebrow at himself. They all set out to lift his apparent melancholy, and when he smiled, each felt personally responsible. He could laugh and dance and charm the hearts right out of their breasts, or so it seemed to them, and then a few days or a few weeks later he would appear at a ball looking just as beset by the blue devils as before.

His grandmother had once told him that he was a true Spaniard—and born under Mercury's sign to boot. "You have the same bit of darkness in you that I do and your mother does," she had warned him. "Do not think you can outrun it, Juan."

Perhaps he had been running from it all his life, sighed Jack. He had thrown himself into sports in school to overcome the stigma of being part Spanish and so different in appearance from all the other boys. He had thrown himself into the social whirl in the same way, always moving, never resting and never admitting to himself that he might be searching for a place to rest, a place where he could be loved for his darkness as well as his light. He had thrown himself into the army and brought himself to Wellington's attention early on. Living among the *guerrilleros* had meant he was always moving.

It was so hard to be *still*, he thought as he resumed his pacing. He had enjoyed the predawn rides and even the hardship of camping out in the desolate Spanish mountains.

Now that was all done with. The adventures were over, and he was faced with the necessity to settle down. It was not that he was an irresponsible man, he told himself. God knew he had taken on enough responsibility in the army. But the everydayness of what he had taken on weighed him down. As he circled the sofa again, he sat down on the edge and this time, gave way to despair. Dear God, he was going to have to charm Miss Anne Heriot into choosing him above whoever else she had singled out. And if he succeeded, he was going to have to live with her for the rest of his life, marooned somewhere in the Pennine hills. How on earth would he outrun the darkness there?

"Oh, how delightful!"

"What is it, my dear?"

"Anne Heriot has arrived in London, Charles."

Lord Faringdon gave his daughter-in-law a fond look. "Heriot? The name is familiar . . ."

"She is my old schoolmate from Miss Page's, though that probably isn't the reason the name sounds familiar to you, Charles. You probably knew of her father, Robert Heriot."

"Ah, yes, the Yorkshire cloth maker. Richer than the Golden Ball, or so rumor has it."

"Mr. Heriot died last year. Anne is out of mourning now and in London on the business of finding herself a husband."

Charles raised his eyebrows. "A most daunting female."

"Elspeth, daunting?" Val Aston asked as he entered the breakfast room and took a plate from the sideboard. "Intrepid, perhaps, but not daunting."

"I was speaking of a schoolmate of hers, Miss Anne Heriot."

Val dropped a kiss on the top of his wife's head and sat down next to her. "Ah, yes, the Yorkshire heiress."

"Yes, and my best friend at school. We stood out like two sore thumbs there, me being army and Anne coming from trade."

"So she has come to London as she promised?"

"I hope it is for longer than a few weeks, for I would dearly love her companionship for the Little Season. I have been away for so long that I fear I have forgotten everything I know about being fashionable, and that wasn't very much to begin with," Elspeth confessed with a laugh.

Anne looked up from the piece of vellum and said with quiet delight, "Elspeth insists I come to dinner tonight, Sarah."

Sarah breathed a sigh of relief. "Then that means she will take you under her wing this fall."

"I am sure of it."

"Thank goodness, for your alternative plan would not have done at all. Interviewing your candidates as though for a position in your household!"

"Well, a husband is that in a way," teased Anne. "But do me justice, Sarah. That was my plan of *very* last resort. I knew Elspeth would come through. Now, what should I wear?"

Since the two women had spent the last week shopping at the most fashionable milliners and dressmakers, the question was not an idle one. Anne's wardrobe was full to overflowing, and now she who was used to wearing serviceable merinos and muslins was daunted by the prospect of selecting from among the silks and lawns and gauze confections they had bought.

"Something quietly elegant. The apricot silk."

Anne nodded. "Thank you, Sarah. You always know just the thing. And what will you be wearing?"

"Surely I am not invited?"

"Not formally, because Elspeth was unaware that you are here with me. But a respectable young lady doesn't go anywhere without a companion. And besides, you are also my friend and I want you to meet Elspeth. I'll send her a note telling her you are coming. You must wear the lilac wool. It makes your eyes look violet."

Sarah blushed. "You were very generous with my own wardrobe, Anne."

"Nonsense. We must both look our best."

It was worth the hours of standing still while the dressmaker had tucked and hemmed, thought Anne when she saw the look of approval in Lord Faringdon's eyes as Elspeth introduced them.

"I would like you to meet my dear friend, Anne Heriot, Charles."

"I am delighted to meet you, Miss Heriot."

"And I you, my lord."

"And this is Val, Anne."

The words might have been simple, but the pride and love in Elspeth's voice brought home to Anne, as Sarah's words had not, just what she would be missing in a marriage of convenience. But Elspeth was lucky. Most marriages were business arrangements, she reminded herself as she smiled at Valentine Aston.

"I have heard a lot about you, Miss Heriot. I understand you made Miss Page's Academy more bearable for Elspeth."

"As she did for me, Mr. Aston."

"Please call me Val."

"Then you must call me Anne." Oh, dear, she thought wryly as she stole a glance at Val Aston's hawklike profile, I do hope none of my candidates is quite so good-looking or I will be hard-pressed to remain rational. She could well understand why Elspeth had overlooked the circumstances of her husband's birth.

"How long will you be in London?" Lord Faringdon asked.

"Six weeks or so," Anne replied. "I don't want to risk icy weather on my journey home," she added.

"We must see that you enjoy yourself while you are

here. Elspeth was very happy to hear you had arrived," Val told her warmly. "The social whirl is rather foreign to both of us."

"Just where in Yorkshire are you from, Anne?" asked Charles.

"Heriot Hall, is just on the outskirts of Wetherby."

"Why, that isn't very far from us, is it, Val?" Elspeth asked.

"Perhaps fifteen or twenty miles. No more than a day's ride."

Elspeth turned to Anne. "I don't think I told you, Anne, but Val will be taking over one of his father's estates. We hope to be there by the beginning of December. I never realized that we would be neighbors."

"For a while, at least," said Anne with an answering smile.

"So you are still determined to buy yourself a husband?"

"Elspeth!" chided Val. He turned to Anne with an apologetic smile. "You must forgive her outspokenness. If you had ever met my father-in-law, Major Gordon, you would know where it came from."

Anne laughed. "Tha must know it is not only the Scots who are plainspoken. In Yorkshire we don't believe in gilding over plain metal. We all know that I am here to find a husband."

"I gather, then, that this Little Season is to be given over to reconnaissance work," Charles commented dryly. "Valentine might be able to help with that."

"I already have a few eligible suitors picked out, and I will appreciate any advice you have for me as I get to know them," Anne said matter-of-factly.

Sarah, who had been trying to make herself invisible, as she believed a good companion should, said without thinking, "Oh, Anne, you are incorrigible!" with a despairing sigh.

"But we are all friends here, Miss Wheeler," said Charles.

"Oh, it is not so much Anne's plain-speaking I

mind, my lord. And Mrs. Aston opened the subject, after all. It is her willingness to settle for a business arrangement rather than. . . . But I am speaking out of turn," said Sarah, feeling terribly uncomfortable. It was one thing to speak frankly with Anne, who made it so easy to forget they were employer and employee. It was quite another to speak as an equal in a social setting, no matter that these were Anne's friends.

"So you believe in romance, do you, Miss Wheeler?"

"I am not a Marianne Dashwood, if that is what you mean, my lord," Sarah replied, thinking that she might as well be hung for a sheep as well as a lamb. " 'I know how full of briars is this working-day world,' " she added.

"And that 'men have died from time to time and worms have eaten them, but not for love'?" Charles counterquoted.

Sarah smiled. "Yes, I know one does not die from love. But I do think it should play a part in marriage."

"I would have to agree with you, Miss Wheeler," Lord Faringdon said approvingly.

"Love and affection are luxuries," Anne said flatly. "It would be lovely to have them, but they are not necessities."

"I can see you are determined, Anne," said Val. "But we will do our best to guide you to someone with whom there would be some possibility of affection."

"And I would be happy with that," Anne replied.

Later in the evening, after their guests had left, the Astons and Lord Faringdon shared a glass of port in the parlor.

"What did you think of Anne, Val?" Elspeth asked.

"I can understand why you two became fast friends. She is as refreshingly blunt as you, my dear wife!"

"And you, Charles?"

"I would have to agree with Val. She is a very bright, attractive, and down-to-earth young woman."

"By 'down-to-earth,' I hope you do not mean vulgar, Charles," Elspeth said defensively.

"Not at all. 'Gilding plain metal' would be vulgar," the earl said with a smile. "Anne Heriot is very comfortable with who she is and very realistic about her situation. I admire her, but whether she was a young lady of the *ton* or a farmer's daughter, I would still wish her some affection in marriage."

"It is not impossible that it can develop," Val interjected. "After all, you came to love Helen very much, Charles," he added.

"I did. But Anne Heriot will be starting with a greater disadvantage, for she is the one taking the initiative. It is unusual for a woman to do that. She will hold the purse strings and therefore some power in her marriage. She will not be the one who is vulnerable. And one must allow oneself to be vulnerable if one is to find love . . . or even everyday affection. I think Miss Wheeler knows that better than her employer."

Elspeth had decided the best way to introduce Anne to Society would be to invite a select group of friends to a musical evening. "There will be a supper beforehand for some of our intimates," she told Anne. "That way, you can get to know a few influential people who may then invite you to their own entertainments."

"You are sure they will be willing to include me, Elspeth?"

"I assure you, Anne, with the earl of Faringdon's sponsorship, you will be welcome anywhere . . ." Elspeth hesitated. "Well, perhaps not to Almack's, but then, I don't expect to receive a voucher either! I hope you don't mind?" she added apologetically.

"Mind? You are all very kind to be doing this much for me. And from what I hear of Almack's, it is too dull for us anyway!"

There were to be twelve at the Astons' dinner, with

another twenty invited for the music afterward. The duke and duchess of Hairston, old friends of Charles's, were the first to arrive, with their oldest daughter, and then the Viscount Forbes and his new wife. Anne and Sarah were shown into the drawing room next, and Elspeth was just finishing up the introductions when there was a stir at the door. All eyes were turned to the newcomers, one a solidly good-looking young officer in uniform and the other a tall, dark man dressed all in black. Anne's eyes slid over the lieutenant, for although he was a good-looking young man, there was nothing in his broad face and open countenance to spark her interest. There was something in the stance of his elegant companion, however, that held her attention. He stood there as though he expected all eyes to be on him, a fact that annoyed her. At the same time, she had to admit to herself that it wasn't an unreasonable expectation. His long brown face with its melancholy look reminded her of a painting of a Spanish saint. Then, as Val approached with an outstretched hand, the stranger's face was transformed. His smile was utterly charming, and his face went from looking ascetic to faunlike in an instant. It was rather disturbing, Anne decided, as she felt an involuntary shiver.

Val brought the two men over. "This is Elspeth's old school friend, Miss Anne Heriot. Miss Heriot, may I present Lieutenant Brook and Jack Belden, Viscount Aldborough."

Anne could have sworn she saw a look of recognition in Lord Aldborough's eyes, though he gave her only a polite hello. So he may already have heard of her, she speculated as she watched Val introduce the two around. She had not yet mentioned her three candidates to Elspeth, so there was no reason to suspect the Astons of inviting him for her. It seemed that Val and he were old comrades from the Peninsula, so it was perfectly understandable that Jack Belden should be here.

Anne was seated between the duke and the lieutenant at dinner and facing Lord Aldborough, who spent the whole meal, as far as she could tell, regaling the ladies on either side of him with his exploits in the mountains of Spain. After dinner, when the rest of the guests arrived, she couldn't help noticing that at least three of the young ladies in the room made every attempt to draw him away from Lord Forbes's side.

As the concert began, Anne told herself that if Lord Aldborough had not already been at the bottom of her list, he would have fallen there tonight, for there was nothing she despised more than a man who was so obviously aware of his own effect on the ladies, particularly young, susceptible ones like Lady Clarise, the Hairstons' daughter. Thank God, she was neither that young nor that susceptible, she congratulated herself. If Lord Aldborough was looking to restore his fortune through her, then he was going to be sadly disappointed.

Jack was very aware of Anne Heriot the whole evening. She was not at all what he'd expected, although exactly what that was he couldn't have said. He supposed he thought that the daughter of a tradesman would be ignorant, loud, and overdressed. He might also have expected her to seek out his company, once she discovered who he was, given what he knew from his solicitor. Instead, she had ignored him.

She appeared to be one of the most self-possessed women he had ever met. He had watched her during supper. She had given her dinner companions equal attention and seemed not at all overawed by the fact that one of them was a most prominent nobleman.

It had been easy to observe her and at the same time appear to attend only to the duke's daughter. Charming young ladies was like breathing for him—he did it utterly unconsciously. It would have been harder for him not to do it, which was one reason he did not consider himself a rake. He never set out to win a young woman's affection. It just seemed to happen.

Yet now there was someone he needed desperately to attract, and he wasn't at all sure how to do it. He could only hope that whatever drew the young women to him would draw Miss Heriot. Surely even a self-possessed young woman would have some vulnerability to his supposedly infallible charm, he told himself ironically.

He had an odd sinking feeling about the whole enterprise, however, which puzzled him, for it seemed to come not from fear of defeat but fear of success. Yet what was there to be apprehensive about? Miss Anne Heriot was more than he could have hoped for. She was a friend of Elspeth's, and that meant a great deal, for Elspeth was one of the most sensible people he knew She was very well educated and very attractive, in a "nut-brown maid" sort of way.

It was her air of being in charge of herself and the situation that bothered him. If he was able to win her, there would be no doubt about who was in control. Jack sighed. Well, why shouldn't she be? It was, after all, her fortune that could save his estate. He had no right to expect more from a marriage. Like love. In his situation, he would not be making a love match.

He had never thought much about love. Oh, he had basked in adoration of the young women over the years and had never lacked for bedmates, English or Spanish. But infatuation wasn't love. The young ladies did not love the real Jack Belden; they loved some exotic creature that they imagined he was.

Anne Heriot did not look like she had a romantic bone in her body, which, he supposed, was a point in her favor. For if she chose Jack Belden, she would be choosing him for his title, which was at least something real!

Chapter Three

Elspeth had been right, thought Anne, as she sat at the breakfast table a few days later going through the modest stack of invitations. She was probably not being included in the most fashionable parties, but she was sure to meet all three men, either at the duke of Hairston's ball or the Ferrons' supper dance. She sighed happily, which caused Sarah to look up from her book.

"Is anything wrong, Anne?"

"No, that was a sigh of satisfaction, Sarah. Thanks to Elspeth, we will be very busy for the next few weeks."

Anne went back to opening her invitations, and after a few minutes, it was Sarah who gave a sigh as she closed her novel.

"A sad ending?"

"No, a happy one," her companion told her with a smile. "But now I must scour the library for a new read. And your father's library offers very little for a woman's taste."

"You don't need to make do, Sarah. We will take ourselves to Hatchard's this very morning."

An hour later, the young women were walking down Bond Street.

"I can never get used to all this chaos," Sarah said, as the sounds of the traffic and street vendors assailed her ears.

"I find it exciting," Anne confessed. "Though I

admit I would not want to live in London year 'round."

Just as they turned the corner, Sarah almost stumbled over a blind beggar. The man sitting there was dressed in a threadbare uniform jacket. He shook his tin cup as he heard them, calling out, "A penny for a poor soldier." Sarah and Anne opened their reticules at the same time, and Sarah dropped in two pennies, while Anne gave him a shilling. Staring straight ahead, the beggar shook his cup next to his ear and said, "Thank you, ladies," with a smile.

"It's the least we can do for one of our veterans. But how did you know we were women?" Anne asked in a sharper tone.

"Yer lovely lavender water, ma'am. Sure, and it perfumes the street. And doesn't the street need it," he added with a grin.

"Come, Sarah. We wish you well, Private."

"Private? And didn't I make sergeant just before Talavera?"

Anne apologized, "I am sorry, Sergeant, but I didn't notice your stripes."

"Ye can't see what's not there, ma'am. I sold 'em weeks ago."

"And that is a sad commentary on the state of our country, Sarah," said Anne as they crossed the street. "A man gives his sight for his country and must then give up his insignia as well. I think it disgraceful."

"And they are everywhere," nodded Sarah in agreement.

It was lovely to lose oneself among the book tables, thought Anne, feeling guilty at how easy it was to shut out the reality of abandoned war veterans as she paged through a book on modern methods of sheep farming. Sarah had wandered to the table where the latest romances were stacked and had already chosen one by the time Anne reached her side. "I have never read Miss Austen's *Pride and Prejudice,* Anne. I am looking forward to it."

"Choose a second book, Sarah, for soon we will be too busy to shop for such practical pleasures. We will be spending all our time at the Pantheon bazaar!"

"A volume of poetry, then," said Sarah with a grateful glance at Anne, for she knew Anne would respect her independence enough to let her purchase the Austen herself, but would be generous enough to pay for the second book.

They were just out the door, carrying their wrapped parcels, when Sarah gasped. "My God, that dray is out of control, and the sweeping boy is right in his way!"

It seemed to Anne that time stopped for a split second. She saw the boy, his back to the wagon, she saw the left front hoof of the draft horse lifting . . . and then it all moved faster than it could have. All she could hear was the clatter of the wagon and the pounding of hooves as she ran toward the boy. She had almost reached him when she felt herself hit and was knocked to the sidewalk. As she lay dazed in the gutter, all she could think was, But the horse hadn't quite reached us. It took her a few seconds to get her bearings and sort out the voices raining over her.

"My God, did you see that?"

"Anne, Anne, are you all right?"

And the one closest to her, whispering into her ear, "That was as brave a deed as ever I've seen in any battle, ma'am. Let me help ye up. I think ye're only scratched and not harmed."

Anne opened her eyes, and the world spun around for a few minutes and then slowly settled. Bending over her was the blind soldier. How had he gotten across the street? And how could she only be scratched if the horse and wagon had hit her? And the boy? "The boy!" she cried.

"Fine and dandy, miss. I'm just sorry I had to barrel into ye."

Anne began to pull herself up. "Stay still, Anne.

Surely she should stay still, Sergeant?" Sarah asked anxiously.

"No, no, I am fine." And she was, miraculously, though she suspected she'd have a few bruises and be very stiff the next morning. She grabbed the sergeant's outstretched hands and let him pull her up.

"So it was you who hit me and not the wagon," she asked, still a little confused.

"Aye, ma'am."

"Thank you for saving both our lives. Where is the boy?" she asked, looking around.

"Run off, the ungrateful little bug . . . er . . . brat, ma'am. His broom got broke in the fall, and I think he's more scared of his master than he was of that horse."

After two gentlemen had assured themselves of Anne's welfare and complimented her on her courage, the crowd melted away, leaving only Sarah and Anne and the sergeant.

"Surely it took a great deal more courage than mine for a blind man to run into the street like that," said Anne with a grateful smile that softened her sarcastic tone.

The sergeant blushed. "I did lose the one eye, miss," he protested, adjusting the eye patch over his right eye.

Anne really looked at him for the first time. He was a stocky man, who appeared to be in his late thirties or perhaps even early forties, judging from the grizzled look of his whiskers. His thick, curly, black hair was also sprinkled with gray and receding slightly from his forehead. His eye was a bright blue and full of humor, which offset the effect of the patch and the scar that ran from his forehead down his cheek.

"You look like a strong, healthy man, Sergeant, aside from your eye."

"I've always had the luck of the Irish, miss. Just that one saber slash in ten years of fighting."

"How are you with horses, Sergeant?"

"Horses, miss?"

"I am in need of a groom, Sergeant. If you work out satisfactorily here in town, perhaps it could become a permanent position when I return to Yorkshire."

"I am good with most animals, miss. I wasn't in the cavalry, but I've handled horses all me life."

"Then it is settled. There's a small apartment over the stables. If you think it an improvement over where you are living, then you are welcome to move in."

"Anything's an improvement over my flea-ridden room, miss!"

"All right, then. Here is my address," said Anne, handing him a card. "I will expect you by five."

"I can't thank ye enough, Miss Heriot."

"Nonsense, sergeant. You saved my life and the life of that ungrateful little bug . . . er . . . brat," she added with a teasing grin. Anne took Sarah's arm and started down the street.

"Miss Heriot, don't ye even want to know me name?"

"Why, of course."

"Ex-sergeant Patrick Gillen at yer service, Miss Heriot," he said, snapping her a fine salute.

Sergeant Gillen arrived at four-thirty, carrying a knapsack that held all his possessions, and one of the footmen showed him to the stables. "Here is where you will sleep, Sergeant," he announced, opening the door on a clean, sparsely furnished room.

Gillen dropped his bag on the cot in the corner and gave a satisfied sigh.

"Miss Heriot told me to tell you that tomorrow she'll send you to a tailor who can measure you for a new suit of clothes."

"She's a fine lady, Miss Heriot."

"She's no lady, Sergeant, but a Cit's daughter come to London to buy herself a title," the footman replied disdainfully.

"So ye mean that her father actually worked for his

fortune, unlike some of those lazy gobshites that call themselves gentlemen?" Gillen said in a deceptively friendly tone.

"It is my ambition to work in one of the great houses in London, sir. This is only my second position, and I see it as a stepping-stone," the footman replied stiffly.

"Well, I recommend ye find yer next stone, for I'll have none waitin' on Miss Heriot that insults her."

"What gives you the right?"

"No one gives me any rights, boyo. I take what is my right. Now I suggest ye pack yer things and be off before I throw ye off," he added threateningly.

The footman, who was one of the servants Anne had recently hired, evidently decided that the job wasn't worth the risk to his person and his dignity, and he was gone before supper.

"I thought Thomas was to help you serve, Peters," said Anne, as her butler served them their soup.

"Thomas has taken himself off, Miss Heriot."

"Taken himself off? He seemed to be very pleased with the position when I hired him."

"The word is, miss, that your new groom made a strong, ah, suggestion to Thomas." Peter's face showed nothing, but there was a hint of humor in his voice as he announced the facts. He had considered Thomas a young snob who didn't know how lucky he was to be working for a fair and generous employer.

Anne raised her eyebrows. "Sergeant Gillen ran my footman off? Please send for him and have him wait in the library."

"Yes, Miss Heriot."

"She wants me in the library, does she?"

"I am afraid so, Sergeant Gillen. Although I was quite happy to see the back of young Thomas, I am not sure Miss Heriot is."

Shite, thought Patrick as he brushed off his trousers

and smoothed his hair. He should have controlled his temper. But that young fool had irritated him, acting as though he was too good to work for a woman who was braver any thirty omadhauns like him.

He presented himself immediately and had to stand and wait in the hallway until Anne was finished her coffee.

"Go ahead on to the drawing room, Sarah, and I will be with you directly," Anne told her companion. "Good afternoon, Sergeant. I hear that I am minus a footman thanks to you."

"Em, yes, miss."

"You are here less than an hour, and you scare off one of my servants! Did I make a mistake in hiring you?"

"No, Miss Heriot. Beggin' yer pardon, miss. I do have a bit of a temper, though, I'll give ye that."

"But what could he possibly have said to make you so angry?"

"He wasn't respectful, miss."

"What do you mean? He didn't salute you? You are not in the army anymore, you know."

"It was not about me, Miss Heriot. He said something about you . . ."

"About me?" Anne was astonished. "Why, Thomas hardly knew me. I am sure he was treated well . . ."

"It had nothing to do with you, miss. I called you a 'fine lady' and he took the trouble to tell me ye weren't one."

"So tha was defending a cloth maker's daughter, then, Sergeant?" said Anne, her voice softening and falling into Yorkshire, as she occasionally did.

"As I told the young shite . . ." Gillen's face grew red. "I beg your pardon, miss, for my language."

Anne knew she should be shocked, but she was only amused. "I have heard the word before, Sergeant," she told him with dry humor.

"Anyway, I told him he should be proud to work for someone whose money came from honest work, and then I threw him out." Gillen hesitated. "Em, thinking about it now that I am calmer, I could have handled it better. Now I've left you shorthanded."

"I suppose I should dismiss you, Sergeant Gillen, but I must confess that I am grateful to you," Anne told him with a smile. "I don't want anyone working for me who is ashamed or unhappy to be in my service. I value loyalty as much as hard work."

"I promise I won't scare anyone else off," Gillen assured her with a grin. "And ye'll get both loyalty and hard work from me."

"I am sure of it. Are you comfortable in the mews?"

" 'Tis luxurious compared to where I've been, Miss Heriot."

"I will have Peters survey it, and if you need any bedding or furnishings, he will take care of it."

"Did you get to the bottom of things, Anne?" Sarah asked when her friend sat down opposite her. "Do you need to hire a new groom now as well as hire another footman?"

"Sergeant Gillen will do very well. Evidently Thomas was unhappy working in a household whose mistress was not a real lady." Anne said it ironically, but Sarah could hear the hurt beneath the irony. "The sergeant 'suggested' that he find a place more to his liking."

"So you have a loyal supporter."

"It seems I do. And I'll need all the support I can get when even the servants here are snobs. I am beginning to get a little nervous about the ball tomorrow night. I will feel like Daniel walking into the lion's den!'

"I will be right behind you, Anne, and the Astons beside you."

"I appreciate your presence more than you will ever know, Sarah."

And truly, without Sarah at her side, Anne doubted she would have made it up the steps of the Hairston town house. Even though she had met the duke and duchess and knew that the Astons would be there, the sight of all the fine ladies and gentlemen going up the steps made her want to turn and run.

"Maybe leaving all this in Mr. Blaine's hands would have been the better way," she said in a low voice.

"Nonsense," Sarah replied briskly, although she herself was inwardly trembling at the thought of the daunting evening ahead of them. "I may not agree with your method of finding a husband, but if it is to be done, 'twere better it were done . . ."

"Quickly," quipped Anne, with a little of her usual humor.

Sarah smiled. "I was actually going to say 'in person.' "

The duke and duchess were very kind to them on the receiving line, giving Anne a minute or two longer than most of their guests, and thereby signaling that she was someone of importance to them. Even so, when Anne heard "Miss Heriot and Miss Wheeler" announced, she froze at the top of the ballroom steps, feeling that all eyes were upon her, most of them disapproving. But she saw Elspeth moving toward her with an encouraging smile, and that broke her paralysis. She descended the stairs with her head held high.

"You look beautiful, Anne," Elspeth told her as she took her friend's arm. "You are so lucky to be petite," she added. "I always feel like a great gawk!"

"But you have such a slender figure," Anne replied. "And I have always wished for more height. Sarah is just perfect, of course."

"I am a bit too old for perfection," Sarah protested.

"Now don't be nervous, either of you," Elspeth said reassuringly as they approached a small group that included her husband and father-in-law. "Val has made sure that his army friends will keep you busy. But not so busy that you don't have room on your cards for anyone else," she added.

Anne was chagrined to see that Lord Aldborough

was a part of the group, but she supposed it was inevitable that she would encounter him first, given his friendship with the Astons. She acknowledged his greeting with a cool nod and then turned to the others as she was introduced around. Within a few minutes, her first few dances were spoken for, between Lord Faringdon, Val, and two officers. By the time Jack Belden requested a place on her card, the only free dance she had was a waltz.

"I am delighted to take your first waltz, Miss Heriot."

"Thank you, my lord," she replied politely, thinking that her strategy of ignoring him had only backfired. She would have been more comfortable with him in a less intimate dance.

"Come, Anne, I see Lord Windham over there. Let me introduce you," said Elspeth.

So Windham was another one on her "list," thought Jack as he watched Anne walk away. He wondered whether the younger man would be a serious competitor. He was classically handsome, in a very English way, with curly blond hair and blue eyes. From everything Jack knew of him, he was a responsible man of honor who had the sympathy of everyone in Society. His father's suicide had been a topic of gossip for weeks. Then Lady Julia Lovett had broken her engagement to the new earl. Everyone knew, of course, that he had gone to her father first and offered to release her from her commitment. Since theirs had had the appearance of a love match, Society was even more sympathetic to Windham's plight.

Now Lady Julia was often seen in the company of the Viscount Barrett and was rumored to be considering him as a possible husband, And her ex-fiancé was likely going to try to rescue his estate by courting Anne Heriot.

Well, Jack had sympathy for the earl too and hated for him to suffer yet another disappointment. But there were other Cit's daughters waiting in the wings. Anne Heriot was going to be Lady Aldborough, or what was the use of his being the Jack of Hearts!

Lord Windham impressed Anne with his quiet friendliness and, she had to admit, his open-faced good looks, and she was glad that she had been introduced just in time for him to put himself down as her supper companion.

When the music began, Anne was claimed by one partner after another. She was very grateful that the first two were Val and his father, for by the time Lord Faringdon turned her over to Captain Scott, she was relaxed and feeling able to hold her own.

When she heard the orchestra strike up the first waltz, however, she felt her initial nervousness return as Lord Aldborough approached her and led her out onto the dance floor.

"You look lovely tonight, Miss Heriot," he said smoothly as he put his hand around her waist.

"Thank you, my lord."

Lord Aldborough was the tallest of her partners, and Anne had to lift her chin in order to meet his eyes. They were so dark and his face so brown from his years in Spain and his Spanish heritage, that she felt almost blond in comparison, she realized with an involuntary smile.

"Does something amuse you, Miss Heriot?"

Anne could have given him some polite nonsense like "I am enjoying the music, my lord," but for some reason she didn't quite understand, she was her more natural, blunt self.

"I am so used to being considered brown that I am quite enjoying the fact that you make me appear almost fashionably fair!"

"I can sympathize, Miss Heriot, having been considered a singular specimen for years." Lord Aldborough gave a sigh, and Anne was sure it was intended to elicit her sympathy and interest.

"But then tha art a man, Lord Aldborough," she told him in her broadest Yorkshire, "and most likely t'young ladies only find you fascinatingly different! In fact, I've heard tha'rt popular with many of them," she added, with a challenging glint in her eyes. Anne felt as though she'd thrown down a metaphorical glove.

Lord Aldborough sighed again, this time with patent theatricality. "I fear my reputation has reached you already. I assure you, it is quite undeserved," he added as he put a little pressure on her waist to guide her away from an approaching couple.

Anne was very aware of the length and slenderness of his hand through the thin silk of her gown, and she stumbled a little in a sudden return of nerves. Lord Aldborough gently shifted his hand, almost lifting her out of her misstep, and then they were gliding easily around the room again.

She had not anticipated being quite so *aware* of Lord Aldborough, and she was grateful when their dance was over and he returned her to Elspeth and Sarah. Of course, someone so practiced with women would be expert at making them aware of him, she told herself as she watched him approach Lady Mary, the younger daughter of Lord Pringle. As he bent over the young lady's hand, Anne saw her face light up. "No, tha reputation is not undeserved, my lord," she whispered with a sense of relief at the return of her objectivity. "But tha practiced moves will do nowt with me!"

When Lord Windham came to claim his quadrille, Anne gave him her warmest smile. As they were brought together by the patterns of the dance, he complimented her on her gracefulness. Although it was what any partner might have said, Lord Windham spoke with such sincerity that Anne felt disarmed. As they went in for supper, Anne noticed a number of ladies looking at her enviously, and she was secretly amused. Under any other circumstances, it was unlikely that Windham would have asked her to dance, much less chosen her as his supper partner.

But as the two of them chatted over their lobster patties, Anne decided that whatever the circumstances, she liked Lord Windham very much. He was open and natural and sounded genuinely interested in Yorkshire.

"I have heard spectacular things about the dales, Miss Heriot," he told her. "One of my old school friends spent a month walking the Pennines. He found the moors quite romantic!"

Anne smiled. "I love my home, my lord. But I have never thought of the hills and moors as romantic. They are cold, windy, and lonely places, hard on sheep and shepherd alike."

"But isn't that loneliness itself romantic?"

"I am as fond as anyone of long tramps, but I am always glad to return home to a warm fire and a hot cup of tea. If you get to know me, you will find I am a very practical woman. Not a bit of romance in me, according to my companion, Miss Wheeler," she added with a smile.

"I hope I may get to know you better, Miss Heriot," Windham responded, flushing slightly.

"I would like that, my lord."

He gave her a teasing smile. "I am sure, Miss Heriot, that I will discover at least a little romance in you."

"Did you have a good time tonight, Sarah?" asked Anne, as they rode home in the early-morning hours. "I noticed that you had your share of dance partners."

"I should have been sitting with all the other companions. It would have been far more fitting. But Mr. Aston and Lord Faringdon insisted on partnering me, and then their friends followed their example. I enjoyed myself very much," she added, with a half-apologetic, half-defiant laugh.

"I am glad, for no one deserves attention more than

you," said Anne, patting her companion's arm. "Perhaps . . ." Anne gave a soft laugh.

"Perhaps what, Anne?"

"I am laughing at myself. Lord Windham insisted that I must have a little of the romantic in me, and perhaps I do, for here I am, hoping that one of your dance partners will be moved to seek you out as a partner for life!"

"Given my age and circumstances, I think that would be highly unlikely. And don't I sound the practical one of us now!" Sarah gave Anne a smile and then sighed. "I want you to know, Anne, that I am aware that things will change when you marry. I am keeping my eyes and ears open for a family who is in need of a governess or companion."

"How can you even think of such a thing, Sarah? As if I would turn you out! Why, I have never said anything because I assumed you knew I could never do without your company. I am very sorry for my stupidity. Of course, you might have worried. But you will always have a home with me."

"I think I knew that, my dear," Sarah reassured Anne. "But your life will be very different once you marry. Your time and attention will be given to your husband and then your children. And it is not likely that a new husband will want to share his wife's time with anyone else."

"If I'm paying the bills, he will have nowt to say."

"Oh, Anne, that is exactly what I am worried about, and why it is better if I go. Especially given the circumstances of your marriage, you'll need time to forge a relationship. And if you want a happy marriage, you will need to learn how to compromise."

"Mine will be a marriage of convenience, and while I hope that some affection may develop between my husband and me, I will still need a friend near me."

Anne's plea was sincere, Sarah knew. Obviously Anne assumed her life would change only a little when she found herself a husband. And it was for that very reason that Sarah knew she must find a new position, although she dreaded the thought of starting all over with strangers. She could not be a crutch for Anne to lean on. Perhaps Anne would not fall in love with her husband. But at the very least there could be friendship and affection—and how could these develop if Anne leaned on her rather than on her spouse. But she was not going to convince Anne of this now. So she only said, "It is good to feel needed," with a catch in her voice.

"Whom else could I count on but you—or trust with my children? You will forget this foolishness now, won't you?"

"At least until I see whom you have chosen," Sarah conceded.

"If I had to choose tonight, it would be Lord Windham."

"I saw you dancing with him, and also with Lord Aldborough."

"Yes, and I found Lord Windham the far more comfortable partner," said Anne with tart humor.

"Life is not a dance . . ."

"No, but Lord Windham was also a delightful companion at supper. We had a comfortable conversation, and he is taking me out for a drive tomorrow to get to know me better. Of course, any man in his circumstances would be bound to say that, but he really did sound genuine."

"From all I have heard, he is. And what of Lord Aldborough?"

"He's far too practiced with women. I couldn't trust him."

"And your other candidate? Baron Leighton?"

"He was not there, or at least I did not encounter him. And I will keep my mind open until I have come to know all three."

Anne had a delightful drive with Lord Windham the next day. They arrived in the park a little early to avoid the late-afternoon crowds, but there were enough people to cause them to stop often and bow to one or another of Lord Windham's acquaintances. Anne was happy to see that he was not at all hesitant to introduce her, and when they stopped to chat with a few of his close friends, she found them engaging. When he dropped her off, he expressed the hope that she would allow him the pleasure again sometime soon.

Anne had to remind herself that she had not yet met Baron Leighton and although her first impressions of Lord Windham were certainly favorable, she did not really know him well enough to rush to a decision.

Chapter Four

It was at the Lovett musicale that Anne finally encountered the baron. She found herself seated next to a very solid-looking gentleman with a broad forehead made broader by a receding hairline. He gave her a nod as she slipped into her seat just as the musicians struck up the accompaniment for the evening's entertainment, a popular coloratura soprano. Anne was fond of good singing, but had always preferred the contralto voice, perhaps because hers was closer to that range. There was nothing that irritated her more than a singer who chose pieces to show off her ability to trill, and when the audience rose to give Madame Bernini a standing ovation for what Anne thought of as interminable warbling, she was taken by surprise. She stood up so suddenly that her program and reticule fell to the floor. She automatically bent to retrieve them, and her head came into sudden contact with her neighbor's as he reached to help her.

Th'art clearly not a lady, Anne Heriot, she told herself. A lady does nowt but wait for a gentleman to help her! She slipped back into her seat and then realized that the audience was still clapping. She stood again, managing to hold on to her reticule but dropping her program again. This time, however, she only smiled gratefully as the gentleman retrieved it for her.

Finally people took their seats and she turned to thank her neighbor. "You must think me a great gawk," she said with a quick smile. "Thank you for rescuing me twice."

"Not at all, ma'am. If I am not mistaken, we share a dislike of musical pyrotechnics," he added, a mischievous glint in his eye.

"Oh, dear, was I that obvious? I assure you that I do appreciate a good soprano voice, but not when it is used only to impress and not express the music."

"I am in absolute agreement, ma'am."

"I will disgrace myself further, sir, and introduce myself. I am new in London and have not met you yet. I am Anne Heriot. A 'miss,' not a 'ma'am,' " she added with a smile.

"I am very pleased to meet you, Miss Heriot. I am Lord Steven Leighton."

Anne's eyebrows lifted in her surprise.

"You have heard of me?"

"Um, I may have heard your name in passing, my lord," Anne stammered.

"Well, I have heard of you, Miss Heriot."

"Oh, and what have you heard, Lord Leighton?" asked Anne, a slightly defensive tone in her voice.

"Nothing but good, I assure you. That you are an attractive and charming young woman. And I can see for myself that the gossips were right."

Anne could only smile a response, for the soprano was going to sing an encore. The baron shrugged his shoulders expressively and whispered, "I believe we are in for another round, Miss Heriot!"

Anne was too caught up in thinking about the man next to her to pay much attention to Madame Bernini. So this was the baron. He was different from what she had expected. She had pictured him as taller—though where that expectation had come from, she wasn't sure. She had also expected him to be more serious. Surely a widower with a daughter should be more serious. Instead, the baron had a fine sense of humor and a down-to-earth manner. Then it came to her—as soon as she had heard he was a widower with a daughter, she had begun to imagine a younger version of her father, and Baron Leighton was nothing at all like Robert Heriot.

After the concert, the audience retired to the drawing room. Anne had just joined Sarah and a small cluster of acquaintances when Lady Lovett came over with Lord Leighton to them.

"The baron has asked me to formally introduce him. Miss Heriot, Lord Steven Leighton."

Anne offered her hand, and he gave it a light but firm squeeze.

"I am pleased to meet you, Miss Heriot. Did you enjoy the concert?" he asked. To anyone else, it would have sounded like a common polite inquiry, but Anne saw the teasing look in his eyes.

"I did, my lord. Madame Bernini is quite the virtuoso."

"Indeed. May I bring you both some refreshment?" he asked. "And perhaps have the pleasure of sitting with you?"

"You are most kind, my lord," said Sarah as Anne nodded her assent.

When he was out of earshot, Sarah turned to Anne. "So, now you have met them all!"

"Yes, and it was quite coincidental that he was sitting next to me. Come, let us find some seats."

They had just settled themselves when the baron returned with two plates. "I'll be back as soon as I fill one for myself," he promised. He had just hurried off when Aldborough appeared. "Is that seat vacant, Miss Heriot?" he asked.

Anne gave him her sweetest smile. "Oh, I *am* sorry, Lord Aldborough, but Lord Leighton will be back in a minute." Anne gestured toward two young ladies who were watching him. "But I am sure that Lady Charlotte or Miss Sinclair would be happy to have you as a supper companion," she added.

"Thank you for pointing that out to me, Miss Heriot," Aldborough said blandly. He bowed and then sauntered over to Miss Sinclair, who blushed becomingly as he took the seat next to her.

Just as the baron returned, there was a clattering as people set their plates down and began to applaud all over again at Madame Bernini's entrance.

"I am *not* getting up this time," Anne declared, looking over at the baron with a defiant grin. "It is one thing to rescue a lady's program and quite another to pick up her supper!"

Many of the other ladies found themselves in the same predicament and also stayed seated as the singer took another bow.

"My, she seems quite impressed with her own talent, doesn't she?" said Sarah.

"I see your companion is as sensible as you are, Miss Heriot. But I assure you that usually Lady Lovett's performers are not as egocentric. Do you like Mozart, Miss Heriot?"

"I have only heard what Sarah plays on the fortepiano. And a few orchestral pieces performed at local assemblies."

"May I invite you to be my guests at the opera, then? The *Magic Flute* is there next week, and although there are coloratura pieces, I assure you they do not detract from the experience!"

"Sarah and I would enjoy that very much," Anne replied, pleased that her plans were shaping up so well.

For the next few weeks, Jack felt he was back in Spain, pursuing an elusive quarry through the mountains. Except that this time it was not a French dispatch officer that he was after but one very elusive woman from Yorkshire. The treacherous terrain was the drawing rooms and ballrooms of the *ton,* where he had to escape the tactics of several young ladies who, despite their parents' disapproval, were clearly set on capturing the "Jack" for themselves.

"Every time I see her," he complained to Val one

afternoon as they walked down St. James Street, "she is with either Leighton or Windham. I may capture her for the odd dance, and then she tells me in that delightfully down-to-earth Yorkshire accent of hers that Miss Sinclair and Lady Charlotte are giving her hostile glances. She is quite determined to see me as nothing but a rake."

"Surely not that!" said Val with mock horror.

"Oh, it is all right for you to be amused, Valentine. You haven't a widowed aunt and two cousins to support!" Jack's words were light, but Val could hear the real concern underneath.

"Are you determined on Anne Heriot, then? Are there not other rich young women in search of a title?"

"There is Miss Crane, the ironmonger's daughter."

Val grimaced. "I see what you mean. No, she would never do for you. Too young and too mouselike. Her father completely rules her. What about some young lady of the *ton* whose father wishes her to marry up?"

"There may be a few available, but believe me, between the extent of my debts, my reputation, and my Spanish grandmother, no father would give me a second thought. Not when there are men like Richard Farrar around."

"And he seems very intent on Anne."

"Indeed."

"What do you think of her, aside from her money, Jack?"

"I find her conversation blunt, if not bordering on the sarcastic, and she is irritatingly impervious to my so-called invincible charms! I am also convinced that she has made it a point to avoid me. That being said . . . I like her very much!"

Val laughed. "Elspeth was sure you'd deal very well together."

"Was?"

"Well, both the baron and Windham have their strong points. The baron has a sense of humor to recommend him, and Windham is an open-hearted young man who has made a good impression on all three women."

"All three?"

"Sarah Wheeler, Anne's companion."

"Ah, yes, Miss Wheeler. I wonder what her plans are when Miss Heriot marries."

"Anne has assured her that she will always be a welcome part of her household. I don't know what the others will make of that. What about you, Jack?"

"What right would I have to complain? After all, I would be foisting three women on Miss Heriot myself. And I like Miss Wheeler very much, from what I see of her."

The two men walked along for a while, then Val broke the silence. "I shouldn't be doing this, and I don't know if Elspeth would approve of my meddling, Jack, but it seems to me that you should at least have an even chance. My wife and Miss Heriot ride together one or two mornings a week."

Jack looked over at his friend inquiringly.

"I happen to know that Elspeth has to cancel tomorrow. Miss Heriot will be alone except for her groom."

Jack clapped his friend on the shoulder. "I will be forever grateful, Val."

Later that afternoon, Val joined his father and Elspeth for a cup of tea. After clearing his throat a few times, he finally turned to his wife and said, "I have a favor to ask you, Elspeth."

His wife smiled. "Anything, Val."

Val grinned. "You may not be so ready when you know what it is. I want you to send our excuses to Anne for tomorrow morning."

Elspeth gave Val a puzzled look. "Why ever should I do that?"

"Because I told Jack Belden you already had and that Anne would be riding alone."

"That was rather high-handed of you, Valentine!"

"Shall I leave you two to fi—figure this out?" asked Lord Faringdon dryly.

"No, stay, Charles," Elspeth reassured him.

"I thought you favored Jack," explained Val. "And he has not had any opportunities to spend time with Anne. She is always with her other two candidates."

"Don't whine, Val. It does not become you," Elspeth told him tartly, but she softened her words with a smile. "I *did* think Jack would be a good choice, but now that I have seen Anne with the other two men, I am not so sure. She certainly doesn't seem to like Jack very much,." Elspeth hesitated. "On the other hand, I don't think she has given him very much time. It isn't a bad idea, but I will feel like I am betraying my old friend, Val."

"Not betraying, Elspeth. Merely giving her an opportunity to, er . . . make a more informed decision."

Elspeth smiled. "I suppose it is not so awful. And I confess, as much as I like Lord Windham, I can't help wondering if he has conquered his feelings for Lady Julia. And none of us has met the baron's daughter. All right, I'll send Anne a note."

Anne opened Elspeth's note before dinner.

"Will you cancel your ride?" Sarah asked when she heard the reason for Anne's disappointed sigh.

"Of course not. I like to ride before the crowds."

"Do you want me to accompany you?"

"That is very kind of you, my dear," said Anne, her overly sweet tone cut by the look of amusement on her face.

"Oh, all right, I admit I have never been an early riser!"

"I will have Patrick, so there is no reason for you to get up early."

"Good morning, Patrick. It will just be you and me this morning," Anne said with a smile as Patrick gave her a leg up.

"Mrs. Aston will not be joining you, then?"

"No, she wasn't feeling well and wished to sleep in."

They rode down the street, their horses' hooves adding to the clatter of the London morning. When they reached the entrance to the park, Anne motioned Patrick up next to her.

"You need not hang behind, Patrick. I'd appreciate the company while we let the horses warm up."

"Thank ye, miss."

After a brisk walk and trot and then a slow canter, Anne reined her mare in.

"She has such lovely gaits. It is like being in a rocking chair. You have a good eye for a horse, Patrick. Did you raise them in Ireland?"

"Me, miss? Raise horses!" Patrick gave something between a snort and a laugh. "Why, an Irishman couldn't even own a horse worth more than five pounds until recently, Miss Heriot."

"I didn't realize that, Patrick."

"I know horses because my father was head groom at Lord Blount's stable before I joined the army."

"Well, you are a natural with them, Patrick."

"Thank ye, Miss Heriot."

"Why didn't you go back home when you were discharged?"

"Nothing to go home for. Me ma died when I was five. Me da and me sisters and brothers died in 1807."

"I am so sorry." Anne could think of nothing else to say, but without thinking, she reached out and rested her hand on his for a moment.

"Was there no one else to go back to?"

"You mean a woman? No, Mary O'Byrne's father sold her to a rich widower."

Anne was quiet, trying to imagine what it would be like to lose everything that made life worth living. She was so intent on Patrick's story that she didn't notice the approaching rider until he was directly in front of them.

"Good morning, Miss Heriot. What a delightful surprise!"

What an annoying man, thought Anne. He always manages to make it sound like the delight should be mine. "You're up early, Lord Aldborough. And after such a busy evening last night, dancing with all the young ladies."

"Not any busier than yours, Miss Heriot. And not *all* the young ladies. Your dance card was full, as I recall. May I join you now?"

Anne gave Patrick a grateful glance as he kept his gelding next to hers while Lord Aldborough fell in on her other side.

"Will you introduce me to your companion, Miss Heriot? I don't think we have met, Mr. . . . ?"

"Gillen. Patrick Gillen, sor."

"Patrick is my groom, Lord Aldborough."

"But he hasn't always been a groom, I would guess—the army?"

"Former sergeant Gillen of the Connaught Rangers, sor."

"A fine regiment. I was not there, but I heard you and your fellow rangers were splendid at Talavera."

"Thank ye, sor."

Now he was charming Patrick! The man was incorrigible!

"Were you in any battles, Lord Aldborough?" she asked.

Her slight emphasis on "any" infuriated Jack, who had met with that attitude often enough. While some members of Society saw him as a dashing and romantic reconnaissance officer, their adulation more often went to those who had been at Talavera or Badajoz. God knows, he didn't need their adulation, nor did any veterans of those bloodbaths. But the attitude that only Wellington and the British troops had anything to do with defeating Napoleon was an insult to all his Spanish *compadres.*

"Only Waterloo, and there I was only a dispatch officer."

"But I have heard that you were with Sanchez, sor," interjected Patrick.

"I was."

"Then Lord Aldborough would have seen many a small skirmish, Miss Heriot. We were most grateful to ye, sor, for keeping the Frogs occupied! Those *guerrilleros* were much more helpful than any of the regular Spanish troops I ever encountered!"

"Indeed, Sergeant Gillen," Jack agreed with such similar disdain that they both looked at each other and laughed.

"Well, 'tis an honor to meet ye, sor," said Patrick, and he gently reined his horse behind Anne's mare.

"You are a traitor, Patrick," she muttered to herself.

"Did you say something, Miss Heriot?" asked Jack, his eyes dancing.

"It seems I have been ignorant about who won the war. Like everyone, I thought it was Wellington. Now I find I am mistaken."

"Lord Wellington is a brilliant commander, Miss Heriot," Jack told her warmly, "but the one thing the British public doesn't seem to understand is how important it was that Sanchez and Mina and their men kept the French troops busy. Wellington would have been outnumbered otherwise."

Lord Aldborough's voice was calm, but Anne could hear that he was keeping his emotions in check. And from what both he and Patrick had said, the Spanish had played an important role, one for which they received no recognition. She had also heard disparaging comments from time to time about Lord Aldborough's Spanish background, and she felt a sudden onrush of sympathy.

"I apologize, my lord. I had no right to talk about the war, given my complete ignorance of military strategy."

Jack was touched by her obvious sincerity. "Thank you, Miss Heriot. Perhaps I wouldn't be so sensitive if it were not for my Spanish blood."

"I know a little of what it is like to be treated dismissively because of one's birth, my lord," she said sympathetically

"So we do have something in common, Miss Heriot," said Jack, giving her his most charming smile. He hesitated and then spoke again. "In fact, I believe we have more than one thing in common."

Anne raised her eyebrows. "And what is that, my lord?"

Sometimes, thought Jack, once one had reconnoitered and found one's quarry, a head-on attack was the best tactic. He threw caution to the winds. "We are both in search of a spouse."

"You surprise me, Lord Aldborough. I would have expected you to be more romantic in your approach." Anne tried to keep her tone light, but she was irritated all over again. She certainly had no romantic illusions about what she was doing, but she appreciated the tact and sensitivity of Lord Windham and Lord Leighton, and she had to admit she felt insulted that the so-called Jack of Hearts was not even going to try to add her to his roster of romantic conquests.

"Sometimes a direct attack . . . er . . . approach is best, Miss Heriot. And from what I have seen and heard, you are a very practical woman. You know something of my predicament?"

"I know that you've inherited a bankrupt estate and the care of an aunt and two cousins, my lord," Anne admitted stiffly.

"I need a wife with money, Miss Heriot, and I understand that you are looking for a husband with a title."

"You're correct, my lord. But you're by no means the only man in London with a title and no money!"

"Oh, I know that all too well, Miss Heriot," Jack replied with a grin. "I realized I'd better let you know that I am as interested in the position as Windham and Leighton are."

"Position! You speak as if I were looking for a servant."

"Well, it *is* you doing the 'hiring,' as it were, Miss Heriot."

"I am doing nowt in London this fall but becoming acquainted with the *ton* and any, er, possibilities that may present themselves, Lord Aldborough," said Anne, stung into a Yorkshirism.

"An admirable strategy, Miss Heriot, to survey the ground before moving in."

It *was* what she was doing, and a sensible thing too. Surely there was nothing wrong in making a considered choice in something that would determine the rest of her life! Yet he was making it sound as though she was unwomanly.

"Since it will be a lifetime bond, I think choosing a husband an important enough decision to take my time over, Lord Aldborough. Now, if you will excuse me, I need to return home. Patrick?"

Patrick reined up to her, forcing Jack to move away.

"Good day, then, Miss Heriot."

"Good day, my lord."

That's torn it, thought Jack. But damn it, it shouldn't have been a disaster. Anne Heriot was a straightforward young lady. She should have appreciated a direct approach, given what she'd set out to do. She *was* shopping for a husband, and since he was selling himself, it seemed stupid not to advertise the goods, as it were. But where was his famous charm when he needed it?

Chapter Five

Yorkshire—November 1815

"I have to let tha out here, lad. Heriot Hall is about two miles down t'road."

Ned Gibson jumped down from the farmer's cart. "I thank tha, sir. Tha saved me a bit of walking!"

" 'Twas nowt. Good luck to tha."

Ned stood there and looked around. He had left Shipton early that morning and after a three-mile walk had been lucky to hitch a ride with a farmer who was going almost all the way to Wetherby. Despite the bumpiness of the ride and the turnips rolling around in the back of the cart, he had slept part of the way. Now here he was, in a long green valley with sheep-studded hills rising on either side. Shipton was not a large town, but the factory dominated it and made one forget that not very far away were the grassy hills that fed the animals that provided the town's livelihood.

He set off down the left fork of the road, feeling hopeful for the first time in months. He was here hours earlier than he had expected, which meant that even if he had to walk home, he might get some sleep before work in the morning. And he felt more and more confident as he took in the fresh air and watched the frost melt, turning the grass from silver to green. Surely Miss Heriot would listen to him. Surely he could convince her to rehire Nancy. And perhaps he could even get her to consider replacing Peter Brill, that tyrannous bastard who made all their lives miserable.

Heriot Hall faced east, and as it came in sight, Ned watched the morning sun turn the windows gold. He had never seen anything larger than the local squire's house, and he was amazed at the size of the hall. So this was the country house Robert Heriot had purchased from an impoverished London family. He stood in the drive for a few minutes, trying to take in the size of the house, the sculptured shrubbery, and the stables to the left, which themselves looked palatial.

He had intended to go right up to the front door, but he was ashamed to confess that he was too intimidated now, so he made his way around to the kitchen entrance and gave the door a few hard knocks to restore his confidence. He waited for a moment and was just lifting his hand again when the door opened.

"We don't feed beggars here," said the young footman who had opened the door, looking Ned up and down distastefully.

"I am no beggar. I'm an employee of Miss Heriot's coom to speak with her. Could tha tell her that Ned Gibson from Shipton mill has coom to call."

The footman laughed. "A mill worker, are you? Why would you think Miss Heriot would see the likes of you?"

Ned's hands clenched, and he had to fight an urge to reach out and shake the overdressed little toad in front of him. "Mr. Heriot was willing to listen to us. I would think that his daughter would do the same."

"Well, she might, she might not."

"Then why doesn't tha ask her and let her decide for herself?" The mincing little bastard, whose only job was to open doors and serve meals and polish silver, was testing Ned's self-control.

"I would ask her if I could. But she's not here."

"I'll wait then till she cooms back."

"You'd wait for a long time," the footman told him with a smile, "for she's in London."

"In London?" Ned was too disappointed to react to the footman's obvious satisfaction.

'Aye. She is there to shop for a husband. Hopes to get herself a marquess or a duke, does our Miss Heriot."

"When is she expected back?"

"Sometime in the next fortnight. I know she intends to travel before the weather turn too bad."

"Then I'll be back," Ned told him, trying not to let his desperation show. He needn't have worried, for the footman had already started to close the door.

Ned walked around the house and stood in the drive, gazing at the shining windows and the spacious symmetry of the hall. He'd been predisposed to like Anne Heriot, but that was just wishful thinking, he now realized. He'd conjured up a sympathetic young woman in his imagination.

But there was no kind young woman here, he decided—and not just because she was gone from home! Any woman who would take herself off to London to buy herself a title could only be hardhearted and mercenary. She wouldn't be the sort to sympathize with the problems of the likes of Ned Gibson and his fiancée.

It was a cold morning and Ned's coat was thin, but he was suddenly so furious that he didn't feel the cold, only the heat of his anger.

Ned was willing to admit that hard work as well as good fortune had made Robert Heriot successful. But Miss Anne Heriot had likely never done an hour's work in her life and was rich enough to go off to London and buy herself a duke! His Nancy was up before dawn to feed and dress her brothers and sisters and get them off to work. He and Nancy themselves had been working in the mill since they were six, and all so Anne Heriot could loll her life away and then go off shopping for a husband.

Ned was almost to the crossroads when his way was blocked by a milling flock of sheep. He heard a high whistle and saw an older man signaling to one of the two dogs that accompanied him. In an instant the dog circled the sheep and forced them into a tight bunch.

"We'll be out of tha way in a minute, lad," called the old man as he climbed down a stile.

"Tha dog is a reet good one."

"Oh, aye, couldn't do anything without her. Th'art not from around here, lad?"

"I'm from Shipton."

"Near t'mill, then."

"I work there."

"So, tha works with t'wool these silly buggers produce!" said the old man with a smile.

"It would take a lot more of them to keep us in work!"

"Aye, I know that. Mr. Heriot, he liked to have t'sheep around just to remind him where he'd coom from, and Miss Heriot's kept them out. What are tha doing so far from home, lad?"

"I came to see tha mistress, but I hear she's gone to London."

"Aye, poor lass."

"Poor lass!"

The old shepherd gave Ned an inquiring look. "Tha sounds angry, lad. Art foolish enough to think that money is t'only thing that can make tha rich?"

"Maybe I am foolish, but that's what I've always heard," said Ned sarcastically.

"Nay, all t'money in t'world won't buy tha happiness or love."

"According to her footman, that's exactly what it is going to buy Miss Heriot."

"She's set off to get herself a husband, lad, but that does not mean she'll be finding love. Does tha have soomone?"

Ned nodded.

"Then tha'rt richer than she is."

"My Nance just got turned off her job in t'mill because of Miss Heriot."

"How does tha figure that, lad?"

"Nance were happy because we'd just got engaged t'night before. She forgot where she was and she started whistling. T'overseer reported her to Mr. Trantor, and she were turned out."

"And tha blames Miss Heriot?"

"I blame Joseph Trantor, but Miss Heriot is t'owner of t'mill, and so she is responsible."

"Come back in a few weeks, lad, and see her. I'll wager tha'll get satisfaction."

"In three weeks, Nance and her family could be in t'workhouse," Ned said bitterly.

"I am sorry for tha troubles, lad."

The old shepherd was clearly sincere, and Ned was touched by his sympathy.

"Thank tha, sir."

"Coom back in three weeks' time, lad. T'weather will be changing soon; I can feel it in my old bones. Miss Heriot wants to be back before t'cold really sets in. How did tha get here?"

"I walked partway and caught a ride for most of it."

"If tha goes down into town and calls at tavern, tha'll find Josiah Croft. He be as regular as clockwork—has an ale and then drives into Shipton to visit his aunt of a Sunday. Tell him I sent tha. At least tha won't have to walk home."

"Tha'rt reet kind."

"And here, lad," said the old shepherd, rummaging in his coat pocket and handing Ned a few pennies, "buy thaself an ale!"

Ned got back home by six o'clock and went directly to the Hart and Horn, where he knew he would find his brother.

"Ah, there's t'sprout," Tom Gibson called out when he saw Ned come in. "Did tha make it to Heriot Hall, lad? Did tha see Miss Heriot? Did she give Nance her job back?" Tom's tone grew more and more sardonic with each question.

Ned slid onto a bench next to his brother. "I got there all reet, Tom. I didn't even have to walk all t'way, going or coming. But I couldn't see Miss Heriot."

"Tha means t'bitch wouldn't see tha."

Ned looked over at his older brother. Tom's face was red from too many ales and his tone had turned ugly, as it did nowadays after his third drink. Ned sighed. He hated to see his brother like this. Once, Tom had been his hero, one of General Ludd's followers, a man who fought for justice. But that was before he was jailed twice for "conspiring" under the Combination Acts and then lost his job at the mills. For the last two years he'd taken whatever odd jobs he could find, but his wife, Susan, had had to assume the support of their family, and the shame of that had driven him to drink more and more. Ned had had to intervene more than once when Tom had gone after Susan after a night of drinking. His brother was always ashamed in the morning, but by early afternoon he was drinking again.

"Miss Heriot couldn't see me because she wasn't there, Tom. She's in London, gone to find herself a husband," he added with a grin, trying to lighten the tone of their conversation.

"To buy herself one, tha means! Doesn't it make tha angry, Ned, to think that she is buying herself a man with money she didn't lift a finger to earn? That she lives in that big house, while we live in matchboxes? That she'll come home, whistling all she wants over her engagement?"

"Oh, aye, it makes me reet furious, Tom," Ned admitted with a heavy sigh. "But there is little tha or I can do about it."

"Tha art reet about that, little brother," Tom replied, his voice full of self-disgust. "We tried, but they sent out more troops against us than they did against Boney, or so it seemed."

"She's coming back before t'holidays. At least that's what her shepherd told me. A reet nice old man. He told me to coom back then to speak with her."

"It will take more than a pleasant conversation over a cup of tea to change things, Ned, and tha knows it. And in t'meantime, what is tha Nance going to do?"

"I don't know, Tom, I don't know."

London

"How did your encounter with Anne go the other morning, Jack?" Val asked his friend later that week at a supper dance.

"I rushed in, Val, like a fool. I suspect that Leighton and Windham have been more careful. But then, I've never been mistaken for an angel!"

Val laughed. "Nor for a fool. What did you do?"

"I thought Miss Heriot might appreciate frankness, so I referred to our common search for a mate. . . . You know, people are always going on about my damned charm, Valentine. I have no idea what it is! I am just myself with the young ladies, but whatever works with them clearly doesn't with Mss Heriot."

"What works with them is that oh-so-mysterious self, Jack. And that brooding look, which changes so quickly to a smile."

"Oh, give over, Val. Truly, I don't set out to win the young ladies, though I must admit I often enjoy doing so. I suppose that makes me as rakish as they say." Jack groaned. "I had thought that for a practical woman like Miss Heriot, the direct approach would be best, perhaps even original," he added with a grin.

"Just because a woman is direct does not mean she doesn't enjoy a little subtlety, or a little romance. I speak from experience. Anne and Elspeth became friends because they are very much alike in some ways. Elspeth is never afraid of speaking her mind.

Of course, she gets that from her father," Val admitted. "And from what I've heard, Robert Heriot was as unlike Ian Gordon as any man could be."

"How so?"

"There couldn't be a warmer-hearted man than Elspeth's father. So while he may be blunt, one always knows that he has the best intentions. Robert Heriot, from what I hear, was a much colder man. Anne doesn't speak much of him. When she does, it is obvious that she holds him in high esteem. But from what Elspeth has told me, there was very little overt affection in Anne's life. Her mother died when she was very young, you know . . ." Val was silent for a minute. "I know what that is like. And I know what it is like to have little affection in one's life. It does not encourage one to show one's deepest feelings."

"Not like Windham, who is blessed with that damned open countenance," grumbled Jack, pointing across the room to Lord Windham and Anne, sitting with their suppers.

"Actually, Elspeth is a little concerned about him. His engagement to Lady Julia Lovett was rumored to be a love match."

"But he hasn't danced with her much at all, that I can see."

"No, he is avoiding her, and Elspeth fears it is not because of indifference, but from lasting affection."

"You two look like you are planning a campaign, or at least a skirmish," teased Elspeth as she joined them.

"Jack was just telling me that Anne very neatly turned back his frontal assault the other morning."

"Oh, dear, then my deception of an old friend was wasted?"

"Perhaps I must just admit defeat, Elspeth," Jack told her with a rueful smile.

Elspeth sighed. "You know, I would advise you to do so, Jack, if I didn't have some worry about Anne's other suitors. They are both very nice men and seem to be genuinely fond of Anne, not just the promise of her money, but I am not at all sure that the baron's daughter will welcome a stepmother after all this time. And Windham . . ."

"I was just telling Jack about your theory, my dear."

"If there had been no deep feeling between them, I think they would be more casual about their contact. But from what I have observed, he takes care to avoid her. Dances with her only when it would be impolite not to. I just don't trust that his heart is free. A marriage of convenience with the possibility of developing an affection for one another is one thing. But I would not wish Anne to marry a man whose heart is given elsewhere."

'I am heart-whole," responded Jack with a mischievous grin.

"Indeed! And there could be another extreme—a man incapable of giving his heart." Elspeth's tone was light, but Jack was stung by the obvious concern beneath her words.

"I have not yet met a woman who touched my heart, Elspeth, but I assure you, I do have one."

"I am sorry," Elspeth apologized. "I do have a habit of saying what I think."

"Yes, and I was just telling Jack how much like your father you are," Val told her with a grin.

"What are you doing for the holidays, Jack?" Elspeth asked suddenly.

"I had planned to spend them with my aunt and cousins, but I have just heard they are invited to Lady Aldborough's sister's."

"We won't be leaving for Yorkshire for a few weeks." Elspeth looked over at her husband, who gave her an approving nod. "Why don't you join us for Christmas and stay to welcome in the New Year?"

"But this will be your first holiday in your new home," Jack protested. "Surely you don't want guests."

"Charles will be with us. And I intend to invite Anne over."

Jack looked surprised and then pleased. "So you do not completely disapprove of me, Elspeth?"

"Despite all appearances, I have this irrational feeling that you and Anne would do very well together," Elspeth told him with an ironic smile.

"Do come, Jack," urged Val.

"All right, I will. And thank you both for giving me an advantage."

It was an advantage Jack was glad to have, for over the next fortnight, Anne Heriot managed to avoid his company very well. He was able to get only two dances from her, neither of them a waltz, and any time he joined a group that she was part of, she gave him only minimal attention. Lords Windham and Leighton, on the other hand, were constantly at her side. It was hard for Jack to tell if she favored one over the other. He knew Lord Leighton had a good sense of humor, and whenever he saw Anne with him, she was smiling. But the baron was older and losing his hair, Jack would reassure himself, as he ran his hand through his own luxuriant crop.

Windham, on the other hand, was more intense. He and Anne often seemed to be involved in serious conversation. She seemed pleased to be in his company, although he was not as amusing as the baron. On the other hand, he had a full head of hair, and it was guinea gold and curly to boot.

Jack decided to hang back and wait. No matter how appealing either man was, one thing he was sure of—Anne Heriot would make no final decision before the spring.

It was true that Anne had no intention of making a choice until she returned for the Season, and when Sarah asked her one morning whether she had discovered a preference, she told her friend that so far she liked both the baron and Windham equally well.

As she went through the daily pile of invitations, she looked over at her companion. "From what I have seen of the weather, I do not think we'll be able to attend the Spencers' rout. I think we had best be on the road by next week."

"I will be happy to be going home," said Sarah. "I am too old for all this gadding about."

"You had better rest up during the winter, then, for the spring will be far worse. You don't really hate it, do you?"

"Not really. Everyone has been most kind to me. Lord Faringdon always makes it a point to ask me for a dance."

"Do you think there is anything special in his attentions?"

Sarah laughed. "Of course not, Anne. We are just good friends. And the earl of Faringdon is not for the likes of me."

"You are the granddaughter of a viscount, Sarah."

"My father was the youngest son. And I have had to make my own living for so many years that I have lost whatever claim I would have had to social position. And to tell you the truth, I don't think I would be happy as a countess! I have grown too used to our quiet life in Yorkshire."

Anne sighed. "I had hoped you would find someone."

"What is more to the point is whether you have. You must have a preference."

"I am not sure I have a favorite, but Lord Aldborough is last on my list, that I can tell you."

"I rather favor him," admitted Sarah with a shamefaced grin.

"The Jack of Hearts?"

"There is something about him, I can't say what, but I understand why all the mothers are afraid of him."

"Why, Sarah, I am disappointed in you to be so

taken in. But then, you *are* a romantic and I suppose he is the sort of man who would make a perfect hero in one of your novels," Anne teased back. "But he is too sure of his own charm to suit me."

"What of Baron Leighton, then?"

"I enjoy his company very much and we have the same humorous outlook on the world. I think I would find him a good companion, but if I were to choose today, it might well be Lord Windham."

"Yet he doesn't make you laugh as much. On the other hand, he has more hair!" said Sarah with a wicked smile.

"That has nothing to do with it!"

"Nor does he have a daughter."

"I do worry about that," Anne confessed. "But I am going to keep an open mind about the two of them. Steven Leighton's daughter will be in town for the Season, although she is too young to socialize. I will have a chance to meet her. And if I like her, perhaps an experienced husband is the better choice after all."

If Anne had had any doubts about the wisdom of hiring Patrick Gillen, he would have put them to rest by the way he organized their trip back to Yorkshire. Despite the help of her butler and housekeeper, she had taken on the major responsibility for their journey south. But when she summoned Patrick to give him instructions, she found he had anticipated most of what she wanted and volunteered to handle many of the household tasks as well as organizing the horses.

"I can see the advantages of hiring a master sergeant, Patrick," Anne told him after she heard his ideas. "You have it all in hand and leave me with very little to do."

"And that's as it should be, Miss Heriot."

Anne smiled. "I suppose so, but I am very used to assuming responsibilities here and at home."

"Ye'll have to let go of some of them after ye're married, miss, so this will be good practice!"

"Miss Heriot's plans for marriage are none of your business, Sergeant Gillen," said Sarah, who had just come into the room.

"Beggin' yer pardon, Miss Heriot, Miss Wheeler is right." Patrick bowed himself out with a patently false obsequiousness. Anne chuckled as the door closed behind her and then turned to her friend. "I am surprised to hear you being so stuffy, Sarah. Don't you like Sergeant Gillen?"

"I am very grateful to him for saving you, Anne. And, to be fair, he is very competent," Sarah admitted stiffly. "But there is something about him—perhaps it is his Irishness—that I find a bit irritating."

"Why, Sarah, I would never have suspected you of such snobbery."

Sarah blushed. "I do not believe I am a snob, Anne. I certainly do not mean to be. Perhaps I am being unfair."

"Well, you don't have to like him. But I confess that I do. Very much."

Although she hadn't liked what Patrick had to say about sharing responsibilities, Anne had a lot of time to think about it as they traveled the long miles home to Yorkshire.

She had lived a very different life from that of most of the young women she had met in London. While they were perfecting their crewelwork, she had been exploring geometry. Her father may have been emotionally distant, but he had recognized her talents early on and had encouraged them. And when his bookkeeper had retired, he had approached his daughter to take over the work.

She had been happy to do it, for it gave her several hours a week with her father, involved with a common concern. It was probably the closest thing to intimacy she had with him, and she suspected that part of the reason he had asked for her help was to spend time with her in a way that was comfortable for him.

She had hated being sent away to school, but he had insisted. "Tha mun learn pianoforte as well as geometry, lass," he'd told her. "Tha will be living the life of a lady someday, if I have anything to say about it."

She knew he was right when she arrived at school and discovered how different she was from the other girls. Not just in rank, although that was the most obvious, but in experience and interests.

When she returned home, she'd had only a year with her father before he contracted pneumonia. She had continued to keep the accounts despite Joseph's protests that it wasn't proper. What would a husband think of a wife who was bored by the pianoforte and planning the menus? Would a viscountess or a baroness be allowed to take over the bookkeeping of the household? To become involved in the running of the estate? Probably not, but at least she would still have the mills, she reassured herself. Certainly Leighton or Windham would not object to her continued involvement, since it helped provide their source of income.

Of course, neither man had seen that side of her yet. They only knew her as a young woman who danced well, conversed easily with all, and preferred a mezzo-soprano to a coloratura! It would have been considered terribly vulgar to speak of her father's business. To speak of her reason for coming to London. To speak of their reasons for courting her.

Of course, Lord Aldborough had had no fear of being vulgar! He had come right out and said it: "You need a husband. I need a wife." But he didn't know who she really was either.

She didn't think she could become someone else. She was used to assuming responsibility for things, and she couldn't imagine letting someone take over her life. If she had to, she would make sure that her marriage settlement had a provision that assured her of some involvement in the mills, if nothing else!

Chapter Six

Anne had been home for less than a week when Joseph Trantor was announced just as she and Sarah had come down for their daily ride.

"I am sorry to disturb you, Anne. I can come back later."

"No, no, Joseph," Anne replied, successfully keeping the trace of annoyance from her voice. "Patrick has the horses ready, Sarah. Would you tell him that I won't be riding this morning. But you go ahead, if you wish."

"I will, if you don't mind, Anne, for if we are going into town later, I won't have time to get a ride in."

"Come into the library, Joseph. There's a good fire there."

Anne wanted to sit behind her desk to give herself some distance from her cousin, but knew it would be rude to emphasize his employee status, so she sat down in one of the armchairs and motioned him to the sofa.

"I hope you enjoyed tha trip to London, Anne?"

Her cousin's question was innocent enough, but Anne knew that what he really wanted to know was whether she had succeeded in her husband-hunting.

"It was delightful, Joseph," she answered as blandly as he had queried her. It was really none of his business whether she had found any suitable candidates for her hand. Of course, he was probably hoping she hadn't, for that would have put a damper on his own hopes, which she suspected would not be dashed completely until she walked down the aisle with someone else. "I didn't expect to see you until Tuesday. Is there something wrong at the mill?"

She was a little surprised when he gave her a worried look and a nod, for she had supposed he rushed over from personal concern rather than on mill business.

"Have any machines broken down? Are we behind in production?"

"Nowt like that, cousin. No, it is just a problem, a slight problem with one of the workers."

"You are usually very good at resolving such things, Joseph." Indeed, for the most part, her cousin rarely spoke much about that part of his job. Their meetings tended to be about production and profits, not men and women.

"It is one young firebrand, a Ned Gibson."

"Whatever does he have to be fiery about? My father's workers have always received some of the highest wages in Yorkshire."

"Much of it is merely personal. I let young Gibson's fiancée go just after you left for London."

Anne gave him an inquiring look.

"Her behavior was not what your father would have approved, Anne," he explained, sounding a little embarrassed.

Anne assumed young Ned and his fiancée had been caught in immoral behavior. Perhaps the young woman was even increasing. But Joseph would be far too prudish to tell her that, of course.

"It sounds as though you may have been justified in your decision, Joseph, but I suppose the young man finds it hard to accept."

"Yes, and unfortunately, a week later, we had an accident in the carding shed. A child got her hand caught in the rollers. She had ignored the safety regulations your father had set up, of course, but that was all young Gibson needed."

"He hasn't been meeting with other workers, has he?"

"I am sure he has, but I haven't been able to catch him at it. If I could, he'd be up before t'magistrate in a second and spend three months in jail like his brother did before him."

"His brother?"

"Tom Gibson. He was one of the most active of General Ludd's troops three years ago, but his second jail term finally broke his resistance. That and his drinking!"

"Does his brother drink too?"

"I want to say they all do," Joseph replied, disgust in his voice. "Always out at t'local pub after work. . . . But to be fair," he added reluctantly, "Ned doesn't seem to be a drunkard."

"Can we just ignore him?"

"That is one possibility. T'other is to let him go too. But I have no real grounds, and he does now have responsibility for his fiancée's family as well as his own."

"Perhaps I should visit Shipton," Anne said thoughtfully.

"No, no, there is no reason for that," Joseph insisted.

"I haven't been to any of the mills since I was fifteen," continued Anne, "and that was only a short tour. I know so much about them on paper. I think it would be good for me to show my concern. In fact, I am sure my presence could diffuse any dissatisfaction Ned Gibson has generated. Perhaps I could even announce a small holiday bonus!" Anne's face lit up at that inspiration. "Then Ned Gibson will only look like a malcontent."

"I still think it wouldn't be proper, and perhaps not safe . . ."

"Not safe? Do you think him violent, then?"

"I have no real reason to believe so, but one never knows."

"Then I will bring Sergeant Gillen with me. I am sure he can handle one young malcontent."

"You can send the mare back to the stable, Sergeant. Miss Heriot will not be riding today," Sarah told Patrick.

"And what about you, Miss Wheeler?"

"I won't have the opportunity unless I ride this morning. You are to accompany me," Sarah added.

Christ, she sounds like a duchess, thought Patrick, as he summoned a stable lad to unsaddle Anne's mare. As though he would have allowed her to ride alone. But he wasn't looking forward to it, for it was one thing to ride behind Miss Heriot and Miss Wheeler when they were chattin' away, and quite another to follow a woman who for some reason that he couldn't fathom didn't seem to like him. For all that she worked for Miss Heriot also, Sarah Wheeler acted like he belonged to another class entirely—a subhuman one. Of course, most of the English looked on the Irish like that, so it shouldn't surprise him.

"Up ye go, Miss Wheeler," he said as he gave her a leg up.

"Thank you, Sergeant Gillen," Sarah replied stiffly, settling herself into the saddle.

It had been very cold for the last week, but the temperature had risen overnight and now there was a mist rising from the earth that gave the silence in which they rode an unearthly quality. It was only as they began to climb the dale that Sarah could see more than a few feet in front of her. Sergeant Gillen was riding in front, and because Sarah was so intent on what was before her, she really looked at him for the first time.

He was a stocky man, but his seat was relaxed and easy. He was wearing what was obviously an old uniform cloak, and the contrast with his new livery made him look a bit raffish. As they reached the top of the scar, the mist lay below them, and Sarah spoke before she even realized she was going to: "It is so beautiful and so mysterious, isn't it?"

Patrick almost laughed out loud in his surprise. The high-and-mighty Miss Wheeler asking for his opinion? But she was right. It looked as if they had emerged from another world, one suspended in time and space.

" 'Tis indeed, Miss Wheeler. But it is no mystery, only the change in temperature."

Sarah felt irrationally hurt. She had been spontaneous and open, and it did look mysterious, whatever the mundane explanation.

"Of course, Sergeant," she replied stiffly.

Dia, the woman hadn't been friendly since he'd been hired and the first time she was, he went and offended her. "Ye were right, though, Miss Wheeler. Ye'd almost expect to see one of the *sidhe* walking out of that mist."

"The *sidhe*?"

"The shining ones, we call them in Ireland."

"Oh, faerie folk. In Northumberland, where I come from, we have a story of a man who spent seven years with the queen of Elfland or Faerie. In thrall to her. I have always loved that phrase."

"It means to be in bondage. So that man was really her slave, wasn't he?" Patrick remarked.

"I suppose you are right," said Sarah thoughtfully. "I never thought of it like that. I always thought of him as caught by her charm, in thrall to *love*."

"Now what kind of eejit would want to make himself a slave for love? Sure, and that's the last thing love is about."

Sarah felt like she had been slapped in the face. Here she was, discussing her feelings with a mere groom and a crude Irishman at that, and he threw them in her face!

"I wonder that you would know anything of love, Sergeant Gillen, having spent so many years at war."

Jasus, the woman was as prickly as a hedgehog. He could easily have countered with something like, "And ye've spent as many years as a spinster, Miss Wheeler, so neither of us is much of an expert!" But he didn't have the heart to insult her like that, so he took a deep breath before he spoke again. "Now, Miss Wheeler, I wasn't criticizing you, but those songs and stories. It's silly to be quarreling about a thing like that."

"I am not quarreling, Sergeant," Sarah replied frostily and, turning her gelding, she rode on ahead, leaving Patrick to trail behind.

Damn the woman, he thought. But there was something about her that made him feel protective despite himself. Perhaps it was her beauty, for she was beautiful in a pale English sort of way. Maybe it was that, despite her age and experience, she seemed in some ways more fragile than Miss Heriot. He admired his employer, he enjoyed serving her, but when all was said and done, she had more choices in her life than Miss Wheeler had ever had. And he knew what it was like to have few choices.

When they arrived back at the stables, one of the maids from the house was waiting with a folded piece of paper for Patrick.

"From Miss Heriot, Mr. Gillen."

"Thank you, Rosie."

Rosie gave Patrick a quick smile before she walked away, making sure to lift her skirts a little so as to keep them out of the muck of the stable yard. And also, Sarah suspected as she watched, so Sergeant Gillen would have a view of her ankles!

Maybe it was something in the air that Rosie had left behind, but when Patrick Gillen helped her down from her horse, Sarah was very conscious of his hands around her waist. They were rough and large, not gentleman's hands, she told herself, but that didn't seem to lessen the sensation of his touch, which lingered even after he let her go.

"Good day to you, Miss Wheeler," he said as he turned away.

"Good day, Sergeant Gillen," Sarah called and lifted her own skirts, as conscious of the fact that he wasn't watching her neat ankles as she would have been if he had!

"Did Patrick get my note, Sarah?" Anne asked her.

"Oh, yes. Rosie was waiting when we got back."

"*Rosie* delivered it?" Anne asked with a smile. "I gave the note to Frank. She must have charmed it out of him. I'll have to watch that girl."

"I thought she and James were courting?"

"I am sure James thinks so, too. Rosie just can't resist the challenge of a single man!"

"You should speak to her, Anne," Sarah said in a sharp tone so unlike her that Anne looked at her curiously.

"For James's sake, of course," Sarah added.

"Of course. I asked Patrick to get the carriage ready. He will be driving me over to Shipton, so I will not be able to go into the village with you. I am sorry, Sarah."

"You are driving to Shipton? Why, you haven't been there since your father took you years ago."

"Joseph came to tell me of some problems at the mill. It seems there is a young troublemaker there who is making the workers feel ill-used. I thought if I showed an interest and announced a small Christmas bonus, I could defuse whatever grumbling he has tried to start."

"Shouldn't Joseph be taking care of that sort of thing?"

"Actually, I am almost glad this came up. It is silly of me to know so much about the mill on paper and never see the real thing. Joseph will be there to meet me. And I'll have Patrick. I think he looks strong enough to discourage any disrespect."

"Perhaps I should go with you?"

"No, Sarah, it isn't necessary," Anne said firmly. "I appreciate your offer, but as owner of the mill I wish to appear as secure in my position as my father was, and bringing my companion would make me look more like I am going to a local assembly than a place of business. Besides, you had shopping to do."

"All right. But please be careful."

The carriage was ready within half an hour. Patrick handed her in and then placed two hot bricks at her feet.

"It may be a bit warmer today, but 'tis a long ride."

"Thank you, Patrick. I appreciate it."

Anne enjoyed watching the scenery change from large, stone-fenced pasture to small rocky fields. She dozed a little, but at last they reached the town. The mill was on the other side of town, but Joseph had arranged to meet her in the courtyard of the local inn. He was there waiting and climbed in with only a nod to Patrick and a look of disapproval for Anne.

"I still think this is unnecessary, cousin."

As they drove through the town, the houses became smaller and poorer, and Anne commented on this.

"Aye, t'north side is where most of t'workers live."

Despite the poverty, many of the houses had small gardens, and Anne was moved by the skeletal rose-bushes and the last frozen greens. Clearly an effort had been made to add something pretty as well as practical to life. But as she looked down the small lanes, she saw other houses, hovels really, in poorer condition.

"And there is one of t'local pubs," said Joseph, pointing to the other side of the road. Anne leaned over to see better, and as she did, met the eyes of a man who had just come out of the Hart and Horn. He was rough and red-faced and looked at her with such hostility that she drew back immediately.

"Tom Gibson," said Joseph. "Drunk before sun-down, as usual."

"He looks so angry. Could he have known who I am?"

"I doubt it. He is angry at everything, Tom Gibson is," Joseph said dismissively.

"Is this Ned Gibson like his brother?"

"He didn't seem to be, but then, violent natures will always show themselves, sooner or later."

When they reached the courtyard of the factory, Joseph handed Anne out of the carriage.

"Will I come in with ye, Miss Heriot?" Patrick asked her after he climbed down from the driver's seat.

"I think it better if you stay here, Patrick. I am in good hands with Joseph."

"We will walk through the weaving loft, Anne, which is on the second floor. I have told the foreman you are coming."

"I had hoped to tour the whole mill, Joseph."

"Oh, I see no need for that."

Anne said nothing, but decided that if she felt the need to go further, she would do so.

As they climbed the stairs, the racket of the looms grew louder and louder, and by the time they reached the loft, Anne thought her head would come off with the noise. She stood in the doorway and watched as an older, heavyset man hurried toward her.

"This is Peter Brill, Anne," Joseph told her.

"Pardon me? I can't hear anything."

"This is your foreman," Joseph said loudly.

"It is a great honor to have you visiting, Miss Heriot," the foreman said. Or at least that's what Anne thought he said. She certainly hoped so, as she replied, "The honor is mine, Mr. Brill." Please God she had heard his name correctly. How did anyone survive the noise? she wondered as they started down the aisle.

In addition to the noise and the frightening speed of the shuttles, Anne realized that what had seemed to be a haze in the room was actually a cloud of lint.

She had noticed some men and women with handkerchiefs tied around their faces, and now she understood why, as the particles in the air tickled her nose and throat.

When they reached the end of the loft, Brill motioned them outside and shut the door, which cut off the noise a little.

"As you can see, Miss Heriot, your workers are happy and productive. And very well paid, I might add," said Brill, with an unctuous smile.

Anne wasn't sure how he could tell they were happy, but she certainly had the impression that they were swift and efficient, and supposed they would have to be reasonably content to achieve that.

"I thought I might surprise them all and order the machines shut down for a minute or two. Mr. Trantor says you have a small Christmas bonus to announce?"

"I do, but perhaps I could see the carding shed first?"

Brill didn't seem to have heard her. Opening the door, he gave a hand signal and all of the machines stopped.

The silence was almost disconcerting after all that noise, thought Anne. She assumed that after a time her ears would have become accustomed to it. Clearly her workers had had years of this, so the silence was probably nothing to them at all.

Although everyone's eyes were upon her, no one had moved from behind their machines, so Joseph led her forward a little.

"We have the honor of a visit from your employer."

There were a few lifted eyebrows, but for the most part their faces remained expressionless.

"She has a few words to say to you."

Anne's knees suddenly felt shaky, and her throat felt even drier, if that were possible. Just as she was about to open her mouth, she felt a tickle in her nose. She wrinkled it quickly and lifted her hand, but she was helpless before the sneeze.

"God bless tha, miss," called an old man two rows down from her, and everyone laughed, breaking the tension.

"Thank tha, sir," she said with a smile. "Soom of tha may remember me, for I visited t'mill when I were fifteen. But that was more than a few years ago," she added with a smile. "I have been keeping t'accounts of the Heriot mills for many years. When I looked at this year's results, I told Joseph I wished to pay another visit and thank tha for all tha hard work."

Many of the men and women smiled proudly, but there were still a number of faces that were unresponsive. Anne was sure her next words would change that.

"I told Mr. Trantor that I wanted to do something to honor my father's memory and reward you. There will be a small bonus added to tha Christmas pay envelopes."

There were certainly more smiles and the old man who had said "God bless tha" added another one. Yet still some of the workers looked at her expressionlessly and Anne, feeling puzzled and a bit hurt that she hadn't been able to reach them, found herself adding something she had not intended to.

"I also have heard some sad news—that a young child suffered an accident a few weeks ago. I intend to pay an extra bonus to that child's family."

Anne could feel Joseph's disapproval, but the nods of approval from the workers in front of her convinced her that she had done the right thing in mentioning the accident.

"We should let everyone go back to work, Miss Heriot," said Brill. "We don't want them to ruin their production rate now, do we?" he added, with an attempt at humor.

"No indeed, Mr. Brill." Anne had barely finished speaking when the foreman gave another hand signal and the noise began again. As she walked down the aisle, looking right and left and smiling her approval, she received a few curtsies and tugging of hair, but most were intent on their machines.

As they started down the stairs, Joseph said, "I didn't think tha was going to mention anything negative."

"It just seemed the right thing to say, Joseph."

"And I think it were, Miss Heriot," said Brill. "Seemed tha were concerned-like. That and t'bonus should take care of any trouble brewing."

"Thank you, Mr. Brill. And now I would like to see the shed where the accident took place."

Both men began to protest, but Anne held up her hand. "I want to satisfy myself that we are taking sufficient safety precautions, Joseph."

There was only the one large machine where the children worked, so the noise was less. Although Anne knew that children as young as six came to work with their parents, she wasn't prepared for the sight of such small bodies busily picking at the wool and pushing it into the carding machine.

"I am surprised there aren't more accidents," she said, as she watched the small fingers coming so close to the rollers.

"They are well trained, Miss Heriot. See how all of them have short sleeves or their sleeves pinned up? The girl who was hurt had let her sleeves down and one caught in the rollers."

"That is enough detail, Peter," Joseph said sharply. "The child was careless, Anne," he added coldly. "We haven't had an accident here in years."

"You are sure the machinery is in good repair?"

"Absolutely."

Anne sighed. She supposed the men were right. A moment of carelessness in any occupation could lead to injury. Her young kitchen maids, for instance, had to be reminded constantly about the danger of burns.

As they walked back to the carriage, Anne asked Joseph where Ned Gibson worked.

"He was in the main loft, Anne."

"So he heard everything I said?"

"Yes."

"Well, then, let us hope he feels satisfied now."

When they reached the carriage, Patrick was not in sight.

"Where is your groom?" Joseph asked, annoyed.

Anne looked around and then spied Patrick reading a poster next to the entrance. Her curiosity aroused, she walked over to see what interested him.

"What are you reading, Patrick?"

"Sorry, Miss Heriot. I didn't see ye come out." Patrick's voice did not hold his usual friendliness, and as he walked back to the carriage, Anne examined the poster. It seemed to be a list of rules for the workers.

ALL WORK WILL BE DONE IN SILENCE.
ANY INSUBORDINATION TO AN OVERSEER WILL BE PUNISHED BY IMMEDIATE DISMISSAL.
ANYONE WITH LIQUOR WILL BE FINED 2 SHILLINGS.
ANYONE SINGING OR WHISTLING AT HIS WORK WILL BE TURNED OFF.

"What is this, Joseph?" Anne asked, motioning her cousin over.

"That was posted by tha father years ago. Obviously we can't have spirits on the premises, given the machinery we use. Or men wandering around t'mill, leaving their work behind."

"But to be turned off for whistling? Or singing?"

"Think about it, cousin. Anyone with time or inclination to whistle cannot be serious about her work—is, in fact, a careless person and probably very liable to accident."

"I suppose you are right," Anne said hesitantly.

"These rules are no different than any other factory owner's, Anne. In fact, tha father was careful to keep fines lower than most. And of course, t'best way to judge is by t'results."

"Of course."

"Well, your visit has proved very successful," Joseph continued heartily. "The news of bonus will spread very quickly, I'm sure."

They dropped Joseph off in the village, and Anne dozed most of the way home.

Sarah had ordered a light supper for them, knowing Anne's appetite was always diminished after a long carriage ride.

"Was your visit successful, Anne?" she asked when her employer came down to the table.

"I think it was. I managed to get to see the sorting shed as well as the looms, even though Joseph wanted to rush me in and out. I announced the Christmas bonus, and most people seemed pleased . . ." Anne's voice trailed off.

"But?"

"It is one thing to add up the price of raw wool and the cost of steam. It is quite another to walk the floor and not be able to hear yourself think! I never realized how noisy the looms are. And yet people seemed satisfied. Or at least, not dissatisfied," she added. "Many of them didn't seem to have any reaction to my visit. I couldn't tell whether they appreciated it or not."

"And the accident?"

"I must confess it is difficult to watch small children feeding the carding machines, but the safety precautions are made clear to them. The child who was injured evidently forgot to roll her sleeve up, and it got caught in the rollers."

Sarah shuddered involuntarily. "It is hard for a small child to remember or even understand such precautions, though."

"Yes, that occurred to me, too. But without the

children's wages, most families wouldn't survive, would they?"

Anne went to bed early and Sarah stayed up watching the fire in the parlor as it died down from flames to glowing orange coals and then began to go out. What would it be like to send your six-year-old off to a mill? she wondered. Or to hear that your daughter's hand had been crushed in the machinery?

Years ago, when she realized she would be forced to hire herself out, when it became clear that despite her education and gentle birth, she would never enjoy any of the privileges associated with either, Sarah had felt very sorry for herself. Although the self-pity had diminished over the years, there were times even now when a wave of it would wash over her, leaving her feeling bereft of hope and joy. Then she would remind herself how lucky she had been. She was treated more like a friend than an employee. Her duties were very light, and she lived in virtual luxury in a beautiful house with plenty of food. And she was well clothed, she thought, fingering her dark blue kerseymere gown.

She had never given much thought before to where wool cloth came from, which was ironic, since she was employed by one of the largest manufacturers in Yorkshire. For all intents and purposes, her clothes came from the shops in Leeds. They would visit the draper two or three times a year and exclaim over his fine wools and muslins and lawns, never once wondering as bolt after bolt was placed in front of them who had woven the cloth, or even, indeed, if it could have been produced in one of the Heriot mills.

Tonight, however, she wondered. Had a child been injured in producing the lovely blue wool she was wearing? She loved this dress. It made her eyes look darker and bluer, it was comfortable and fashionable at the same time. But once upon a time before it became cloth, this wool had been fleece and had been fed into a carding machine by six- or seven-year-old hands.

But children worked all over England, Sarah told herself. If not in factories, then in mines or in chimneys. She remembered the chimney sweep who had come in just before they left London. His boy was a wizened little creature who scrambled his way up the chimney as though the devil were after him. As she recalled his master's face, she wondered if the devil had indeed gotten after him. Sarah sighed as she scattered the coals. Families needed to live. She was helping her mother in both the house and the garden by the time she was six. It was the way things were. But as she made her way up the stairs, she wondered why the phrase "the way things were" always seemed to refer to the hardest aspects of human life and those associated with the poor.

Chapter Seven

"Did tha see t'bitch, Ned? I saw her coom in through t'village, though I didn't recognize her at t'time. If I had, I would have stopped her and told her a thing or two," Tom added.

"She visited our floor and the sorting shed," Ned answered quietly. He took a long swallow of ale and sighed appreciatively as it eased his throat, which was, as usual, dry and irritated after a day at the loom.

"I hear she announced a Christmas bonus," his brother jeered. "That's to show that Ned Gibson is a wrongheaded troublemaker to take notice of accidents and such. To show they couldn't have a kinder employer than Miss Anne Heriot of Heriot Hall. Things aren't so bad at t'mill, are they? Tom snorted and drained his glass. "And they'll believe it, like the sheep they are."

"It is not as though anyone cheered her," Ned replied mildly, with an ironic smile. "And she did insist on seeing the shed. I'm sure Trantor wanted to hurry her in and out."

"Does tha still think a polite conversation will enlighten her, then, lad?"

"I don't know. I wanted to cheer her for coming, on one hand, for I'm sure no one wanted her here. And I also wanted to shake her till her teeth rattled. There she is, all dressed like a lady while my Nance makes do with twice-turned dresses. Driven in her own carriage and going to marry some sort of lord."

"Once she does that, then tha'rt in the hands of

Joseph Trantor, good and proper. She'll be off on some big estate, enjoying herself in London, and never coom back here. If tha wants her attention, the time to get it is now."

"You're right, Tom," Ned admitted. "I'll have to go back."

The next day when Anne and Sarah appeared at the stable for their morning ride, Patrick was very quiet as he handed them up onto their horses. Usually he had something to say—a comment on the weather or a funny story he had heard in Wetherby.

It was a beautiful morning, cold and clear, and after warming up their horses, they had a fine canter along the top of the scar. Anne welcomed the exercise, for it took her mind off the mill. Although she knew her workers were treated well, the noise of the looms and the sight of the children in the shed had stayed with her.

Patrick was a silent presence behind them the whole ride, however, and finally Anne broke the silence.

"You are very quiet this morning, Patrick. Are you feeling all right?"

"I am fine, Miss Heriot, now that ye ask, but after reading that poster yesterday, I wondered if I should be talkin' at all." The underlying sarcasm in his voice was so patently out of character that Anne looked back, surprise on her face.

"I believe that the rules make sense at the mills, Sergeant Gillen," Anne told him stiffly.

"Sure, and ye probably couldn't hear yerself think in that place anyway, so why be wastin' yer breath on conversation?" This time Patrick's sarcasm was full-blown.

"My father's workers are well paid and well treated. If they weren't, our production levels wouldn't be so high."

"Beggin' yer pardon, miss, but they are not yer father's mills anymore; they are yers. And if all that concerns ye is how they produce, then ye're clearly thinking of yer workers like ye think of yer sheep, Miss Heriot."

"I will overlook your comments this time, Sergeant, because you are an excellent groom and because you saved my life. But I will not be lectured to by anyone on how I manage my factories."

"What I am afraid of, miss, is that it isn't you that does the managin'." Patrick's tone was softer, but Anne was still stung.

"Thank you, Sergeant. I will take your expert views into consideration."

Sarah smiled as Anne spurred her horse ahead of them. Sergeant Gillen ran a poor second when it came to the use of sarcasm. She was surprised at him, though, for he clearly liked and admired Anne. She was also surprised at herself, for she should be indignant for Anne's sake, but instead she was very curious to know what the sergeant had been referring to.

"Did you accompany Miss Heriot on her tour of the mill, Sergeant?" she asked him.

Patrick turned his good side toward her as she pulled her horse next to him. "No, Miss Wheeler. I was waitin' just outside. But ye can hear the racket from there, I promise you. And I had plenty of time to read the rules that are posted. Can ye imagine what it must be like not to share a word with yer mate while ye work? To be dismissed for whistlin', for sweet Jaysus' sake. . . . And I thought the bleedin' British Army was bad!" When he realized what he had said, Patrick blushed and apologized.

"It is quite all right, Sergeant," Sarah replied. "Is Anne aware of these rules?"

"Indade, because I pointed them out to her."

"Are they unusual, do you think?"

Patrick sighed. "Likely not. I believe Trantor in that."

"You don't like Mr. Trantor?"

"I don't."

"Neither do I," Sarah was surprised to find herself confiding in Patrick. "Anne's father was a stern man. He had worked hard to raise himself up, and he believed in hard work. But he was a fair man. I don't think that Joseph Trantor is." Sarah hesitated and then went on. "He wanted to marry Anne."

"God help her if she got into the hands of that one."

"If he had Anne, he would have everything."

"Then I hope she finds herself an earl or a duke quickly," said Patrick with a wide grin.

Sarah gave him an answering smile, then spurred her horse ahead to join Anne.

Maybe Miss Wheeler wasn't as much of a snob as he had thought, mused Patrick, as he watched her join her employer. And maybe he had better keep his gob shut, or he'd find himself out of a job!

It was unfortunate that Ned Gibson chose the following Sunday to make another visit to Heriot Hall, for Patrick's comments had made Anne defensive. She had admired her father and would not allow an employee of hers to criticize his policies, especially when she knew they were no different—no, in some ways, more generous—than others. She pushed down the small stirring of doubt and concern she had felt when confronted with the noise of the looms and the sight of those small fingers feeding the rollers. So when Ned was announced just before Sunday lunch, Anne made him wait in the hall until she had finished her meal and only then had him shown into the library.

He was young, close to her own age, she would guess. He had dressed carefully in what was probably his Sunday best. His suit was clean, although the cuffs were threadbare. He was a pleasant-looking young man, with reddish hair and hazel eyes that looked right into hers, although his face was expressionless.

"What did you want to see me about, Mr. Gibson?" she asked him in her coolest tones.

"I came a few weeks ago, Miss Heriot, while tha was in London. I wanted to talk to tha about t'mill."

"I spoke with my workers on Tuesday, Mr. Gibson. I believe you were there."

"Aye, but tha workers had no chance to speak with tha."

"So you wish to thank me for the Christmas bonus, then?"

Ned was almost stung into telling her what she could do with her bonus, but he reminded himself that he was here for Nance's sake. He'd be damned if he'd act like a grateful child, though, even if she clearly expected him to.

"Nay, Miss Heriot. I coom about Nance, my fiancée. She were let go a month ago."

"I think Mr. Trantor may have mentioned her to me. It was for unwomanly behavior, I believe."

"It were for whistling the morning after we got engaged, miss. She were so happy that she forgot where she was." Which said a lot about Nance's love for him, thought Ned, for it were near impossible to forget tha was in t'mill!

"I don't think it was for whistling, Mr. Gibson, though I understand that *is* one of the offenses you can be turned off for. Mr. Trantor told me, and I do not wish to be critical of your fiancée, but he implied she was dismissed for improper conduct."

Ned's face flushed with anger, and it was all he could do to keep himself under control.

"My Nance is as good a lass as any in Yorkshire. She is responsible for her brothers and sisters, Miss Heriot. She needs her thirty shillings a week. We need it, or we can't marry. I thought you could speak to Mr. Trantor for us."

"Mr. Trantor is empowered to act for me, Mr. Gibson. If I interfere with his actions, I only make his job more difficult. I am afraid his decision will have to stand. But I do not wish any family to suffer at the holidays. I will make sure that Nance gets her Christmas bonus despite the fact she is no longer employed."

Ned wished that she had handed him the money there and then so he could throw it in her face. But God knew, Nance needed it. His voice was shaking with suppressed anger as he said, "There is something else. Little Jenny Warren had her hand crushed by t'rollers in carding machine."

Anne flinched at the picture his words conjured up. "I know, Mr. Gibson," she answered in a softer tone, "and I have asked Mr. Trantor to continue her wages until such time as she can return."

"Does tha think money can give her back her hand? T'doctor said she was lucky not to lose it, but she won't be good for much now but cleaning the sheds. If tha stopped thinking of thaself as 'Lady Bountiful' and had t'old machines replaced, it would do more for us than tha damned bonuses. But tha will only replace machines with ones that replace us," he added bitterly.

"I do what has to be done to keep the factory profitable, Mr. Gibson. You should be thankful profits are steady, because all your jobs are dependent upon them."

"Tha profits are dependent upon *us,* Miss Heriot, and not t'other way around."

"I have nothing further to say, Mr. Gibson. You may count yourself lucky you still have a job after such an outburst," she added, reaching over to pull the bell rope next to her. When Peters opened the door in response, she merely said, "Please show Mr. Gibson out."

Ned turned on his heel and was out the door without a "Thank you for seeing me" or any such acknowledgement that he was lucky to have such a receptive employer, thought Anne. Well, she was not going to think of Ned Gibson again. She would concentrate on getting ready for her visit to the Astons.

* * *

"But, Sarah, you must come with me."

"Is that an order, Anne?" Sarah asked, trying to tease her friend out of her disappointment.

"If it is, it is the first I've given you, you must admit!"

"I know. But I truly would prefer to stay here, and you don't really need a companion for a visit to such close friends. You and Elspeth don't need me haunting you."

"You know we both enjoy your company," Anne chided.

"I just feel that I would enjoy having some time alone after all the socializing we did in London. I can't really explain it."

"Then there is no need to, Sarah. I am sorry for pressuring you. After two months in London, you deserve to have the kind of holiday you want. But if you change your mind and feel lonely, I want you to promise you will have Patrick drive you over."

"I promise."

"All right, then. Now, which dress do you think I should pack for Christmas Day?"

Sarah was happy to turn her attention to whether green sarcenet or gold silk was more appropriate, for she hadn't wanted to be pressured into saying anything more about her decision. It had come to her a few nights ago that for some reason, after all these years—and even after a very enjoyable time in London—she could not bear the thought of spending another holiday as an appendage. Oh, she knew she was genuinely welcome at the Astons' and trusted that they liked her for herself. But the thought of being neither fish nor fowl, family nor friend, was suddenly unbearable. Heriot Hall was the closest thing to a home she had, and she wanted to spend Christmas there, even if it was alone. In fact, she was beginning to realize she was more and more dreading the idea of Anne's marriage and the subsequent move. It occurred to Sarah that she might even eventually ask Anne if she could make a permanent home here at the hall. Perhaps she could act as housekeeper, rather than look elsewhere for employment. Mrs. Pendrake was getting old and close to retirement. She would consider those decisions when she came to them; for now, she would have almost three weeks free.

She was surprised at the relief she felt when she used that word. She had never felt that bound. She loved Anne, had loved her from the beginning when she came to act as her governess. But her life had been given over to Anne for many years. Once Anne had a husband, Sarah knew suddenly, but deeply, she wanted to reclaim her own life. It might be constrained by lack of money and opportunity, but at least it would be her own.

Anne set off to the Astons' three days before Christmas, with James, her coachman, driving. Her stated reason was that she wanted Patrick in charge while she was away, but truly she decided she did not want to be reminded of her trip to the mill. She wanted to enjoy her holiday with no thought of looms or carding machines.

Not that Patrick had said anything more to her. He had gone back to being his usual friendly self, or so it seemed on the surface. But Anne thought she could detect a reserve, a holding back, perhaps even disappointment. Well, let him stew in his disappointment, she thought as she put her head back against the velvet squabs of the carriage, after waving good-bye to Sarah and her critical groom.

Ripley was only twenty-odd miles from Wetherby, so it was a pleasant day trip broken only by a stop for lunch. They arrived just after dark, as the moon was rising, and when the carriage pulled up in front of the house, the door opened into a hall filled with warm golden light, profiling Elspeth and Val, who were waiting to greet their guest. Val's arm was around his wife's shoulders, and for one moment Anne felt a wave of loneliness engulf her. Then she was pulled into the warmth and light and shook herself, as though she were shaking the cold and dark away.

"You must be chilled," said Elspeth. "And hungry. Supper is waiting."

"I'm not that cold, but I am ravenous," admitted Anne with a grin.

"Here, let me take your cloak, and Elspeth will show you your room. If she can find it," Val added. "We are still trying to get used to all this space!"

"Yes, after years in army tents, I am suddenly responsible for a mansion," laughed Elspeth. "I only know my way around a part of the house so far. Lucky for you, it included the guest bedrooms."

Anne was shown into a charmingly decorated room, hung in blue, with a small fire blazing on the hearth.

"There is warm water on the washstand, and I can send Lucy up if you need a maid. But don't think you need to change for supper. It is only the three of us."

"I'll just wash up then, Elspeth. I am too hungry to waste any time on my dress," Anne said gratefully.

"Then we'll see you downstairs shortly."

Anne brushed her dress off and, tying a linen towel around her shoulders, splashed her face and hands. Even though it had been a short trip, it was good to be able to stretch—and wonderful to be visiting friends. It would have been a lonely Christmas at home. Not her first one without her father, but the first when the household would not be in mourning. She was glad to be here.

When she was shown into the dining room, she found Elspeth and Val sitting opposite each other. "Come and join us, Anne. We've saved the head of the table for you. Would you like some wine?"

"No, thank you. I might just fall asleep on you if I did."

"I hope supper does not seem too light," Elspeth apologized. "It is only a clear soup and then roast chicken and vegetable. Even that seems a lot to me after army fare. But it is nothing compared to those dinners we have been consuming in London."

Anne laughed. "Yes, and I must have put on five pounds my first week there. I am happier with plain fare myself."

"We will have to lay out a better table for my father and Jack, of course," Val reminded his wife.

"Jack?" asked Anne, trying to remember if some cousin or other had been mentioned as a guest.

Elspeth gave her husband an exasperated look. "Jack Belden. Lord Aldborough. His parents are away, and we extended him a last-minute invitation. I hope you don't mind?"

"Of course not," Anne replied evenly. What could she say? The Astons certainly had the right to invite any guests they chose, and Aldborough was a friend of Val's, as she was a friend of Elspeth's. It shouldn't feel like a conspiracy . . . but it did. For a moment she felt very disappointed. Then she rallied. Tha will not let tha Christmas be spoiled by that man, Anne Heriot, she told herself firmly.

"When do they arrive?" she asked brightly.

"My father will be here tomorrow, and we expect Jack by Christmas Eve."

"I am sorry Sarah did not come," added Elspeth. "She would have evened out our numbers. Charles very much enjoyed her company in London. Was she feeling ill?"

"No, but London tired her out," Anne replied. "I made her promise to have Sergeant Gillen drive her over if she felt lonely."

"Well, she would have plenty of time to rest here, for we are planning a very quiet Christmas," Elspeth told her friend apologetically. "We are not well acquainted with our neighbors yet, although we have received a few invitations for the holidays. I hope you don't mind?"

"Not at all. This is only the second Christmas I have spent without my father, and I am happy just to be with good friends."

As Anne got ready for bed, however, she hoped they would attend some local parties, for a quiet holiday with Val and Elspeth was one thing, but an intimate Christmas with Jack Belden was quite another.

Chapter Eight

"You are sure you don't want to use the chaise, my lord? The wind is blowing from the north-east, and I wouldn't be surprised if we had snow by Christmas."

"I'm sure," Jack told his groom. "I am quite used to long, cold rides, you know."

"Then I'll have Sancho ready for you early tomorrow morning."

"Thank you, John."

"But why you want to ride in this weather is beyond me," muttered his groom as Jack left the stables. "You'd think three years in Portugal and Spain would have been enough for you!"

Jack could have given him a reason or two, had he asked. First, it would be much cheaper. Taking the chaise would mean changing teams and patronizing larger inns, those that could handle the carriage trade. Riding meant he could stop at the smaller taverns.

God, it was depressing to be constantly worried about funds. He hadn't needed much money in the army. And he hadn't spent any of his pay, except to treat Sanchez and his men to wine every now and then. It seemed that all he'd thought about, worried about, since he'd returned to England was money, or rather the lack of it.

And coming here to Aldborough, he'd had to face his uncle's wife and her hesitant, apologetic questions about the two girls, who would be coming home from school for the holidays but didn't know if they would be returning?

Thank God, his aunt and cousins were going to her family in Surrey. And thank God for Val's invitation, or he might have been tempted to run off and reenlist, the title be damned. The thought of sitting here for two weeks, worrying about the three women who depended upon him and his marriage for their future. . . . He had to move, he had to ride; he had to do something or he'd fall into a black hole of despair again.

Jack was up early the next morning, feeling more like himself than he had in a long time.

"It's good to be on the road again, eh, Sancho," he'd said as his gelding gave a happy shake of his head and almost danced down the drive. "We may not be after the Frogs, but we do have an important mission: to convince one reluctant Yorkshire lass that marriage to yours truly would be far preferable than to any of her other suitors. Surely winning Miss Anne Heriot can't be any more difficult than defeating Boney!"

By the end of the first day on the road, the temperature had dropped, and Jack was very happy to see the light of a small tavern winking out at him. He settled Sancho himself and then happily joined the other customers around the taproom fire. He was wearing an old military cape that he'd wrapped around him many a cold night in Spain, so the men around the fire saw only a returned soldier. It was wonderful to let the title slip from his shoulders. In fact, it was so good not to be Lord Aldborough that Jack drank a little more hot punch than he had planned to and woke late, with the kind of head one gets after drinking cheap liquor. It took several cups of strong coffee before he was ready to leave.

By now, the wind was blowing directly into his face and his pace was slower. He wrapped his long wool muffler around his face, but by late afternoon the bones in his forehead were aching from the cold, and his hands, despite sheepskin gloves, were stiff.

It took much longer to get to the next town where he had planned to lodge, and by the time he arrived he was frozen through, thoroughly miserable and thoroughly happy. He had been right not to take the chaise. This was exactly what he needed—to push himself, to keep moving despite cold or discomfort until he got to that place where one existed only in the present moment, in the next breath, the next gust of wind, the cramping of the fingers, the air so cold that the nostrils stuck together with each breath. All else was forgotten in the need to go on.

And then, of course, when one stopped and found shelter and warmth and light, there was such a sensation of calm, of floating in the moment rather than struggling through the moment. Every bit of consciousness became focused on the now, and all else fell away.

The way to climb out of that black hole, thought Jack, as he fell asleep on his lumpy bed, is to keep moving, to distract from the mind's discomfort by providing the body with some.

It was snowing when he started out the next morning, large crystal flakes that fell softly and silently at first, glittering like diamonds in the early-morning sun. But by noon the wind was up, the sun was completely gone, and the flakes had shrunk to stinging pellets. Sancho's head was down as he picked his way carefully over the road that soon became a narrow path over a corner of the moor.

They were very close to Ripley, but these last few miles would be the most difficult, Jack realized, as the sky grew darker and the snow was driven into their faces. He finally dismounted so he could lead Sancho and feel for the path himself. Thank God he was one of those men who had something like an inner compass, a sense of direction that rarely failed him, or he would have been worried.

He was worried a little later when he realized that a "moment's rest" had turned into a quarter hour of dozing against Sancho's shoulder. It would be ironic to have survived years of winter in the Pyrenees only to sleep himself to death in West Riding! He clapped his hands together and stamped his feet and, pulling at Sancho, forced them both into a quicker pace.

"We should be very close," he told the gelding half an hour later. His face was so stiff he could hardly talk. But for the next fifteen minutes he began to doubt himself. And curse himself. "You're a bloody fool, Jack Belden. *Soy loco, verdad,* Sancho?"

And then in the whirling whiteness, he saw a light and then another. At first he wondered if he was imagining things, but then a recognizable shape formed.

"Gracias a Dios," he whispered fervently. *"Somos aqui!"*

He went right up to the front door and began pounding.

"Who on earth could that be in this weather?" Elspeth exclaimed. She and Val and Charles were in the drawing room, waiting for Anne to come down before they went in for supper.

"If I were a betting man, I'd say Jack. But even he couldn't be so mad as to set out in this."

"We were expecting him today," Elspeth told Charles. "But we assumed he would be a day or two behind schedule because of the weather. No carriage could have made it through the snow."

The door sounded again. "I am too curious to wait, Val," said Elspeth, so they all trooped out into the hall.

The door opened on an apparition in blue and white.

"Are you going to keep me standing out here in the cold, then, Val, because I'm a few hours late?" Jack could feel the joy bubbling up from deep inside. He was here! He was alive!

"My God, you are a madman!" exclaimed Val. "How ever did your carriage get through?"

"I didn't drive. I rode, and I need to take care of Sancho before I do anything else."

"Summers, get Bob out here immediately to take care of Lord Aldborough's horse."

Jack protested, but Val just grabbed his friend and pulled him in. "Get in here, Jack. You must be near frozen."

"I am frozen," laughed Jack. "I'll have to thaw off here in the hall, or I'll ruin the furniture," he added as he stamped his feet. "I apologize, Elspeth, but they are blocks of ice."

"Let me get some warm water, Jack. Sit down on the bench and take your boots off. Charles, Val, help him, please. The last thing we need is a guest with frostbite."

"You are an amazing woman, Elspeth," said Jack appreciatively.

"Quite," declared Charles with a quiet irony as he and Val pulled at the boots.

"Here, this should be big enough for you to stand in," announced Elspeth, as she and a footman came in with a roasting pan from the kitchen and a pitcher of water. "Take his cloak, Samuel. And here, Jack, take my shawl," she added, pulling the plaid wool off her shoulders and wrapping it around him.

Anne had heard the pounding as she was getting dressed. When she came down the stairs, she was greeted by the sight of Jack Belden standing in the front hall, his feet in a roasting pan, his shoulders draped in plaid wool, and his face turning from livid white to beet red as he warmed up.

Anne was so struck by the absurdity of the scene that she sank down on the third step from the bottom and gave herself over to laughter.

All four turned to her in surprise.

"Oh, dear, I am sorry, Elspeth, Lord Aldborough,

but you look so . . ." She went off into another gale of laughter.

It took only a moment before they were all howling with her, Jack included.

Finally their hysteria subsided and after catching her breath, Elspeth asked, "How are your feet, Jack?"

"Burning like the devil."

"Good. That means you won't lose anything. Not that you don't deserve to! Whatever made you do something so foolish?"

"Don't ask, my dear. I thought I could outride the weather."

"Well, you are here and safe and that is the important thing. Are you hungry?"

"Ravenous!"

"Why don't we be very informal tonight, Elspeth?" said Val, his eyes twinkling. "We can have a small table set up in the drawing room and that way we can have Jack's . . . er . . . roasting pan with us."

"Oh, God, don't start me laughing again," complained Jack. "Enough of me is hurting as it is. And I think my feet are thawed enough to leave the pan behind. Just give me some stockings from my bag and I'll hobble into the dining room."

After her uncharacteristic lost of control, Anne felt very self-conscious. She didn't know Jack Belden well, and she had never laughed at anyone before. Though she hadn't been disposed to like him very much, one thing she had to admit was that he had one quality to recommend him—the ability to laugh at himself.

But what on earth would make a man want to ride in this weather? Surely it was not sensible to risk your life on a routine peacetime journey. One did not expect someone who looked like a Spanish saint to be setting off on irrational adventures.

After supper they all returned to the drawing room, where Elspeth had port and biscuits sent in.

"When did you decide to ride, Jack?" asked Val.

Jack, who had settled himself into a comfortable armchair, looked over at his friend. "Don't you ever get bored, Val? Do you never miss riding out on reconnaissance?"

Val gave him a quick grin. "There *is* something about constant danger that makes one feel more alive, I have to admit."

The combination of a full stomach, the warm fire, and the port were having a strange effect on Jack. He felt like he was floating above himself and able to say anything. "I needed to move. I needed a purpose. And I didn't have the damned money for the coaching inns," he added with a sleepy grin.

Elspeth and Val traded quick, concerned glances.

"If you are in need, Jack, you have only to ask."

"No, no, 'tis only that I am at the end of the quarter. The estate still brings in a little income."

There was an embarrassed silence, then Anne turned to Elspeth. "Where are your parents this Christmas, Elspeth?"

"Still in Spain, I'm afraid. They will be here next month. I would have loved to see them at Christmas, though. Especially this Christmas," she added, giving Val a little smile. "So I am particularly happy to have you and Charles. And Jack."

When there was not even a polite murmur from Jack, they all looked at him, then exchanged smiles with each other. Jack's eyes were closed and his head slumped back against the chair.

"I'm not surprised," said Val. "He must be exhausted."

"Shall I wake him?" asked Elspeth.

"No, let him sleep. He'll probably awake later. I'll have a footman on duty to show him up to his room."

"Well, I am about ready for bed myself," said Charles.

"And I," Anne agreed.

Elspeth pulled a small throw off the sofa and tucked it over Jack's knees.

Anne stood there watching her. No, the truth was, she was gazing at Jack Belden. The combination of shawl and coverlet should have made him look ridiculous again, but somehow it did not. There was something in the bones of his face, in the long, slender fingers that rested on the arm of the chair; there was a tension in the air around him, despite his apparently relaxed state. She could imagine him as a soldier or a buccaneer—asleep, but with some part of him vigilant. She supposed it would take a long while for a soldier to lose that vigilance.

"He is one of a kind," murmured Elspeth. "And a very handsome one to boot," she added, as they left him there by the fire. "It is a shame you don't find him attractive, Anne."

"Isn't it?" murmured Anne with a light touch of irony in her voice. She gave Elspeth a good night and made her way upstairs.

But later, as she settled herself in bed, the image of Jack sleeping came back to her, and she felt an overwhelming urge to touch those long, sensitive fingers.

When Jack awoke the next morning, he found himself in what was presumably his room with no memory of how he had gotten there. The late-morning sun was pouring through the half-opened curtains and he got up, grimacing at his stiffness, and walked over to the window. The snow had left a sparkling blanket on the trees and lawn. It was not as deep as he had expected, however, which surprised him, given his struggles of yesterday.

He looked down at his feet. They were intact, thank God. He had been lucky to reach the house when he did. And lucky that Elspeth was so quick with her roasting pan of warm water. He had looked ridiculous. No wonder Anne Heriot had gone off into gales of laughter. So much for getting her to fall for his charms these next few weeks. If she hadn't responded to him in London, then she certainly would not after seeing him last night.

He still had on his shirt, but someone had stripped off his breeches. He trailed his fingers in the basin of water on the washstand. The water was warm, and he took his time washing and shaving. Someone had been by this morning, for his maroon jacket was hanging in the wardrobe, brushed and pressed, and his corduroys were folded over the chair. He dressed quickly and glanced in the pier glass. He still looked a bit travel-worn, but other than that, he saw no reason that Miss Heriot should find him amusing!

Chapter Nine

If Jack had not known it was Christmas Eve, he would have guessed it from the delectable spicy smells coming from the kitchen, which started his stomach grumbling. He found his way into the breakfast room, where Val's father was still seated.

"Good morning, sir."

"Good morning, Jack. Are you recovered from your ride?"

"Almost. My legs are still protesting. I haven't spent three days in the saddle for a while," Jack admitted with a rueful grin.

"Val is in the library. He told me to tell you he'd be free at lunchtime. Elspeth and Anne are in the kitchen, helping the cook stir the Christmas pudding."

"The smell reminds me of when I was a boy. I can't remember my last Christmas in England."

"Yes, it is wonderful to have 'peace on earth' become a reality and have . . . all of you home."

Jack knew from the slightly hesitant and wistful tone that the earl was thinking of one who hadn't made it home.

"You must especially miss Charlie at this time of year, Charles," he said, with quiet sympathy.

"I do, Jack, I do. I will never get used to his loss. But I am very grateful to have had my oldest son spared to me."

Jack helped himself to a generous plate of ham and eggs.

"Coffee or tea, Jack?"

"Tea, please. God, there is nothing better than to sit down to a good breakfast after a long march."

"You miss the army?"

"Oh, I don't know," Jack said with a confused smile. "I do miss the challenge and the sense of purpose, and even sometimes the danger. Everyday life feels somewhat like a let-down, although I know that sounds absurd and ungrateful."

"No, I think I can understand."

"There are few people who do. And my war was a very different one from that of the everyday soldier. Val is one of the few who knows what it was like, which is why it is so good to be here."

"Not to mention the pleasure of Miss Heriot's company," Charles added teasingly.

"I may appreciate her presence, but I very much doubt she'll take pleasure in mine."

"The famous charm not working, eh?" asked the earl, with an ironic lift of his eyebrows.

"Whatever it is that draws the young ladies has no effect on Miss Anne Heriot, I assure you. And looking like an old granny last night did not help!"

"Oh, I don't know," said Charles with a laugh. "She seemed to appreciate the scene."

"God, I did look ridiculous, didn't I? Ah, well, maybe I'll have to seek out another heiress in the spring," he added, with an only half-humorous sigh.

After breakfast, Jack wandered into the library, where Val was still examining the account books.

"It's Christmas Eve, Val!"

"I know. That's what Elspeth says. But I feel like I need to get a handle on the estate as quickly as possible. I promise I'll be finished in half an hour, Jack."

"Don't worry, I'll find something to read." Jack pulled down a volume of poetry and wandered out to the hall, where the kitchen smells were even more intense. He couldn't help it; he had to follow his nose.

Elspeth and Anne were standing by a large copper basin, taking turns stirring the Christmas pudding.

"Good morning, ladies."

"Jack, just what we need! Another arm to give it a stir," said Elspeth with a welcoming smile.

"Have you put the charms in yet?"

"They are right here," Elspeth told him, pointing her spoon at the little silver objects.

"Well, drop them in, Elspeth, and I'll make sure they are thoroughly mixed," said Jack, taking off his coat and rolling up his shirtsleeves.

Anne watched as the charms disappeared into the batter, and then her attention was drawn from the raisin-studded pudding to the strong arm mixing it. Lord Aldborough might be on the slender side, but his arms rippled with well-developed muscles as he stirred. Anne stepped back as she felt a warmth flood her that she suspected had less to do with her proximity to the stove and more with the closeness of that brown arm. She fussed with the copper bowl intended for cooking the pudding.

The cook returned just as Jack gave one last stir. "Na then, my lord, let me do the pouring," she said as she shooed them away.

Jack shrugged his coat back on, and he and Elspeth went out, leaving Anne struggling with her apron strings.

"Tha can't concentrate, eh, lass," teased the cook. "I don't blame tha, what with that handsome gentleman around."

"It's just tied too tight," Anne replied. As she was folding the apron she saw the slim volume that Jack had left on the table. "Lord Aldborough must have brought this in," she said.

"Well, tha had better return it, then, lass," the cook told her with a wink.

Elspeth had wandered into the library to see if she could drag Val out, and Jack had just been heading into the drawing room to read when he realized that he'd left his book behind. He met Anne halfway down the corridor.

"I believe this is your book, Lord Aldborough," she said.

"Ah, there is my book . . ."

They both spoke at the same time, and Anne gave a nervous little laugh.

"I was just about to take advantage of the fire in the drawing room, Miss Heriot. Would you care to join me while we wait for Elspeth to drag Val away from the accounts?"

Anne could hardly refuse the invitation, so she preceded him into the room.

"I was lucky to find a volume of verse in the library," Jack told her politely once they were seated on either side of the fire.

"You like poetry, then, my lord?"

"I do. And you also, I am sure. Most ladies do."

"Not particularly," Anne admitted. "I would rather deal with numbers than words any day. I know where I am with numbers."

"And you don't with words?"

"*Some* people's words," Anne replied with an edge to her voice. "Especially poets' words. They're always saying one thing and meaning another. Writing some exaggerated folderol about love."

"You do not believe in love?" Jack lifted his eyebrows and gave her a mischievous glance. She wanted to lower her eyes but was determined not to give way to his attempts at roguish charm.

"Of course I do. I loved my father. I love my friends. I just don't believe in that romantic twaddle the poets write about."

" 'Folderol' and 'twaddle'! Let's see if I can find a good example of either. This seems to be a collection of verse arranged historically." Jack paged through the book from back to front. "Now, Miss Heriot, I cannot believe that you are immune to Lord Byron."

"Completely, my lord," Anne said briskly.

" 'She walks in beauty like the night, of cloudless climes and starry skies . . .' " Jack read the lines dramatically.

"There, you see what I mean! What does that *mean*, anyway?"

"I must confess I am not sure," Jack admitted with a grin, "but it sounds beautiful."

"Oh, aye, I'll give you that."

" 'She was a phantom of delight . . .' "

Anne giggled.

"Mr. Wordsworth does not impress you either, I see."

Jack paged forward in the book. "Wait a minute, here is one . . . Uh, no, I think I will not read Andrew Marvell after all."

"You had better not," said Anne with a mischievous look in her eye. "They made sure at school that we did not have that poem."

"So you have read it?"

"Well, you cannot forbid something and expect a lass not to seek it out, my lord."

"Well, here is one, although I am sure you'll have something against this one also:

> It lies not in our power to love or hate
> For will in us is overruled by fate.
> . . . .
> Where both deliberate, the love is slight;
> Whoever loved, that loved not at first sight?

Anne gave him a superior smile. "I find Mr. Marlowe the most fatuous of all."

"So you don't believe in such instantaneous attraction, then?"

"I do not believe that such attraction is love, my lord. As usual, the poet exaggerates."

"I think I must yield to your practicality, Miss Heriot. I confess myself to be more a romantic than you are after all."

On the surface, their conversation was merely the sort of banter one used to pass the time, but Anne knew she had conveyed an unspoken message: "Don't try your charms on me, my lord. Poetry will not convince me any more than your frankness did."

Jack was by no means oblivious to Anne's message. She was the most exasperating young woman he had ever encountered. On the other hand, there was a crackly tension in the air that he was sure did not emanate from him alone. He continued paging through the book until he was at the very beginning and without thinking, he read aloud the first lyric:

> Western wind, when wilt thou blow?
> The small rain down can rain?
> Christ, if my love were in my arms,
> And I in my bed again!

Anne's eyes met his in surprise for a split second, and then she lowered her gaze and blushed. "I have never heard that poem before," she said softly.

"I suspect your teachers would not have approved of "Anonymous' any more than they did of Marvell," said Jack with a grin. "He is very plainspoken, though, Miss Heriot. No folderol here."

"I must agree with you, my lord. But there is no proof, is there, that the author is a 'he'? It may have been written by a woman." The words were out of Anne's mouth before she thought, and she couldn't believe she had said them.

"I suppose it could have been," Jack admitted. "Perhaps a woman like you, direct and plainspoken."

Just then the door opened and Elspeth walked in. Anne had never in her life been so grateful to see another person.

"We were just reading some poetry, Elspeth," said Jack, his words innocent but his tone full of mischief.

"Poetry? I am surprised you did not put Anne to sleep. It was her least favorite subject at school."

"So Miss Heriot informed me. I see you can't pry Val loose."

"He has *promised* me that he will be here at any minute."

"And here I am, my darling wife," said Val, coming in behind her. "Now, what are the plans for this afternoon?"

"I thought Anne and I might go for a ride. The snow was lighter than it looked. Does either of you wish to join us?"

"I have a few errands in the village," Val said vaguely.

"And I want to give Sancho a day of rest," said Jack.

"We could mount you easily, Jack," Elspeth offered.

"I must confess I am giving *myself* a day to rest also."

After the women left, the men settled in front of the fire.

"You don't seem to be in a hurry to do your errands, Val. If you need a companion, I'd be happy to walk into Ripley with you."

"I don't have any errands, Jack. I have arranged a surprise for Elspeth, and I am waiting for them," Val confessed with a smile.

"For them?"

"Yes. Her parents. I asked Ian to request an earlier leave. If it hadn't been for the weather, I'd have expected them yesterday."

"I am sure Elspeth will be very pleased."

"I shouldn't be saying anything, but Elspeth and I have an announcement to make tomorrow, and I wanted her parents here."

"An announcement?"

"She is increasing," said Val, with a sheepish look.

"Why, that is wonderful, Val! My God, you'll be a father!"

"You had better have a believable look of surprise on your face tomorrow," Val warned his friend.

"I will, I promise. What does it feel like?"

"Terrifying. I have no idea how to be a father, Jack, never having had one myself."

"Charles came into your life rather late, didn't he?"

"And I resented the hell out of him. We didn't become close until Charlie died."

"I am lucky. My father is a good man and spent more time with us than most parents. Speaking of fathers," continued Jack, trying to sound casual, "what sort of father was Robert Heriot?"

Val gave his friend an amused glance. "From what Elspeth says, he loved his daughter but was not very good at showing it. Their most intimate moments were spent over the account books."

"Perhaps that explains why Miss Heriot is such a relentlessly practical woman," said Jack with a sigh.

"They're two of a kind, Elspeth and Anne, two plainspoken lasses. But even the most practical woman has a romantic side. Don't give up. Elspeth is sure you were made for each other."

"So you've told me," Jack said dryly. "Your wife is more of a dreamer than you think, Val, if she supposes Miss Heriot to be vulnerable to my wooing. Why, reading poetry to her only led to a discussion of how wrongheaded poets are about love!"

The two men spent a comfortable half hour in front of the fire, and then they heard a muffled clattering in the drive.

"It must be the Gordons," said Val. "They made it!"

It was indeed Elspeth's parents, and Val and Jack hurried out to greet them.

"I am so glad to see you, sir," Val exclaimed. "How were the roads?"

"Not that bad, Valentine. The snow squalls we had

yesterday were deceptive. They looked worse than they were."

"Unless you were riding in them," said Val, gesturing at Jack, who was helping Mrs. Gordon down.

"So it's Captain Belden! Or I should say, Lord Aldborough. You didn't get enough of cold rides in the army, eh, lad?"

"Well, yesterday might have convinced me of the benefits of retirement, sir!"

"Oh, Yorkshire can be wild, and the storm was coming from the north . . . but nothing like Scotland, eh, Peggy?" said Major Gordon, pulling his wife close to him and dropping a kiss on the top of her head before letting her go.

That quick little gesture of affection touched something in Jack. He had friends who were engaged and a few who were in good marriages, like Val. But to see that the Gordons still expressed their love for one another so easily and spontaneously after all these years together moved him profoundly. For the first time, he imagined himself dropping a kiss so easily, leaning over to touch his lips to dark brown hair threaded with gray. He stood there for a moment as the others went inside, struck by the fact that the woman in his fantasy came up only to his chest. The woman in his vision of long-married bliss was Anne Heriot.

"Are you coming, Jack?"

Val's voice brought him out of his reverie, but it occurred to him as he went in the door that he couldn't replace Anne Heirot's image with any of the women he'd been with over the years or any of the young ladies whose hearts he had unwittingly won.

Anne and Elspeth were out for a good two hours, and when they returned Elspeth wondered aloud at the strange carriage.

"Who could be visiting us so late in the day, and

on Christmas Eve? Whose carriage is this?" she asked their groom.

"I don't really know, Mrs. Aston," said the groom, who had been sworn to secrecy.

When Elspeth got to the house, she asked the butler and got a vague answer: "Someone on estate business, madame. Mr. Aston is closeted with them, er, him in the library."

"Well, tell my husband I will be down shortly and remind him we are dining early because it is *Christmas Eve.*" Elspeth's annoyance at Val's obsessive concern with the estate accounts on a holiday eve was clear. "Come, Anne, we are going to dress for dinner, and then we are going to drag Val out of his cave!"

When Elspeth and Anne came down half an hour later, there was no one in the library.

"Where on earth is he?" muttered Elspeth.

"I hear voices in the drawing room," Anne told her.

"If he has invited this person to stay, I will be annoyed."

Anne smiled. "Will be" was hardly accurate. Elspeth was very annoyed now, and she opened the door to the drawing room with an angry push, and then stopped so suddenly that Anne almost bumped into her.

"Valentine, how could you!"

Anne could tell from Elspeth's tone that whatever Val had done, she was no longer annoyed.

Then all was a flurry of "Mama, Papa." "There, there, ma wee lassie," and "Darling, we are so happy to be here . . ." and Anne watched in amusement as Elspeth rested her head for a moment on her father's shoulder and then turned to Val, her voice breaking. "Oh, Val, how ever did you get them here and how did you know what a perfect Christmas present this would be?"

Anne stood in the doorway, not wanting to interrupt the family reunion. Jack, who had been standing with his back toward her, suddenly turned and gave her a smile that lit his whole face and made her catch her breath. It was a smile one friend might give another. It conveyed his happiness for Elspeth, as well as his enjoyment at seeing her shaken out of her usual sangfroid.

It was also a smile that communicated more than just fellow-feeling. It held all of the charm that Jack Belden was famous for, and for the first time since she'd seen that charm, it had its effect on Anne. She had to take a deep breath to steady herself before she approached the Gordons.

"Why, there's ma wee Yorkshire lass," said Major Gordon, coming over and grabbing Anne's hands in his.

"It is good to see you again, Major Gordon. I am pleased that you remember me."

"Of course I remember you, Annie. It wasn't that long ago, after all, and ye haven't grown an inch!"

Everyone laughed. "Anne is the true 'wee lass,' Father, not me," Elspeth said dryly. "Val, could we have some wine?"

"Samuels is on his way, Elspeth. In fact, here he is. But with champagne, not sherry," added Val, standing next to his wife and putting his arm around her waist.

"Champagne!" exclaimed Mrs. Gordon.

"It is Christmas Eve, Peggy," said her husband, "and we're all here together."

"And Val and I have an announcement to make," said Elspeth.

"First a toast!" said her father.

"Hush, Ian," said Mrs. Gordon, a knowing gleam in her eye. "Elspeth has something to tell us."

"Val and I are going to be parents," announced Elspeth, her face pink with both pleasure and self-consciousness.

"Ye're to be a mother!" exclaimed her father joyously. "When is my grandson expected?"

"Or granddaughter, Ian," his wife reminded him.

"Sometime in June," replied Val.

"Congratulations to both of you," said Charles.

"What a lovely night for such an announcement," Anne said after they had drunk their toast.

"I had been planning to tell you all over Christmas dinner, but I couldn't wait, not after seeing Mother and Father."

"Have you picked a name yet?" asked Major Gordon.

"We have talked about it already," said Val. "It is to be Margaret if it is a girl," he said, nodding at Elspeth's mother.

"And if it is a boy?" Jack asked him.

Val looked over at his father. "Charles," he said. "Perhaps 'Charlie' for short."

"Thank you, Valentine," his father said softly, but everyone could hear the emotion in his voice.

Just then a footman appeared in the doorway. "Supper is ready," announced Elspeth.

After a light supper, the carriages were brought 'round to take them to church for Christmas Eve services. Anne was happy to see that the church, although beautifully decorated, was plain, and the service closer to her own chapel background than she had expected. The hymns were all the familiar carols, and as Anne lifted her voice on "God Rest Ye Merry, Gentlemen" she could hear Jack Belden's resonant baritone behind her. He had a beautiful voice, she had to admit, and he sang with feeling.

The moon was almost full and though the night was cold, it had warmed up from the day before, so the parishioners lingered a little in the doorway, wishing one another a Merry Christmas.

Anne found herself next to Jack as they waited for the carriages to be brought 'round.

"It is a beautiful, clear night, Lord Aldborough," she remarked politely.

"The stars are all so bright, aren't they?"

"The church looked very beautiful, so filled with light, although I am not used to so many candles."

"We need the light in this dark time of year."

Their words could have been spoken by any polite acquaintances, yet Anne was aware of an undercurrent between them. It was as though Jack Belden's presence made her more aware of the bright moon floating above them and the stars' coruscating brilliance. She was very grateful that she ended up in the carriage carrying the Astons, while Jack took his place beside the Gordons.

When they got home, they were welcomed by more candlelight, and Elspeth had port served before they all took themselves off to bed. Anne lay awake for a while, wondering what it was that drew her attention to Lord Aldborough almost against her will. Whatever it was, she was determined not to succumb to it. She was not like those silly widgeons in London, so vulnerable to a glance or a smile. She was a grown woman who knew what she wanted: a comfortable marriage with someone like Lord Windham or Baron Leighton. She could imagine herself with either of them, developing an affectionate partnership over the years, their lives together as calm as a meandering stream.

She might also, unfortunately, be able to imagine herself enjoying a kiss of Jack Belden's, but thank God, she could not form a mental picture of him as a husband. The man she would choose would be steady and practical and wouldn't dream of riding the Yorkshire moors in a snowstorm. And above all, he would not constantly be drawing the attention of other women!

Satisfied that her feelings of attraction were but an aberration and hadn't deflected her from her purpose, Anne fell asleep.

Chapter Ten

Christmas morning was leisurely, with a late breakfast after which Elspeth announced that presents would be opened in the morning room. Anne's father had celebrated Christmas, of course, but usually their exchange of gifts on Christmas Eve involved only a few small trinkets. Anne was amazed at the pile of brightly wrapped parcels piled up in front of the fire. She was a little anxious, for she had brought only one present for each guest. And she hadn't known Elspeth's parents would be there.

But as names were called out and wrapping and ribbons piled up on the floor, she let go of her worries. Most of the presents were small, and Major Gordon was so charming when he handed her a box containing a flask of French perfume that she didn't say a word of apology for not having a gift for him.

Anne was happy that Val was so grateful for the leather-bound account books she gave him, and Elspeth's exclamation of pleasure as she fingered the length of soft green wool was enough for Anne. Lord Faringdon gave her a warm smile when he opened his gift from her—a volume of history.

There was no question of exchange between her and Jack Belden, of course, but his smiles of approval at her gifts made Anne almost forget her resolutions of the night before.

"Dinner will be early today, for we are all invited to a supper dance at Squire Leveret's," Val announced. "But there is plenty of time for walking or riding . . . or relaxing in here with a new book."

Lord Faringdon chose to read his book, but Val, Elspeth, and Mrs. Gordon were eager for a ride.

"Will you ride with us, Anne? Jack?"

"I think I prefer to walk today," said Anne.

"And I'll join Miss Heriot on her walk, if she doesn't mind."

"What about you, Ian?"

"I'll keep the young folks company, Peggy," said Major Gordon, and Elspeth sent her father a grateful glance.

"There is a path at the back of the house that leads to the moor," Val told them.

They set off after waving good-bye to the riders. Both Major Gordon and Lord Aldborough were wrapped in their army cloaks, and Anne was glad that she had thought to bring her old broadcloth cape and a warm pair of brogues. No one spoke much as they climbed, but when they reached the moor, they all stopped to admire the view.

"Is this at all like Scotland, Major Gordon?" asked Anne.

"Something like it, but flatter."

The sun was strong and the day warmer than the past few, but a cold wind blew across the moor and they all pulled their cloaks around them and started walking to keep warm.

"I hear ye couldn't resist a long, cold ride, laddie," teased Major Gordon. "Do ye miss the war that much?"

Jack laughed. "Not the war, certainly. But there is something about danger that keeps one feeling alive."

"Oh, aye, I know what ye mean. I don't know how Peggy and I will deal with retirement."

"So you are saying good-bye to the army, sir?"

" 'Tis time. The war is over and I did my part to help win it. And now that I have a grandson on the way . . ."

"Or granddaughter," Anne reminded him tartly.

Major Gordon smiled. "Or granddaughter—it will be good to be close to Elspeth and Val." He turned to Jack. "But inheriting a title and managing an estate should be challenge enough, Jack."

"I am not sure 'challenge' is the right word, sir. At least in the army I had some hope of success, of my efforts counting for something. My uncle was almost bankrupt when he died, and he left his widow and two daughters to provide for."

"I'm sorry, lad. I didn't know." Major Gordon clapped Jack on the shoulder. "You'll just have to find yourself a duke's daughter. It shouldn't be hard, not with your reputation."

There was an embarrassed silence, and the major looked closely at Jack's face.

"It is precisely my reputation that works against me, sir."

Major Gordon laughed. "The mothers don't trust you, eh? Why, then, what about someone like wee Annie," teased the major, putting his arm around Anne and drawing her close. "She's a practical lass, experienced at managing things, aren't you, Annie? But she might feel just like those mothers, that a man known as the Jack of Hearts may make a poor husband!"

"Indeed she might," Jack said dryly. He was usually amused by Major Gordon's tendency to plain-speaking, but even though he knew the major had been joking and knew nothing of the situation, he was ready to throttle him.

"You are shivering, Annie," said the major as he felt Anne shaking. "Let's get you home."

They had wandered a way out onto the moor, but at least on their way home the wind was at their backs. When they finally reached the house, Anne made her escape, saying she wished to repair the damage to her hair and clothes from the wind.

Ian Gordon and Jack found their way to the drawing room and stood close to the fire, warming their hands.

"I was only teasing you out there, lad, but I kept thinking about it as we walked home, and it seems to me that you and Anne would do well together. Her father educated her above her station, and if I remember correctly, was planning on looking for a title for her. You couldn't find a better lass."

"I would have to agree with you, sir. In fact, Miss Heriot has decided to honor her father's wishes and is, er, looking for a title for herself. In fact, I have tried to suggest that I would be a good candidate, but she distrusts my reputation."

Major Gordon looked at Jack, his embarrassment written clearly on his face. "Oh, laddie, Peggy would have my head for this. I didn't know anything about your situation, and there was Annie, and she is such a sweet lass and a pretty one . . . and a rich one, Jack, and could solve all your problems."

"Elspeth and Val look at it in the same way, which is why I was invited, to give me an advantage over Leighton and Windham."

"Leighton? I don't know much about him. Old title. But Windham? Wasn't he engaged to be married?"

"He had to break it off when his father lost everything in a bad investment and shot himself."

"It was a love match, if the gossip was right. I'd hate to see Annie married to a man whose heart was given elsewhere."

"It is hard to tell whom she favors, except that it most certainly is not me!"

"What about your heart, lad? Have you ever given it?"

Major Gordon had the knack of disarming one's defenses by humor and then suddenly taking the conversation to a deeper level, thought Jack, as the major looked at him seriously.

"No, I don't think I ever have. My liaisons have always been friendly and left me heart-whole."

"Aside from her obvious financial suitability, what do you think of Anne Heriot?"

Jack turned his gaze to the fire and watched the flames flicker and dance around the logs that fueled them. Love was often compared to a fire, he thought, and yet he had never experienced the flaring of anything but desire. Off in the corner, there was a small piece of half-burned wood, not on fire, really, but resting on a pile of orange ash that threw out bright little sparks. Jack knew that sooner or later the wood would catch, and suddenly, it seemed to him a good image for his feelings for Anne Heriot. He certainly had not gone up in a conflagration of "love at first sight," but he had to admit that in her presence he felt the spark of something. Attraction? Yes. Admiration? Certainly, for as he learned more about her background, he could see what an accomplished young woman she was. Affection? Yes, he was beginning to like Anne Heriot very much indeed.

He turned back to Major Gordon. "I confess that my initial interest in Miss Heriot was sparked by her fortune. Now that I know her better, however, I am drawn to her for other reasons."

"Aye, she is a pretty lass."

"And a smart one."

"So you might come to love her, then? Annie needs someone to love her after that cold father of hers."

"Well, it is all speculation, anyway," said Jack, with a rueful grin. "I am last on her list, after all!"

"Things can change, lad, things can change."

Christmas dinner was as elaborate as Christmas Eve had been simple, and by the time the pudding was brought to the table, they all groaned in chorus.

As each slice was served, Anne said a little prayer that she would be spared a silver charm. Any other time she would have enjoyed the teasing that went along with it, but here, with Lord Aldborough at the table, it would be too embarrassing.

Then Jack yelped, as with one of his last spoonfuls he almost swallowed a little silver trinket.

Everyone turned to look at him, and he flushed.

"Married within the year, Jack!" cried Val.

"Ye can relax, laddie. All your problems will be solved," added Major Gordon.

"Are you sure that is what it means?"

"It is a time-honored prediction, Jack," Elspeth assured him, with a straight face but twinkling eyes.

No one looked at Anne, for which she was truly grateful. It would have been awful to have received knowing looks that suggested a link between Jack Belden's fate and her own. Major Gordon's comments on the moor had been bad enough.

"Well, I suppose that means some mama has had a change of heart and thinks I'd be the perfect husband for her daughter," laughed Jack. "I will go into the Season with renewed hope," he added. "Do I get to keep the charm, Elspeth?"

"Of course."

"Thank you," said Jack as he slipped it into his pocket.

Anne gave a soft sigh of relief. She was very grateful to Jack for his indirect message. He had clearly resigned himself to the fact that she would never choose him.

Squire Leveret's house was already full when the Aston party arrived. Val and Elspeth were whisked off at the door to meet their new neighbors, and the others made their way into the drawing room, which had been cleared to become a makeshift ballroom. It was hung with evergreens. And mistletoe. Finding that his wife was standing under one little branch, Major Gordon drew her to him and gave her a loving kiss. "There, Peggy. Now make sure I am the only one to find you under one of these."

"They are tuning up. May I have the first dance, Anne?" Lord Faringdon asked her.

"I should be delighted, sir."

Jack watched as the couples moved off. Standing there alone, he was struck by a wave of melancholy that seemed to come out of nowhere. He supposed it had to do with the failure of his plan to capture Miss Heriot's hand over the holiday. Or perhaps it came from seeing the obvious affection between the Gordons.

It didn't matter where it came from, he told himself. It only mattered that he get away from it. He searched the room and found what he was looking for—a possible dance partner in a simply dressed young woman sitting with some older ladies in the corner.

He made his way over as quickly as he could. "May I have this dance?" he asked.

She looked up at him, surprised pleasure on her face. "I would love to, sir, but we haven't been introduced."

Jack turned to one of the older women next to her and, giving her his most charming smile, said, "The musicians are almost finished their tuning, ma'am, and I will never find my hostess in time. Would you introduce me?"

"I will be happy to, if you will only introduce yourself to me, sir!"

"Jack Belden, Lord Aldborough, ma'am."

"Lord Aldborough, may I introduce Miss Susan Blakely."

"Come, Miss Blakely, before the sets are filled."

"Should you have done that, Martha? I have never seen you so unconventional," said one of the woman's companions.

"Oh, I suppose I shouldn't have, but I felt sorry for Susan. I gave her a dance with the most attractive man in the room."

"But who *is* he?"

"A friend of the Astons'. And for some odd reason, I felt sorry for him, too," she added.

* * *

Susan Blakely, who was governess to the squire's children, found that her dance with Lord Aldborough brought her to the attention of several young men from the neighborhood and she danced more that evening than she had the whole of last year.

Jack himself was not disappointed, for she was a good dancer. The musicians went from one vigorous country dance to another, and by the time they stopped, he felt his black mood lifting. He thanked Miss Blakely most sincerely and went to find some refreshment.

Anne was having a very satisfying evening. After her dance with Charles, she had been sought out by a number of men. One of her most enjoyable partners was the squire himself, who was a most graceful dancer, despite the fact that he was short and rotund. It was a perfect end to a lovely Christmas Day, and after their dance, she had relaxed her vigilance and unknowingly stopped under one of the ubiquitous branches of mistletoe.

"May I get you a glass of punch, Miss Heriot?"

She hadn't noticed Lord Aldborough until he was in front of her.

"Thank you, my lord. I *am* thirsty," she confessed.

Just as Jack was about to move away, however, a loud cry went up from a small group of the younger guests, who were too old for the nursery and too young to dance. They had been amusing themselves all night by keeping an eagle eye out for those who stopped under the kissing boughs.

"You must kiss the young lady first, my lord," cried a young man whose shirt points reached his ears.

It seemed to Anne that the whole room must be watching them. Damn the man! She'd thought he'd given up on his unrealistic hopes and here he was, trapping her in front of everyone.

"I swear I didn't see it, Miss Heriot," Jack muttered, giving the young man his darkest look. "But since we are caught," he added, turning back to Anne with that smile that changed his whole face, "why not enjoy it?"

Jack had intended only to drop a quick kiss on Anne's cheek, but she was standing so much like a martyr at the stake that in a streak of contrariness, he put a finger under her chin to lift her face to his and, leaning down, pressed his lips to hers.

Anne had been expecting that he would immediately draw back, but he lingered a moment, gently coaxing a response. To her surprise and against her will, her mouth opened under his, and she released an involuntary sigh of pleasure that turned into one of disappointment when he pulled away.

"Well . . ." said Jack, as surprised by her response as she was.

"You need not have lingered, Lord Aldborough," Anne protested after the young people wandered off in search of another victim. But she was almost angrier at herself than at him.

"I am not sure it was only my lips that did the lingering, Miss Heriot," replied Jack, with a gleam in his eye.

Anne was not sure what she might have said next had not Elspeth come to her rescue.

"I saw you were caught too," she told them with a laugh. "That young jackanapes actually caught me," she added. "He had to stand on tiptoes, so he ended up being the one embarrassed."

Anne laughed. "He deserved that."

"He did indeed, after ambushing others. I've relaxed my guard now that I'm out of the army," Jack added.

"Val has sent for the carriages. Shall we find our cloaks, Anne?"

Anne tried not to look like a scurrying rabbit, but she wanted nothing more than to get away from Jack Belden. Except, perhaps, she was ashamed to admit, another kiss from him!

* * *

Sarah had wondered if she would regret her decision to stay at Heriot Hall for the holidays. The first morning after Anne left, she felt restless, as though there was something she should be doing. It was an odd feeling, for her position wasn't onerous when Anne was home. They lived together more like friends than like mistress and employee, but Sarah never allowed herself to relax into a position of equality, much as Anne might have wished her to. She was rarely at Anne's beck and call, and it was strange to find herself wandering aimlessly, seemingly missing something that existed only in her own standards for herself.

But finally she found it utterly luxurious to feel responsible to no one, especially her own sense of what was necessary.

She and Anne had done a little decorating, but the tradition at Heriot Hall was a more austere holiday than Sarah had ever liked, so she woke up on Christmas Eve morning determined to ride over to a small spinney to cut a little holly.

"Would you tell Patrick that I will be riding this morning?" she told Peters when she came down for breakfast.

Sarah gazed out the window. It was a gray day, and the sun was only a dim disk hidden behind a veil of clouds. She couldn't tell if it would succeed in fighting its way through, but it didn't seem that more snow was imminent.

When she finished her breakfast, she walked down to the stable yard where Patrick had her mare and his own gelding saddled. She would have liked to ride alone for once, but she'd need his help to bring back the evergreens.

"I wanted to ride over to the little wood to collect some holly, Patrick. In my family we celebrated Christmas more festively than the Heriots."

Patrick fetched clippers and a sack from the stables and gave Sarah a leg up. He kept his horse behind hers, and Sarah felt increasingly uncomfortable. It seemed silly to have him act the groom with her, so she motioned him up beside her.

"It looks like the sun may come out, Patrick."

"Yes, and weren't we lucky the snow wasn't as heavy as it looked yesterday, Miss Wheeler." He hesitated, then continued, encouraged by Sarah's friendliness. "There is nothing lovelier than the deep green of the holly leaf and the red berries, unless it is a rope of ivy. Me mother and sisters would always try to have a little in the house, especially since the priest wouldn't let it in the church!"

"It is not allowed here either," Sarah told him with a quick smile. "I suppose I can understand why they forbid mistletoe, but holly seems innocent enough."

"Ah, but 'tis a pagan tree, holly. And the bush in which we find the King of All Birds."

"The King of All Birds?"

"The wran."

Sarah smiled at the thought of the smallest of the birds being made "king."

"In Ireland, we go out on Saint Steven's Day to hunt the wran out of the holly."

"Do you actually kill the poor little thing!"

Patrick tried to look properly ashamed, but he had a twinkle in his eye when he said, " 'Tis an old, old tradition, Miss Wheeler. The wran boys carry around the corpse and go house to house to collect money. Ah, but 'tis a fine thing, hearin' the drum and knowin' they're on their way," he added wistfully.

"When did you leave Ireland, Sergeant Gillen?"

"When I was sixteen. It's been twenty years since I was home."

"That's a long time," Sarah said sympathetically.

"What about you, Miss Wheeler? How long have you been here?"

"Since Anne was thirteen. Nine years."

"And is any of your family alive?"

"No, my parents died within six months of each other five years ago."

"I have heard that happens, when there is a great love between two people."

When they were almost to the wood, Sarah shifted in her saddle to face Patrick, and suddenly she felt it begin to slip sideways beneath her. At first she didn't know what was happening, and then instinct took over and she just managed to unhook her leg as she went over.

"Jaysus!" cried Patrick as her mare, terrified by the strange thing bumping at her side, took off at a canter. He jumped off his own horse and ran to Sarah's side. "Are ye all right?"

Sarah tried to pull herself up and then fell back with a moan. Her right arm wouldn't take any pressure. "I think I must have landed on my arm," she whispered.

Patrick knelt down beside her, and putting his arm around her, lifted her to a sitting position. "Here, now, let me see it."

It was very odd, thought Sarah, who was still too dazed to react, to be sitting on the cold ground while Sergeant Gillen carefully slipped off her cloak and examined her arm. "Can ye straighten it at all, miss?"

Sarah could only stretch her arm out halfway before she gasped in pain. "It's the elbow," she said.

"Ye've jammed it, I think, but nothing seems broken. A bad sprain is all . . . though sometimes that hurts worse than a break," Patrick told her. "What about yer legs?'

"They are fine," Sarah told him quickly. It was one thing to have Sergeant Gillen feeling down her arm, but quite another to have him examining her ankles. "Just give me your hand, Sergeant."

Patrick grasped Sarah by her left arm and pulled her up. She swayed and for one embarrassing moment found herself leaning on his chest, waiting for the ground to stop spinning.

It was a wide, solid chest, she realized, and smelled

faintly of pipe tobacco and Patrick. It would be very nice to rest there, she thought, her mind still confused, her guard down.

Miss Wheeler's head reached his shoulder, Patrick realized, and he could just rest the top of his chin on her hair. It felt very sweet to have her there against him, clinging for balance. He wanted to put his arms around her and hold her closer. He wanted to brush the grass out of her hair. He wanted to . . .

He stepped back. "How is yer head?"

"Spinning. Or the world is. I am not sure which. But it is getting a little slower." Sarah looked up at Patrick and gave him a dazed smile.

"Take my arm and we'll walk a few steps and see how ye feel."

Sarah was shaken, but aside from the pain in her arm, she was all right. Her head cleared quickly. "I am fine, Patrick—I mean, Sergeant Gillen," she told him after a few steps.

"Ye can call me Patrick, Miss Wheeler."

"Then you must call me Sarah."

"All right, Miss . . . Sarah." Patrick grinned. "Whatever happened? One minute I was talkin' to ye, the next, ye're on the ground."

"I don't know. I felt the saddle give a little and then begin to slide. I got my foot free just in time," said Sarah with a little shudder.

"Thank God ye've got good instincts, for yer mare would have taken off with ye, and I hate to think what could have happened."

Sarah started to shake again as the whole thing hit her. If she had not unhooked her leg, she would have been dragged upside down, her head hitting the rocks. "Dear God," she whispered.

"Here, now, let me get yer cloak around ye and have ye up on my gelding. Ye need to be gettin' something strong into ye, and I don't mean tea!"

Patrick brought his horse over and grasping her waist, started to lift her into the saddle.

"I'd rather ride astride, Patrick. I'd feel more secure."

"All right, then." Patrick tried not to look at Sarah's ankles as she mounted. He let her get settled in the saddle and then mounted behind her.

It was a short ride back, but both Sarah and Patrick were conscious of every minute of closeness. His arms had to encircle her to hold the reins, and it was impossible for her not to lean back for support. By the time they got to the house, Sarah was no longer shaking. In fact, her temperature was very much warmer than when they had set out, and she was certain it was not the result of a sudden fever!

Patrick handed her over to the housekeeper. "Get her some brandy, Mrs. Collins. No, ye must," he added firmly when Sarah protested that hot tea with a lot of sugar would be fine. "Ye're in shock, whether ye realize it or not, and I'll not have it on my conscience if ye get ill! I must be out after yer mare. I'll come and check on ye later."

Sarah choked on the brandy, but Mrs. Collins stood over her and made sure she got it down. "Tha must swallow all of it, lass. T'sergeant is right. And then I'll see to yer arm."

Patrick *was* right. The warmth of the liquor flooded through Sarah, replacing the warmth of his arms. Surely she shouldn't be thinking of his arms. And what about her own arm? She winced as Mrs. Collins took it gently and straightened it. "Don't worry, lass, I won't take it farther than that," the housekeeper reassured her. "I'll fix tha a sling to support it."

When Patrick returned an hour later, he found Sarah dozing by the morning-room fire, her arm supported in a sling that had been fashioned from a challis scarf. She was a very beautiful woman, Miss Sarah Wheeler, he thought, not for the first time. He watched her for a few minutes and was about to turn and go when her eyes opened and he felt himself drown in their intense blue.

"Patrick! I tried to stay awake, but all that brandy you had Mrs. Collins pouring down my throat made me sleepy."

"Ye were glad of it while she examined yer arm, I'll wager."

"I was," admitted Sarah. Then she realized that he was standing there holding a few holly branches, with a rope of ivy vines hanging from his arm.

"Why, Patrick, you went to the wood!"

" 'Twas where the damned—I beg yer pardon—the mare ended up. It seemed silly to let our outing go to waste. I'll give them to Mrs. Collins, and ye can tell her where to put them."

"Thank you, Patrick."

" 'Twas nothing . . . Sarah."

"Why don't you sit down and have a glass of brandy? You must be cold."

Patrick laid the greens on a side table and sat in the chair opposite.

"Did you find my saddle?"

"Halfway up the hill. But it wasn't yer saddle."

"What do you mean?"

" 'Twas Miss Heriot's saddle ye used this morning because Jacob hadn't cleaned yers yet."

"I didn't notice. But Anne's is not much older than mine," mused Sarah. "And Jacob has always kept things in excellent condition."

"The girth wasn't worn out—it was cut."

"Cut! What if Anne had been riding!"

"And what if she hadn't been as quick to react as ye were? Even if she had, she could have been hurt. You were."

"Not badly."

"But ye were lucky, Sarah."

"Are you saying someone was deliberately trying to hurt Anne?"

Patrick sighed and leaned forward, his hands on his knees. "I don't know. I'd guess whoever did it would have been happy either way. But one thing's fer sure—he meant harm."

"But who on earth would want to do such a thing?"

Patrick sat back and looked over at Sarah. "There's that young hothead at the mill. He wasn't very happy after his visit to Miss Heriot, was he?"

"No, he went away very dissatisfied," Sarah agreed reluctantly. "I wish Anne wasn't so attached to the memory of her father and how he did things. Their only way of making an affectionate connection was over the factory, and I think she needs everything to stay the same in order to hold on to him. But under Joseph . . ."

"It's Mr. Heriot's rules that are posted," Patrick pointed out, trying to keep the anger out of his voice.

"Oh, Mr. Heriot was no radical, Patrick. But unless it hindered production or threatened someone's safety he often overlooked his own rules. Joseph Trantor, on the other hand, is a cruel man. No, maybe that is not fair to him." Sarah was quiet for a moment. "And Anne's refusal didn't soften him any."

"Does he care for Miss Heriot or does he just want to marry her for her fortune?"

"Both, I think. But I would guess his greed is stronger than his love. But again, maybe I am being unfair, for I have never liked him."

"He knows that Miss Heriot aims to find a husband in London," mused Patrick. "If she does—well, his hopes are finally dashed. But if she died, he would inherit everything, wouldn't he?"

"I think so. Anne has no other relatives that I know of."

"Sure, and that's a strong motive, isn't it?"

Sarah shuddered. "Much as I dislike Joseph Trantor, I don't know that I can see him as a murderer. But his motive is stronger than Ned Gibson's."

"Well, I'd like to be investigatin' that young man a little further myself, just to make sure," said Patrick.

"What will we tell Anne?"

"The truth," said Patrick. "And with no delay. I don't want to ruin her Christmas, but I will be ridin' over to Ripley on Saint Stephen's Day."

"I am sure all the wrens in the vicinity will be relieved that you will be too busy for hunting," Sarah teased him.

"So ye remember my story?'

"Of course." She hesitated. "I am glad that you will be here tomorrow, Patrick. I wonder . . . I was not planning to have anything elaborate, but would you care to join me for Christmas dinner?"

Sarah couldn't tell whether Patrick's face was flushed with embarrassment, pleasure, or the heat of the fire. "Of course, if you had other plans . . ." she hastened to add.

" 'Twould be lovely, Sarah. When were ye planning dinner?"

"At about one."

"Then that would give us time to walk into Wetherby and see the mummers. That is, if ye're feeling up to it."

Sarah smiled. "I would like that. Anne and I always go, but since she wasn't here this year, I wasn't sure what I would do."

"Well, if ye'd accept my escort?"

"I would be delighted, Patrick."

Sarah had a hard time sleeping that night. It was difficult to find a comfortable position. She had taken the sling off and kept the arm close to her side, but she would relax in her sleep and stretch it and then wake from the sudden pain. When she would try to get back to sleep, she would start worrying about Anne. Surely whoever had cut the saddle girth would not attempt anything else, she told herself. Ned Gibson might be furious at Anne's unsympathetic response, but a young man would not risk his freedom just for revenge. And Joseph? Joseph did worry her, for he had something to gain besides simple revenge.

When she wasn't worrying about Anne, she was thinking about Patrick. She had not approved of Anne's hiring him so quickly, and at first she had not liked him very much. Maybe just because he was Irish. Anne had accused her of snobbery, and perhaps she'd been right. But his devotion to Anne and his job was impressive, and the shock of this morning's accident had awakened her to other things, like his strong arms. It had felt so good to be enfolded in them, to be able to relax in a way she hadn't in years. To give over all responsibility to someone else.

It probably wasn't proper to invite him to dine with her. But he was the head groom, and she was a companion, so perhaps it wouldn't look odd. Mrs. Collins found him charming, so perhaps she wouldn't think too much of it. And if the footmen and maids gossiped—well, why should she care?

Chapter Eleven

When Patrick arrived at the kitchen door early the next afternoon, the cook sent him into the morning room. He stood in the doorway, reluctant to enter as a guest. He wondered whether Sarah regretted her invitation to him. He was standing by the fire when she entered, and as she came toward him, her hand outstretched in welcome, he carefully released the breath he had been holding.

"Good afternoon, Patrick. You look splendid in your uniform."

"Good afternoon, Sarah. And ye look lovely."

It was no empty compliment. She did look lovely in her dark blue wool, her blond hair pulled up, revealing a long white neck. She was wearing what looked like sapphire and diamond earbobs. She looked too fine for an old soldier like him to be having dinner with. His nervousness made him brusque when he asked her about the absence of her sling.

"My arm is feeling much better, so I thought I'd try to do without it for a while," she told him. Actually, she'd thought the sling ruined the effect of her gown, so she'd dispensed with it, despite the twinges of pain that occurred whenever she let her arm relax. Seeing the approval in Patrick's eyes, she was glad she had.

"Dinner is ready, Miss Wheeler," announced Peters.

"Would you like some wine, Patrick?" Sarah asked once they were seated at the dining room table.

"No, thank ye, Sarah."

As dinner was served, they were both uncomfortably silent, except for occasional commonplaces like how good the soup was. Sarah was finally driven to say, "I am sure the rest of Mrs. White's meal will be equally delicious, Patrick. If we agree on that now, perhaps we can find another topic for conversation?"

Patrick looked over at her, and his face relaxed. " 'Tis just that I am not used to sitting at a gentleman's table, Sarah."

"And I am not used to playing hostess, so we are both a little out of our element."

"Oh, not you, miss. Ye're a lady, all right."

"I admit my father was the son of a viscount. But he was only a country vicar. He married beneath him, so his family made sure he received only a second-rate living. I did not grow up in a house like this, I assure you. And I have been supporting myself for years."

"Where did ye work before coming here?"

"I had spent some years as governess for Lord and Lady Beresford's children."

"So ye were used to moving with the quality."

"I was used to avoiding Lord Beresford's oldest son," Sarah said caustically. "I was very grateful to find a position here. For all his faults, Mr. Heriot never once treated me with anything but respect. And Anne has always been generous and loving. Why, look at her present to me. They are really too fine for a companion, but she knew I would love them," Sarah added as she fingered the diamond-and-sapphire earrings.

"They have a lovely sparkle," agreed Patrick. His eyes held hers for a moment, and Sarah wasn't sure if he was talking about her earrings or her eyes. She looked down in confusion.

By the time they finished their meal, Sarah and Patrick had relaxed enough to share memories of their childhood Christmases. After dessert and a small glass of port, which made Patrick feel that he had joined the decadent aristocracy, they walked down to the village with the rest of the servants to see the mummers perform.

Wetherby was a village that had its own band of mummers, and Patrick enjoyed trying to guess who it was beneath the costumes. Was that Timothy, the butcher, dressed up as the buxom older woman? And Dr. Carter as the fool?

It was an English custom, to be sure, but somehow it made Patrick feel at home, for the story came from the same roots as the wren ritual: during the darkest time of the year, something had to die, and the darkness had to become even darker for a while in order for the light to return and the earth to come back to life.

When Timothy pranced around, emphasizing his "bosom," Patrick heard Sarah giggling, and without thinking, he put his arm around her shoulder and drew her close. He leaned down and whispered, "I like a woman who can laugh." He was about to drop a kiss on her lips when he remembered he was no longer in the army, teasing one of the laundresses, but holding Miss Sarah Wheeler, the granddaughter of a viscount. He let her go immediately and was so embarrassed by his lapse of manners that he turned his attentions to Rosie, who was standing on his other side.

Sarah, who had been warmed down to her toes by Patrick's embrace, grew cold all over again when he withdrew his arm and let Rosie pull him into a conversation. And later, as they all walked back to the house, she had to ask herself just why it bothered her so much that she was caught between Mrs. Collins and the cook while that saucy little baggage had both James and Patrick leaning down to catch her every word.

Patrick saddled his gelding early the next morning and arrived at the Astons' a few hours later. Samuels made him wait in the front hall while he went to the morning room to announce him.

"Mr. Aston," he whispered into Val's ear.

"Yes, Samuels?"

"There is an . . . Irish person here to see Miss Heriot. He claims he is her groom."

"Sergeant Gillen?"

"I believe that is his name, sir."

"Then show him into the library, Samuels."

When the butler had left, Val went over to the sofa where Anne was sitting, working a small square of embroidery.

"Anne, Patrick has ridden over to see you."

Anne looked up in alarm. "What would Patrick be doing here today? There must be something wrong at home." Anne jumped up, scattering her silks over the rug.

"Do you want Elspeth or me to come with you?"

"No, let me talk to him alone."

Patrick was standing by the fire when Anne entered.

"I am really sorry to be interruptin' yer holiday, Miss Heriot," he apologized when she came in.

"Is it the mill, Patrick? Or is Sarah ill?"

"I suppose it is a bit of both, miss. Why don't ye sit down and I'll tell ye."

Anne sank onto the sofa. "Sarah is ill?"

"No, no, Sarah is fine. But she might not have been."

Anne barely noticed that Patrick was calling her friend by her first name. "Tell me, Patrick."

"We went out on Christmas Eve in the morning to gather a little greenery for the house."

"But we decorated the hall before I left."

"Em, yes, but Miss Sarah said she wanted some holly and ivy for the drawing room mantel, and I offered to help her. We were halfway there when her saddle gave way."

"Gave way?"

"Started slidin' off. Luckily she felt it happenin' and kicked free before the mare took off."

"Was she hurt?" Anne asked anxiously.

"Just a little. A sprained elbow."

"Thank God. But what has this to do with the mill, Patrick?"

"Ye see, Sarah was using yer saddle, Miss Heriot. And when I examined it, I found the girth had been sliced halfway through."

"How could that have happened?" asked Anne, not quite able to grasp what Patrick was telling her.

"Someone cut it very carefully. Since it was yer saddle, ye would have been the one hurt, the next time ye went for a ride."

"I still don't see how the mill comes into this," said Anne, and then her puzzled expression changed. "Ned Gibson? Do you think Ned Gibson had anything to do with this?"

" 'Tis a possibility that occurred to me."

"But what good could it do him if I were hurt?"

"Sarah was lucky that she freed herself so quickly. It could have been much worse if the rider had been dragged along. 'Tis very rocky out there . . ."

Anne closed her eyes and shuddered as a picture of Sarah or herself, foot caught on the pommel, head hitting the ground over and over, took shape.

"She could have been seriously hurt. Or even killed. I could have been," Anne whispered. "But could Ned Gibson have been that eager for revenge?"

"Ye don't really know him that well, do ye?" Patrick hesitated. "He was me first suspect, but then another person came to mind—Mr. Trantor."

"Joseph! Why ever would he want to hurt me!"

"He has a very good motive, Miss Heriot. Miss Sarah tells me he wants to marry ye, but ye're looking elsewhere."

"He was disappointed, I know. Even angry that I was going to London. But Joseph could never be a murderer. I can't believe it."

"He inherits all if something happens to ye, isn't that true?"

"Yes, he's my father's only living relative aside from myself."

"Sure, and that's reason enough, I'd say."

"But how could he be sure I'd be killed, Patrick? After all, Sarah escaped serious harm. No, it can't be Joseph. It must be Ned Gibson, out for revenge." Anne was quiet for a moment. "But how can we prove anything?"

"I'd like to do a little investigatin', Miss Heriot. Take a trip over to Shipton. Have an ale or two at one of the pubs. Maybe I'll hear something more about our boyo."

"But they know who you are, Patrick. Why should anyone talk to you?"

"I can complain about what a hard mistress ye are, miss," said Patrick, giving her a quick smile.

Anne rose from the sofa. "Patrick, I want you to come and tell Mr. Aston your story. Perhaps he will have some ideas."

Anne led Patrick over to the cozy little circle of chairs around the morning-room fire. "You all know Sergeant Gillen."

"You must be cold after your ride, Sergeant. Will you have a cup of coffee?" Elspeth offered.

"I'd love some tea, ma'am."

Elspeth rang for a pot of tea and more scones.

"Now, come over here and sit down, Sergeant. Anne, you look worried. What has happened at Heriot Hall?"

Elspeth's easy way of taking charge calmed Anne a little.

"Patrick has just told me of an accident that Sarah had."

"Miss Wheeler is all right, I hope," said Lord Faringdon.

"Yes, sir, I mean, my lord," Patrick answered.

"But it wasn't really an accident," continued Anne. "Her saddle girth was cut—except it wasn't her saddle, it was mine . . ."

"What are you saying, Anne?"

Anne gave Elspeth a rueful smile. "I know I am being a little confusing, but I haven't taken it in yet myself."

"So you suspect that someone intended harm to Miss Heriot, Sergeant Gillen?" Val's tone was that of someone used to getting information quickly and efficiently.

"Yes, sor. And Miss Wheeler was very lucky to escape serious injury."

Jack Belden stood up and walked over to lean against the mantel. "Have you any idea who would do this, Sergeant Gillen?"

Before Patrick could say anything, Anne quickly replied, "There is a young man at the mill who came to see me just before Christmas. He was very upset that his fiancée had been dismissed."

"What did he want from you, Anne?" Val asked quietly.

"I suppose he wanted me to intervene with Joseph for her and have her rehired. But of course I wouldn't do that. It would create all sorts of problems if I went over Joseph's head. I told him that I would make sure she got a Christmas bonus despite the fact that she was let go before I announced the bonuses."

"What was his reaction?"

"He was still very angry," Anne admitted.

"At you personally?"

"I suppose so. Certainly at Joseph."

"What was the girl dismissed for, Anne?"

"Whistling."

"Whistling?" Val said incredulously.

"I suppose it does sound minor, but my father's rules made sense as Joseph explained them to me. And they are no different than the rules set by the other mill owners," Anne said defensively.

"Is Trantor a hard man?" Val inquired.

"Not an unjust one," Anne said with some annoyance in her voice. *She* was beginning to feel interrogated, which felt unfair, given that she had been the intended victim.

"So you admit he is hard?"

"Surely Miss Heriot doesn't have to admit anything, Valentine. She was, after all, the probable target." Jack smiled as he mildly rebuked his friend.

"I apologize, Anne," Val said stiffly. "I worked under a hard man myself as a boy and encountered my share of 'just' officers when I served in the ranks. It's difficult for me not to feel sympathetic to your workers."

"You are not suggesting that Ned Gibson is justified in putting someone's life in danger!" exclaimed his wife.

"Of course not, Elspeth. I was just thinking about motive. Wouldn't he have more reason to go after Trantor?"

"And then there is Mr. Trantor himself," Patrick pointed out.

"I am *sure* Joseph would never wish me harm," Anne protested.

"But if ye're looking for motive, Mr. Aston, then Trantor's got one. He wants to marry Miss Heriot. Beggin' yer pardon, ma'am, for speaking of yer private business."

Anne sat there, irrationally furious that Jack Belden was hearing all this. She felt she had suddenly become the center of a sordid drama, through no fault of her own.

"He is your father's second cousin, Anne. He would inherit everything if anything happened to you, wouldn't he?" Elspeth reflected.

"Oh, Elspeth, not you too. Joseph cares about me. I admit I have disappointed his hopes, but he would never harm me. I am sure it is Ned Gibson. His family has a history of following General Ludd, and we all know the violence they brought to Yorkshire."

"I understood it was mainly directed at machines," said Val.

"William Horsfall was shot to death, all because he was bringing in a new steam engine," Anne told him.

"But hasn't it all calmed down over the past few years?" Elspeth asked.

"There may still be a few men who are resentful," commented Jack, his tone conciliatory. "This Gibson may be one."

Anne looked over at him gratefully. "Thank you, my lord. I was feeling that I was the one on trial, merely for running the mills the way my father ran them!"

"I don't think a discussion on the labor question is one we want to continue, is it, Val?" Jack continued smoothly. "I think the question here is to find out who did this and why. Obviously, Ned Gibson is the one to start with."

"Thank you again, my lord," Anne said warmly.

Jack smiled at her and then continued apologetically, "We cannot overlook your cousin, Miss Heriot. But we will start with the person who is the most obvious suspect."

After Anne left the room to see Patrick off, Elspeth looked at her husband. "You were hard on Anne, Val. You sounded as though you were cross-examining one of your men."

Val ran his hand through his hair. "I know. I'll have to apologize. It is just that I know what it is like to work for a living and be at the mercy of the one who is your master." He hesitated. "You must admit, Elspeth, Anne has never had to worry about anything. Her father's mills have provided her with the life of a lady."

"That's not her fault, Valentine," Jack protested.

"I am not saying it is a fault, Jack. It is just that

Anne would have a hard time imagining the life of a mill worker."

"Her father knew, and he didn't seem to let it get in the way of his profits," countered Jack.

"No, but I'd be willing to bet Trantor is much harder on the workers. I think a visit from Patrick is a good idea."

"And what about Trantor?"

"I think we must trust Anne's perception that he is too fond of her to wish her harm."

"Surely he only wants to marry her to gain control of her fortune," Jack said indignantly. "If she married elsewhere . . ."

Val gave Jack an ironic smile. "Your anger is a little out of place, Jack. You yourself need to marry Anne for her fortune, after all."

It took all of Jack's self-control not to respond to Val's thrust. And why was he so furious, he asked himself, as he took a deep breath and turned to stir the fire. He clenched his hands on the warm iron poker. When he turned back to Val, however, his tone was bland. "Touché, Val. I suppose I am a little annoyed to have to add a fourth to Miss Heriot's list of suitors."

"Oh, stop, both of you! Joseph Trantor is most certainly not one of Anne's suitors—not that it is any business of yours, Jack." Elspeth turned to her husband. "And since she has turned elsewhere for a husband, it could well be that her cousin is behind the attack, Val," she added worriedly.

Val gave his wife an apologetic smile. "I know I was hard on Anne, Elspeth, and I will ask Patrick to keep a careful watch on her."

Elspeth gave him a quick kiss on his cheek, saying, "Come, you can make your apologies to Anne and invite her to join us on a ride. Do you want to come, Jack?"

"Thank you, Elspeth, but having just stirred up the

fire, I think I will take advantage of it and read my book."

Jack stared at the pages blankly for a while, then finally gave up trying to read. He leaned over and gave the fire an aimless poke. Why *should* he resent Trantor so? Especially since it was clear that Anne Heriot would never entertain the man's suit. Val was right. How was he any different from her cousin, pursuing Anne for her money?

He pushed at a fallen log. Somehow his feelings for Anne Heriot were beginning to change. Or, to put it more accurately, he was beginning to have feelings for her. He certainly had had none at the beginning. He had seen her only as a means to an end, as a woman with whom he was trying to negotiate a business arrangement.

Some negotiator he'd turned out to be. Not only had he failed in convincing her that he would make the best husband, but he was beginning to think that she would make a very good wife indeed, with or without her fortune. Didn't that make him some kind of a fool, starting to care for a woman who had no interest in him? He poked at the fire again.

"If you keep doing that, Lord Aldborough, you are going to make it go out altogether!" said an amused voice behind him.

Anne sat down on the chair opposite, and Jack gave her a rueful smile. "You are right, Miss Heriot. I am stirring things up too much," he agreed, replacing the poker and then wishing, for some reason, that he had something else to do with his hands.

"I wanted to thank you for supporting me, my lord," Anne told him quietly.

"It seemed to me that Val was being a bit harsh. I am sure your father was fair to his workers."

"I know he was. Especially compared with some of the other owners." Anne sighed.

"I am sure you must miss your father, Miss Heriot."

"I do. I trusted all his decisions about the mills. But I had only seen the mills on paper, you see. It is very different to examine account books than to walk through a weaving loft." Anne hesitated, then looked up at Jack, her confusion clear in her eyes. "Have you ever been in a factory, my lord?"

"No," Jack admitted.

"It is very noisy . . . so noisy I don't know how one can think. There is a rule against talking, but that seems unnecessary to me," said Anne with an ironic smile, "for I can't imagine how you could carry on a conversation with the looms going. And then there is the sorting shed. It's where the children work, pulling the wool and feeding it into the rollers. I found out that one little girl had her hand caught . . ." Anne was silent for a moment. "Do you know something, my lord?"

Jack could hear from her voice that she was on the verge of tears. "What, Miss Heriot?" he asked gently.

"I have tried to put all this in the back of my mind. I have tried to tell myself it is the same everywhere. That, in fact, it is possibly better in the Heriot mills and our workers are lucky to be there . . . as indeed they are," she added, her confusion almost palpable. "But how can I call anyone fortunate who is deafened by the looms, or a child who is always in danger of crushed fingers or worse?"

"Yet without their jobs, where would your workers be? There is not enough work on the land for them all. It is no longer easy to support oneself as a hand weaver. Their future is in the mills. Without them, they would be begging along the highways."

"Yes, I keep telling myself that. But I never realized before that everything that was given to me came from their hard work."

"And your father's. He started out in the mills, didn't he?"

"Yes." Anne sighed again. "I just wish I knew what was the right thing to do."

"Let Sergeant Gillen investigate, Miss Heriot. He can find out just who Ned Gibson is and how justified his complaints. In the meantime, I suggest you enjoy the rest of your holiday."

Anne gave him a grateful smile. "I suppose you are right. I can't do anything until Patrick discovers more. And I will enjoy the holidays, but not here, I am afraid," she added regretfully. "I must get home to see how Sarah is. I can't leave her alone after such a frightening experience."

"I will be sorry to see you leave, Miss Heriot," he told her, and the sincerity in his voice was obvious.

"Thank you, my lord. And thank you for listening to me."

After she'd gone, Jack went to the window and looked out. The day was a gray one, with an occasional breakthrough of wintry sunlight. It didn't look like snow, and he realized that he was wishing for it. Hoping for a regular blizzard to keep Anne Heriot at the Astons'.

He had jumped to her defense automatically, his protective instincts aroused by Val's attack. It wasn't that he agreed with what she was saying, however. At some level he was disappointed in her unwillingness to see that Ned Gibson or her workers had any cause for complaint.

He had been a Whig before Spain, but his time with the *guerrilleros* had strengthened his radical tendencies, for most of his comrades were peasants, fighting for their land and livelihood. He had lived closely with them, and any notions he might have had about the supposed natural superiority of the upper classes had been dispelled early on. He'd known that one day he would inherit his uncle's title, but he had not expected it to be for years. And since he did have to assume the privileges of birth and rank, he was determined to find ways to better the lives of his tenants.

So it wasn't support of her ideas that led him to Anne Heriot's defense. Perhaps it was his intuition that underneath her words lay the confusion she had just revealed to him.

He admired her for asking those painful questions. He liked her for it. Perhaps he was even beginning to love her for it. Bloody hell, what a ridiculous thing to have happened! Why was he becoming vulnerable to the one woman it seemed he couldn't win?

Because he admired her straightforwardness and courage in coming to London without a father's protection and setting out to get what she wanted. Because he couldn't charm her! Because she was direct and honest about her own faults. Because she was both strong and vulnerable, hard and soft. And because when they danced, had he been able to pull her closer, she would have fit right against his heart.

Chapter Twelve

Anne left the next morning and was home by afternoon tea. She found Sarah in the drawing room, wrapped in a wool shawl, half dozing by the fire.

"Why, Anne, what are you doing home?" she asked.

"I came as soon as I heard what happened. I couldn't leave you alone after such an experience. How is your arm?"

" 'Tis much better. I'm able to move it a little."

"But you look tired."

"I am. I think it is the aftermath of the shock. I slept late yesterday and today and find myself napping in the afternoon. But I *am* fine, Anne. You needn't have interrupted your holiday, although I am grateful for your care."

Anne sat down, and when James came in with the tea, she poured for Sarah and herself.

"How was your Christmas, Sarah? I hope not too lonely."

Sarah blushed a little and hoped that Anne didn't notice. "It was very peaceful . . . well, as peaceful as it could be after what happened. We—that is, all of us—walked into Wetherby for the mummers, of course. And yours?"

"I very much enjoyed being with Elspeth and her family. But there was one fly in the ointment."

"Oh?"

"Lord Aldborough. I felt a little uncomfortable, of

course." Anne hesitated. "Patrick is sure it wasn't an accident, that it was aimed at me."

"I think he is right, much as I hate to frighten you. I went out and looked at the girth myself. It was definitely cut."

"We got into a discussion of possible suspects, which led us to the topic of the mills." Anne hesitated. "Do you think my father was an unfair master, Sarah?"

"Why, no, he was always very generous to me, in his own way."

Anne gave her a wintry smile. " 'His own way' was rather understated, wasn't it?"

"It was. But I don't think I've ever heard a servant complain in all the years I've been here."

"And what of the factory?"

"I don't know, Anne. I've never had contact with any of the workers. From all I could tell, your father was no worse than any other owner, and perhaps better."

"I had a very uncomfortable conversation with Val," Anne told her. "He was sympathetic to the workers because of his early years. I defended my father and Joseph, of course, but later I couldn't help but think of what it must be like to work in the mills. Lord Aldborough came to my defense." It was Anne's turn to hope that the warmth of the fire was explanation enough for her reddened cheeks. "I told him I was very grateful, of course."

"Of course," Sarah said, keeping her tone serious, although she was tempted to smile. "You thanked him and then rushed right off?" This time she couldn't keep the amusement out of her voice.

"I couldn't leave you alone, Sarah."

"I am not precisely alone," Sarah protested mildly.

"Should I *not* have come home to see how you were for myself?"

"Not at all. I am very grateful, and you know it. I was just teasing you a little. It's only that your initial unhappiness with Lord Aldborough has seemingly been transformed into something else."

"Yes, and I suppose I am confused by it. And by him," Anne admitted. "Not that I have changed my mind about him, mind you."

"Of course not."

"Sarah, do stop teasing."

"I am sorry, Anne."

"As well you should be, for I am feeling very confused about a number of things that I was so sure of—the mill, Joseph, Lord Aldborough. He kissed me, you know."

"Lord Aldborough kissed you!"

"Oh, it was only because of the mistletoe, and it was in front of half of Yorkshire. But I must confess that I enjoyed it very much."

"Perhaps you should reconsider him, then?"

"No, I still prefer Lord Windham's warm straightforwardness to practiced charm. Lord Aldborough may have been kind to me and he may give expert kisses, but it is just that expertise that I don't trust. It is how he earned his nickname, after all!"

Anne walked down to the stables early the next morning and found Patrick grooming Sarah's mare.

"Good morning and welcome home, Miss Heriot."

"Good morning, Patrick. Would you show me my saddle? I want to see the girth myself."

Patrick pulled her saddle off its hook and hung it over an empty stall door. "See here," he said, lifting the girth up.

Anne ran her fingers over the break. "It is too smooth to have just worn through, isn't it?"

"The leather isn't that old, and has been well cared for, miss. There is no reason it would split on its own."

"I was sure you were right, Patrick, but I needed to see for myself. Now that I have, I am even more upset. Sarah could have been badly hurt."

"Or yerself, Miss Heriot."

Anne shivered. "I don't like to think someone would hate me that much."

"Well, if ye can spare me tomorrow, I'll ride over to Shipton and see if I can get anyone to talk to me."

"Ned Gibson was very upset when I didn't offer to overturn Joseph's decision. He showed no respect for my cousin and very little for me. I am sure he is the one responsible for this."

"It would seem so," Patrick said blandly.

But as he rode over to Shipton the next day, Patrick had to admit that he preferred Joseph Trantor to Ned Gibson as the culprit. Not that he really knew either of them, he reminded himself. But the little he'd heard of Trantor he disliked. And inheriting a fortune was an even stronger motive than revenge.

When he reached the town, it was early afternoon and as he rode through, he was struck by the difference between the center and the outskirts, where the factory workers were housed.

He tied his horse up at the Hart and Horn and entered the dark taproom. He hadn't shaved this morning and had dressed in his oldest clothes in hopes that he wouldn't stand out too much. He would be obvious enough as a stranger.

The taproom was empty except for a very old man dozing by the fire, his snoring punctuated only by bouts of coughing that Patrick was surprised he was able to sleep through.

Patrick took his tankard of ale to the corner and sat there nursing it, wondering if the barkeep was a talkative sort. Then the door opened and a man walked in, heading straight for the bar.

"Good day to tha, Tom. Wot'll it be?"

"Tha asks me that every day, Ben," growled the customer, "and tha knows t'answer: a pint of stout. And another as soon as I'm finished," he added, slapping his money down on the counter. He drank the first pint quickly while standing at the bar. The barkeep stood there with his hand on the tap, and as soon as the last drop was drained, he started pouring another. The man took his pint and headed toward Patrick's corner.

"Tha'rt sitting in my seat."

"Am I now?" Patrick said mildly. "I'll be movin', then." He'd come for information, not a fight, so he slid onto the next bench.

"Tha looks familiar. Do I know tha?"

"I don't think so. But I have been in town before. Maybe ye saw me then. I work for Miss Heriot."

The man slammed his pint down. "Tha has soom nerve, cooming in here."

"Well, I have a day off, and I was curious about the mills my mistress owns."

"Tha mistress!" the man said contemptuously. "A reet bitch, to my way of thinking, living well while her workers starve."

"Beggin' yer pardon, but ye don't know what starvation is," said Patrick. "But I'll agree she can be hard sometimes, the mistress. I'll give ye that," he added.

"Tha will, will tha," his companion said sarcastically.

"I've heard that her father was a hard man, but a fair one."

"As owners go. But seeing what owners are, that isn't saying much. Is it, Ben?" he added, turning to the barkeep.

"Tom here fought with General Ludd," Ben told Patrick.

"Ye did, did ye? From what I've heard, your boyos shared the same hatred of tyranny that our Whiteboys and Ribbonmen did in Ireland," said Patrick, nodding his approval.

"I don't know about t'bloody Irish, but in Yorkshire we almost won . . . till they started throwing us in jail for having a pint together. Isn't that true, Ben?"

"Tom there, he went to jail twice for conspiracy."

"And I'm proud of it," Tom declared. "Another pint, Ben."

"Let me," offered Patrick, putting his hand on Tom's shoulder as he started to get up. "I'll take another one too."

He waited until Tom had drunk half of his third pint before saying casually, "From what I hear, there's still some good men willin' to stand up to the owners. Why, the butler at Heriot Hall told me that someone walked all the way there to protest to Miss Heriot."

Tom turned and looked at Patrick, suspicion in his eyes. "Did he tell tha t'lad's name? Or his reasons?"

"No, only that Miss Heriot was gone the first time and sent him away angry the second. 'Tis hard to know what to think, ye know, as I'm new to her service."

"He's a young fool, Ned Gibson, and I should know, because I'm his brother."

Patrick didn't have to feign his surprise. "Ye don't say. But why do ye call him a fool?"

"For thinking he could get anywhere by talking. The only thing t'owners understand is action. But he learned his lesson. He knows now tha has to act to get attention."

"And what was he wantin' from Miss Heriot?"

"He's going to get married, my little brother. And his fiancée, Nancy, coom into t'mill so happy after he asked her that she were whistling soom old tune. She were turned off in less than ten minutes, and her with brothers and sisters to support."

"Just for whistlin'? Jaysus!"

"T'foreman is Trantor's creature. And Miss Heriot will not question her cousin. Another pint, Ben, and one for my friend here. A corporal, were ye?" Tom asked, after looking at Patrick's old uniform jacket.

"Ex-sergeant."

"A sergeant! I never was in army myself, except for General Ludd's," Tom muttered. He looked up as

Ben delivered the two pints. "We all thought t'lass would marry him."

"Ye mean Nancy broke off her engagement to yer brother?" Patrick asked, confused by the turn in the conversation.

"No, tha idiot, *Miss Heriot.* Or maybe t'other way around. We all thought he'd be marrying her. Then Ned hears she's gone south to buy herself a husband. I tell tha, Sergeant, it didn't make Trantor any easier to work for!"

"Do ye think Miss Heriot knows how hard he is?"

"If she doesn't, she should. Especially after hearing Ned. He's a good lad, our Ned," said Tom Gibson, the easy tears of the drunkard filling his eyes.

The old man by the fire started his coughing again, but this time it was such a long fit, it woke him up.

"Give Jed an ale, Ben," Tom called out. "Coughing his lungs out," he muttered to Patrick. "As we all will be soom day. 'Tis from t'lint. Gets into lungs and tha can't cough it out after a while. I have cousins up north who go down into pit. I used to thank God my father and mother moved here, but t'lungs go here, too—slower, but just as sure."

Patrick stayed for another half hour, nursing his second ale while Tom Gibson drank another and then finally passed out. Then he walked slowly toward the mill, a plan forming as he went. He could wait till closing time and hope that Ned Gibson came into the pub. But suppose he went to the mill and told the foreman he had been sent by Miss Heriot to talk to Gibson? That way, he'd have him alone and get a better sense of what sort of man he was and what sort of action he might be driven to.

For Patrick had to admit that he sympathized with Ned Gibson. Or any of the mill workers, for that matter. At least in the army, as hard and as dangerous a life as it was, you could defend yourself against your enemy. Here, the "enemy" might be the very man who was paying your wages and helping you feed your family.

He was able to bluff his way in by being every inch the master sergeant and staring the foreman down after he'd questioned Miss Heriot's failure to send a written request.

"Sure and she didn't know who could read and who could not, Mr. Brill," explained Patrick blandly, but his posture told the foreman he wasn't going to move until his mission was complete.

He had to wait only a short time for Ned Gibson to be shown in. Ned looked about ten years younger than his brother and a stone lighter, although he was by no means a slight man. He came in and gave Patrick a hard stare.

"Do ye want to sit down, lad?"

"I'd rather stand. Tha has a message from Miss Heriot?"

"I do, but first I have a few questions for ye."

Ned's heart had sunk when the foreman pulled him away from his loom and told him there was a visitor to see him. The only time a worker was released from his work was to be let go or because of an emergency. But when Brill opened the door to the room where his visitor waited, he only said, "This is Sergeant Gillen, Miss Heriot's groom."

When the man offered him a seat, Ned refused. What on earth was he here for? If he was to be sacked, Brill or Trantor would have been the one to do it. What kind of questions could the Heriot groom have for him, anyway?

"I understand ye visited Heriot Hall twice this year?"

"Aye."

"And what would have been yer purpose?"

"I went to ask Miss Heriot if she would consider rehiring Nance Hutton, my fiancée."

"But Miss Heriot was in London," said Patrick. "And lucky for me she was," he added with a quick smile. " 'Twas there she hired me."

Ned stared at him, not about to respond to the change in tone.

"But ye came back again, didn't ye?" asked Patrick.

"I saw Miss Heriot in December," Ned said stiffly.

"Did ye ask her about Miss Hutton?"

"If tha cooms from Miss Heriot, tha knows I did, Sergeant."

"She refused to help ye?"

"Tha knows that too. Oh, she made sure that Nance got her Christmas bonus, but she was not about to overturn her cousin's rules," Ned responded with bitter sarcasm.

"So ye're angry with her?"

"I'm angry with myself, that I expected her to have a heart."

"And didn't she show some generosity in givin' a bonus to someone no longer workin' for her?" Patrick asked mildly.

"T'bonus will only keep Nance out of the workhouse for a little longer. She needs her *job.*"

"But she broke the rules?"

Ned snorted. "T'rules against *whistling*! T'rules against being human."

"I saw them posted," Patrick said slowly. "They've been up for years, haven't they, lad?"

"Oh, aye, but Mr. Heriot's foreman would never have reported Nance. And if he did, Trantor would probably not have dismissed her. He'd only have fined her, were Mr. Heriot alive. He was a fair man, Mr. Heriot. He knew all his workers. He knew Nance was a good girl, never the sort to make trouble."

"Unlike yer brother," Patrick said quietly.

"What does tha know of my brother?"

"Mr. Heriot put him in jail twice, from what I've heard."

"Aye," Ned admitted slowly. "T'damned Combination Acts. All t'owners were using them against their workers."

"So ye have some good reasons to hate the Heriot family."

"They ruined Tom, that's the truth. But I think there is a difference between righteous anger and hatred, Sergeant. I don't *hate* Miss Heriot."

"Ye wouldn't be wishin' any harm on her, then?"

Without thinking, Ned gave something between a snort and a laugh. "If owt harmed Miss Heriot, what good would it do me or any of us? Tha must know Trantor would get everything and we'd be even worse off!" Then Ned fully took in what Patrick was implying. "Art tha saying Miss Heriot's been hurt?"

"Not Miss Heriot, for she was away from home for Christmas. Something ye may not have known. But her companion had a riding accident, which could have been much worse than it was."

"And tha thinks that I had something to do with this?" Ned asked incredulously.

"Ye've got a grudge against her, so I couldn't help but think it, lad."

Ned wasn't about to get pulled in by Patrick's quiet tone. "And when would I have a chance to do anything? I was here working." Ned's voice trailed off.

"Ye were saying, lad?"

"I was working all week, except I got sick late on t'day before Christmas Eve. And since we only work half day on t'eve, I stayed home. I had to; I couldn't get out of bed, t'legs were so weak. And Nance can vouch for that, Sergeant."

"Sure and she would, wouldn't she?"

Ned wanted to punch the soft-spoken Irish bastard in the face. The more he implied, the stronger his brogue.

"I swear to tha, Sergeant, I did nothing to harm Miss Heriot."

"For now, I'll have to be takin' yer word for it." Suddenly Patrick's voice grew hard. "But if I find ye had a hand in it, boyo, I'll hang ye myself with the greatest of pleasure."

Patrick got home in time to get a few hours of sleep before his morning duties. When he brought the horses up to the door for Anne's morning ride, she looked at him closely. "Did you get enough sleep last night, Patrick?" she asked sympathetically.

"Yes, ma'am."

"Well, I only have time for a short ride, anyway," she said, although she was eager to take advantage of the good weather and ride up on the moors.

She motioned Patrick next to her. "Did you discover anything in Shipton yesterday?"

"I found out that Tom Gibson is a great drinker, miss."

"But what about Ned?" Anne asked impatiently.

"I saw him. I must admit I have some sympathy for the lad."

"Do you indeed, Patrick?" asked Anne, her tone cool.

" 'Tis hard to see someone ye love facing the poorhouse."

"He may have every reason to be angry, Patrick, but that does not excuse violence."

"I'm not sayin' it does." Patrick was quiet for a minute. "But he didn't strike me as a violent lad, Ned Gibson. He *was* angry; but as he pointed out, and very cool he was about it, if something happened to ye, yer cousin would have even more power over them. Now he only has what ye give him. Though that has been enough to ruin Nance Hutton," Patrick added.

"I can't reinstate her now, Patrick. Not after that attack. And if I had done so before, it would have looked as though I didn't trust Joseph. If I do something now, then it means whoever did this has succeeded in frightening me."

"Yes, miss," Patrick said flatly.

Anne reined in her mare. "I know you think me

unsympathetic to this woman's plight. I am not," said Anne, her voice low and strained. "It is only that I have never been confronted by this kind of situation before. It was so much easier just to see the mills on paper."

"And in an account book things are all black and white."

"The figures add up or they don't," agreed Anne. "I have always been good with numbers. My father took care of the rest."

"Maybe 'tis time ye did some thinking of yer own, Miss Heriot." And this time with yer heart, Patrick added to himself.

Anne spurred her mare and for the next quarter hour rode as though the devil were after her. But on the way home, as they walked their blown horses, she turned to Patrick and said, "But could we find some way to help this Nance? Perhaps she could take in laundry for a local inn, or some such thing. We could arrange it anonymously and make it worth an employer's while to hire her."

"That would be a generous thing to do, Miss Heriot. And I am sure I could find something for her."

"About Ned Gibson . . ."

"He says he was home sick and that Nance will vouch for him, but he could have done it."

"But you can't find proof. We will just have to be extra careful, then. Maybe hire another lad to keep watch on the stables. I am sure that this was just an act of revenge on Ned Gibson's part. If Nance is taken care of, even if he doesn't know it is by me, perhaps his anger will cool. And I will be in London soon anyway."

Chapter Thirteen

Over the next few weeks, however, Anne found her thoughts straying to her conversation with Patrick, especially when she was working with the accounts. She had always been as precise in her recording as she was in her calculations, but as she carefully filled out the columns in her ledger, she did not find the same satisfaction that she usually did. It had always given her great pleasure to see how even her columns were. She loved filling in the clean white space with black ink and was an expert at keeping her pen sharpened so that it would never blot. She hadn't had very many smudges in the books since she had started keeping them.

Now she couldn't look at the black and white without thinking of the gray that Patrick had spoken of. People weren't numbers. Nance Hutton's name might be crossed off the list of employees, but she couldn't so easily forget about the girl's existence.

Nance had been happy about her engagement—so happy that she came in whistling. Was that enough reason to threaten her livelihood? What would her father have done? Anne wondered. The rules had been posted for years, but had they been as strictly enforced? Was Joseph harder than Robert Heriot?

Finally one morning in late January, she left the accounts unfinished—something she had never done before—and went off in search of Sarah.

"She had errands in town, miss. She said to tell you

she would be back in a few hours, should tha want her," Rosie told her.

"Did she take the carriage, Rosie?"

"No, miss. She had t'sergeant with her to carry her packages and all. He'd do owt for her. He doesn't even look at me anymore," Rosie added with a sigh.

Anne wasn't surprised at Rosie's outspokenness, for she had always been somewhat lacking in decorum. To tell the truth, Anne had always enjoyed that about her. She was surprised, however, at Rosie's suggestion that Patrick had developed a liking for Sarah, but she only said, "Why, Rosie, I thought you had an understanding with James?"

"Oh, I do, miss, but t'sergeant is ever so romantic with his eye patch and his uniform. It makes a girl forget he is Irish."

"Yes, well, thank you, Rosie," Anne said dryly.

Too restless to go back to her accounts, she tried to settle down with her embroidery, but found herself pacing the rug in front of the French windows. Sarah and Patrick Gillen? She wasn't sure she approved, much as she liked Patrick. He was a good and trustworthy man, certainly. And attractive, she'd have to admit that. But Sarah was the granddaughter of a viscount, no matter how poor her father had been. Anne had had great hopes for her after the Little Season, when Sarah had been accepted as much for herself as for her position as Anne's companion. Surely she and Elspeth could have found someone—one of the older officers who kept Sarah's dance card close to filled. Sarah Wheeler married to an Irish groom did not fit Anne's plans for her in the least.

She was at the window when they returned. Sarah's cheeks were flushed a becoming pink, but that could have been from the cold or the exercise, Anne told herself. When Patrick handed over Sarah's parcels, however, they lingered for a minute or two. Of course, it could have been innocent chatter, but that didn't explain the way Sarah lifted her eyes to Patrick's face and then lowered them quickly, as though she was shy about what he might read there.

"Tha had better be careful, Patrick," Anne muttered as he turned away. "If tha hurts Sarah Wheeler, tha will answer to me!"

By the time Sarah came down to the morning room, Anne was settled calmly by the fire, intent on her embroidery.

"Did you have a nice walk, Sarah?" she asked.

"Yes, I did, and a very successful shopping trip as well."

"Rosie tells me Sergeant Gillen accompanied you. I am glad you had someone to carry your parcels."

"It is none of Rosie's business who accompanies me to town," exclaimed Sarah without thinking.

"No, of course not. Although you usually bring James, don't you? Perhaps she only noticed because of that."

"James was busy with the silver, and Patrick had some things he wished to pick up also."

Anne lifted her face and said blandly, "You have no need to explain, Sarah. I am glad Patrick was free to accompany you."

"Yes, so was I," said Sarah, pouring the tea.

"I like this new Darjeeling, don't you?"

"Especially for afternoon tea," Sarah agreed, thankful that the conversation had turned to a more comfortable topic.

"I need your advice, Sarah," Anne said after a minute, with such seriousness that Sarah looked at her in surprise.

"What is it, Anne?"

"I am thinking of making another visit to the mill."

"Do you think that wise? What if Ned Gibson was the one who caused my accident? You might be putting yourself in danger."

"Not if he's busy at his machine and Patrick is by my side."

"Why do you want to go back?"

"I have not been able to stop thinking about the mill since I was there. When I was at the Astons' I was very resistant to Val's point of view, but he did make me think about things."

Sarah only looked over at Anne inquiringly and said nothing. It reminded Anne of when her friend had been her governess and would introduce a controversial historical topic and then wait to hear what Anne's stance was.

"You never were one for giving me the right answer, Sarah!"

"I have always thought the questions we ask ourselves more valuable than the answers."

"One question I have been asking myself is why I have taken everything I have for granted and never given a thought to where it comes from. The mills have always been about numbers to me, Sarah, not about people." Anne hesitated. "I have been asking myself whether my father enforced all his rules as strictly as Joseph does, or whether the sorting shed is safe for those children. Or what it would be like to lose your job merely for expressing joy?"

"They are certainly challenging questions," agreed Sarah.

"What should I do, Sarah?" Anne pleaded.

"I don't have the answers, Anne. I think you need to find out for yourself, and so perhaps another visit would be helpful."

"This time, I will not tell Joseph. I'll choose a day he is at market so that no one can control whom I talk to and what I see."

Anne poured herself more tea and then said more calmly, "I have asked Patrick to help Nancy Hutton find another position."

"Yes, I know," said Sarah with an approving smile.

If Sarah knew, it was because Patrick had told her. Anne could only hope that the relationship that seemed to be developing was simple friendship and not something more.

The morning after Anne and Sarah's conversation, the weather was wet and wild, and it ushered in almost a fortnight of bad weather. Finally, the first week of February, the sun returned and the road dried enough to make the journey.

When Anne arrived at the mill, it was lunch break and some of the workers were scattered around the yard with their pails. Some of them watched her curiously, and a few gave her openly hostile looks. As she climbed the steps to the weaving loft, she could hear their voices buzzing behind her.

Brill was in his office and looked up in surprise when Anne walked in.

"Why, Miss Heriot, what a surprise. Joseph didn't tell me tha was coming . . ." His voice trailed off as he stood there, clearly unhappy at her presence.

"Joseph didn't know my plans, Mr. Brill. I would like to interview a few of the workers."

"Tha would what?"

"You heard me. As owner of the mill, I think it is important that I get to know my workers better."

"Why, of course. 'Tis a good time, lunchtime. I'll see that a few men are sent up."

"Oh, no," said Anne, "I don't want to deprive anyone of his break. Perhaps I might use the office? Would you mind?"

"Of course not."

Patrick, who was standing behind Anne, had a hard time keeping his face straight. Now that Brill had gotten over his shock, it was clear that he minded very much, but without Trantor's authority, he was clearly at a loss as to how to stop Anne.

"I would like to interview a few of the older workers—those who have been here since my father's time, Mr. Brill," Anne said as she settled in behind the desk. "And make sure at least one of them is a woman."

"All right." The foreman's face brightened for a moment, and Patrick realized that he saw an opportunity to monitor exactly what Anne heard and saw.

"I'll wager ye have records of the wages ye've paid over the years, with fines and such like," put in Patrick. "Why don't ye bring Miss Heriot one from ten years ago. Then she can choose whom she wants to see. Would that be all right, miss?" Patrick added with false obsequiousness.

"Why, that is an excellent idea, Patrick," Anne said, giving him an approving smile as soon as Brill was headed out the door.

When he returned, Anne quickly picked out a few names.

"Jonathan is dead, Miss Heriot," Brill informed her solemnly. "But t'others are still here."

"Then send them in to me, one at a time."

"Yes, miss."

The first to be shown in was Bert Swain, a man of about fifty. His eyes remained expressionless as Anne greeted him.

"Now that my year of mourning is over, Mr. Swain, I have decided that a continuing way to honor my father's memory is to become more familiar with the workings of the mill. I have made one visit already, but I didn't have a chance to speak with anyone. I understand you have been here a long while."

"Aye, onto twenty years."

"So you knew my father?"

"Oh, aye."

Swain gave nothing away by his tone or expression, so Anne had no idea whether he approved or disapproved of Robert Heriot.

"Are you satisfied with the present management of the mill, Mr. Swain?"

Swain raised one eyebrow. "It isn't for me to say,

miss. 'Tis more to the point whether tha art satisfied," he added, the faintest trace of irony in his voice.

"There are two things important in managing a mill, Mr. Swain. One is assuring the owner a profit. Joseph Trantor has done that for my father and is doing it for me. The other is making sure the workers are treated fairly." Anne surprised herself by the strength of conviction in her voice. Over the past few months her concerns about the mill had broadened, and she realized that the token generosity of her initial visit had been transformed into something much deeper.

"What was it like to work here when my father was alive?"

"Ah, Mr. Heriot was a hard but fair man."

"I have seen the rules posted outside."

"Oh, aye, t'rules are pretty much t'same everywhere."

"They seem rather strict to me. No talking. No whistling."

"There has been some talking and some whistling in the past, miss," Swain told her noncommittally.

"Were the offenders dismissed?"

"I'm still here," he said, with a slight movement of his mouth that on anyone else might have been a grin.

"So tha has done a little talking," said Anne with a smile.

"Not lately, miss."

"I see. Perhaps Mr. Trantor enforces the rules more strictly now that my father is gone?"

"I don't know as I'd want to say that, miss."

It seemed clear that Mr. Swain was not going to give her much more, so Anne thanked him and let him go. The next worker was a tall, thin man who had been at the mill for ten years. He was as resistant as Swain and could hardly speak for coughing.

"It sounds like you should be at home in bed with that cough, Mr. Walters."

"Oh, no, miss, there's nowt wrong with me but t'lint."

"The lint?"

"Aye, tha breathes it in all the time. 'Tis not as bad as coal dust, though. I'm very grateful to be in t'mill, miss. Under such fine management and all."

After he left, Anne turned to Patrick. "Patrick, that man sounds like a consumptive and it's all from working here, and he won't say a word against Joseph."

" 'Tis one thing ye can't blame on Trantor, Miss Heriot. And Walters doesn't want anything gettin' back to his 'fine manager' for fear of losin' his job."

"Even though it is making him ill?"

"What else would he do?"

Anne's last visitor was Mrs. Martha Talbot, a small woman who looked to be in her early thirties.

"There must be a mistake in the ledger, Mrs. Talbot," said Anne with a smile. "You can't be much more than thirty."

"Twenty-nine, miss."

"But it says you started working here twenty years ago."

"Aye, I started later than some. I were nine."

Anne thought of the children she'd seen in the shed. "Were you a sorter to begin with?"

"Aye."

"It seems like a dangerous job for a child."

"T'machine makes it easier to get caught, miss. Sorting and carding were a bit easier when I was young. And ye have t'softest hands from pulling at t'wool," she added with a quick grin.

"I was here before Christmas, you know, Mrs. Talbot, but I didn't have much time to talk to people."

"I wouldn't think so, miss, not with Mr. Trantor keeping tha in tow. I was surprised tha made it to t'shed."

Anne gave a little sigh of relief. At last, here was someone who would speak to her openly.

"Tha Christmas bonus was a great help, Miss Heriot," Mrs. Talbot added.

"I hope to be more of a help to the workers here,

but I cannot do that unless I know what some of the problems are."

"Then I'll be telling tha, Miss Heriot."

"So there are problems? Why would no one else speak frankly?"

"If tha needs t'job, tha keeps quiet. I'll be leaving t'first of next month. My George has got himself a small farm," she announced proudly.

"How have things changed since my father died, Mrs. Talbot?"

"Tha must understand, no mill is a good place to work, Miss Heriot. Not one owner would listen to us, and t'Combination Acts got rid of those who tried to do something. That and t'troops."

"Were you in favor of General Ludd, then?"

"Not in favor of killing, miss. But there wasn't much of that. General Ludd's men mostly went after t'machines."

"But that cost the owners money. What is wrong with improving a mill, Mrs. Talbot? Better machines mean better production, which then means higher wages."

"Higher profits for t'owners, more like! And those that brought in steam engines will end up laying off workers. Replacing them with machines that do t'work of a few men."

"But isn't that a sign of progress?" Anne asked. "Surely if machines can do the work of several men . . ."

"Then what? There will be nowt for them to do. They can't go back to home weaving. There's very little land for farming . . ."

"I hadn't thought about it in that way," admitted Anne. "And I don't know what I can do about it, for the steam engine is here, whether we like it or not. But I *can* deal with what goes on in this mill," she added.

"Aye, if tha is ready to get rid of Peter Brill and

maybe Trantor too. But then, he is tha cousin, so tha could hardly do that!"

"Tell me about Brill."

"He is a nasty piece of work, and he gets a percentage of any fines he imposes."

"Why, that means he'd be looking for infractions."

"He's on us day and night, miss, for things tha father would have let go."

"Was he foreman under my father?"

"No. Tha cousin raised him up."

"I see. So Mr. Trantor is far stricter than my father."

"Tha father was a fair man, though he was an owner. At least he knew what it was like to work a loom. Mr. Trantor, he coom from a shop, I believe?"

"Yes, his father and mother were shopkeepers. And I cannot fire my cousin, Mrs. Talbot, nor would I want to," Anne added. "He has been a loyal friend to my father and to me."

"Aye, and word is, he'd like to be more than that."

Anne raised her eyebrows. "My private life is not the business of my workers, Mrs. Talbot," she said coolly.

"Only if it means tha are under Trantor's thumb, which would make life harder for us," Martha Talbot fired back.

Mrs. Talbot was irrepressible, and Anne couldn't help but like her because of her honesty. "So you recommend that I fire Brill?"

Mrs. Talbot's face lit up. "Tha would do a good thing if tha did that, miss."

"And who would you put in his place?"

Mrs. Talbot thought a moment. "I'd say Ned Gibson, but he's too young yet, though he's been here so many years."

"Ned Gibson?" Anne's tone was cool again.

"I think tha has met him."

"Aye, he came to see me about his fiancée."

"And tha gave her a bonus instead of her job back."

"I could not reverse Mr. Trantor's decision. It would have set a precedent and ruined discipline."

"I don't agree with tha, since he made a bad decision. But I can see summat of tha point. If tha puts a man in charge, tha must abide by his decisions. Which is why it is so important who tha has under him."

"I am glad you can see something of my side, Mrs. Talbot," Anne said ironically.

Martha Talbot smiled. "Oh, aye, even though we are only mill workers, we can see t'sense of things." Her tone became more serious. "It is too bad Ned doesn't have a few more years. He is the only one able to see both sides—some of t'time, at least," she added with another smile.

"And yet his brother was jailed twice for conspiracy."

Mrs. Talbot shook her head and sighed. "He were a fine man, Tom Gibson, till they took him off to jail. That was tha father's doing, Miss Heriot. We didn't expect it from him, but it was only after Arkwright died."

"Then the Gibson family has every reason to hate me," Anne said quietly.

"I wouldn't say hate, Miss Heriot. But there's anger there, all right."

Anne stood up and Mrs. Talbot quickly did too. "I am very grateful for your honesty, Mrs. Talbot. I assure you, I will consider your advice very carefully, and though I would like to keep you here, I wish you and your husband well on the farm."

After she left, Anne sank down in her chair.

"What do you think, Patrick?"

"I liked the woman," he said with a wide grin.

"So did I, but I meant what did you think of her advice?"

"Getting rid of Brill seems a wise move to me. When a man makes a profit off other's troubles, 'tis not good for anyone."

"I'm sure Joseph won't approve," Anne said with a sigh. "But I can't dismiss my cousin."

"I agree, miss. Ye have no good reason to. We have no real evidence against him . . . or against Ned Gibson."

"Do you suspect one over the other, Patrick?"

" 'Twas interesting to hear more about Tom Gibson. He's had a strong influence on his younger brother, I'm sure. But on the other hand, Tom seems a broken man, drowning himself in ale, so his influence may be less these days."

"Yet Ned Gibson may blame my father for turning his brother into a drunkard."

" 'Tis the man who lifts the tankard, Miss Heriot. Others have spent time in jail and not become like Tom Gibson." Patrick hesitated. "I still think yer cousin has a strong motive. If ye marry someone else, he has a fortune to lose."

"But he was left a very generous legacy in my father's will. And is well paid as a manager, I assure you," protested Anne.

"Some men are never satisfied with what they have. And some turn a little mad with jealousy. It may be both love and greed, Miss Heriot. Trantor may feel if he can't have ye, no one should."

"I can't believe Joseph's feelings for me are that extreme."

"Ye never know, miss. Love can make a man do things he'd never have imagined."

Chapter Fourteen

By the time Anne returned home, she was so tired from her day that she asked Sarah if she would mind having supper alone. "All I want is some tea and a muffin in my room. Could you have them sent up, and I'll see you in the morning?"

"Of course, Anne."

Sarah ate her supper slowly, noting how the light was lasting longer these days. It meant that spring was coming and they would be on their way to London soon. She wondered what Anne had discovered at the mill and whether Patrick knew the details.

She had found herself thinking a lot about Patrick these past weeks. She supposed that was not surprising, given his solicitousness after her accident. What was more surprising was the *way* she was thinking. Despite her disclaimers to Anne, she had entertained the occasional fantasy in London. Captain Scott had danced with her twice at the Hythes' ball. And what if Sir David Bertram's interest was more than friendly?

How could an avowed romantic not have such fantasies amid the whirl of London society! But she had no such dreams of ex-sergeant Patrick Gillen. Was it easier to be romantic about men who were more present in one's fantasy life than in one's real life? Sarah wondered. And if her feelings for Patrick weren't romantic, then what were they?

She couldn't imagine him sweeping her away from her life at Heriot House. For one thing, she would choose to stay, if it weren't for Anne's marriage plans.

And for another, Patrick was only a head groom, not a baronet or a retired army captain. He had no means to sweep her away.

No, whatever was drawing her to Patrick Gillen was not the part of her that reveled in Cinderella-like tales. It was something she couldn't quite articulate even to herself, except to say that she was drawn to him as though he were a sort of lodestone.

After she finished her supper, she sat for a few minutes sipping a small glass of port. She didn't want to wait for the morning to hear what had happened at the mill. She wanted to find out now. And there was no reason she shouldn't. It was about the time that the horses were being settled for the night. She would walk down to the stables and see if Patrick was there.

He was, and just finishing up his evening work.

"Good evening, Patrick."

"Good evening, Sarah," he said with a welcoming smile. " 'Tis a bit late for ridin', don't ye think?" he added teasingly.

"Anne went right up to bed, and I was too curious about what happened today to wait until morning to find out."

Patrick looked around. "I can't offer ye a seat in the stable, but I could offer ye a cup of tea and a biscuit, if ye wanted to come up to my rooms, if you think it would be the proper thing to do," he added.

"I think at my age and so far away from Society, it would be safe for me to accept your offer without compromising myself," Sarah said humorously.

Patrick's rooms surprised her. She'd expected that a man on his own might be living in a bit of a mess, but the rooms were spotless, and Patrick's few possessions were arranged with great care.

He sat her down in the room that he obviously used both as "parlor" and bedroom, but the alcove with his cot and washstand was halfway screened off so

Sarah was able to convince herself that she wasn't really sitting in a man's bedroom.

"Here ye are—some of Mrs. White's ginger biscuits and tea."

Sarah took a sip and looked up in surprise. "Why, the tea has a ginger flavor too!"

"I got a taste for it in the army. 'Tis a good settler of the digestion. I hope ye like it," he added worriedly.

"It is delightful."

Patrick took the chair opposite and tilted his head a little to the right. Sarah had unconsciously taken in that habitual tilt, but only now did she realize that it was compensation for the loss of his eye. Without thinking, she said, "I have never thought much about your injury, Patrick. Your right eye must get tired, doing all the work."

"Sometimes. But the hardest thing about it is that ye can't judge the depth of things."

"What do you mean?"

"Ye need two eyes to see things as they are. With only one, things sort of flatten out, but because ye know how things *should* look, yer brain helps ye out. At any rate, I only have trouble when the place is unfamiliar. Then it takes a minute to 'see' where a wall ends and a chair begins! 'Tis a good thing I'm a groom and not a butler."

"I am sorry. I didn't know there was more than the obvious difficulty," Sarah said softly.

" 'Tis nothing. Except once in a while, ye want to touch something, just to see the all of it," Patrick said quietly, looking at her face with such concentration that Sarah knew Patrick wasn't talking about chairs. There was something between them that was almost palpable.

She put her cup down and clasped her hands, trying to keep them still, and asked the question she had come to ask. "What happened at the mill today?"

Patrick sat back in his chair. "Miss Heriot interviewed several of the workers. I don't think any of them like Joseph Trantor. But the one they want to get rid of is the foreman, Peter Brill, who gets a percentage of any fine he levies."

"But that means Trantor has given him an incentive."

"Yes, but Miss Heriot is determined to dismiss Brill and hire someone at a higher salary, so there will be no reason to respond to Trantor's offers." Patrick smiled. "One woman even suggested Ned Gibson."

"Ned Gibson!"

"This Mrs. Talbot spoke highly of him, though she admitted he is a bit of a radical."

"Anne would never hire Gibson after what has happened. But do you think she will dismiss him?"

"There is no reason to, Sarah. Not yet. His Nance will vouch for him, so there is no proof that he was over here."

"And what about Joseph?"

"There is no evidence against him, either. And wouldn't he have known Miss Heriot's holiday plans?"

"I don't know that Anne told him when she was leaving for the Astons'. And I can't imagine he would have done the deed himself, anyway. He could have hired someone who delayed. And Anne would have used the saddle, sooner or later."

" 'Tis a good explanation, but I think we'll just have to watch and wait."

"Well, we will be in London soon, where Anne will be safe."

"Are ye both lookin' forward to the balls and breakfasts, then?"

Sarah gave him a smile. "I think Anne is. I enjoyed the Little Season, but the closer Anne comes to choosing a husband, the more I realize how my life is going to change."

"Wouldn't ye stay here?"

"I could, I suppose, but if Anne and her husband choose to spend much of their time here, I would not feel comfortable. And if they didn't, I think I would come to feel lonely and useless."

"Aye, I understand that. But ye might just meet someone at one of these balls, Sarah," Patrick suggested with a quick grin.

"Oh, I don't think so, Sergeant Gillen," said Sarah, stung into formality by his apparent belief that this would be a good thing. She stood up, and as she moved away, her knee jarred the small table between them. Patrick's teacup rolled off and shattered on the floor.

"Oh, dear, I'm so sorry." Sarah went down on her hands and knees and started brushing the pieces together with her fingers, when Patrick's hand covered hers. "Leave it, Sarah, or ye'll be cuttin' yerself on the splinters. I'll get it later."

"No, no," Sarah protested. "It was my fault. Let me clean it up." Patrick was kneeling next to her, and the closeness of his shoulder to hers distracted her so that she got a small sliver of china stuck in her hand and gave a little gasp of pain.

"There now, will ye give over?" said Patrick, sitting back on his heels and taking her hand in his. He held it close to his good eye and gently brushed it with his thumb.

"Damn, I can feel it, but I can't see it well enough to pull it out."

"It is all right, Patrick, really," said Sarah, knowing she should stand up, but unwilling to pull her hand away.

"Wait a minute—there, I got it!" Patrick declared. "I don't think it went in deep, but it is bleedin' a little."

Sarah gently withdrew her hand and raised it to her lips to suck the small wound, the way she had with childhood scrapes. "It is fine," she said and was about to rise when Patrick reached out and found her face, cupping it gently in his broad hand.

"Sure and I've been wantin' to do this for a long

time," he said, as he traced a finger gently over her lips. "But I wasn't sure I would be findin' them," he added, with a glint in his eye. He tilted her face and gave her a gentle kiss on the lips.

Sarah sank back on her heels as he slowly increased the pressure, and her mouth opened under his. She lifted her own hand and reached up to run it through Patrick's thick hair. "And I've been wanting to do this for a long time," she whispered.

"Ye're a beautiful woman, Sarah Wheeler."

"Thank you, Patrick," she said softly, her face flushing with both embarrassment and pleasure.

"And I can't understand why such a beautiful woman hasn't a home and husband of her own."

"Beauty doesn't make up for lack of money, Patrick."

" 'Tis sad that the men ye have met have felt that way, for to me, beauty is almost everything."

"Almost?"

"Sure, and even beauty is nothing without a loving heart. But ye've got that, Sarah."

Sarah pulled herself away and stumbled up. Patrick's words had touched her so deeply that she didn't know what she might do. No, that wasn't true, she thought wildly. I would kiss *him* this time.

Patrick looked up at her for a moment and then stood up. "I shouldn't have done that, Sarah."

"I am glad you did, Patrick. It is a moment I will cherish. But I must go now."

She was down the stairs before he could say, "But I'd be happy to give ye more moments to cherish, Sarah Wheeler." Yet how could I be doin' that? he asked himself. She might be an employee like he was, but there was a greater distance between them than that between the stables and the house. She was a lady, no matter her station in life. A true lady, for she could have made him feel he had stolen something from her, and instead she'd left him feelin' that he had given her something.

* * *

As she hurried across the yard, Sarah realized she was thirty-three years old and had at last received her first real kiss. She wouldn't count the slobbering of the Beresfords' son.

How pitiful that it had taken this long. And yet how lovely it had been. She could still feel Patrick's lips on hers, the feel of his hair under her fingers, and she grew warm at the memory. She would cherish the moment, as she had told him. It would be something to hold on to, wherever her life took her.

At breakfast the next morning, she listened to Anne's account of her visit as though she were hearing it for the first time.

"So you intend to fire Brill?"

"Definitely. Joseph will not like it, but when all is said and done, as the owner, I make the final decision."

"I am proud of you, Anne," Sarah told her. "It is never easy to begin questioning our long-held assumptions."

"Thank you, Sarah, but you are giving me more credit than I deserve. It is a relatively small thing to fire a foreman."

"But it will make a big difference in your workers' lives." Sarah hesitated. "Did you speak with Ned Gibson?"

"No, I trusted that Patrick got as much out of him as I would have." Anne laughed, and Sarah looked over at her with surprise.

"I am only remembering how we met Sergeant Gillen, Sarah. I am very grateful to that sweeping boy for bringing him into our lives. Not only did I get myself an excellent groom, but someone whose experiences are very useful in a situation like this."

"Yes, Patrick makes me feel safe," Sarah said without thinking. "That is, I am sure he can keep you safe, Anne."

"Yes, I know what you mean," Anne said with a quizzical smile. "From what Rosie says, you and he are becoming fast friends."

"Rosie should mind her wagging little tongue," Sarah responded sharply.

"Why, Sarah, that is not like you at all. Did I touch on a tender subject? Is there something between you and Patrick?"

"Would you mind if there was? Not that there is," Sarah hastened to add.

"You know how much I like and admire Patrick. But he is only a groom, and you are . . ."

"Granddaughter to a viscount, yes. How could I forget?" Sarah said with uncustomary irony. "And much good it has done me!"

"My father would never have hired you otherwise, so it has done *me* much good," Anne said quietly. "And I was hoping that I could give something back to you, Sarah. There was more than one man in London who sought you out. Captain Scott or Sir David would be very appropriate for . . ."

"The granddaughter of a viscount," Sarah intoned, but this time humorously, and they both laughed. "Don't worry, Anne. Sergeant Gillen and I may have become friends, but it is no more than that." On his part, Sarah continued to herself. For her own part . . . well, Patrick Gillen had made his way into her dreams, waking and sleeping.

When Joseph Trantor arrived for his fortnight meeting with Anne later that week, he did not immediately sit down to go over the accounts. Instead he stood, his back to the fire and his face closed and angry. "I heard that you visited the mill without my permission, Anne."

"I hardly need your permission to visit my own mill, Joseph," Anne responded with barely controlled anger.

Her cousin flushed. "Forgive me, cousin," he apologized stiffly. "Of course tha art right. But it would have been a courtesy to let me know. I would have joined tha."

"But then my visit would have been managed, Joseph, as it was the last time. I wanted to talk to some of the workers by myself. It was enlightening, I must say."

"I can't imagine Swain or Walters had much to say to tha?"

Of course Brill would have told Joseph whom she had seen. But the worried note in his voice told her that he had no idea what had been said, and she silently blessed the two men for keeping their mouths shut. It had annoyed her, but their reticence benefited her now.

"No, they were both reluctant to discuss anything of substance with me, probably because I am a woman."

"I hope tha were not too disappointed, then?" Joseph asked with patently false sympathy.

"A little, but then I spoke with Mrs. Talbot."

Joseph lifted his eyebrows. "Oh? I thought she was off to be a farmer's wife."

So Brill had neglected to mention Mrs. Talbot? He probably thought a woman wouldn't know anything, thought Anne.

"It was her last week. She was very helpful to me in making a decision, Joseph. I want you to dismiss Peter Brill."

"Dismiss Peter? Why, he's invaluable! I appointed him after James Brand retired."

"James was a fair and honest man; Brill is not."

"Are you accusing me of hiring a thief?" Joseph asked indignantly.

"I am accusing tha of nowt, Joseph," said Anne, falling into broad Yorkshire for a moment. "Though I might accuse tha of encouraging tha foreman to punish petty infractions by letting him collect a percentage from the fines."

"He has been a loyal employee, Anne. It seemed

to me that a little reward for his vigilance was not unreasonable."

"If Peter Brill deserved a higher salary, you should have paid it directly."

"That would have cut into our profits, Anne."

"You have been thinking too much of 'our' profits, cousin," Anne said coolly. "They would be 'our' profits only if you married me." She reconsidered and gave him an ironic smile. "No, they would be *tha* profits if we married, wouldn't they?"

"Tha'rt not suggesting I wish to marry tha merely for monetary reasons, Anne! Tha knows I am very fond of tha, not that tha has let me speak of it before."

Anne's face softened. "I know, Joseph. But you're also a good businessman, as I am a good businesswoman. If I am interested in what marriage to an earl might bring me, why shouldn't you be interested in what I bring tha? I don't fault you for it."

"I see us as having rather different motives, Anne. After all, tha don't care for any of your earls or dukes, while I do care for tha."

"I appreciate your caring, Joseph, but my mind is made up. I will find my husband in London, and you will dismiss Brill. And before I leave, so that I may consult with his replacement."

Joseph opened his mouth as though to protest and then closed it again. "Of course, Anne."

"Thank you, Joseph. Shall we turn to other business? The price of Irish wool has gone down. Should we buy some?"

Anne breathed a sigh of relief when her cousin finally left. The tension between them as they did their work had been so strong that she was exhausted from trying to screen it out and concentrate on wool prices and the output of the mills.

She sat down in front of the library fire with a glass of sherry and waited for the Amontillado to relax her. She was sorry for Joseph. Clearly he did care for her.

But did that mean she was more unfeeling than he? She wasn't intending to marry someone she disliked, after all. She liked both Leighton and Windham very much. She was sure that with either of them there was the potential for the growth of affection and perhaps even love.

Then why, she wondered, as the warmth of the fire and the sherry began to have their effect, was it Jack Belden's long-fingered hands that she could almost feel around her waist and the pressure of his lips on hers? And why was it that whenever she imagined how the Season would unfold, it was Jack Belden who was always her dance partner in her imaginary waltzes?

There was little curiosity at the mill when Trantor closeted himself with Peter Brill the next day, until those closest to the foreman's office heard the raised voices even over the noise of their looms. Trantor and the foreman had not had a disagreement in anyone's memory, and the men looked at each other, raising their eyebrows and shrugging their shoulders expressively. When Brill came out, carrying his few personal belongings, the surprise and then the satisfaction on the men's faces was obvious.

"We knew," said one of the men, telling the story later in the Hart and Horn, "that soomthing was up, but it weren't till our Peter came out with his old coat and his tea mug that we guessed what were going on!"

"But why would Trantor let him go?" asked Ned. "Brill was his source of information at the mill. It doesn't make sense."

"Aye, but it does," George Talbot piped up. "My Martha told me that Miss Heriot listened to all she had to say. She didn't give away nowt, but Martha thinks she were sympathetic. I'll wager it were she that ordered him dismissed."

Tom Gibson snorted derisively. " 'Twere more

likely Trantor and Brill had a falling-out. Maybe he was holding money back."

The men nodded. "Aye, tha makes good sense, Tom."

"I still think my Martha is right," Talbot insisted stubbornly.

"Well, tha can think what tha bloody well like, George," Tom said with a laugh. "But I know what I know, and that is that there is nowt a Heriot would do for t'workers."

Chapter Fifteen

Gibson's cynicism seemed confirmed a few days later. Ned had gone outside to relieve himself, when he heard screaming from the sorting shed. He was there even before Girton, the children's supervisor, and he took in the situation at a glance. Little Katie Hyland's skirt had become caught in the rollers and she was pulled back tight against the machine. She was frozen there, too frightened to cry. It was the other children around her who were screaming, for they remembered the last accident all too well. It was clear they were expecting the roller to swallow her up.

"Hush now," murmured Ned as he slowly approached Katie. She was safe for the moment, but the machine had caught enough of the material so she could not be torn free. As long as she was frozen by fear, she was in no danger of injury. If she moved a hand, however, and the machine caught the edge of her sleeve . . .

Ned knelt a few feet in front of her. "Now, then, Katie, tha'rt caught fast, I know, but that machine can do nothing to tha if tha stays still. Does tha understand me?"

The child was in shock, but she finally nodded.

"All right, then. Jimmy," Ned called to one of the older boys who had been trying to quiet the little ones.

"Aye, Ned?"

"Tha must run up to t'loft and get me some shears. Does tha think tha can do it quickly, lad?"

"Aye, Ned." The boy was gone, and Ned stayed where he was, murmuring soothing words to Katie.

Before Jimmy got back with the shears, however, Girton burst into the shed. "What on earth is all that caterwauling? What art tha doing here, Gibson?"

"Shut tha face and listen." Ned said quietly but forcefully. "Tha needs to shut off the machine."

"I can't do that without Mr. Trantor's orders. T'machine runs all day, tha knows that."

"Not if it is eating up Katie's dress, it doesn't! Shut it off, or I will feed tha to it," said Ned, staring Girton down.

"All right, but tha will be responsible for this. The child could be cut out."

"Before Jimmy gets back with the shears, she might be dead from shock or move and lose an arm, tha sheep-buggering bastard."

A few of the older boys snickered.

"I'll report tha for this, Ned Gibson," said Girton as he walked to the back of the machine. When it finally stopped, Katie slipped into a faint, and Ned moved forward to hold her up. "There there, sweetheart, tha was a brave lass and will be free soon."

A few minutes later Jimmy burst in, carrying a heavy pair of shears. "Here, Ned."

"Tha did well, Jimmy. T'danger's over now, but t'only way to get her out is to cut her out."

It took some effort to cut through the bunched and twisted fabric, and by the time Ned succeeded, Katie was conscious again. When she was finally free, she gave a little moan and Ned opened his arms. "Tha needs soom fresh air and maybe a sip of tea, lass," he murmured, and he scooped her up and carried her out.

"Jimmy, go get her mother. She's on t'second floor."

Ned was in the yard in the center of a crowd of children when Joseph Trantor rode in.

"What the devil is going on here, Gibson?" he demanded.

"Aye, t'devil truly has something to do with it," Ned responded. "That devil machine. 'Tis old and needs replacing, as tha well knows. Katie Hyland got caught in it."

"Is she hurt?" asked Joseph, in a softer tone.

"No, no thanks to tha or Miss Heriot," Ned announced angrily.

At that moment, Mrs. Hyland, white-faced and trembling, came out the mill door. "Where is she? Where's my Katie?"

"She's right here, Mrs. Hyland. She's not hurt, just a little frightened. She's a brave lass, your daughter. She stood still till we got her out."

"Oh, thank God," cried Mrs. Hyland, pushing her way through the children and taking her daughter into her arms. "Thank God! And thank tha, Ned Gibson," she added with a sob.

Joseph had dismounted. "Get back to work." In a gentler tone he added, "Mrs. Hyland, tha may stay with tha daughter for a few minutes."

"Thank tha, Mr. Trantor," she said, bobbing her head.

After she left, Girton came hurrying out. "Mr. Trantor, thank goodness tha'rt here."

Trantor turned to him. "What happened here? Why isn't t'machine running?"

"Gibson threatened to feed me to it if I didn't turn it off, sir," Girton whined. "I told him we could have cut her out."

"And I told tha if she moved she could have lost a hand. It's not like tha could do anything till t'lass was free, anyway, tha witless bastard." Ned turned to Trantor. "Tha knows t'machine is old and needs replacing. But it seems we only buy new machines if it will get rid of some workers, not save them."

"And how did tha get involved in all of this, Gibson?" Trantor demanded.

"I was outside, taking a piss when I heard t'children screaming."

"Why didn't you get Girton?"

"There wasn't time."

"Well, tha may or may not have saved t'lass from injury, Gibson, but tha has lost thaself tha job. Get tha things and go."

"What for?"

"For threatening a supervisor, for one, and for disrespect to me, for another."

"I have nowt to collect, Trantor, and I'm glad to show this place my back." Ned clenched his hands to keep himself from punching Trantor in his self-righteous face. It was bad enough he was losing his job; he didn't need to add a jail sentence. He turned his back on them both and walked out whistling the same tune Nancy had been whistling the day she was let go.

His whistling stopped soon enough. As soon as he was out of earshot, his shoulders slumped. "Tha'rt a fool, Ned Gibson. Tha might have gotten off with a fine from staying away too long from t'loom if tha hadn't called Girton a sheep-buggering bastard. Now there's two Gibsons out of work."

He made his way through the narrow lanes till he came to the Huttons' house. Nance's shock at seeing him there in the middle of the day turned immediately to worry. "Tha'rt not hurt, Ned?"

"No, lass, I'm fine. Can I coom in for a cup of tea?" he asked with a rueful smile.

"How does tha have time for a cup of tea, Ned? What are tha doing here in t'middle of afternoon?"

"I've been dismissed, Nance."

Nance gave a helpless laugh. "Just when I thought things were looking up, tha gets thaself dismissed. I don't see how we will ever get married."

"What does tha mean, looking up?" Ned asked.

"Just today I got word that Mr. Yates in north part of town is looking for help—soomthing between a maid and a shop girl. I'll be keeping his rooms clean and helping with the stock."

"You got t'job?"

"It were almost like it were made for me. And t'pay is what I were making at t'mill, and I'm free after four o'clock on Saturday!"

Ned sighed in relief. "Thank God tha'll be all right, Nance. I'll have to start looking tomorrow. I won't find anything in town, by t'time word gets around. But maybe one of t'local farmers . . ."

"But then tha'll be traveling long hours back and from work, Ned," Nance protested.

"Sometimes a farmer boards his help, Nance," Ned said slowly.

"Oh, Ned, then we'll never see one another, married or no. Whatever did tha do?"

"Little Katie Hyland got caught in t'rollers, Nance. I made Girton turn t'machine off. And I told both him and Trantor what I thought of them and their damned machines."

"Then there is no chance of doing work at any other mill?"

"No, word will get out. I'll be like Tom."

"Oh, no, tha won't! I will not let tha turn into an ale-soaked do-nothing, Ned."

"Now, Nance."

"I know he's tha brother, Ned, but tha'rt willing to look for other work, where Tom gave up."

"But I've never been to jail, Nance. I don't blame Tom for what he's become. But, by God, I do blame that damn Miss Heriot and her cousin."

Nance nodded in agreement. " 'Tis true, Ned. T'mill has never been easy, but Mr. Heriot would never have let tha go for soomthing like this. He'd have fined tha or even suspended tha. But it seems Miss Heriot is t'spoiled bitch Tom thinks her."

"Mrs. Talbot thinks she's behind Brill's dismissal," said Ned, in a halfhearted attempt to consider another side.

"And she's t'only one! We all know 'tis more likely he and Trantor had a falling-out." Nance hesitated.

"But does tha think if tha approached Miss Heriot . . . ?"

"I did that once and what did it get me? No, I have other ideas for Miss Heriot and Trantor, Nance," he said, his face suddenly hard and closed.

"Tha won't do anything foolish, Ned?"

"Don't worry. I won't."

Joseph Trantor rode over to the hall the next day and met Sarah, Anne, and Patrick as they were returning from their ride.

"Good morning, Joseph. This is a surprise."

"I did not wish tha to go back to London without my good wishes, Anne."

"Thank you, cousin. I appreciate that," Anne told him warmly.

"I also needed to inform tha about a situation at the mill."

"Not another accident, I hope!"

"Only a minor one, Anne. In the sorting shed."

"Was another child hurt?"

"No, the Hyland lass's skirt got caught in t'rollers, but Girton turned t'machine off so she could be cut out."

"Thank God for that!"

"And I had to let Ned Gibson go," Joseph added.

Patrick, who had been riding in front, turned all the way 'round in his saddle when he heard that. "And why did ye need to do that, sor?" he asked quietly.

"Because he threatened Girton and was insubordinate to me. And may I suggest that the management of the stables and not the mill is tha business, Sergeant Gillen?"

"Patrick has been very helpful to me in a number of ways, Joseph. Why did Gibson threaten Girton?"

"Because he wasn't sure the machine needed to be turned off."

"So it was Ned Gibson who saved the little girl?"

"They were going to cut her out, Anne. It was only her skirt that was caught."

Anne shuddered as she tried to picture what it would be like to be trapped so close to that threatening machine. "The child must have been terrified," she whispered.

"I am sure it was frightening," Trantor admitted. "But it wasn't her hand or arm, after all. At any rate, we are lucky to get rid of Ned Gibson at last."

"What will he do, Mr. Trantor?" Sarah asked.

"He'll never find work in a mill again, I'll make sure of that. Happen he'll get something on a sheep farm soomwhere."

Anne took a deep breath. "I can't ask you to rethink your decision, Joseph, for I have no time to hear both sides out. We are leaving for London the day after tomorrow. But I am not sure I agree with it. Despite his insubordination, it sounds like Ned Gibson did the right thing." Anne hesitated. "It also sounds like we need to replace that machine."

"Now, Anne, a new machine would be an enormous expense."

"Yet we are considering a steam-powered loom?"

"But that will pay for itself," Trantor protested.

"I want you to have the machine inspected. I also want you to visit some mills that have the newer machines. I am sorry to add this to your responsibilities, Joseph."

Anne could see that her cousin was angry, but he merely said politely, "Of course, cousin."

"Do you have time to join us for nuncheon?"

"I have too much to do already, and given tha requests, I'd better decline. I wish you well in tha London, er, ventures."

"I want you to know that I appreciate your good wishes and your hard work for me, Joseph," Anne told him. Despite her sincerity, however, she was relieved to see him go.

Anne never slept well before traveling, but she got

hardly any sleep the night before they left, what with her usual nervousness and the horrifying images of a child caught in the carding machine.

"You look dreadful, Anne. Did you sleep at all?" Sarah asked her sympathetically the next morning.

"Very little," Anne confessed. "I could not help thinking about the accident at the mill. I hate leaving all that unfinished business behind. And leaving Patrick here! I'll have to hire an interim groom in London, but I want someone at the hall who is capable of dealing with any trouble that may arise. Ned Gibson has even more reason now to wish to harm the Heriot family."

"I had already thought of that," Sarah admitted.

"Well, there is nothing he can do to either of us once we are safely on our way, and Patrick will inform me if anything happens at the mill."

After Anne went upstairs to see to last-minute packing, Sarah walked over to the window. She supposed she should be excited at their return to London, but instead she felt reluctant to leave Yorkshire. The truth was, as she was well aware, she, too, was reluctant to leave Patrick behind.

It wasn't that she expected anything more from him. In London, the social distance between them would have been more emphasized, for she would be taking part in the Season, albeit peripherally, while he would be restricted to taking care of the horses and accompanying them on rides in the park. Where it was possible they would meet a prospective suitor, like Captain Scott.

She had never expected anyone to take much notice of her, but Lord Faringdon and the Astons had made sure that a few suitable men had sought her out. The trouble was, she didn't want any of those suitable men. She wanted someone utterly unsuitable—a one-eyed Irish soldier whose kiss had stolen her heart. And she hadn't even had the opportunity to say good-bye to him.

Sarah could feel her heart beating a little faster. Her packing was done. There was no reason in the world she couldn't walk down to the stables to bid her mare good-bye. And if Patrick Gillen happened to be there . . . well, then, she would say her farewell to him too.

Patrick was nowhere in sight. "I just wanted to wish Gypsy a good-bye," she told the stable lad, feeling very self-conscious.

"Sergeant Gillen has got her out back, Miss Wheeler. She picked up a stone and he's picking it out."

"In for a penny, in for a pound," she whispered and made her way to the paddock.

Patrick had Gypsy's hoof on his knee and was probing it with his hoof pick.

"Good morning, Patrick."

He looked up in surprise. "Good morning, Sarah. I thought ye'd be packin' yer last ball gown this morning."

"I wanted to wish Gypsy good-bye."

It seemed the flimsiest of excuses to Sarah, but Patrick only smiled, and releasing Gypsy's hoof, led her over to the fence.

Sarah reached out and stroked the mare's nose. "I'll miss you while I'm in London," she murmured. She felt so foolishly obvious that she actually started blushing.

"I'm sure she'll be missing ye, too, Sarah. Sure and we all will," Patrick said with a smile.

Sarah took a deep breath and, keeping her voice steady, said, "I am very sorry you won't be with us, Patrick."

"To tell the truth, Sarah, I'm not," he confessed. "I had enough of London to last a lifetime, and I'm needed here."

Sarah blushed even deeper. Clearly Patrick Gillen wouldn't miss her at all. The few moments that she cherished probably meant nothing to him. She reached out and patted Gypsy again, muttered a good-bye, and turned to go.

"I suppose ye're lookin' forward to it? 'Tis the world in which ye really belong, isn't it?"

Patrick's tone was light, but Sarah heard something more in his question. She could ignore what might be there or she could take a risk. She turned back and, looking at him directly, said quietly, "I have been very happy here this winter, Patrick. And I will miss you as well as Gypsy." She extended her hand.

He captured it between his, warming her with his body heat and something else entirely. "I will miss ye too, Sarah. I wish the best for ye." After a moment or two he let her go, and mumbling another good-bye, Sarah hurried away.

Patrick looped the reins over Gypsy's neck, and she turned and nuzzled his shirt. "She deserves the best, yer mistress. I should be hopin' she meets someone in London, someone better suited for her than an old soldier like me. But God forgive me, I can't, for I want her for myself."

Chapter Sixteen

Once again, they were fortunate in the weather. There was one rainy day on the trip, the last, but the rain was light and intermittent and the roads stayed fairly dry. But it seemed they had brought the rain with them to London, for the whole first week it rained every day. By their third day in the city, Anne knew Sarah was going crazy, but she herself was quite satisfied to stay in bed until late morning and return to her bed in the afternoon for a nap. All her excitement over the Season and deciding on a husband and the direction of her new life seemed to have drained away, leaving her uninterested in anything. She knew part of her strange lassitude was a result of the trip and the dreariness of the weather, which kept them from morning exercise. But she also suspected that her mood had something to do with the unsolved problems she had left behind. Now that her eyes were opened to the realities of the mill, she couldn't close them again. At the same time, she had no idea what she could do. Children shouldn't be working in such dangerous circumstances. But if she didn't hire the children, their families would lose much-needed income and send them to work elsewhere anyway. She could replace the carding machine and perhaps even reduce their hours without reducing their wages, but whatever small changes she made would hardly affect the British factory system. Surely more widespread reforms were needed, but how could she help make them? She couldn't vote, couldn't run for Parliament.

The only influence she might have would be through her husband.

But where on earth had her sense of satisfaction from being in charge of her own destiny disappeared to? The practical Anne Heriot who had come to London in the fall and matter-of-factly drawn up her list of prospective mates seemed to have disappeared, and in her place was a reluctant young woman who only wanted to pull the covers up over her head.

Anne's behavior was so unlike her that by the fourth day Sarah decided she needed to address it.

"Are you quite sure you are not coming down with something, Anne?" she asked her employer at breakfast.

"Other than a severe case of the blue devils, I don't think so," Anne replied with a painful smile.

"Can you talk to me about it?"

"I don't know what to tell you. It is the mills, in part, and my worries about Joseph. And this weather! If t'bloody rain doesn't stop soon, I will scream!"

"And I will join you," Sarah said lightly, ignoring Anne's swearing. "But it has to end sometime, and these invitations are beginning to pile up. Aren't you looking forward to seeing Lord Windham again? Or even Lord Aldborough?" she added teasingly.

"I thought I was. Oh, I am sure I will be, once the weather clears and we can ride and walk again." Anne sighed. "But it seemed very simple in November, Sarah. Make a list, meet the men on it, decide upon one, and marry him!" Anne laughed. "Now that I look back, I think I was being much more naive than practical. I was thinking so much about what I was moving toward that I forgot what I might leave behind. Or be putting into another's hands."

"The mills?"

"I have been thinking, Sarah, that I want to institute some reforms in the mills. Perhaps even go so far as to cut the hours, but not the wages, of the children," she said hesitantly.

Sarah gave Anne a warm smile. "An excellent idea."

"But perhaps not a practical one, Sarah," Anne said, a little spark of humor back in her eyes.

"I doubt that it would cut into your profits excessively, so we can acquit you of being impractical," Sarah responded, happy to see some life back in Anne's eyes.

"Yet a very small change when one takes into account all the children in all the factories. I'd like to do more, but once I am married, I will only be able to make changes through my husband."

"So now you have an added consideration in making your choice. Is that part of what is bothering you?"

"Yes. I have no idea what Windham's or Leighton's opinions are."

"And Lord Aldborough?"

"From our conversations over the holidays, I think he might be open to my ideas. But I cannot imagine the Jack of Hearts as a reformer, can you?"

"I think you will need to question all three of them."

"I suppose you are right." Anne looked over at her friend and smiled. "Putting all this into words has been helpful, Sarah. Thank you." She glanced out the window, where the rain seemed finally to be letting up. "You know, despite the fact that we will get a soaking, I am inclined to send for the carriage. We could have a drive to Hatchard's or the bazaar."

Anne was right. Even with their pattens, cloaks, and umbrellas, they were wet just walking from the carriage to the front door of Hatchard's. She didn't mind the discomfort, however, for it was so good to be out and moving again after her unusual lethargy.

They were so intent on avoiding the deeper puddles that she ran right into a departing customer as they approached the door.

"I beg your pardon," she apologized.

"Not at all, miss. Why it is Miss Heriot, isn't it?"

"Lord Windham! What a delightful surprise," said Anne.

"You cannot stand here in the rain, Miss Heriot." He held the door open for them and ushered them inside before he folded his umbrella and followed them in.

"When did you return to London?"

"The end of last week, my lord. And we have been prisoners of the rain ever since," said Anne with a smile. "We had to get out today, no matter how wet it is."

"I know what you mean. I have been keeping myself busy with paperwork and estate business, but there is only so much energy one can devote to that. I needed a diversion. Are you looking for anything in particular? Can I recommend Mrs. Radclyffe's latest? My cousin tells me it is delightful."

"Then Sarah must have it," said Anne. "I am torn between educating myself in the poetic tradition and the newest ideas on labor reform," she said lightly, but she watched Lord Windham's face very carefully.

"You are interested in reform, Miss Heriot?" he asked, his curiosity apparent. "But, of course, you have been very involved in your father's mills. I forgot."

"Then you don't think it odd for a woman to concern herself with such things?"

"Not a woman like you, Miss Heriot," he answered warmly. "Of course, at some point in the future, I am sure your husband will want to share these concerns."

"Indeed, I am hoping so, Lord Windham."

"Well, this table holds the latest in poetry, Miss Heriot. Did you want to read a contemporary, like Mr. Wordsworth?"

"I suppose I should become more familiar with his work, but for now, I am looking for a collection."

"Here is one."

It was the collection Jack Belden had been reading,

and for some reason Anne had been hoping to obtain a copy.

"Thank you, my lord. That looks just the thing."

Sarah, who had been paging through a book on the other side of the table, said, "I think I will choose poetry this time also, Anne. Here is a volume of Robert Burns's work."

"One of Elspeth's favorite poets, Sarah. I don't know if I can stand it if you start reciting in broad Scots, though, the way Elspeth does!"

"I doubt I can roll my *'r's* the way she does, not having been born to it," said Sarah, attempting a Scots accent as she spoke.

Lord Windham laughed. "You do very well, Miss Wheeler. Mr. Burns is not to everyone's taste, of course, but if you are familiar with him . . ."

Anne, whose warm feelings for Lord Windham had become stronger at his seemingly favorable response to her talk of reform, found herself a little irritated by his protective stance. She knew that Mr. Burns had written some very bawdy poetry, because Elspeth had recited one to her at school. They had both gasped and giggled. "Wherever did you learn that, Elspeth?" she had asked her friend. "My father has several volumes of Burns's work. Of course, I was forbidden one of them, but that only made me more curious."

But Burns's more explicit poetry was hardly likely to be on display in the middle of Mayfair!

"I think it is refreshing to read a workingman's thoughts, don't you, Lord Windham?" Sarah asked sweetly.

"Why, yes, Miss Wheeler. And Burns is quite a popular poet."

"As popular as Lord Byron?" Anne asked with feigned innocence.

"I believe Lord Byron's popularity has waned recently," Windham responded.

Anne was about to ask, "Oh, why is that?" when Sarah, familiar with her sense of humor, gave her a warning look. Anne may not be familiar with his poetry, but she was very familiar with his reputation and knew he was not a proper topic for conversation.

"May I escort you two ladies to Gunther's for a cup of tea and some pastries?" Lord Windham asked after Anne paid for their books.

"Another day I would be delighted, my lord, but I don't want to keep the coachman in the rain too long," Anne replied.

"Then I will hope to see you at the Hairstons' supper dance?"

"I look forward to it, my lord."

"Lord Windham seemed genuinely happy to see you, Anne," Sarah declared once they were settled in the carriage.

"As I was to see him. He has always been my favorite, and today he expressed some openness to my ideas." Anne gave Sarah a mischievous smile. "He seemed overly proper in his attitudes toward poetry, though."

"I am glad I caught your eye before it was too late. There was no need to embarrass him."

"You must admit, it would have been amusing to see him trying to explain Lord Byron's fall from grace!"

Sarah smiled. "Indeed, it would have."

"He is a thoroughly nice young man," Anne said emphatically.

"Is that a problem?" Sarah asked humorously.

"I don't think so. And he is a full year older than I am. But his sense of humor is not as well developed as Leighton's."

"Perhaps you will end up preferring humor and experience over seriousness after all," Sarah responded lightly.

Anne had left most of her new wardrobe in London over the winter, so it was almost like shopping all over again to rediscover her evening gowns and walking dresses. For the supper dance, she'd decided on a dark rose silk with a smoky gauze overdress and a bodice embroidered with jet and crystal. Although young women usually wore pastels, she had fallen in love with the color at first sight and decided that since she was not really a member of Society, she could get away with something darker.

She was very happy with her choice. She wanted to sparkle on her first appearance of the Season, and in this dress she would do so quite literally, she thought, as she appreciated the tiny fires flashing from the crystal embroidery.

They arrived a little late due to a horse's lameness and were greeted only by their host, the duchess having just gone downstairs to join her guests. Anne apologized, explaining their delay.

"There is no need to worry, Miss Heriot. Indeed, I am happy that your off-wheeler went lame, for now I have the opportunity to take you down to the ballroom myself and claim your first dance. I am honored to be with the most scintillating young lady at the ball," he added with an approving smile.

Anne smiled back, and she and Sarah went down the steps arm in arm with their host. Sarah was quickly whisked away by Captain Scott, who had been watching for her.

"Miss Wheeler seems to have made a conquest last fall," commented the duke as he led Anne into a country dance.

"Two or three men became quite fond of her, I suspect. It is just what I was hoping for. But I am not sure any of them have captured Sarah's interest," she added.

"Well, they have all spring to do so. As do your admirers," he added with a smile.

"Look, Val, there is Anne with Hairston. She looks lovely, doesn't she?" Elspeth added. "How I wish I could wear a dress like that. But it is not at all my style or color."

Val looked at his wife and smiled. "Ah, but you look even lovelier in your green, Elspeth. And I prefer simplicity."

Elspeth was indeed looking elegant in her gown, which brought out the green flecks in her hazel eyes.

"I am lucky Madame Celeste was able to alter the bodice for me. I have gone from being slender to . . ."

"A most becoming fullness," said Val, caressing her with his eyes. Elspeth felt liquid and warm under his gaze. She had had a few weeks where she hadn't been able to keep any food down and felt exhausted all the time. Val had been very supportive, holding the basin for her and reassuring her that just holding her in his arms was enough, when she apologized for her lack of interest in lovemaking.

Now the worst was over, however, and her desire for her husband seemed to have returned tenfold. These days, if she took to her bed in the afternoon, it was not alone and certainly not to sleep, she thought with a blush. In fact, she was hoping to persuade him to leave early tonight!

As though he'd read her mind, Val groaned softly and whispered, "You are going to exhaust me, Elspeth. I will be dead before our child is even born!"

"We had best make the most of this time," Elspeth said with a smile, "because I suspect that the baby will change everything."

"You are blooming tonight, Elspeth," said Jack Belden as he joined them.

"I was just telling my wife the same thing."

"I see Miss Heriot is looking lovely also," Jack said blandly. "When did she arrive in town?"

"She has been here for a week."

"Do you know whether Sergeant Gillen was able to discover who was behind that riding accident, Val?"

"Our journey to London took far longer than we expected because of the rain, so we have only been here a few days ourselves. Elspeth hasn't had a chance to visit with Anne yet."

"Though I expect to tomorrow, and I will make sure to ask her," said Elspeth.

"Or you might ask her yourself," suggested Val.

Jack smiled. "If I stay here, she is sure to come over, and perhaps I will be lucky enough to take her in to supper."

Anne had already spied the Astons, and when their dance was over, she asked the duke to lead her to them. She had seen Jack, of course, but there was no need to avoid him. They had established a rapport over the holidays, and she had no rational reason to feel embarrassed by a ritual kiss under the mistletoe, she told herself.

"Here you are, Miss Heriot," said the duke. "I regret that I can't have the next dance, too, but I must see to the rest of my guests," he apologized as he bowed his farewell.

"You are looking wonderful, Elspeth," said Anne.

"I have received more compliments this evening than ever before in my life. It is an odd thing to finally be considered attractive, and all because one is increasing."

Anne gave her friend a sympathetic grin and then asked, "When did you arrive in town?"

"We were just telling Jack how the weather delayed us."

"Sarah and I made it just before the rain, but it has been as dreary a week in town as it would have been traveling."

"It almost felt at times like we were back in Spain, crawling along at a snail's pace," joked Elspeth. "We got stuck twice and ended up in some rather unpleasant inns. I would have been more comfortable in an army tent!"

"When did you arrive, Lord Aldborough?" Anne asked politely.

"I have been here for several weeks, Miss Heriot, getting my aunt and cousins settled."

"Is one of your cousins coming out this spring?"

"No, thank God, since I couldn't afford it, but it is a treat for them, since Lincoln can be quite bleak in the winter."

"That was kind of you, my lord," Anne told him approvingly. "How old are your cousins?"

"Lydia is eleven and Helen is almost seventeen."

"Then they are young enough to enjoy Astley's. And Lady Helen is old enough for the theater and museums," said Elspeth with a smile.

"Yes, I'll have to keep them busy with sight-seeing and away from the Pantheon bazaar, although I am sure shopping is high on their list of preferred activities," Jack responded ironically. "Perhaps you would like to join us on one of our outings, Elspeth? Miss Heriot? I would greatly appreciate the support."

"We would be happy to, wouldn't we, Anne?"

Anne nodded. She could hardly refuse, and accompanying his cousins was hardly encouraging him in his suit.

"Is your supper dance taken, Miss Heriot?"

Anne glanced at her card, although she knew it wasn't. "No, it doesn't seem to be."

"Then may I claim it?"

"I would be delighted, my lord."

Anne's card filled quickly, and she was very happy that Lord Windham and the baron were among the first to approach her. Both asked for the supper dance, and it was frustrating to have to tell them it was already spoken for.

When the time came for her dance with Leighton, he looked down at her with a twinkle in his eye and said, "Miss Heriot, much as I would enjoy dancing with you, I am wondering if you would enjoy a walk around the room instead? I had hoped to be your supper partner and have the opportunity for some conversation."

"I would be very happy to skip a dance, sir," Anne confessed.

Leighton took her arm, and they strolled around the periphery of the dance floor.

"Did you and your daughter enjoy the holidays, my lord?"

"We did. We spent them at my late wife's parents. I have always thought it important for Eliza to keep in touch with her grandparents."

"That is very good of you," Anne said warmly. "It must have been painful at first?"

"It was. Eliza was only five when my wife died."

"I am sorry. I know what it is like to lose a mother."

"Well, it was a long time ago, Miss Heriot. But because of Eliza's youth, I have tried to keep her interests to the fore. Now that she is older, however, I am able to think more of my own needs." Leighton put a subtle emphasis on "own" and covered Anne's hand with his.

"How old is Eliza?"

"She is fifteen and very impatient to grow up," laughed the baron. "She is in London with me this spring, you know, and I am hoping that the two of you could meet."

"I would very much like that."

"Good. I want you to get to know each other, for Eliza is getting to the age when she could use a . . . friend to look up to. I have already told her how much I admire you."

Anne flushed with pleasure.

"But enough of my concerns. How were your holidays?"

"I spent them with the Astons, who are not too many miles from Heriot Hall." Anne hesitated. "But I returned home to some disturbing news."

The baron gave her a concerned look.

"My companion, Miss Wheeler, had a riding accident, which was not an accident at all. Someone had cut the saddle girth."

"Why would anyone wish to harm Miss Wheeler?"

"It was my saddle she was using."

Leighton stopped and looked down at Anne with shocked concern on his face. "Miss Heriot, why would anyone wish to hurt you?"

"There has been some trouble at one of my mills. Sergeant Gillen, my groom, suspects one of the men there, whose fiancée was recently dismissed."

"I hope this man has been dismissed too!"

"He has, but not by me," Anne added ironically. "There is no proof that he had anything to do with the accident. And there is another suspect—my cousin, Joseph Trantor. He managed the mills for my father and has continued doing so."

"What would his motivation be?" asked the baron, a puzzled look on his face.

Anne hesitated. She and Leighton had hinted at their mutual interest in one another, but they had never spoken directly of it.

"Joseph would like me to marry him, but I have discouraged him from proposing, for I don't love him."

"Yet love is not, I believe, your prime consideration in marriage," the baron commented delicately.

"No, but some sort of liking and compatibility should be. I don't dislike Joseph, mind you, but our ideas are very different, and he has no sense of humor. A sense of humor is necessary in marriage, don't you agree?"

"You know that is one of the things I most enjoy about your company, Miss Heriot."

They continued walking, and Leighton said solicitously, "I am glad you are here in London and out of personal danger, Miss Heriot. Whenever you decide to marry, your husband will be able to take the weight of the mills off your shoulders. A lovely young woman like yourself shouldn't be carrying such a burden."

"Oh, but I don't see the mills as a burden, my lord.

I am beginning to think that I need to become more involved. In fact, I have visited twice and am determined to institute some reforms."

"I see," Leighton said thoughtfully. "Of course, it is a way to occupy yourself before you have a family, Miss Heriot."

"Indeed."

When the baron returned her to Sarah, Anne realized she was feeling very much in charity with him on some points. The way he so obviously cared for his daughter, for instance. And the way he had sounded genuinely concerned for her own safety. On the other hand, she was irritated by his assumption that the mills merely served to fill her time until she had children of her own.

"You look distracted, Anne. Didn't you enjoy your stroll with Baron Leighton?" asked Sarah.

"I did, Sarah. I like him more and more. But I like Windham also," Anne confessed with a rueful smile. "And both of them have hinted at their interest in becoming more than friends."

"But neither of them is as precipitate as Lord Aldborough?" Sarah commented with a twinkle in her eye.

"Hardly!" Anne laughed.

"Speak of the devil and here he comes," teased Sarah, as Jack approached them.

"Good evening, Miss Heriot, Miss Wheeler. I trust you have been enjoying the ball? I noticed you did not dance this last set, Miss Heriot. If you are fatigued, you and I could take a turn about the room also."

Damn the man! There was a veiled challenge in his voice and an amused look in his eye, and she was never one to turn down a challenge. She wasn't sure she wanted another waltz with him, but she would not let him get away with his subtle criticism of her stamina or her last partner.

"I am quite looking forward to our dance, my lord."

"Do we leave you alone, Miss Wheeler?"

"Not at all. Here comes Captain Scott to claim his dance."

Chapter Seventeen

Anne told herself she should be able to control her response to Lord Aldborough, but as soon as he put his arm around her waist, she felt that unwelcome yet terribly pleasurable warmth emanating from his fingers.

"Captain Scott seems very interested in Miss Wheeler," Jack commented as they glided over the floor.

"Yes, I am hoping something might develop."

"Scott is a good man. But I don't see the same gleam in Miss Wheeler's eye that I see in his when they are together."

"I am afraid she may be more interested in another soldier," Anne told him without thinking.

"Oh? I haven't noticed anyone else in uniform in her company."

"I mean my groom, Sergeant Gillen," Anne said, her tone clearly disapproving.

"And you are not happy?"

"I would love to see Sarah settled with someone who would give her what she deserves as the granddaughter of a viscount."

"And is marriage always a business transaction to you, Miss Heriot? What if she cares for the sergeant?"

Anne pulled away a little in irritation, but Jack's hand held her firm.

"As a member of the *ton,* who only view marriage as a business transaction, I hardly think you have the grounds to criticize me, my lord. I am very fond of Patrick, but Sarah deserves more."

"Perhaps Miss Wheeler wants love as well as security." Jack looked down at Anne with a gleam in his eye. "My grandfather married for love. So did my father. Indeed, it is a tradition in my family." His voice was teasing, but his eyes were warm with something other than humor, and Anne had to lower hers.

"It is sad, then, that you have to break the family tradition, my lord."

"It does seem that way," Jack replied easily.

Anne was not quite sure what to make of the subtle emphasis he placed on "seem." Had it been anyone else, she might have wondered if he was attempting to convey a message. But Jack Belden was notorious for collecting hearts, not giving his away. She decided that the turns of the waltz and the disturbing sensations she felt when he held her had made her a little giddy.

They finished their waltz in silence, and then Jack found them a place near Elspeth and Val. "I will be right back with your supper plate, Miss Heriot."

Anne looked around her. Sarah was off in a corner with Captain Scott, and she gave a little smile of satisfaction and hoped that the captain was as competent at wooing as Lord Aldborough thought he was at soldiering.

Val and Elspeth were opposite and were involved in conversation with Lord and Lady Hythe, so when Jack returned and sat next to her, Anne had no recourse but to be drawn into what felt like a tête-à-tête.

After a few commonplaces about the quality of the lobster patties, Jack's tone became more serious.

"Has Sergeant Gillen had any luck with his investigations?"

This was one topic that Anne felt comfortable discussing with Lord Aldborough, given their conversation at Christmas.

"Patrick spoke with Ned Gibson, who claims he was ill in bed and has his fiancée as a witness."

"Not necessarily the most trustworthy of witnesses, you must admit," Jack commented.

"No. But nothing further has happened . . . that is, no further attempts to harm me have occurred," Anne corrected herself. "But I decided to visit the mills again myself. I spoke to several of the older workers. The men didn't say much, but one woman was very outspoken. Mrs. Talbot was quite persuasive, and on her advice I decided to sack Peter Brill, the foreman." Anne hesitated. "She was also a great champion of Ned Gibson."

"Then you kept him on?"

"I did. But this last week another accident occurred in the sorting shed, and Ned Gibson saved a little girl from injury. In the process, however, he was insubordinate and threatening to both my cousin and the overseer, so Joseph dismissed him."

"Did you let it stand?"

"I felt I had to. I had no time to make further inquiries myself, since we were leaving for London the next day."

"I think I have more doubts about that cousin of yours than about Ned Gibson," said Jack ironically.

"I confess that I believe him too harsh myself." Anne grew silent and looked down at her plate, where her lobster sat half-eaten, and then over at Jack. "I am letting our conversation become too serious, my lord."

"Not at all."

Anne hesitated again and then said, "I have been doing a lot of thinking about the mills since our last conversation."

Jack looked down at her, and the combination of genuine interest and sympathy in his eyes encouraged her to continue.

"I was very resistant at first, but the more I thought about my workers, especially the children . . . Doesn't it seem wrong to you that small children should be working such long hours and at such dangerous jobs?"

"Actually, it is something I have given some thought to, ever since I saw a new chimney sweep, who couldn't have been more than six, being beaten on the soles of his feet to make him climb."

Anne shuddered. "And yet without the children's wages, families would suffer. The only solution I can think of is to cut their hours without reducing their wages."

Jack raised his eyebrows. "A rather radical solution, and one that would no doubt cut into your profits, Miss Heriot. What will your cousin think? And for that matter, what if your future husband doesn't approve?"

"I would make it clear that decisions about the mill are mine."

"Yet legally a husband controls his wife's property."

"I will have it written into the marriage contract, then," Anne said stubbornly.

"That could lead to unhappiness were you in serious disagreement. And you also challenge one of society's most deeply held beliefs."

"Which is?"

"Why, that the production of goods and wealth are of the highest value, not people."

"I have never before questioned society's values or examined my own. I am ashamed to think that all these years the labor of little children has contributed to the ease of my life."

"Don't be too hard on yourself, Miss Heriot. We all benefit from the labor of others. I admire you very much for your willingness to question things," Jack said quietly, but with such warmth and approval that Anne blushed.

"Nonsense, Lord Aldborough. 'Tis little enough I intend to do. And it will make very little difference in the larger picture. There is not much a woman can do to change things. Except through her husband, of course," Anne added tartly.

"Which is why choosing a husband should be done carefully." The seriousness of Jack's tone was tempered by one of his most charming smiles.

"Indeed," Anne agreed blandly, not rising to his bait.

Jack was about to say something else when Elspeth leaned over and addressed them both. "Val and I were just talking about our plans for later this week. We have never been to the Tower and were wondering if you wanted to invite your cousins to accompany us. I am sure Lady Helen especially would be enthralled by the romance of the place, and Lady Lydia should enjoy the menagerie."

"I don't know that I'd call it romantic to visit someplace where so many have lost their heads, Elspeth!" said Anne.

"I think it is just what the girls need—a little taste of English history and a mangy lion or two," said Jack with a laugh.

"Then let us do it. What about Thursday morning, Anne?"

"I have been only once, years ago when my father took me. I was probably the age of your younger cousin, Lord Aldborough. I do remember getting the shivers, but whether that was from the cold and damp or the guard's stories, I can't recall!"

They all laughed and agreed that the Faringdon coach could accommodate the six of them. The conversation then turned to the recently announced engagement of Hairston's daughter. Anne was relieved, for she had been led into a far more intimate conversation than she had meant to have with Jack Belden.

When she was lying in bed later that night, she realized that of the three men she was considering, Jack Belden seemed most in sympathy with her concerns. As a practical woman, she did not think she had viewed any of her candidates through rose-colored glasses, but she had to admit that before this, she had seen nothing to criticize in Lord Windham or Baron Leighton. Now she felt a little disappointed in both of them.

Were they so important to her, then, these questions about the mills? Could her decision about a husband hinge on them? After all, there were likely to be many areas of disagreement between a husband and a wife.

But tha whole life has revolved around tha father's business, she reminded herself. Indeed, her life and the life of the mills were interwoven in such a way that she did not see how she could ever be free from them, even if a husband took control out of her hands. What she was struggling with was a reevaluation of her connection to her father's business and her father. For if the mills were so important to her life, it was because of her father. Making any changes would be painful. Had already been painful, because changing something that her father had established seemed almost as much of a separation from him as his death.

But she couldn't turn back now. She was not a young girl anymore. She was a grown woman who had to make her own decisions—about the workers, the mills, and a husband.

"It would be so much easier if tha was choosing for love," she told herself, and with something between a laugh and a sob, she blew out her light and lay there in the dark, trying to banish her memories of the interest and sympathy on Jack Belden's face.

She would have been amused to know that Jack was having just as much difficulty getting to sleep as she was, and for a similar reason. Oh, he was thinking of how it felt to have his hand around her waist and the curve of her breast, which had called out for his hand to caress it. But most important was how much her willingness to open up to him had touched him. She had allowed him a glimpse of her struggle to work out her beliefs about personal and societal responsibility. He had wanted to say, "Marry *me,* Anne, and we will take on these problems together."

In the beginning, he hadn't thought much about marriage except as a means of relieving his financial dilemma. Then, of course, he realized that he was attracted to Miss Anne Heriot. Was falling in love with her. But until tonight, he hadn't thought much about what he wanted from marriage. He wanted a partner, he realized. A woman who would open her heart and one to whom he could open his. He wanted Anne Heriot in his bed, of course. But more than that, he wanted her by his side, working out their own concerns, as well as assuming the responsibilities of what they had both inherited.

What happened to her mills was important to her. He would have a place in Parliament, a certain amount of power that he had never had before. He hadn't thought much about taking his seat in the House of Lords, but with Anne by his side, he could imagine a life filled with challenge. Not the same challenges he had faced as a soldier, but in some ways even more important ones.

He was convinced marriage to Anne Heriot was what he most wanted and needed. Now all he had to do was convince her!

Lady Lydia, Jack's younger cousin, was thrilled by the plan to visit the Tower, but Lady Helen, having already been to the Tower several times, thought their day would be dull beyond words. She was eager, however, to meet Miss Heriot, the young woman in whose hands their future rested. Without Anne Heriot's money, she and her sister might never have a Season or find a husband.

When the Faringdon coach arrived, Liddy jumped in, and after shyly acknowledging Anne, began chatting excitedly to the Astons. Helen gave Anne a friendly smile, but was careful to maintain her air of sophistication as she complimented Anne's walking dress and commented upon the weather.

When they arrived, Liddy put her arm through Elspeth's and Val's and pulled them along, leaving Jack and Anne with Helen.

The guard who was to guide them through greeted them unenthusiastically but became much more animated after Val slipped him a few coins. By the time they got to the courtyard where beheadings had taken place, Anne was ready to swear he had been on the stage at some point in his life. She was amused to note that Lady Helen had slowly lost her air of indifference and had tears in her eyes as they heard the story of the little princes.

"What an evil, evil deed!" she exclaimed. "I am glad such a monster died so ignominiously."

"Richard was a Yorkshire man, and I have never believed he had anything to do with the murders," Anne declared.

"Mr. Shakespeare is quite clear about it," protested Helen.

"Ah, but he would have to be, wouldn't he?" Anne replied. "Given that his queen traced her ancestry back to Henry Tudor."

"Why, I never thought of it like that. In school we were only taught that Richard got what he deserved."

"I don't think any man deserves to be hacked to death," Anne said, a note of sadness in her voice.

Helen's eyes opened wide. "Why, that is horrible!"

"War is always horrible, no matter if it is justified or not," Jack interjected somberly. And then, in an instant, his tone changed. "But I brought you here so that you could enjoy yourself, Helen. We need to find those lions."

But the mangy, sad-looking, smelly lions to whom Liddy threw scraps she had brought from home only depressed Helen more.

"Would you like to step out with me, lass? I need a breath of fresh air," Anne suggested. "My father brought me here when I was your sister's age," Anne told Helen when they got outside. "I was just as excited as she is, but it all looks very different now."

"My father brought me here four years ago. I enjoyed it then, but the stories seem so much sadder to me now."

"Aye, and perhaps you were thinking of your father? I know I was," Anne told her, taking Helen's hand and giving it a sympathetic squeeze.

Helen's eyes glistened with unshed tears. "Thank you for understanding, Miss Heriot," she said quietly.

"I don't know what else your uncle has planned," Anne said briskly, "but I think we should take you girls for an ice at Gunther's."

Helen smiled. "I would like that very much."

When Liddy came bouncing out with Jack and the Astons, Anne and Helen walked over to them.

"I know you were thinking of taking us to a tearoom, Lord Aldborough, but I have developed a sudden craving for a lemon ice," Anne told him, her eyes twinkling.

"Then Gunther's it is, Miss Heriot."

They were all settled at a window table and had given their orders when Anne looked up and saw Steven Leighton and a young woman who was obviously his daughter sitting across from them.

He smiled and nodded, and when they had finished their ices and cakes and were on their way out, he stood and approached them.

"I am sure you saw that I am with my daughter, Miss Heriot. I had hoped to introduce you to her in more formal circumstances, but would you come over now?"

"Of course."

Anne stepped over to their table.

"Eliza, I would like you to meet a lady of my acquaintance, Miss Anne Heriot. I have told you about her."

Eliza Leighton looked up and, giving Anne a cool nod, said, "Yes, but I understood you to say that Miss Heriot is not a lady, Papa." Lady Eliza made her statement with an air of innocence, but it was so obviously an insult that Anne caught her breath.

"Eliza! You will apologize to Miss Heriot."

"Have I said something wrong? Oh, dear, I suppose it might have sounded insulting. I am sorry, Miss Heriot, of course I did not mean that you are not respectable. Merely that you are not a lady by birth. I am sure you told me, Papa, that Miss Heriot is the daughter of a mill owner," Eliza said plaintively.

"I am sure he did, Lady Eliza, for it is true," Anne said coolly. "It is a pleasure to meet you after hearing so much about you from your papa. He is very proud of you."

"I know," said Eliza, giving her father a dazzling smile.

"I will call on you soon, Miss Heriot."

"I look forward to it," Anne replied.

After she left, Leighton looked over in shocked anger at his daughter. "I am not proud of you this afternoon, Eliza. That was a very insensitive comment."

Eliza reached across and grabbed her father's hand. "I *am* sorry, Papa. I truly didn't mean it as an insult."

"I admire Miss Heriot very much, Eliza, and I am hoping you will come to like her too."

"I am sure I will, Papa, if you do," Eliza said softly.

Anne's cheeks felt as warm as if she had been physically slapped. Indeed, Lady Eliza's words were a virtual slap in the face, she thought, as she rejoined her party outside.

Jack couldn't help noticing what appeared to be a becoming flush, and he took Anne's quietness on the ride home as a sign that she was still pleasantly distracted by their chance meeting with the baron. He felt his heart sinking. Perhaps she had more feeling for

Leighton than he had thought. He had been viewing Windham as his chief rival.

Jack's mood, which had been optimistic earlier, changed suddenly, and it took all his energy to nod and chat and smile a good-bye when they dropped Anne off.

Sarah, who had stayed home for the day, was reading in the morning room when Anne arrived home.

"How was your day, Anne? Do you want some tea?"

"No, thank you, Sarah. We stopped at Gunther's and I am full," Anne replied with a quick smile. "As for our little excursion, I enjoyed it very much . . ." Anne's voice trailed off.

"You don't sound that enthusiastic."

"Our visit to the Tower was delightful—well, perhaps 'delightful' is not the right word," said Anne, correcting herself with a smile. "After all, the Tower is dank and cool, and I doubt anyone has had a moment of happiness there in the last few hundred years, including the lions! But Aldborough's cousins were very sweet. The younger, Lady Lydia, was enthralled by our guide, and the bloodier his tales, the more she liked them. And of course, she brought scraps for the lions."

"I remember when you insisted collecting leftovers for them yourself," Sarah reminded her.

"Yes, the Tower brought back memories to me and to Lady Helen. She is lovely. I'm sure she'll be a big success her first Season."

"If she has one."

"Now, Sarah, don't try to make me feel responsible for her. It is not my fault that her uncle inherited a bankrupt estate." Anne was quiet for a minute. "We met Steven Leighton and his daughter at Gunther's."

"How lucky. You have been wanting to meet her."

"And now that I have, I am not sure I want to

again," Anne said with her characteristic dry humor. "She was very frank about my lack of birth."

"She insulted you!"

"Oh, all very innocently and subtly. 'Why, Papa, I did not mean to be insulting . . .' And pigs fly," Anne said flatly.

"What did the baron do?"

"He scolded her, of course, and she apologized. But I did not detect an ounce of sincerity in her words. Of course, it must be difficult to think about having a new mother, especially when you have had your father to yourself all these years. I know I would have been very angry had Papa remarried."

"I suppose you are right. You will have to give her a chance to get to know you."

"I just wish she were Lady Helen and Lady Helen were the baron's daughter, if you know what I mean," said Anne. "I liked both of Lord Aldborough's cousins so much."

Sarah sighed dramatically. "It is too bad, isn't it, that you are not drawn to Lord Aldborough in the least, then."

Anne laughed. "Oh, Sarah, I am willing to admit he is a very attractive man. And I am not impervious to his charm." Anne reconsidered. "No, that is not quite true. It is not his charm that has affected me, but other aspects of his personality. He has been very understanding about my concerns around the mills."

"The Aldboroughs have been Whigs for generations, so it doesn't surprise me. Captain Scott is a great admirer of Lord Aldborough. He says that no one has fully appreciated the part the *guerrilleros* played in the war. And that when Aldborough came home, his opinions about this were frowned upon, for they seemed to take away from Lord Wellington's glory."

"Surely he wasn't speaking against Lord Wellington?"

"Of course not. Merely pointing out that he had

some help from the Spanish peasants. So, clearly, he would be sympathetic to the plight of workers."

"Be that as it may, I am resolved to resist him, for I still think that Windham or Leighton would make a better husband."

Chapter Eighteen

The next evening, at the Suttons' musicale, Leighton approached Anne as soon as she arrived.

"Miss Heriot, I am very glad to see you. I wish to apologize again for my daughter's behavior."

"There is no need, my lord," Anne assured him.

"I do want the two of you to become better acquainted and was hoping you could join us for a stroll in the park tomorrow?"

"I would love to."

The baron cleared his throat. "I know we have not spoken directly about our mutual purpose in coming to London. But it is very important to me that you and my daughter form a friendship."

"As it is to me, Lord Leighton," Anne reassured him.

Oh, dear, thought Anne as the baron left, looking very satisfied with himself, I hope he doesn't take that as some sort of admission that I prefer his suit above any other.

Lord Windham arrived late that evening, but he made sure to seek Anne out after the musicians had retired.

"Did you enjoy the concert, Miss Heriot?"

"I always enjoy Mozart, my lord. The pianist was very talented and made my attempts at playing seem quite infantile."

"Did you take lessons when you were younger?"

"Yes, my father wanted to make sure I had all the accomplishments of a young lady. Unfortunately, the one thing I excelled at—mathematics—was not considered to be a ladylike subject!"

"And I always hated doing my sums at school and have a passion for music, Miss Heriot. So we are both unfashionable in our tastes," responded Lord Windham with a smile.

"I love music and I get much satisfaction out of keeping the accounts, but I must admit that I consider neither a passion," admitted Anne. "Mine is a very practical nature, I am afraid."

"Oh, surely not entirely practical, Miss Heriot. And you seemed quite passionate when you spoke of reform the other day."

"How would you define passion, my lord?" Anne asked him.

Until now, the tone of their conversation had been light, but Windham's voice became more serious as he answered her. "I would say that we all have likes and dislikes that come from ourselves, as it were. But to me, passion is a feeling for someone or something that seems to come from elsewhere—a pull or an attraction quite beyond our control."

Windham spoke with an intensity that Anne had never heard from him before, and it seemed to her, an underlying sadness. It made her wonder how much he was speaking from experience. Had he wanted to do something with his music, perhaps—which would have been quite impossible for a member of the nobility?

"I suppose there is an element of that in my concern over the mills, something that draws me into issues I have never thought of before," Anne said thoughtfully. "But I have never experienced such feelings before, certainly not for any person."

"Then you are lucky, Miss Heriot," the viscount told her with an ironic smile. "But look, the musicians have returned, the next piece of music is by Haydn, and there will not be a hint of passion in it," he said with a laugh.

Lord Windham had steered their conversation out of deeper waters, but as Anne let the patterns of the music soothe her, she wondered what it would be like to be married to a man whose nature was passionate when the basis of their relationship would so clearly be practical.

"Are you sure you don't want to join us, Sarah?" asked Anne the next day, as she slipped into her pelisse.

"You don't need me with Lady Eliza there, Anne. And I think it best for the three of you to spend some time together."

"The Leighton carriage is here, Miss Heriot," Peters announced.

"Wish me luck, Sarah!"

"I am sure it will all go well," Sarah reassured her.

Anne was not so sure, judging from the blank-faced young woman who sat opposite them in the carriage. Lady Eliza gave her a polite smile, but then pointedly turned her gaze out the window while her father chatted nervously about the weather.

Anne had never seen Steven Leighton nervous before, and it rather marred her picture of him. He had always exuded self-confidence. On the other hand, she had to admit that introducing an almost-grown daughter to a potential stepmother would make the most insouciant man afraid!

When they reached the park, it was just beginning to become crowded with the usual late-afternoon crush of riders and carriages, and the baron steered them carefully to those paths used almost exclusively by walkers. They bowed to acquaintances and stopped two or three times to chat. Once or twice Anne even caught an animated look on Lady Eliza's face when she encountered a family friend.

"There are benches by the lake," Leighton said, "and Eliza brought a small bag of crumbs for the ducks."

"You made me bring it, Papa," Eliza protested.

"Yes, and Eliza made *me* carry it," he joked to Anne.

"I am not a child anymore, Papa."

"I know," Leighton said with real sadness. "And I hate to admit it, Eliza." For a moment, Lady Eliza's closed face opened as her father held out his hand and she grasped it, with a loving smile that brought a pang to Anne's heart.

"I remember becoming very exasperated with my father, Lady Eliza, when he would forget that I was almost a young lady."

Lady Eliza's face closed again, and she said nothing in reply.

When they reached the lake, the baron held out the bag to his daughter.

"No, Papa, it was your idea. You feed the ducks yourself." Lady Eliza's statement was leavened by her teasing tone, and Anne was gratified to see some feeling under her sullen countenance.

"We will sit down on the bench and watch you in dignified silence, my lord," Anne said with a twinkle in her eye.

Leighton heaved a dramatic sigh and said, "Well, then, I will go and make myself look foolish." He wandered down to the water's edge and began to sprinkle crumbs, which drew a covey of ducks away from a little boy and his nurse, farther down the bank.

"I've run out of crumbs, luv," the nurse told her charge, who had a heartbroken look on his face as his web-footed friends coldly deserted him. When the baron realized what had happened, he walked over and, kneeling down, offered the child his bag.

"That was very sweet of your papa," Anne said.

"It won't do, you know," Lady Eliza said quietly. Anne was taken aback by the fierceness in her tone.

"What won't?" she asked calmly.

"You know what I mean, Miss Heriot. I won't let

you buy Papa. He deserves better than someone in trade."

Anne sat quietly for a minute and then said, "If it is not me, it will be someone else, Lady Eliza. And that someone else will most likely also be a Cit's daughter," she added dryly.

"Papa need not marry at all," Lady Eliza declared.

"I rather think he does. His title is old, but his estates are quite impoverished. And he wishes to do well by you," Anne added in a softer tone. "To make sure you have a proper Season."

"I don't need to find a husband. I have one in mind already. Lord David Spence and I have known each other for years and are very much in love. As soon as he comes of age next year we will be betrothed. And Papa will not have to marry anyone at all then. He will have all the money he needs."

"A lot can happen in a year, my lady. And then there are Lord David's parents. They might have something to say about him marrying a dowerless young woman." Anne hesitated. "I think I know how you feel, Lady Eliza," she said kindly. "My mother died when I was young, and my father and I were each other's only family for years. I would have found it hard had he ever planned to remarry."

"You can't know how I feel, Miss Heriot. The situation of a mill owner's daughter is quite different from mine."

"Tha has a lot to learn, lass, if tha thinks the human heart beats differently under different roofs," Anne chided, stung into broad Yorkshire.

"I don't intend to learn it from you, Miss Heriot," said Lady Eliza, and she got up and walked over to her father. With her sweetest smile on her face, she helped the little boy throw out the last crusts.

Well, tha'rt soom actress, lass, thought Anne. I'll bet tha father would never guess what a strong-willed lass he has on his hands. But I suppose with a doting father and grandparents, tha has never had anyone cross tha.

Given Lady Eliza's age and upbringing, Anne knew the girl's meanness shouldn't have bothered her. But it did, and though she was as good an actress as his daughter, she was very glad when the baron suggested they make their way back to the carriage.

"I hope you both had a chance to get better acquainted?"

"We did, Papa."

"Yes, I feel I know Lady Eliza very well now," Anne told him, her face as bland as blancmange.

They were halfway to the carriage when Anne heard a voice calling her.

"Miss Heriot! Over here!"

It was Lady Lydia, waving wildly, while her older sister was obviously trying to get her to behave in a more dignified manner.

"How nice to see you," said Anne. "May I introduce you to Lord Leighton and his daughter, Lady Eliza."

"It is a pleasure," Helen said shyly, while Liddy bobbed up and down in a curtsy.

"Were you feeding the ducks?" she asked when she saw the empty sack in the baron's hands.

"We were," he said with a grin.

"*You* were, Papa," Eliza said, rolling her eyes and sighing.

Lady Helen looked at her with sympathy while Liddy chattered about the clutch of ducklings that had swum over to them.

"Surely you are not here alone, Lady Helen," Anne asked.

"No, no, Miss Heriot. My cousin is with us, but he met someone and let us go on ahead."

"Here is Aldborough now," said the baron.

Jack hurried across the grass toward them. "I cannot believe you girls deserted me like that," he teased.

"I couldn't stand the way Miss Perry and Lady

Mary were batting their eyes at you, Jack," said the irrepressible Lydia.

"Neither could I, Liddy, but at least I was polite," Jack laughed.

Having established that their carriages were in the same direction, the three grown-ups fell behind while the girls walked ahead.

"Do you know Miss Heriot well?" Lady Eliza asked Helen.

"We spent a day sight-seeing together. I liked her very much."

"I suppose she is nice enough for someone of so common a background," Eliza said coolly.

Helen was shocked into silence by Lady Eliza's dislike.

"My cousin Jack is trying to get her to marry him, so she cannot be *that* common," said Liddy, warmly defending her relative.

"My father is also hoping to marry her," said Eliza, "but I hope your cousin wins her, for I have no need of a stepmama."

"Well, we hope she marries him, too, don't we, Helen?"

Helen grabbed her sister's hand and squeezed it tight. "It is not ladylike to be indulging in such *common* gossip," she said pointedly and, turning the subject to something more innocent, noted Lady Eliza's flush of embarrassment with pleasure.

Later, when they had finished their tea and Liddy was in the corner with her mother playing a hand of piquet, Helen looked over at Jack. "May I ask you something personal, cousin?"

"Of course," he said, looking at her curiously.

"Do you think Miss Heriot intends to accept you?"

"I don't know, Helen. What do you think?" he responded, a quizzical look on his face.

Helen did not immediately answer his question. "Lady Eliza says her father wants to marry Miss Heriot also."

"Since we are speaking frankly, I may as well tell you that Lord Windham is yet another suitor."

Helen looked serious for a moment. "Oh, dear, that is a problem. Lord Richard is so handsome," she said, without thinking.

"And I thought only Liddy was brutally frank!" said Jack with a laugh. Helen rushed in to reassure him. "Oh, but he is not rumored to have captured as many hearts as you have, Cousin Jack. And you have that brooding look that ladies like."

"Another hit!"

"Why, that was not an insult!"

"In Miss Heriot's view it is, my dear. The very thing she likes least about me is my ability to collect ladies' hearts."

Helen patted his hand reassuringly. "Well, I don't think you will have to worry about Lord Leighton."

"Oh, and why is that? They were walking along as though they were a family already."

"Lady Eliza is the reason. She was quite insulting to Miss Heriot. I think she is a spoiled girl who will not tolerate anyone else's claims to her father's attention."

"I certainly hope you are right," said Jack, regarding his young cousin with respect. "And may I say that I have always appreciated your good sense and lack of spoiled behavior."

Helen laughed. "Who could be self-important with Liddy around!"

Jack chuckled. "Yes, I see what you mean." he hesitated. "So you like Miss Heriot?"

"I do. But the more important question is, do you?"

Jack felt himself grow warm under her inquiring gaze. "As a matter of fact, very much. But the most important question before us is whether she will accept Windham because of his blindingly handsome face!"

"You are very handsome in your own way," Helen

began seriously and then saw the twinkle in her cousin's eye. "You are funning me!"

"Only a little. I do hope you are right about the baron, but I suspect I am still last on Miss Heriot's list."

Anne had done a very good job of hiding her anger and hurt on the way home, but once she was inside the house, she went looking for Sarah. She found her in the library, in front of the fire.

"It has grown surprisingly chilly this afternoon," said Sarah, "so I came in here."

"Yes, I was very glad of my pelisse," murmured Anne. She sat down for a moment and then popped up again, walking over to her desk and riffling through some papers.

"You seem restless, Anne. Wasn't the walk enough exercise for you?" Sarah asked, knowing Anne's love for long tramps.

"We stopped to feed the ducks," Anne told her with a wry smile.

"Why, that is very sweet. I would have thought Lady Eliza a little too old for that."

"Oh, Lady Eliza *is* too old for it. Her papa did the honors while she and I sat on a bench and watched. And got to know one another better. Believe me, Sarah, Lady Eliza is not sweet at all."

"What did she say to you?"

"Oh, only that she would not want to see her well-bred papa married to someone as common as a mill owner's daughter."

"Why, what a disrespectful little chit!" exclaimed Sarah. She could hear the pain as well as the anger in Anne's voice.

"Yes," Anne said dryly. "I was prepared to overlook a lot, for you know I can understand it would be difficult to share her father. But she threw my sympathy right back in my face!" Anne sighed. "I don't think I could live with that kind of meanness. It might be different if the baron and I were making a love match. But as much as I think he likes me, I suspect his loyalty will always be with his daughter." She was quiet for a moment. "We met Lady Helen and Lady Lydia on the way out of the park." Anne smiled. "Lydia is so adorably natural. And Helen a real lady."

"I could imagine you becoming Aunt Anne very easily."

"If only it didn't mean marrying their Cousin Jack!"

"So it is to be Windham after all?"

"It would seem so. I just wish he had understood my concerns about the mills better. But I am sure he will come around."

"Yet Lord Aldborough was very much in sympathy on that score," Sarah said pointedly. "You like his nieces, and he is certainly not physically repellent to you!"

"Give over, Sarah. I know you favor him, but I'm sure Windham will make the better husband. Even without love—especially if there is not love—there needs to be trust in a marriage."

But later, as Anne dressed for supper, she thought about the two men. Lord Windham had everything to recommend him: He was a handsome, intelligent man who had treated her with great respect. They had become comfortable with one another almost immediately, despite the differences in their temperaments. And she felt safe with him, for he had never done anything to impose himself on her physically. He may have described himself as a passionate man, but he had never let passion intrude upon their companionship.

That was a good thing, she told herself. In a marriage of convenience, mutual affection was preferable to one-sided passion. Surely she didn't want Lord Richard to feel passionate about her? No, but she had to be honest: she might not want that, but she wondered, albeit illogically, why she didn't inspire it.

Jack Belden, on the other hand . . . Anne was not sure if he was a passionate man. He had certainly never described himself that way. The fact that his fingers seemed to burn through her, and that he had prolonged his kiss under the mistletoe, meant nothing. How else does a man go about collecting hearts than by convincing a woman that only she makes him feel this warmth and desire?

Be fair, lass, she admonished herself. Maybe 'tis nowt but tha own desire. She grew warm thinking about it. But a moment of lust meant nothing. It wasn't a safe way to choose a husband.

That was it, realized Anne. She wished to feel safe. She was drawn to the baron and Windham because she knew they could never touch her deeply. And that made good sense, for if a man was going to marry her for money, she didn't want to be vulnerable to him.

She wouldn't be safe with Jack Belden. She would be vulnerable, if only on a purely physical level. When he touched her, he *touched* her. She could not afford that. And since she was, after all, the buyer, she would buy what she could afford: a kind man whom she could bed safely and keep at a distance.

Having finally settled on Windham, Anne was eager to see him. When she received a bouquet of violets and a short note asking her to save him a waltz at the Preston rout, she was pleased. Perhaps Thursday night she could let him know that she preferred him. The formal arrangement would be made by Mr. Blaine, but if she dropped a hint to Lord Richard, she hoped he would make a more personal approach.

"You look especially lovely tonight, Anne," Elspeth told her when she and Sarah arrived at the Prestons'.

"As do you."

Elspeth lowered her voice. "I have had all my gowns altered, for the bodices have all grown too small. I should be thankful, I suppose, that that is the only sign I am increasing," she added with a wry smile. "Have you come any closer to a decision, Anne?" she asked as they waited for Val to join them.

"I think I have, Elspeth. Leighton . . ."

"Oh, not the baron!" Elspeth protested.

"If you will let me finish! Leighton is no longer a candidate. But what did you have against him?"

"Nothing personal, only I thought it would be more difficult to begin a marriage of convenience with the added complication of a stepdaughter."

"Well, you were right, Elspeth. Lady Eliza is spoiled and snobbish. She doesn't want her father to marry at all. In fact, she assured me he will not have to, for she has an understanding of sorts with one of her neighbors," Anne told her friend.

"So she is headstrong as well. It sounds like you are well out of that family, Anne!"

"What family is that?" asked Val as he joined them.

"Anne has dropped the baron from her list," Elspeth told him. "It seems Lady Eliza is dead set against having a stepmother."

"Then it is Windham or Jack?" asked Val.

"It is Windham," Anne informed them.

Elspeth opened her mouth as if to say something, and Val gave her a quick, warning glance. "Does the lucky man know yet?"

"I am hoping to drop a hint tonight. I may be a practical lass, but I find I would like a proposal before contracts are drawn up," said Anne.

"Here he comes now," Val told her.

"Yes, he has the first waltz."

As Anne and Windham moved off, Elspeth looked over at her husband. "Nothing is working out as I wish, Val. I *know* Jack and Anne would suit," Elspeth complained.

"Well, we did our best, my dear," Val told her with a smile.

"I know. But what will Jack do now, Val?"

"He will have to find some other Cit's daughter."

"But I'd like to see both of them happy, not merely settling for what they can find."

"You don't think Anne can be happy with Windham? He seems to hold her in the highest esteem. And there is no spoiled daughter to complicate things," Val added with a grin.

"But there is Lady Julia," Elspeth said thoughtfully.

"I know you were worried about his attachment, but she is rumored to become betrothed any day now. Whatever they felt for one another, I am sure it is over."

"Would you have forgotten me that quickly, Val?"

"Never," he said so fiercely that Elspeth grew warm.

"And there is no reason to suppose we are the only passionately faithful lovers in the world, Val, much as I would like to think it."

Chapter Nineteen

Now that Anne had made a decision, she hoped to discover if Windham and she would be compatible physically. She might not want a grand passion, but neither did she want a sterile marriage.

His hand felt pleasantly warm against her waist, and the fingers of her hand nestled comfortably in his.

"We dance well together, Miss Heriot," he said after a few turns around the floor.

"I have always thought so, my lord."

Anne was pleasantly relaxed by the time the music stopped, and when Lord Richard suggested a stroll in the garden, she agreed happily. It seemed he was taking the initiative without her having to hint at all.

There were other couples enjoying the air, but Windham guided her down one of the deserted paths. At the end was a small wooden bench, and he asked if she would like to sit for a while.

"Thank you, my lord, my slippers are a bit tight tonight," Anne told him. Her slippers, in fact, fit perfectly, but she would not turn down the opportunity of few minutes alone with him.

He sat next to her and they were quiet for a moment, drinking in the sweet smell of lavender that perfumed the air around them.

"I have always marveled that a Mediterranean plant does so well in our wet climate," Anne remarked, breaking the silence.

"At Windham, one whole side of the house is bordered with lavender, and in June we open the door to the breakfast room to let in the fragrance."

"It sounds lovely. I would love to see it."

"And I would love to show it to you," he said quietly. "Windham has been in my family for more than three hundred years, and each generation of Farrars has only grown more attached to it," he added with a sweet smile.

"It must be very hard for you to know it is at risk."

"Yes. Yet as much as I love it, I would not marry just anyone to save it, Miss Heriot. I wish you to believe that." He hesitated and then continued. "I know I am speaking very frankly, but I feel you will not mind."

"I welcome it, Lord Richard, being a straightforward Yorkshire lass," Anne reassured him with a smile.

"I may need a rich wife, Miss Heriot, but I also want one who can be a friend and companion. I hadn't really hoped to find a person like that until I met you," he whispered, and leaning forward, dropped a kiss on her lips.

His lips were warm, and when he felt her respond, his kiss became warmer as her mouth opened under his. Yet, somehow, at the heart of it, it was a cool kiss, Anne realized when he pulled away. And so, when he took her hand and said, "Miss Heriot, I am hoping . . ." she raised her hand to stop him. "I am afraid our absence will be noticed, my lord. I think I can guess what you are about to say and hope you will call on me this week?"

He let go of her hand instantly. "You're right, Miss Heriot. I should get you back. But I will call on you tomorrow, then?"

"I will look forward to it."

As they walked back, Anne wondered at herself. She had come to this ball intending to get Lord Windham to the point of proposing. He had been about to do just that, yet she had stopped him. The only reason she could come up with, she realized as they reached the ballroom, was that his kiss, given in the most romantic of settings, had not warmed her to the center of her being the way Jack Belden's very public Christmas kiss had. Well, it didn't matter; she would have a chance to say "yes" very soon.

For the next few hours, Anne did not have any time to think, since her dance card had filled early. She was almost relieved, therefore, when the young marquess of Hythe stumbled and spilled half a glass of punch on her dress.

"Oh, I say, I am terribly sorry, Miss Heriot," he stammered, his face red with embarrassment.

"It is all right, my lord. My dress and the punch are almost the same color," she said with a reassuring smile. "But you will excuse me? I wish to deal with the stain right away."

Anne quickly made for the ladies' retiring room. She had hidden her distress from young Hythe, but the rose silk was one of her favorite gowns, and she hoped a quick sponging would rescue it. She was behind a screen cleaning her skirt when she heard two young ladies come into the outer room.

"I do not think I can bear it, Maria," said one, clearly on the verge of tears.

"But you yourself are about to be betrothed, Julia. I thought you had finally put Richard out of your mind."

"I thought I had too, but it became very clear to me tonight that I have been deceiving myself. When I saw him go out into the garden with Miss Heriot . . ." Lady Julia Lovett gave a little sob.

Anne had been about to announce her presence when she was frozen in place by the mention of her name.

"He *has* to marry someone with money, Julia, you knew that," her friend said sympathetically.

"Of course. It is why he had Father break off our

engagement and if he has to marry someone in trade, Miss Heriot is better than some of the other young women shopping for husbands. From what I have seen of her, I would like her myself."

"You know he doesn't love her."

"Do I?" Lady Julia whispered brokenly. Anne, who had been standing as still as a deer caught in torchlight, told herself to take a breath. Tha must not faint, lass, and be discovered.

"Don't cry, Julia," her companion said helplessly.

"I'm trying not to, Maria. It is just that the reality of it all hit me tonight. And he hasn't spoken to me except for polite conversations since last July," she added despairingly.

"I am sure he is avoiding you for your own sake, Julia."

Lady Julia sighed. "Yes, that would be quite like Richard. I just wish he didn't have to be so bloody honorable!"

"Julia!"

"Oh, no one can hear me, Maria."

Anne could hear the rustle of their gowns as they rose. "I must go back out there. If he can be honorable, I suppose I can be too. And I am glad he took Miss Heriot out to the garden. I would have continued pretending that I didn't care anymore. Now that I know how much I still do, I can never marry Lord Broome."

"Don't make any rash decisions, Julia," counseled her friend. "Tonight has upset you, but things will look better in the morning."

When Anne heard the door close behind them, she let out her breath in one long sigh. She had never heard of any engagement between Windham and Lady Julia. Why had no one *told* her? She stepped out from behind the screen and sat down on the loveseat. Lord Windham had loved Lady Julia, probably still loved her.

He was as nice a man as she had believed, Anne thought with painful irony. He'd ended his betrothal to free Lady Julia when he had been ruined by his father's recklessness. And he had made a complete break of it. Anne knew Lady Julia by sight, of course, but she would never have guessed from Windham's behavior that he had ever known her intimately, much less been betrothed to her.

An honorable man. And one she could never marry. She might not be expecting love in her marriage, but she'd be damned if she would enter into a union where the possibility was hopeless from the beginning. It was one thing to take the chance that her husband might not be able to give her his heart, but quite another to marry someone whose heart had already been given to someone else.

An honorable man! If Lord Richard was such an honorable man, then why hadn't he spoken of his betrothal, she thought angrily. Had he ever planned to tell her?

Now, lass, be fair. He could hardly have announced it on your first meeting. Most likely he was planning to tell you tomorrow. Or at least, before the wedding.

Anne looked down at her dress. The wet spot was dry enough for her to see that the gown was still slightly darker from the claret punch. She sighed. She supposed a lady wouldn't have tried to save the dress, but gone home immediately. But she was a practical lass from Yorkshire, so of course she had to attempt to rescue it! If she weren't so damned practical, she would never have overheard a conversation meant for no one's ears, especially hers. She would have been dreaming of a betrothal-sealing kiss.

Instead, there she sat, knowing there would be no betrothal. In one short week, it had become clear that if she was to marry this year, it would be Jack Belden or no one!

When she returned to the ballroom, she sought out Elspeth immediately. "Would you walk me to the cloakroom, Elspeth? My gown is ruined. Please tell Sarah I have gone home, Val."

Elspeth gave her husband a puzzled look as Anne slipped her arm into hers and started for the cloakroom.

"Why didn't you tell me Windham was betrothed to Lady Julia Lovett last spring?" Anne demanded, her tone at odds with the smile on her face.

Elspeth stopped and turned to her friend.

"No, lass, keep on walking. We would not want to attract any attention!"

"It was almost a year ago, Anne. I had hoped Windham was over his attachment. He has hardly spoken to Lady Julia since."

"But his avoiding her could have been because he still felt too much!"

"I did consider that," Elspeth confessed. "But I didn't really think you would choose him anyway, Anne. I had hoped . . ."

"I know what you hoped. You hoped I would fall in love with a confirmed rake!"

"You are being unfair to Val and me, Anne. Jack is no rake, and we would never invite him into our home if he was."

"All right, I apologize," Anne said reluctantly.

"And until you met his daughter, the baron seemed as likely a choice for you. But how did you find out about Lady Julia?"

"I overheard her talking to a friend. Evidently she was very upset by our tête-à-tête in the garden."

"I am so sorry you had to find out in that way," said Elspeth.

Anne sighed. "Yes, and I am sorry for jumping on you, Elspeth. Of course, I can never marry Windham now."

"But you weren't looking for a love match, Anne."

"No, but neither do I want a marriage where love would have no chance of growing."

"What are you going to do?"

Anne gave her a painful smile. "I could go home and hope that someone else is ruined next year. I could marry my cousin . . ."

"You would never do that!" protested Elspeth.

"Or I can tell Joshua Blaine to contact Aldborough's solicitor and have the contracts drawn up. That should make you happy."

"I don't want you to marry Jack to make me happy, Anne, and you know it. I truly believe he has the potential to make *you* happy."

"I know, and I am being a witch with you, Elspeth," Anne admitted. "I am not sure what I am going to do, only what I am not going to do: marry either the baron or Lord Windham."

When Windham was announced the next morning, Anne had Peters show him into the morning room. He was standing by the window when she came in, and he turned and greeted her with a welcoming smile.

It was a genuine smile, which gave Anne an unexpected pang of regret. If she hadn't overheard Lady Julia, she would have been very hopeful about a marriage with the young man in front of her. He was kind and affectionate, and she knew he enjoyed her company. Many a marriage started out with far less. But a simple moment of clumsiness had altered her life irrevocably.

"Please sit down, Lord Richard," she said as she settled herself on the sofa.

"You left the ball early last night, Miss Heriot. I hope it was not because of illness?" The concern in his eyes was as real as his initial pleasure at seeing her.

"It was only an accident with a glass of punch, my lord."

Windham cleared his throat. "Miss Heriot, I think you know what I am here for. I hold you in the highest esteem and am hoping you will agree to become my wife. I know this marriage would benefit both of us in some, er, practical ways, but I also believe a potential for lasting affection is present."

"I believe you're right, my lord. Our liking for one another might have developed into affection. But not, I think, into love."

Windham's face looked surprised. "I had not thought that was something you expected from marriage, Miss Heriot."

"Isn't it something that you would be looking for, my lord?"

"No, I would not be," he told her reassuringly.

"Yet I believe you had found it in your previous betrothal."

Windham's face colored.

"You see, before I left the ball last night, I chanced to overhear a conversation that revealed the fact you had planned to marry a woman with whom you shared passion as well as affection."

"That is true," he admitted stiffly. "But it was before my father's . . . demise and the subsequent bankruptcy. As an honorable man, I had to release her from the betrothal."

"Were you ever going to tell me about Lady Julia, my lord?"

"I suppose so," he said slowly. "But it was over almost a year ago, and she is about to be engaged to another."

"I think she is not," Anne said softly.

For one fleeting moment she could see the joy and relief in his eyes before it faded, and any lingering doubts she may have had about refusing him faded just as quickly.

"It does not matter," he told her, "for it is you I wish to marry, Miss Heriot."

"Or is it me that you *must* marry, my lord?" Anne sighed. "Until last night, I did not mind the practical foundation of our union. In fact, like you, I was sure a strong affection had every chance of developing between us. But that was when I thought you were heart-whole. Now that I know your heart is given to another, I am afraid I must refuse you."

"I assure you, I have hardly spoken to Lady Julia since breaking off our betrothal."

"I know that, my lord," Anne said kindly. "You are a good man who has done the best he could under difficult circumstances."

"I will not demean either of us by begging, Miss Heriot," Windham told her quietly. "But I assure you, I truly believe we could make a good marriage."

"I know you do, my lord. But I believe your love for Lady Julia would always be a barrier to happiness." Anne stood up, and when Windham rose, she offered her hand. "I regret this, my lord, and I wish you well."

"And I you, Miss Heriot," he responded, his voice strained. He bowed over her hand and was gone.

Lady Julia Lovett was not the only one who had noticed Anne's sojourn in the garden with Lord Richard. Over the course of the Season, Jack had become very aware of Anne and whom she talked with and danced with. After his conversation with Helen, he was not really surprised to see that Leighton had sought Anne out only once during the past few nights. He suspected that Lady Eliza was beginning to work on her papa, and if she was as spoiled as Helen thought, she would probably win. At any rate, if he had likened their competition to a horse race, he would have said that Windham had suddenly moved up on the inside rail and was a full length ahead of the baron. He, of course, was still in last place, he told himself with a rueful smile.

But it was one thing to dismiss oneself with humorous images and quite another to imagine Windham and Anne in the garden. He awoke the next morning in one of the darkest moods he had endured for a long time. Windham had kissed Anne in the garden, Jack had no doubts about it. If he hadn't proposed last night, then he was probably doing it right now. And he, Jack Belden, despite all his skill at reconnaissance and fighting, was absolutely helpless before this "enemy."

He usually dressed for breakfast, but this morning he only tied his dressing gown around him before going down. He sat at the table, looking bleakly at his unopened newspaper and fingering the pile of unopened invitations on the tray next to him. At least one good thing would come out of this, he told himself. He hated the social round, and now that his main reason for attending was gone, he would throw all future invitations into the fire. His solicitor would just have to get busy finding him some Cit's daughter to marry—and sooner rather than later.

But, oh, God, how he dreaded his future, and how he hated his helplessness. He *had* to marry, and the one woman he wanted to marry preferred a blond Adonis to his blue-deviled, long-faced self. And who could blame her? He was useless back in England. The war had given his life meaning. It was a terrible thing to admit, but there it was.

He got up from the table and began to pace. He would visit Stebbins today and tell him to find a woman—any woman—and engage him to her. And then he would ride out of London tomorrow and not stop until he had outrun his dark mood or ridden off the north coast of Scotland—whichever came first.

He was about to go upstairs when Val Aston was announced.

"Good morning, Val. What brings you here today?"

"I wanted to know if you wished to ride. You left the ball shortly after Miss Heriot, looking as if you were on your way to a funeral. I came to cheer you up."

Jack sighed and gave his friend an ironic grin. "I felt like I was going to my own funeral, Val. Although it is only marriage, somehow it feels like the same thing."

"What do you mean?"

"I am going to tell Stebbins to find me the richest man he can and engage me to his daughter! I have to make sure Helen and Lydia are taken care of."

Val sat himself down at the table and poured himself a cup of coffee, took a muffin and began to butter it.

"You look like the proverbial Charlotte, eating bread and butter, Val," Jack told him with plaintive humor. "Don't I rate any sympathy as a disappointed lover?"

"The thing is, Jack, I am not so sure you are going to be disappointed," Val said casually, seemingly intent on evenly spreading cold butter without crumbling his muffin.

"Oh, I saw Anne Heriot and Windham going off into the garden. If he didn't propose last night, he will be doing it soon and she'll accept him. My heart is broken and all you care about is your damned muffin!" Jack spoke humorously enough, but Val heard the underlying pain in his friend's voice.

"I think Windham intends to propose, but I don't think Anne will accept him."

"She's not going to take on that spoiled chit of Leighton's?"

"I rather think she plans to take on *you,* Jack!"

"I don't mind your teasing, Val, but this is going a bit too far." Jack's face grew warm. "I love her, you know," he said, his voice tight with emotion.

"I know you do," Val said seriously. "I shouldn't have joked about it. But it is true. Anne was planning to accept Windham's proposal last night or whenever it came. But then she discovered that his heart had been given elsewhere."

"Do you mean to tell me she didn't know about Lady Julia?"

"No. She was angry with Elspeth for not telling her,

but all in all, I think Elspeth was right in not speaking. Their betrothal ended almost a year ago."

"Would you forget Elspeth in a year?"

"Not in ten thousand," Val answered instantly.

"Nor would I Anne Heriot. It wasn't my place to mention Lady Julia, but I thought she'd known about it from the beginning."

"Well, she didn't."

"But she wasn't looking for passion, our Miss Practicality from Yorkshire," Jack added with a grin.

"No, but she won't marry where there is no potential at all for love." Val hesitated. "Evidently she is planning to visit her man of business today and have him . . . er . . . make you an offer."

Jack's face reddened as though he had been slapped.

"Yes, I know," Val said softly. "A cool way to do it. That's why I came over to poke my nose in. Elspeth and I thought you deserved a more personal announcement first. You will accept her?"

"Of course," Jack said stiffly.

"Elspeth and I still think that you and Anne have a chance for a happy marriage, Jack."

"You and your wife are damned romantics! And so am I, God help me, or this wouldn't hurt so much," he said, looking at his friend with such pain in his eyes that Val winced. "Anne would wander out into the garden with Windham and no doubt be happy to have one of his kisses, but then she handles a betrothal to me the way she would a bloody mill merger! Windham is probably well out of it, if he has any heart left to him."

"Anne is not a cold woman, Jack."

"Perhaps not, but she did her calculations early on and decided that because I've been rumored to have collected so many hearts, I have none of my own."

"Did you ever try to prove her wrong?"

"Oh, she likes me better than she did, I'll grant you that. But what chance have I had for more than mistletoe kisses when she's been spending most of her time with Windham and Leighton?"

"Well, now you have your chance, Jack. And whether you win her heart before or after the wedding, I believe you finally will if you don't let your wounded pride get in the way."

So the other horses are out of the race, and the dark horse has won, Jack told himself as he dressed to go riding. But if he had won, then why did the victory seem so meaningless?

Chapter Twenty

Jack had planned to visit Stebbins first thing that morning, but after Val's news he decided to wait till later in the afternoon. If the Heriot solicitor *was* going to approach his, then he would give him time.

He and Val rode in the park and after a few brisk canters, his black mood lifted. By the time he set out for Stebbins's office later that afternoon, he was more resigned to what had happened.

"Lord Aldborough, this is a fine coincidence!" said Stebbins as he ushered him into the office. "I was about to send a note over asking for you to meet with me tomorrow. I have very good news for you. Miss Heriot's solicitor approached me this morning and wishes to write up a marriage contract."

Jack let out an imperceptible sigh of relief. Ever since Val had spoken to him, he had wondered whether Anne might change her mind. But it seemed Val and Elspeth were right. She would rather marry a man whom she believed had a wayward heart than one whose heart had already been given.

"You don't seem surprised, my lord. But I suppose you were aware that your wooing had proved successful," Stebbins said with a knowing smile.

"Indeed," Jack murmured.

"You will find the proposed settlements most fair . . . actually generous, my lord," Stebbins told him, handing over the papers.

Jack scanned them quickly and breathed a deeper sigh of relief. The Heriot money would save Aldborough and offered an allowance to Lady Aldborough and her daughters. He smiled when he came to a clause about the management of the mills. "I see Miss Heriot wishes to keep control over her father's business."

Stebbins frowned. "Yes, that is the only sticking point I can see, my lord. It doesn't seem appropriate to me, but evidently she is adamant on that point."

"I am sure she is," murmured Jack. "And so she should be. I have no difficulty with that provision."

"She has provided quite generously for you also, my lord," Stebbins pointed out.

"So I see."

Stebbins cleared his throat. "In matters of this sort it is always preferable that a husband has some sort of independent income. Of course, under law, all that is hers is yours, but she was wise, I think, to write it this way. Independence on both sides bodes well for the future, don't you think, my lord?"

Jack gave Stebbins a quizzical smile. "Do you go home at night and entertain yourself with romantic fantasies about the matches you've made, Stebbins?"

Stebbins chuckled. "Not at all. But from what I know of you and Miss Heriot, there could be worse fates for both of you."

"Another romantic, God help me!"

"Hardly, my lord. But if Anne Heriot were my daughter, I'd rather she be married to you than to take on a spoiled stepdaughter or a man whose heart was given."

"You are well informed, Stebbins," Jack said dryly.

"I have to be to do my job well, my lord. Though Lord Windham may be heart-whole shortly. Blaine told me—and this is between you and me and the lamppost, my lord—that Miss Heriot intends to pay off Windham's debts."

"Why, they are considerable!"

"Your future wife is a very wealthy woman. And a very warmhearted one too. Evidently she was touched by Lord Windham's predicament. It means he can offer for Lady Julia Lovett. But no one else knows. Windham will be told that a distant relative in the West Indies died suddenly and left him some money. He will still have to work hard to keep the estate going, but if Lady Julia is willing to take him, he'll have a loving wife to help him."

So Miss Anne Heriot has a more romantic heart than she herself would admit to, thought Jack when he left Stebbins. It was too bad he couldn't praise her for her generosity or tease her about her romantic gesture.

Instead of hailing a hansom, he decided to walk. As he made his way through Covent Garden, he passed a flower stall and decided he would call on Miss Anne Heriot this very afternoon.

"I would like a bouquet of roses, please."

"And wot color, gov?"

There were several bunches of pink roses, but somehow they didn't seem strong enough for the occasion. And the deep red roses spoke more of passion than he would feel comfortable with. But there was one bouquet of ivory roses tinged with a deep pink. "I'll take those," he said, pointing.

" 'Ere you are, then, and I 'opes yer lady loikes em," said the woman with a broad wink.

"I'm sure she will."

Jack wasn't so sure as he stood in the foyer of the Heriot town house while Peters announced him. He had not asked for permission to call. In fact, he would be lucky if Anne was even at home at this hour. She was often out driving with either Leighton or Windham. But of course she wouldn't be with either man now. She was an engaged woman, he thought with deep irony.

Jack felt a surprising surge of anger. He had thought he'd gotten over his hurt, but goddamn it, here he was, standing like a fool, a bouquet of roses in his hand, intending to do what? Propose? Thank Anne Heriot most humbly for accepting his hand, which she'd never given him a chance to offer? If her father had been alive, he would have made sure there was at least a charade of a proposal. But not Miss Anne Heriot—she took care of the business herself and made sure to forestall any declarations, sincere or otherwise! Jack looked down at his flowers and was tempted to hurl them on the floor and leave. But then Peters was back and leading him down to the drawing room.

Anne and her companion were reading when Jack was shown in. Miss Wheeler took one look at the roses and, putting aside her book, excused herself quietly, giving Jack an encouraging smile as she passed him.

"Good afternoon, my lord. Won't you sit down?"

"Actually, I was considering dropping to one knee before you, Miss Heriot," he said sarcastically, "but perhaps it is more appropriate for me to humbly accept *your* offer."

"You have seen your solicitor, then?" Anne kept her voice steady, but she had been wondering all day how and when Jack Belden would acknowledge their betrothal.

"I have just come from his office."

"And was everything to your satisfaction, then?"

"You were most generous, Miss Heriot."

"Not at all, especially since I keep control of the mills."

"I have no objection to that, as I think you would have guessed from our conversations."

"But you sound like you have *some* objection to raise."

"If your father were alive, no doubt he would have arranged the practical details of this match. But I'd have been given an opportunity to speak to you alone about our marriage."

"We are alone now, my lord," Anne pointed out.

"Yes, and I'd sound the complete fool, wouldn't I, if I asked you to marry me, now that you've already 'proposed' to me! You have left no room for sentiment, Miss Heriot, and you have taken my consent for granted."

"You *do* wish to marry me, my lord? And I had not thought it was primarily for sentimental reasons." The slight hint of irony in Anne's voice infuriated Jack even further.

"Of course, I wish to marry you, damn it. But you've made it very clear to me that I was your last choice. It was a surprise to find myself the first and without even a hint from you."

Anne's hand tightened over the book she held. She *had* acted quickly, mainly because she had been so upset over Windham.

"Somehow I doubt that you would have treated Windham this way," continued Jack. "I'm sure you would have given him some subtle hints that you would be open to a proposal—perhaps during your time in the garden last night."

"What I did or did not do in the garden is none of your business, my lord," Anne replied angrily. She always reacted defensively when accused of anything she knew herself to be guilty of. He was right—she had given Windham the opportunity to propose in a proper manner. She had been so upset by her disappointments, one right after the other, that in the end she had only wanted to settle the issue quickly. She hadn't thought much about Jack Belden's feelings at all, and she had treated him shabbily.

"Of course it is none of my business," Jack replied stiffly. "But I think, given our conversations on various occasions, you might have dealt with me more personally and less practically."

"Tha knows I am no romantic, my lord." Anne was trying to be humorous, but even as she spoke, she knew her words were all wrong.

"I know it all too well," said Jack, standing suddenly. "God knows why I ever brought these," he said, and dropping the roses into the fire, he gave her a quick bow and left.

Anne sat there speechless, watching the flames lick at the moist petals, retreat, and then finally, slowly, consume them.

"What was tha *thinking* of?" she whispered as the roses were reduced to ashes. Why *had* she approached Jack Belden through his solicitor, as though she were her father? It wasn't a love match she would have been arranging with either of the other two men, but she would have given them a chance to approach her as a woman. Why hadn't she given Jack Belden the same opportunity?

He was right. They had developed a sympathetic connection. But she'd chosen Windham over Jack because she felt him to be more trustworthy. She laughed. She had trusted Lord Windham because he was not a ladies' man like Jack. Had she married him, she would have been placing her heart in the hands of someone far more dangerous to her happiness, one whose heart was already given.

As long as she was being honest with herself, she would have to admit Jack Belden had always stirred a stronger physical reaction than either of the others. Had he been her last choice because she thought she couldn't trust him? Or because she couldn't trust herself? Had it felt safer to deal with their marriage as only a business transaction because of what he made her feel?

He had been right to be angry with her. She laughed again. Tha is in a reet pickle, lass, she told herself. Betrothed at last and t'announcement in t'paper tomorrow and tha fiancé in a fury!

Anne knew Jack was likely to be at the ball that night, and she was tempted to plead a headache and stay home. But that would look very odd the next morning, once people learned about the betrothal. Of course, it would look even odder if she and her soon-to-be fiancé were there but not speaking to one another!

But she was no coward. She would hope Jack had the generosity to appear and to be courteous. And if he didn't ask her to dance, she would ask him herself!

Jack himself had been tempted not to appear. If Miss Anne Heriot wished to approach marriage in the same way she would approach purchasing a mill, then let her be alone the night before their "business transaction" was made public. Let people wonder the next day why they had not attended the ball together.

But his temper, which was hot and quick, was also quick to cool, and after he got home and had a brandy, he realized he was as hurt as he was angry. He loved Anne Heriot, God help him, and while he had not expected her to treat him as a lover, he had hoped she could at least treat him as a friend.

Well, he wasn't going to wallow in either anger or wounded affection. He would go to the ball and dance with his intended and take her into the garden himself if he had the chance. That would certainly confound the gossips, he thought with an ironic grin. And all those who were still wagering on Windham might well wish they had backed the long shot!

When he saw Anne standing with Miss Wheeler and Captain Scott any remaining anger drained away. She looked absolutely lovely tonight in a pale gold gown, with a diamond pendant nestled in the hollow of her throat. He felt a surge of desire as his gaze was drawn to her breasts. He had wanted her even before he loved her, and now the two forces combined to leave him breathless at the thought that this woman was to be his wife.

He approached her casually and asked whether her card was full or if she had a waltz free.

Anne blushed. "I have saved a waltz just for you, my lord."

Captain Scott looked over at her curiously. All the gossip he had heard had led him to believe that if Miss Heriot was going to save a waltz for anyone, it would be for Windham. Yet here was Aldborough acting as though he'd expected her to reserve a dance for him. The captain was not given to betting, but perhaps he would seek out Preston and lay a hundred guineas on Aldborough!

Luckily, their waltz was the next dance, for Anne did not think she could have waited too long. She needed to apologize, and the sooner she had the opportunity, the better she would feel.

As they moved off across the floor, however, Anne was unable to lift her eyes above Jack's third shirt button, or say anything at all. Finally, tightening his hand around her waist, he broke the silence between them.

"I apologize for my behavior this afternoon, Miss Heriot."

Anne finally lifted her head. "Oh, no, my lord, it is I who should apologize. You were right. I treated you thoughtlessly, and I cannot even offer you a reasonable excuse except to say I was upset about Lord Windham and wished to settle things quickly." Anne stopped. "Oh, dear, I suppose I am making things even worse."

"You made it clear all along where your preferences lay."

"Yes, but we had begun to be friends, my lord, and I treated you like a stranger."

"What's done is done," said Jack. "But I thought it best we appear interested in one another tonight, given that the announcement goes into the paper tomorrow," he said with a smile. "Perhaps I might secure another dance?"

"I saved the next one," Anne confessed, "for I, too, was worried about appearances."

"Ah, yes, for appearance is all that counts with Society."

"You should know better than I," Anne said tartly. "After all, it was just the other evening I was in the garden with Windham, which I'm sure made some people jump to certain conclusions."

"Ah, yes," Jack said thoughtfully. "Perhaps we should make our own visit to the garden," he suggested, as seriously as if he was considering military strategy, but his eyes twinkling.

"Is that a challenge, my lord?" asked Anne, her own eyes sparkling.

"Merely a suggestion."

"I *am* feeling quite warm after such a vigorous turn about the floor. And it will be amusing to confound people's expectations."

As they made their way through the crush to the French doors that opened out onto the garden, Anne fluttered her dance card in front of her face and made sure to complain audibly about the heat. When she pressed her hand to her brow and reached over for Jack's arm as though for support, Jack leaned down and whispered, "Doing it much too brown, Miss Heriot!"

The Worth garden had only one long path leading through a bed of roses, on which various couples were strolling. As Jack led her down toward the end, Anne found herself wishing they were in the other garden, with the opportunity for privacy. Of course, it didn't matter, she told herself; it was enough for people to see them leave together. She was surprised to find that although the path narrowed as it moved away from the house, it did not end, but led to a small side garden surrounded by boxwood hedges, with a small stone bench in the middle.

"I think this should do for us," Jack said. "If we sit here a few moments, people will be nodding their heads over our announcement tomorrow, saying, "I told you their behavior meant either marriage or scandal."

The garden surrounding them was a circular herb garden, but there were four white rosebushes marking each quarter, and as she admired the roses, Anne remembered the ones Lord Aldborough had tossed into the fire and felt ashamed of herself all over again. "I *am* sorry, my lord. You brought me roses today, and I drove you to destroy them before I even had a chance to appreciate them."

Jack looked down and felt his heart stop. This was the Anne Heriot he'd fallen in love with, the one who'd shared her dilemmas, the vulnerable Anne usually hidden under a practical exterior.

"I chose the flowers carefully," Jack told her quietly. "Pink roses seemed too childlike and insipid for you. Yet red roses were not right either. But the white ones, with that tinge of red at their hearts, seemed just the thing."

Anne sat very still and wondered at his subtle message. Red roses usually stood for passion. Pure white flowers were about the purity of love. His flowers combined both, and she wondered if he had been trying to convey his desire or hinting at her own.

"Miss Heriot . . . Anne," Jack whispered, and she looked up at him, her question in her eyes. His mouth was open to say, "I love you," but he stopped himself just in time and leaned down to capture hers, this being a more realistic goal than capturing her heart.

For a moment, Anne tried to observe and compare the kiss to Lord Richard's. But as her mouth opened under Jack's, she was flooded with the most delicious sensations of warmth and weightlessness. It was as though she had disappeared and only the sensations existed.

When he felt her response, Jack put his arm around her waist, pulled her closer, and deepened the kiss. Anne gave a little moan of pleasure, and he let his hand go where it wanted—to lightly caress her breast for a brief moment before releasing her.

"Oh, dear," whispered Anne, and then blushed at

her foolishness. Jack gently lifted her chin with one long, slender finger and dipped his head again. This time, her arms went around his neck and she buried her hands in his hair. Jack pressed her close against him, but when he realized how aroused he was, he let her go and sat there almost shaking with his sudden exercise of control.

"I think that we have given Society enough time to gossip about us, Anne, don't you?"

Anne was breathless and could only nod her agreement.

"Perhaps we should, ah, rearrange ourselves and stroll back?" he added, restoring his cravat to its former precision. Anne patted at her hair and pulled at the bodice of her dress.

"You are right, we'd best go back, my lord," she whispered.

"Surely we can be Anne and Jack to each other now," he said lightly as they rose and she took his arm.

"Of course . . . Jack." But calling him Jack reminded her of his nickname, and as they made their way back down the path, she wondered how many young women he had kissed. With kisses like that, it would not surprise her if he had captured a full suit!

Jack was right. When their announcement appeared, the gossips were saying, "I told you Aldborough would carry the day," as though a few nights ago they hadn't been convinced Miss Heriot was on the verge of choosing Windham. And Captain Scott, who had followed his instincts, was several hundred pounds richer, for the odds against Jack had gone up after Anne and Windham's tête-à-tête.

The Astons were lingering over a late breakfast when Charles pointed out the announcement. "Given what you told me, Elspeth, I am not surprised that Anne has chosen Jack, but it all happened so fast. I wonder he even had time to propose."

"I know Anne wanted to settle things quickly," Elspeth said, attempting to defend her friend, although she too had been taken aback. "And as much as we might have wished differently, it does not seem to be a love match."

"They certainly tried to make it look like more than a business arrangement last night. They were in the garden long enough to settle any last-minute contractual details," Val said with a grin.

"Anne did look a little pink upon her return to the ballroom, so perhaps the garden was a little warmer than she expected it to be," Charles agreed, his eyes twinkling.

"Well, we must do something for them. Might we have a supper dance, Charles, to celebrate their betrothal? I know you haven't entertained much in town since Charlie died . . ."

"But this would be a perfect occasion, if it isn't too much work for you, Elspeth. I would be delighted for us to take the place of Anne's family."

"Are you sure this won't tax you too much, Elspeth?"

"I am with child, Val, not suffering from illness. And I can ask my mother to help me."

"Well, if the formidable Mrs. Gordon takes charge, it's sure to be a success," joked Charles and they all laughed, for after life in the army, where the unexpected was the rule, Mrs. Gordon was a most talented organizer.

"I'll call on Anne this morning and make sure she approves the idea," said Elspeth happily.

When Elspeth called later, Anne had been up for hours. She had awakened in the middle of a dream kiss, but try as she would, she could not get back to sleep and dream herself back into Jack Belden's arms. She lay there as the sun came up, remembering the night before, realizing that for all her distress over

Lord Windham, at least she was taking a husband whose heart was in his kisses.

Despite her lack of sleep, she was restless, and when Elspeth arrived, she suggested they go for a walk.

"I would be happy to, Anne," her friend agreed as she retied her bonnet. "Val has been insisting that I ride and walk only at a sedate pace, and I need some vigorous exercise."

They chatted about inconsequential things along the way, but once they reached the park, Anne turned to Elspeth and said, "I suppose everyone has read the notice by now."

"And we may encounter some who are throwing themselves into the lake, having lost all by wagering against Jack," Elspeth teased.

"Oh, dear, I had forgot how gambling-mad Society is. In Yorkshire we are more careful of our money!"

"I was happy to see that you and Jack had some time alone last night. He must have been taken by surprise, after all."

"I did not handle things well, Elspeth, if that is what you mean. Lord Aldborough—I mean, Jack—was upset at first, and rightfully so, but I think we have come to a better understanding."

"What are your wedding plans?"

Anne looked at her friend and laughed. "Do you know, I have been so intent on choosing a husband that I have not thought much beyond a betrothal."

"You could wed before the end of the Season, although that would take a bit of doing."

"I've felt more welcome in London than I ever expected to, but I don't think of myself as part of Society, Elspeth. I think I would like a small wedding at home in the chapel at Wetherby."

"I suspect Jack would prefer something like that as well, but you will need to consult with him."

"I am so used to being in charge of my life that it is hard to get used to the idea of consulting anyone."

"It takes a while to get used to, but when you love someone, it gets easy as time goes on." Realizing what she had said, Elspeth stammered, "Of course, I was thinking of Val and me."

"Don't get thaself into a twitter, lass," Anne replied lightly. "Jack and I agree friendship isn't a bad basis for marriage, and I think we have that."

The two women walked along quietly for a bit, and then Elspeth said, "You know, Anne, if your father were alive, he'd be arranging some sort of betrothal celebration. Val and Charles were wondering if you would let us take the place of family?"

Anne stopped and turned to Elspeth. "I am very lucky to have such good friends. But are you sure it isn't too much for you?"

"I'm feeling very well, and I have my mother to help."

"Then I would be very grateful, and I'm sure Jack will be, too."

It was so odd, Anne thought as they walked on, to be speaking of Lord Aldborough as Jack, as though they had been intimates for years. It was also strange to think there was someone else she would need to consider when decisions were made. She was very much her own woman. Her father may not have given her much affection, but he'd given her something almost as important—independence. He had treated her as a partner, and the day he turned the accounts over to her had been one of the proudest moments of her life.

So far, Jack Belden had seemed to respect and admire her independence—if not her practicality! But that had been when he was presenting himself as a suitor, when he needed her. Now that he had her, she wondered if things would change.

When she told Jack about the Astons' offer, he seemed as pleased and grateful as she was. And when she raised the issue of a wedding date, he looked at her in much the same humorously rueful way that she had at Elspeth. "I must confess, I hadn't thought much beyond a betrothal and I hadn't much hope of succeeding . . . ! But you must have some thoughts on it, Anne. After all, you knew that you would be planning a wedding no matter who ended up as your groom!"

From another man, this might have verged on insulting, but Jack gave her one of those heart-stopping smiles of his, and Anne had to laugh.

"You're shamelessly frank, my lord."

"Well, it is the truth, you must admit."

"I will admit I hadn't thought much about it either until I spoke to Elspeth, but I think I would prefer a small country wedding in Yorkshire with friends and family. What do you think of that? Or would you prefer a Society wedding?"

"Not at all. A small wedding seems more appropriate for us."

Anne was surprised to feel a little hurt by his phrasing. Was a more private wedding appropriate because theirs was a marriage of convenience? Or because he didn't like large weddings? And why should she feel hurt if it did? She didn't expect "for us" to mean anything more, did she? Or could it be that, though she wasn't expecting it, she was beginning to want it to mean something more.

Jack had meant it in all three ways. He had no desire for a big public ceremony. And given their reasons for marriage, he would prefer a small wedding. But most of all, he wanted the ceremony to be as meaningful as possible under the circumstances. He wanted to take Anne Heriot to wife in a place she cared about, surrounded by people she loved. She may not love him now, but if she ever did come to love him, he wanted her memories of their union to be as warm as possible.

Chapter Twenty-one

The Astons announced their supper dance for the week after the betrothal announcement. Jack was more grateful to them every day, for the informal acknowledgments of his engagement tended to be variations on "You sly dog" or "The dark horse came in first!" He hated to think of what people were saying of Anne. A formal celebration, sponsored by Faringdon, would give their betrothal at least the appearance of something more than practical.

His older brother had inherited the diamond-and-sapphire necklace that traditionally went to the eldest son's bride. Jack was sure his grandmother had a few small pieces she had saved for his eventual marriage, but he preferred she give them to Anne herself on the occasion of their first visit to her. He wanted Anne to be wearing something from him at her betrothal ball.

The question was whether he could afford it. Oh, now that their betrothal was public, he could charge the crown jewels based on Anne's fortune. But he didn't want her paying for her own engagement present, damn it. He wanted the gift to be something he paid for himself. But the question was, with what? He had a little money left from selling out, but he'd have wedding expenses to think of. He had sold a number of things already from the town house and there wasn't much left, except for a small painting that had hung in the library since he was a child, a portrait of a Spanish ancestor whom he greatly resembled. He went in and stood before it, just as he had many times over the years, feeling comforted and strengthened by the portrayal of such an obviously admirable man who was so un-English. It meant a great deal to him, this picture, and he sighed as he took it down and wrapped it carefully in brown paper. It was more important that Anne wear something from him next Tuesday evening than he keep this small portrait. There was another and more formal one at his grandmother's. It didn't hold the same meaning for him, but then, he was no longer a young boy in need of reassurance.

He got a good price for the painting, and the next morning at the breakfast table, he asked Helen if he could have her help in making a purchase.

Helen looked at him with surprise. "Why, of course, Jack, but I didn't think you were very fond of shopping?"

"I wish to get Miss Heriot an engagement present. I thought you might be better at knowing what would be attractive on her."

Helen's face lit up. "I would love to help you!"

"I thought so," said Jack with a grin. Helen had been delighted by the betrothal—and not merely for selfish reasons. His marriage to Anne meant that she and Lydia would have a future, but he also knew Helen had come to like Anne for herself.

Helen lifted her eyebrows when Jack stopped in front of Rundell and Bridges, for it was the most exclusive of jewelers.

"Are you sure, Jack?" she whispered. She didn't want to come right out and say, "Are you sure you can afford it?" but he guessed what she meant and gave her a reassuring wink.

The clerk showed them a few trays of ostentatious necklaces, and Helen shook her head as he pointed to several. "Something smaller and simpler in design would suit Miss Heriot much better," she told her cousin. "What about this one?" she asked, pointing out a delicate gold necklace set with garnets and small diamonds.

"Garnets are only semiprecious stones, my lord," the clerk informed him.

"Yes, but there are the diamonds," Helen declared. "And deep red is much more flattering to Miss Heriot's coloring than emeralds or sapphires. Are there earbobs to match?"

"These would complement the necklace very well," the clerk told them, drawing out a pair of diamond earrings.

"We'll take them," said Helen, then looked at Jack apologetically as the clerk left to wrap them up. "I *am* sorry, Jack. Did you want to look at anything else?"

"No, your taste is excellent, Helen, which is why I brought you along," he told her with an approving smile. "I liked that necklace best, but I wouldn't have trusted my judgment, especially with the clerk making me feel that garnets would be an insult!"

When the clerk returned with their package, Jack pointed out a smaller pair of diamond studs. "I would like these in a separate box, if I may."

"Certainly, sir." When he handed Jack the smaller package, Jack turned and said to Helen, "A small thank-you gift. I would be proud to see you wear them at the Astons' supper dance, Helen."

"Oh, Jack, you shouldn't have. I thought they were another gift for Miss Heriot."

"No. I know you must sit on the sidelines this year, but there is no reason you can't sparkle, is there?"

They walked slowly down the street, enjoying their window-shopping. As they gazed into one of the windows, Helen turned to her cousin and said hesitantly, "I love my gift, Jack, but I am a little worried . . ."

"Whether I could afford it?" Jack asked with a quizzical grin.

"Well, Miss Heriot's money makes anything possible, but I hate spending her money on her betrothal gift."

"It's not silly. I felt the same way, so I paid for all of it out of my own pocket. I sold a small painting—the one in the library."

"But that is one of your favorites!"

"Yes, but so is Anne, and so are you. Live relatives are more important than long-dead ones, don't you agree?" Jack replied teasingly.

Helen gave him an impulsive hug. "Anne Heriot is very lucky to be getting you as a husband, Jack. And she should be grateful that you saved her from that witch, Lady Eliza."

"I only hope she feels the same way, Helen."

Jack sent the necklace and earrings over to Anne with a short note saying that he hoped his gifts pleased her and he would be proud to have her wear them at the supper dance. "Of course, if they do not complement your gown, I will understand completely," he added in a postscript.

Anne turned to Sarah, who was sitting with her in the morning room when the package arrived.

"It is an engagement gift from Lord Aldborough," she said, gazing down at the package in her lap.

"How thoughtful of him. Do open it, Anne."

Anne unwrapped the paper slowly and, lifting the lid, gasped with pleasure. "Look, Sarah, it is exquisite. And the earrings are a perfect match."

"It is perfect for you. Not too fussy and just the right color. The filigree work is very unusual—spare and strong and yet it appears quite delicate."

"He hopes I will wear it Tuesday evening, Sarah. But the necklace doesn't match what I planned to wear. He adds he would understand if I didn't wear them."

Sarah sat silently, wondering what Anne would do. In any other circumstances, the choice would be obvious. If one cared for one's fiancé, one would wear a different dress.

"I had so wanted to wear my new, yellow silk,"

Anne murmured. "But these go perfectly with the embroidered overslip on the ivory gown."

"Which doesn't look as good on you," Sarah pointed out gently.

"Well, I will just have to rely on the necklace to garner compliments, Sarah," Anne declared. "I cannot hurt Lord Aldborough's feelings."

And so, when Tuesday night arrived, Anne had the pleasure of seeing Jack Belden's eyes light up with appreciation of the way the sparkling necklace rested in the hollow of her neck and with gratitude that she had worn his gift.

"You look very beautiful tonight, Anne," he told her as he led her out for the first dance.

"Thank you, my lord, and thank you for your lovely gift."

"It matches your gown perfectly."

"I wanted to do justice to the necklace," she said softly.

"I appreciate your thoughtfulness, Anne," said Jack, his voice warm.

His obvious depth of feeling surprised her. She had worn the dress less from a desire to please and more from the wish not to hurt, but she found herself very happy to have pleased Jack Belden.

Anne made sure to visit with Lady Aldborough and her daughters, who were sitting off to the side.

"I hope you are all enjoying yourselves. I would be very happy to sit with your daughters for a while if you wish to visit with friends."

"Thank you, Miss Heriot, but I am so recently out of mourning that I feel more comfortable just watching tonight."

"You look lovely, Miss Heriot," said Helen.

"Especially your necklace," piped up Liddy. "Helen helped Jack pick it out, you know. And Jack gave her her first diamonds!"

"Hush, Liddy."

"I noticed the sparkle from across the room," said

Anne with a smile. "They are as lovely as my own, Lady Helen."

"He sold a painting to buy them, you know," said Liddy. "It was his favorite, although I don't know why. The gentleman in the picture looks even more melancholy than Jack!"

This time, Helen turned to her sister and said fiercely, "Hush, Liddy, or I will have Mother send you upstairs."

Lydia sat back with a red face and muttered an apology.

"There is no need to apologize. What picture was this that Jack sold, Lady Helen?"

Helen considered sparing Jack embarrassment by downplaying his sacrifice. But he had made such a thoughtful and romantic gesture that she decided his fiancée needed to know about it. Especially since they were marrying for such unromantic reasons.

"My cousin had a small portrait of our great-great-grandfather. Jack looks very much like him."

"I hope it wasn't the only likeness!"

"There is a larger one at my grandmother's home. But I know this was his favorite. I believe Jack wanted to make sure that his engagement present was a true gift," Helen added, trying to be as subtle as possible.

"I understand, and I very much appreciate it," Anne told her softly.

"But I am sure he didn't want you to know, which is why I am so angry at Liddy."

Anne smiled. "She is a delightfully open child, but openness can sometimes cause embarrassment. I will keep this our secret, at least for now. And I wish you would call me Anne, now that we are to be related, Lady Helen."

"Then you must call me Helen. I want to tell you how happy I am you chose Jack over Baron Leighton. His daughter was not as respectful as she might have been . . ." Helen's voice trailed off.

"Tha means she was a right witch, doesn't tha?"

replied Anne with dry humor. "And I suspect tha was as much of a long-tongue as tha sister when tha was younger, lass."

Helen blushed. "Mother despaired of ever teaching me manners. But I haven't disgraced myself in years."

"You are a daughter to be proud of, Helen, and I am happy to call you cousin," Anne told her warmly.

Elspeth and Val had been so busy with their guests that Anne had no chance to visit with them until later in the evening. "I cannot thank you enough, Elspeth," she told her friend. "Your party has been the perfect way to celebrate my success. All my favorite people are here and none of the spiteful gossips."

"That doesn't mean no one is gossiping, Anne," Elspeth warned her with a smile.

"But not spitefully!"

"No, most have been talking about how beautifully your necklace complements your gown."

"It *is* beautiful, isn't it? It was Jack's engagement present."

"I know. The first thing he said to me tonight was 'Do you think I chose well, Elspeth?' "

"I understand Lady Helen had a hand in choosing it." Anne hesitated. "Are people assuming that Jack spent my money, Elspeth?"

"No one here would be that crass, Anne."

"But I am sure they are wondering."

"Do you care? Everything Jack has will come from you."

"I care only because it does him an injustice, Elspeth. Lady Lydia blurted out that he sold a painting for it."

"That child is incorrigible!"

"I like her. In fact, she reminds me of you!"

"I was never that blunt," protested Elspeth.

"Almost as bad when we were at school." They both laughed their agreement, and then Anne said seriously, "It seems Jack valued this painting very much. It was a portrait of his Spanish great-great-grandfather."

"It was likely all he had left to sell."

"I am touched he would make such a sacrifice for me."

Elspeth wanted to say, He loves you, so he was happy to make it, but it wasn't her place to reveal Jack's secret. "He is a sensitive man, and whether people would know or not, he probably felt it more honorable to make sure his gift was truly a gift."

"It's a gesture I wouldn't have expected from him," Anne confessed. "I think I have had an image of him from our first meeting that I have never quite let go of."

"The devil-may-care 'Jack of Hearts'?"

"He seemed like a man not overly careful of women's feelings."

"Only if you listen to the gossips. Or did not see that the young ladies whose hearts he supposedly stole were quite eager to hand them over to any man who fit their fantasies."

"You and Val have always painted a different picture, but Leighton and Windham appeared so much more trustworthy."

"They are both likable gentlemen, so there is no need to apologize for preferring them at the time. But now that you're marrying Jack, I'm glad you are beginning to see him more clearly."

Anne looked across the room at Val and Jack, chatting with Captain Scott. Val Aston was a striking man, with his hawklike nose and broad shoulders. Captain Scott was another good-looking man, very handsome in his regimentals. But Jack Belden, whose face changed like quicksilver, was one of the most attractive men she had ever met. She could admit it now and felt a stirring of desire. It would seem that whatever one's motive for marriage, one could so easily be deceived by external appearances. She had only seen the positive qualities of Lord Leighton and Lord Windham. What if she had married either one of them and then found out about Lady Eliza or Windham's wounded heart?

With Jack, she had seen only the negatives, the aspects of him that were most on the surface. Although all three men had the same motive—her fortune—she had allowed herself to see the others' feelings of affection for her. But she had never taken Jack Belden seriously. She had dismissed him early on, and despite their growing friendship, had never completely let go of her early suspicions. But any man who would make such a sacrifice was a man who cared for her.

She was very grateful, she realized, for she might well have made a match that gave her more than she had hoped for.

As though he was aware of her eyes on him, Jack turned and smiled. His smile was so warm, so approving, that Anne felt she was melting in its warmth. She found herself hoping they would find some time alone before the night was over.

Jack was hoping the same thing, but unfortunately, it was a chilly night and the Faringdon town house had only a small garden. There was a conservatory, however, and he intended to maneuver Anne there as soon as possible.

It took almost all his patience to wait through the next few dances, but finally the musicians announced a break. "I am going to claim some time with my fiancée," he told Lord Lovett, her last dance partner, and he whisked Anne away from him.

"Have you seen Lord Faringdon's conservatory, Anne?"

"No, although I have heard it is quite lovely." Anne sounded calm, but in fact her heart was beating erratically at the thought of being alone with him.

The earl had imported several small orange trees from Spain, and the scent of their blossoms was intoxicatingly sweet. As they walked slowly around the perimeter of the semicircular room, Anne was disappointed to see that there seemed to be no place for two people to sit. But finally they reached a small window seat.

"This is not very comfortable, but it will have to do," Jack muttered as he pulled her down next to him and then almost immediately leaned down and kissed her. He did not begin with gentle exploration, but took possession of her mouth with a hunger that stimulated her own. One moment, she surrendered herself to him, and then, in the next, she was demanding as much from him as he was from her. Soon she lost all sense of who was kissing, who was being kissed, for they seemed to have become one person.

The kiss went on forever and at the same time ended too soon.

"God, I've been wanting to do this all night," Jack murmured, his face buried in her neck.

"And I have been wanting you to," confessed Anne, ducking her face in embarrassment.

"So you enjoy our kisses," he teased.

"Very much. Too much."

"Too much?"

"I'm afraid I'll get lost in them and never find my way back."

Jack pulled away and looked down at her. "Back to where, my love?" he asked softly.

"To solid ground, to what is familiar . . . kisses aren't practical," Anne said wildly, knowing she was making little sense.

"The ever-so-practical Anne Heriot," said Jack with a teasing grin. "Sometimes you have to let go of solid ground, Anne. Sometimes you have to lose in order to gain. I hope I can show you that with more than kisses," he whispered, as his long fingers slipped beneath her bodice and cupped her breast. As his thumb circled, she felt again a flood of warmth deep within and wanted something more from him, though she was not sure what that was.

When he took his hand away, she gave a little moan, for she thought he was going to pull away from her. Instead he gently lifted her gown and trailed his finger up her thigh. She gave a little gasp of surprise and then pleasure when his finger slid into her. How had he known just where she was melting down to? As he began to stroke, she was very still, and he began to lift her up and up, only to bring her down shuddering in his arms.

Jack had always taken pleasure at bringing a woman pleasure, but he had never before been the first, never before felt a woman he loved trembling in his arms. He wanted to take her then and there, but at the same time he marveled at how he didn't need to, because her pleasure felt like it was his own.

Well, almost didn't need to, he thought with ironic humor as he shifted a little so he was not so close to her. He hoped his arousal would subside, for they would have to return to the ballroom soon. They were betrothed, it was true, but he didn't want people gossiping any more than they were already.

"Are you all right, Anne?"

Anne didn't know what to say. She had never felt so much herself in her life, and yet she had never dreamed herself capable of such abandon. She couldn't look at Jack, couldn't let him see her, so she kept her head down as she nervously straightened her gown and smoothed her hair.

"Yes, I am fine, but shouldn't we be getting back?"

"Yes, in a minute or two." She could hear the ironic humor in his voice and realized what he meant. She had grown up in the country and was not ignorant of male anatomy, but she hadn't been thinking much of him at all, just of the delightful things he had been doing to her.

"I am sorry. Should I have been doing something for you . . . ?" Her voice trailed off, and Jack gave such a delighted laugh that Anne finally relaxed and laughed with him.

"There will be many opportunities in the future, I hope, so you can even out the debits and the credits, my dear, if that is what you are worried about."

His image was so absurd and yet so apt that Anne could not get it out of her mind as they finally made their way back to the ballroom. Column one: kisses. There the sums added up. They were even. Column two: intimate caresses. Oh, dear, she was in debt there. Column three: exquisite and indescribable pleasure. His credit was so large she couldn't imagine how she could ever make it up, but only hoped she would find a way.

Chapter Twenty-two

Anne fell asleep quickly that night and slept much later than usual. When she awoke, she could hear the patter of raindrops against the window and burrowed under the covers. The rhythm of the rain was lulling her into a delicious state between waking and sleeping, where she could imagine herself in Jack's arms, when she heard a knock at her door.

"What is it?" she called, annoyed at the interruption.

"Begging your pardon, miss, but Miss Wheeler told me to tell you that Sergeant Gillen is here."

Anne shook her head to clear it. "Sergeant Gillen? He can't be here, he's in Yorkshire."

"He rode all the way, miss, and a right mess he is too. It looks like he hasn't slept for days."

"Hand me my wrapper, Mary." What on earth had brought Patrick Gillen to London? Anne worried as she tied her dressing gown around her.

"Where is the sergeant, Mary?"

"In the kitchen, miss. Miss Wheeler is trying to get him to eat something, but he says he can't relax until he speaks to you."

Anne hurried down to the kitchen and there was Patrick Gillen, looking just as exhausted as Mary had described. He was standing by the stove, warming his hands while Sarah sat and watched him.

"Whatever are you doing here, Patrick?" Anne exclaimed.

"I am sorry to break in on ye in such a state, Miss Heriot, but I couldn't trust the news to anyone else."

"Sit down, Patrick, and tell me." Anne slipped into a chair and motioned him into another.

He sat down at last and, running a hand through his hair, turned his head so his good eye faced her. "There's been trouble at the Shipton mill, Miss Heriot."

"What kind of trouble, Patrick?"

"A fire in the sorting shed, which burned it to the ground."

Anne gasped. "The children?"

"No, no, they're all right. It was at night. Yer cousin thinks it was Ned Gibson, miss, and he has all the bloody troopers in Yorkshire out lookin' for him."

Anne was quiet for a minute, then said regretfully, "I should have settled this before I left. I should have done something about Ned Gibson."

"He certainly had a motive, Anne," Sarah said quietly.

"Revenge for being let go," agreed Anne.

"Or determination that the machine would be replaced," Patrick said coolly. "But this time I am not sure Ned Gibson is behind it at all."

"But who else would have a reason, Patrick?"

"Yer cousin, for one."

"Joseph! Why, he would never do anything to slow production," responded Anne with a touch of humor.

"Under usual circumstances, no. But the news of yer betrothal might have driven him to it."

"What do you mean, Patrick? He has known I wouldn't marry him for months."

" 'Tis one thing to know something and another entirely to see it become real."

"I know you don't like Joseph, Patrick, but you are letting it cloud your judgment," Anne said disapprovingly.

"I don't think Ned Gibson is a violent man." Patrick hesitated. "Yer cousin has written to you with the news of the fire, but I wanted to make sure you heard it from me first. If you return to Yorkshire before you're married and another 'accident' occurs, then Trantor inherits everything."

"What do you recommend, Patrick?" Anne asked coolly.

"I don't know when ye're planning to get married, miss, but I suggest ye don't return to Yorkshire until ye've tied the knot!"

"I am planning to marry in the Wetherby chapel, Patrick," Anne said stiffly. "I don't believe my cousin is capable of harming me."

She stood up. "Make sure the sergeant gets some food into him, Sarah. And order hot water for a bath. You look about ready to collapse, Patrick," she continued, her tone softening. "I may not agree with you about my cousin, but I'm grateful for your loyalty."

"Bloody stubborn woman," exclaimed Patrick after the kitchen door closed behind Anne. "She should not go back to Wetherby until she is Lady Aldborough. At least she chose Jack Belden. She's a smart lass in everything but this."

Sarah busied herself at the stove, filling the teapot and dishing out a bowl of porridge, which she set in front of Patrick.

"Do you really think she would be in danger?"

Patrick looked up from his porridge, which was half eaten already. "By God, I was hungry! As for Joseph Trantor . . . I don't know, Sarah. But 'tis better to take no chances, don't ye agree? If she comes back as Miss Heriot, he still has a chance . . ."

"To do what, Patrick? To kill her?" Sarah shivered.

"Maybe not. Maybe only to frighten her into marrying him."

"Why wouldn't he have done that sooner?"

"I don't have any answers, Sarah. But there are enough questions to keep her in London till she is Lady Aldborough."

"On that part, we're agreed."

"So ye'll convince her?"

"Yes, and you might work on Lord Aldborough. But not until you've had time to rest."

"I'm not fit to be showin' myself to anyone this way," muttered Patrick. "I didn't expect to be seein' ye here in the kitchen, Sarah," he added with an embarrassed smile. "I thought ye'd be enjoyin' yer rest after a night of dancin'. I'm assumin' ye've been doin' a good deal of dancin' here in London."

"I have been fortunate enough to meet a few gentlemen who make sure I am not holding up the wall," Sarah told him stiffly, hurt that he seemed to be *pleased* that she'd been enjoying herself.

Patrick stumbled up. "I'm just goin' to fall into bed, so don't ye bother with the hot water till later," he told her.

"Just tell Mrs. Collins when you want it, then, Patrick."

Sarah sat there after he left, looking down at her cup of tea. It had been weeks since she'd seen him, and he'd hardly looked at her. Here she had been foolishly missing him, and he had clearly forgotten her and the kisses they'd shared.

Anne dressed quickly and had a footman bring her some tea and muffins in the morning room. She sat in front of the fire, listening to the rain beat down against the window, nibbling absentmindedly at her muffin. She *couldn't* believe her cousin would wish to harm her. She had never believed it. He might be a harsh man, but surely he had a fondness for her, not just for her fortune. No, Ned Gibson was the most likely culprit. She would have to leave London as soon as possible. It wouldn't look good to go so soon after her betrothal, but she couldn't worry about the gossips. They would think that she cared nothing for Jack, that she had gone home as soon as she'd gotten what she came for. But they would have thought that anyway, she told herself, whomever she married and however she married him. She hoped Jack would understand why she had to go. The mills were as important to him now as they were to her, albeit for different reasons.

She sighed. She had to admit to herself, at least, that she didn't want to go, that for once in her life she didn't wish to be practical. She had wanted to play the lady this morning, to stay in bed and imagine what it would be like to lie there on a rainy morning with Jack Belden beside her. She had wanted to dream about his kisses, to lose herself in the memory of the pleasure he had given her. And to daydream of the musicale tonight, where they might have found some time to be alone together. She wanted another few weeks of enjoying just how compatible she and her husband-to-be were, at least in one area of marriage.

Now she would be leaving him behind. How much this would affect the fragile beginning of their relationship, she didn't know. But she had no choice and could only hope he would understand.

Patrick slept for only a few hours and then sank gratefully into the tub that had been brought up to his apartments. He would have given anything to stay and soak the stiffness out, but he was in too much of a hurry to see Jack Belden. He only had time for washing, he reminded himself, not for lolling around.

He set off for the Aldborough town house, praying that Jack would be in. When the butler admitted him and showed him into the library, he breathed a sigh of relief.

"Good afternoon, Sergeant Gillen. I was surprised to hear you announced," Jack said with a welcoming smile that offset the puzzled look on his face when he saw Patrick.

"I am sorry to be disturbin' ye, sor, but I've just ridden down from Yorkshire on a matter of some importance to Miss Heriot. And may I add my congratulations, my lord," Patrick added with a wide smile. "I was hopin' all along that she would choose ye. But then, I should have trusted Miss Heriot. She's a sensible woman . . . except for now, when she's bein' so stubborn. Which is why I'm here."

"What *does* bring you here, Sergeant?"

"There was a fire in one of the mills, sor."

Jack frowned. "You must think there is some connection to what happened this winter, or you wouldn't be here, Patrick."

"I do, sor. And we still don't know who's responsible for that, either, do we?"

"But you have your suspicions?"

"I do. Joseph Trantor has a very good reason to do something that would bring Miss Heriot back before she has a chance to marry."

"Yes, Miss Heriot's fortune has always been a believable motive," mused Jack. "I know you don't like him, but do you really think this Trantor capable of murder?"

"I don't know. But as I've told Miss Heriot, Ned Gibson never struck me as the violent sort."

"What do you suggest I do, Sergeant Gillen?"

"Marry Miss Heriot immediately, sor."

"There is nothing I would like better," Jack murmured. "But she will have something to say about that."

"She already has, sor. She's leaving for Yorkshire tomorrow!"

"Is she at home now?"

"Yes, sor."

"Then let's continue planning our strategy with her."

So Anne would leave him behind in London, thought Jack as they walked. He didn't care that much about *ton* gossip, but he had to admit it would be rather humiliating to be left behind only a few days after his betrothal announcement. It made him feel rather like a parcel that Anne had come to town to purchase and was going to have shipped to her later!

Anne and Sarah were in the morning room when Jack walked in on them unannounced. "Sergeant Gillen is in the library, Miss Wheeler. Perhaps you would like to make sure that he has some refreshment?"

It may have been phrased as a suggestion, but Sarah

knew an order when she heard one. With an apologetic glance at Anne, she left.

"I suppose Patrick told you all," Anne said quietly.

"The question is, were *you* going to tell me or just go haring off to Yorkshire alone?"

"I was going to write you a letter, explaining why."

"Perhaps you would like to explain it to me now?"

"I *have* to go—you must understand that."

"I know the mills are very important to you. And I agree we must discover who is behind this vandalism. But why disregard Patrick's advice? Marry me before you go, Anne. I'll get a special license, and we can be wed and on our way in a few days."

"I want to wed from my home, Jack, just as we planned. And I don't see how marrying in a rush here in London will help."

"It might save your life, damn it!"

"I cannot believe that Joseph would ever hurt me."

"And what if you're wrong?"

"Suppose I am wrong? Then what will marrying now accomplish? We'll never really know if Joseph was behind this or not. And . . ."

"And what?" Jack asked quietly.

"And we could both be in danger."

"I appreciate your concern for my safety, my dear, but I think I can handle one rebellious Yorkshireman," Jack said with a touch of sarcasm that annoyed Anne.

"Tha might or tha might not. At any rate, I am going home, and I am going home as Miss Anne Heriot. We will marry as we planned, in Wetherby, as soon as this matter has been settled."

"Do you really think I will let you go alone?"

"You cannot stop me, Lord Aldborough," Anne said frostily.

"I am not trying to stop you, but I am going with you, so come down off your high horse, Annie!"

Anne couldn't help smiling. No one called her Annie except her old nurse and Elspeth's father. "You can't leave your aunt and cousins, Jack. I am sure I will be fine. It is Ned Gibson behind this, and once he is arrested, the danger will be over."

Ignoring her, Jack stood up and started pacing. "You are right, I can't leave my aunt and the girls tomorrow, Anne. I have to make sure they are taken care of while I am away. Once I am up there, I'll not come down again before the wedding. I'll need to make travel arrangements for them, too," he added thoughtfully.

"I want to leave tomorrow, Jack. And wouldn't it look better if you followed after me?"

Jack laughed. "I think we have to give up worrying about appearances, Anne. The gossips will enjoy themselves whether we leave separately or together."

"I'll have Patrick and Sarah with me, Jack. I want to get *home.*"

Jack sighed. "All right," he agreed reluctantly. "I won't be that far behind you if I am riding," he admitted. "But I don't like it."

Anne was so grateful for his understanding that she got up and went to him. "I know this might make you look a little foolish, Jack, and I thank you for understanding my need to go."

"You think that's what I'm worried about? That I'll look a little foolish? I am worried about you, damn it," he said angrily and grasping her by the shoulders, he leaned down and kissed her.

It wasn't like the other kisses. It was hard and fierce and shook her with its intensity. It communicated far more than desire, and he let her go before she could respond.

"I am sorry for my roughness, Anne," he told her, his face shuttered. "I will see you in Yorkshire."

He was gone before she could say good-bye, and she stood there for a moment, knowing that he had told her something very important with that kiss, something she knew she should understand but wasn't quite sure she did.

Chapter Twenty-three

The journey home to Wetherby was exhausting for all of them, but particularly for Sarah, who suffered from motion sickness. By the time they reached Heriot Hall, she had been ill off and on all the last afternoon, and Anne sent her right to bed.

"You should be getting some rest, too, Miss Heriot," Patrick told her. "I pushed us hard the last thirty miles."

"I will, Patrick, as soon as I can relax a little. I want to visit Shipton tomorrow." Anne looked at him appraisingly. "You are looking pretty exhausted yourself. Will you feel up to driving?"

"Ye're not goin' anywhere without me, miss. Don't worry, I'll be ready."

Anne slept late the next morning and smiled when she awoke to the sound of birdsong and the occasional sheep bleating in the field behind the house. She enjoyed London, but it was good to be home. If she had her way, she would spend most of the year in Wetherby. But now that she was marrying Jack Belden, she supposed she might well be living at Aldborough. Or perhaps Jack preferred the city? But they didn't have to live in each other's pockets, she reminded herself. She could likely spend more time there and make extended visits to Lincoln or London.

But the idea of a long-distance marriage, one in which her life did not change very much, wasn't as appealing to her as it had been last fall. Now that she had tasted Jack's kisses, she wasn't at all sure she wanted to be without them for long periods of time. It would be good to have help with the mills. And to give him her support if he decided to play an active role in the House of Lords. London would be more appealing if she had some real purpose for being there. Acting as her husband's hostess would mean that she could aid in influencing government policy on issues like child labor and mill safety.

Her marriage to Jack Belden was becoming more and more appealing. She was beginning to think she was very lucky to have ended up with her last choice, and not just because of his kisses. She could imagine a partnership, something she was now increasingly sure she would not have had with either Leighton or Windham.

She gave a little sigh of satisfaction, and then frowned. Today was not a day she could spend dreaming about her future with Jack. She needed to take care of problems in the present.

She and Patrick left after a late breakfast.

"Are you sure it wouldn't be better to wait for Joseph to advise you about the situation?" Sarah asked anxiously.

"I want to investigate for myself, Sarah, and be able to ask questions without Joseph beside me."

Anne's carriage was recognized as Patrick drove through Shipton, and the news spread quickly. What was Miss Heriot doing back from London so soon, people were asking one another. And was she still Miss Heriot? Had she found herself a husband or would she end up with her cousin after all? No one had any answers, of course, but everyone was looking forward to closing time when they would learn what she was doing at the mill from their husbands and daughters and sons.

As the carriage pulled into the courtyard of the mill, Anne heard Patrick say, "Good afternoon, Mr. Trantor," and her heart sank. She had been hoping to avoid Joseph.

The door opened, and there was her cousin, his hand extended to help her down.

"Thank you, Joseph," she told him calmly.

"Whatever art tha doing here, Anne?"

"I came to see the results of the fire myself."

"But I wrote tha exactly what happened." He frowned. "But how could tha have gotten my letter and made it back home so quickly?"

"Patrick rode down to London to make sure I had the news right away."

"That was thoughtful of you, Sergeant Gillen, but there was no need of such heroics," Joseph said sarcastically. "I have things completely in hand, Anne. Ned Gibson was behind all this, and t'troops will have him any day now."

"And ye're sure it was Mr. Gibson, sor?" Patrick asked mildly.

"Isn't it obvious? He is sacked because of an incident in the sorting shed, and after drinking and brooding about it, he burns the shed down."

"I had thought his brother was more the drinker in the family," Patrick murmured.

"It runs in t'family, I'm sure." Trantor turned to Anne. "This is most upsetting, cousin. I have an appointment and can't stay to show tha around. Why doesn't tha coom back tomorrow?" he added, trying to make his tone conciliatory.

"I appreciate your concern, Joseph, but Patrick and I will do fine. Perhaps you can call on me tomorrow?"

"Of course. Tomorrow, then." Trantor climbed into his own carriage and with a wave of his hand set off.

"I'm glad he had that appointment, Patrick," Anne said as they made their way to the shed. Or where the shed had been. It was now an empty shell, the floor half gone and the carding machine crushed under one of the ceiling beams that had obviously been eaten through by the fire.

"Thank God this happened at night," Anne whispered.

"Amen to that, Miss Heriot," said Patrick, as he surveyed the destruction. "I don't think it's safe to go in, miss," he added as he stepped a little closer and tested a floor board, which sagged under his weight.

When they made their way up to the loft, Anne was very glad she had not announced her visit, for the surprise on the workers' faces gave her hope that she might get some spontaneous response from them. But although she interviewed a number of men and women, they knew nothing. Or denied that they did, at any rate. When she asked specifically about Ned Gibson, their faces closed and they only told her, "Ned would never do soomthing like that, miss," or "He hasn't been seen at mill since he were sacked, miss."

"I don't know what to think, Patrick," Anne complained when he joined her in the office after she had interviewed everyone. "The fire certainly accomplished one thing—it destroyed a machine that has caused several accidents. We will have to replace it, and that might have been motive enough for Ned Gibson."

Patrick nodded thoughtfully. "Ye make a good point. But it also means quite a few families are short of money until the machine is replaced. Would he want to cause such hardship?"

"Maybe in the short run, if he thought the long run would make things safer." Anne sighed. "If he did do it, I must admit I have a certain sympathy for him."

"I do, too, miss, but destroyin' things is never the answer."

"What *is,* Patrick?"

"Creatin' new ways, miss, so ye're leavin' the old behind, not burnin' it before ye."

"I intend to create new ways, Patrick," Anne said determinedly.

"I know ye do. I knew ye were a woman of courage since the first day I saw ye."

Anne dozed off on the way home, still tired from her long journey from London. But she awakened with a start when the carriage stopped and she heard Patrick give a loud curse.

"What is it, Patrick?" she called out the window.

"There's somethin' in the road, Miss Heriot. You stay right where ye are while I take care of it."

The "something" was a large limb of a tree, dragged across the road. There was no way around it, unfortunately, for there were ditches on either side. "It wasn't there a few hours ago," Patrick muttered as he climbed down, and then laughed at himself as he leaned over to pull it away. "Of course it wasn't, ye feckin' eejit, or else we wouldn't have gotten by." The branch was heavy, but not immovable and he had just started to shift it when suddenly his head exploded from behind and he went down like a felled branch himself.

"Patrick?" Anne had heard him muttering to himself, and the scraping sound of the obstacle being moved, and then a loud noise as something fell. Had he dropped whatever was blocking the road? She couldn't just sit in the carriage if he needed help.

Just as she reached for the handle, the carriage door opened and she found herself peering into a stranger's face.

"There tha are, lass."

The words were simple enough, but the man's tone held so much hostility that Anne shrank back.

"Art tha cooming out thaself, or do I have to pull tha out?"

Anne stepped down carefully and looked up at her accoster. "I don't have much money with me today, if that is what you are looking for. But then, if you were a common thief, I don't think you'd let me see your face," she added calmly.

"Tha'rt a smart lass, like I've always heard. Too bad tha'rt such a hardheaded one."

"Who are you and what do you want from me?"

"All in good time, lass. All in good time." The man grabbed her arms and, pulling them in front of her, tied them quickly with a rough piece of rope. Then he attached another piece so that he had her on a sort of leash. "Now tha can coom easy or hard, lass, it's tha choice. But coom with me tha will." He turned and pulled Anne with him. As he stepped over the ditch, Anne, who had been looking back in horror at where Patrick lay over the limb of a tree, found herself on her knees in the mud.

"Get up, lass, and pay attention. We have a ways to go."

Anne climbed slowly to her feet and helping herself as best she could with her hands, climbed out. The rope was thick and harsh and when her captor jerked it again, she pulled back without thinking from the pain.

" 'Tis no good to resist. I'll sling tha over my shoulder if I have to," the man growled and then began to climb the hill.

Anne did her best to keep up, so that there would be slack in the rope, but the man's strides were longer, and every now and then she would be jerked almost off her feet. And she was in shock. In only a few minutes she had gone from being Miss Anne Heriot, traveling home in her own carriage to being a woman whose only concern was keeping up with a madman so her wrists would not be torn to shreds.

She was sobbing and gasping for breath when they finally reached the top of the scar, and she was pleased to see that her captor also needed to rest. He was blowing out deep breaths, and from the smell of them she could tell he was a heavy drinker. Maybe he was drunk and had mistaken her for someone else. She made herself look at his face. She didn't know him, she was sure of that. And yet . . . there was something familiar in his face.

"Do you know who I am? Are you sure you have the right woman?" she asked when she finally caught her breath.

"Oh, aye, I know who tha are, all reet. Tha'rt Heriot's bitch of a daughter."

Anne couldn't help herself from shrinking back at the hatred in the man's voice.

"You knew my father, then?"

"Aye, and he knew me well enough, too."

"But I have never met you." Anne paused. "Though you look familiar to me for some reason."

"Perhaps because tha has met my brother."

Then it came to her. This must be Ned Gibson's brother. They probably had looked even more alike before Tom Gibson had given himself over to drunken hopelessness.

"Tha'rt Tom Gibson?"

"I am, lass."

"But what do you expect to get out of this?" Anne asked him, lifting her hands.

"I intend to keep tha until tha calls troopers off our Ned and promises to give his job back."

"But I can't do anything for him as your prisoner, Mr. Gibson."

"I've heard tha'rt reet good at figures, Miss Heriot. I've no doubt tha can write also," he added sarcastically.

"There's no place to hide up here. You'll be caught and hung, and then where will your brother be? And your wife and family?"

"Neither tha father or tha cared much for my wife and family before, miss. And don't worry, tha won't be found until I want tha found. Coom on."

It seemed to Anne they went on for hours, but in truth, it was well before sundown when they reached what appeared to be a tiny valley on top of the dale.

Clearly someone had lived here once, for there was a crumbled ruin that Gibson led her over to.

"But I will freeze to death if you leave me here," she protested.

"Don't tha worry tha pretty head, lass. Tha'll be warm and dry." He pulled at the grass, or so it seemed to Anne, until she realized that he was actually pulling at a hidden handle of a cellar door.

"Get thaself down, then."

Anne looked at him in horror.

"Don't worry, tha'll not be bothered by anything. How does tha think we kept ourselves out of troopers' hands before now?"

Anne climbed carefully down worn stone steps, with Gibson following behind her. There was a small stream of light cutting across the darkness, and as her eyes adjusted, she saw that she was in some sort of root cellar and that the light came from a gap left by fallen stones.

There was a small rickety table and three chairs in the middle of the room, and when Gibson struck a lucifer and lit a rusty lantern, Anne almost sobbed with relief.

Her captor unslung a knapsack from his shoulders and, reaching into it, brought out half a loaf of bread, a heel of cheese, and three bottles of ale as well as a tin plate and what appeared to be a tin version of a chamber pot. Anne's heart sank. Clearly the man had come prepared to keep her here a while.

"Now, then, lass, tha'll stay here for a day or two, while everyone is looking for tha, and then tha shalt write note," Gibson told her as he pulled out a wrinkled piece of paper.

"Don't you want your brother back at the mill sooner rather than later?"

"I want them all worried enough. Tha cousin would as soon spit on Ned as look at him. He won't be easily convinced."

Anne took a deep breath. "Mr. Gibson, I just came from the mill . . ."

"Aye, I know. I saw tha carriage go by, and then it came to me." Gibson uncorked one of the bottles of ale and guzzled it.

"So you never *planned* to do this?"

"Oh, I planned to do soomthing, I can tell tha," Gibson told her, his eyes beginning to glaze over.

Anne realized that she was dealing with someone who was so far gone in drink that he was almost as irrational as a madman. Her heart sank. There were all sorts of reasons why Gibson couldn't get away with this—indeed, would harm his brother more than help him, but Tom Gibson had left rationality behind years ago. Yet she had to try to reach him.

"I was at the mill to investigate the fire, Mr. Gibson, to see if my cousin was right in sacking your brother."

"Ned was never one of us, and tha cousin should know that. Ned doesn't believe in machine breaking; he believes in organizing and protesting. But protesting gets tha nowt, I told him. Nowt but a jail sentence. My Sally lost a babby while I were in prison," Gibson told her, his eyes filling with the easy tears of the drunkard. "And it were all Robert Heriot's fault."

"My father was a fair man, Mr. Gibson, and paid a good wage."

Gibson pounded his fist so hard on the table that Anne thought it would shatter. "Tha father, Miss Heriot, were willing to put in t'new machines that displaced workers, but never to replace t'old ones for safety reasons. 'Twould interfere with his profits, and his profits kept tha nicely fed and dressed and eddicated, didn't they? And able to buy thaself a husband in London, eh?"

Anne took a deep breath and said calmly, "I have been thinking a lot about the condition of the mills, Mr. Gibson. I wish to change things, if you would give me the chance."

"Oh, aye, easy to say that now, lass, when tha wants out of here!"

"But they will catch you, and you will hang for kidnapping, Mr. Gibson," Anne pleaded desperately. "How will that help you?"

"Tha will give Ned his job back and tha will settle money on me, enough so Sally and I can leave here—maybe go to America."

"I see. What if I promised to do that anyway?"

Gibson laughed. "Does tha take me for a fool, lass? No, Ned gets his job and I my money before tha gets out of here."

"How long do you intend to hold me, then?" Anne asked quietly, trying to keep fear out of her voice.

"A couple of days should do it, lass. Don't worry—tha has bread and cheese and ale, a workingman's diet, to keep tha going. I'll leave lantern; tha'll have light till t'oil burns down."

"Will you untie me, at least?" Anne pleaded, hating herself for begging, but how else would she manage?

"T'cellar is secure enough so I suppose I could do that," agreed Gibson, looking around. It was a stone cellar, and the door looked relatively new, for it had been replaced a few years ago when they started using the place for their meetings.

Gibson looked longingly at the two bottles of ale, but shook his head and smiled. "I'll leave tha both," he told Anne, "for I will be at tavern all night drinking anyway." He reached into his pocket and, drawing out an old knife, sawed away at the rope. When her hands were finally free, he picked up his knapsack and said, "I'll be back soon, lass, with more food for tha."

"Wait!" Anne cried, but he just climbed out of the cellar and closed the door behind him, leaving her in semidarkness. She could hear him securing a padlock, and her heart sank.

Dear God, she was completely at the mercy of a drunkard who hated her. Maybe he wasn't planning to come back at all. Panicking, Anne scrambled up the steps and pushed at the door. It moved an inch or so, giving her another band of light, enough to see the strong chain that held it shut, but still she pushed and pounded on it, yelling for help until she realized how useless it was to waste her energy.

She climbed down and looked at the pitiful supply of food on the table. Gibson had left the lucifer, which surprised her. But then, why not? She could hardly burn her way out. The door was wood, it was true, but even if she succeeded in setting it on fire, she would die from the smoke before she got out. At least she could extinguish the lantern and save oil, knowing she could light it again. Though there was still light coming through the gap in the wall, she didn't have the courage to do it. It was close to sundown, she reasoned. She would turn the lantern down when she went to sleep. Oh, God, how was she to sleep here?

Holding the lantern up, she surveyed her small prison. She hadn't noticed before, but in one corner was a pile of wool sacks. She could lie on those and even pull some of them over her. But that would be later. Now she had to act as though this were somehow normal. She put the lantern on the table and picked up the tin pot distastefully. She would put that in the corner next to the door where some air might come through to take away the smell.

So, now she had a water closet, a bedroom, and a dining area, she told herself, trying to look at her situation humorously. It was chilly and damp, but at least she wasn't exposed to the elements. Nights were cold in Yorkshire, even in early summer. She carefully sat down on one of the chairs and although it swayed a little under her weight, it held. She couldn't believe it, but she was actually hungry, and the bread and cheese looked better to her than any of the fancy suppers she had had in London. She decided to eat while there was still some natural light and broke off a piece of cheese and placed it on the tin plate. The bread was dry, and she was thirstier than she had ever been in her life. She supposed it was a combination of shock and fear and the climb up the scree. She opened a bottle of ale and tried sipping it slowly, but it was impossible. She gulped almost all of it down, till she realized that she had better save some. There was only the one other bottle, and who knew when Gibson would be back.

The ale gave her warmth and a little courage. After rewrapping the bread and cheese and corking the bottle, she sat there, watching the lantern flame. She had never realized how beautiful such a simple thing could be. She held her hand close to it for warmth and then looked at her wrists for the first time. They were rubbed raw and bloody and could quite easily become infected, she realized, with no way to wash them. She hated to do it, but the only way to disinfect them was with the dregs of the ale from the first bottle. She poured carefully, gasping aloud at the pain, and then she tore a few strips off her petticoat and tied them awkwardly around her wrists. There was one swallow left in the bottle and she finished it off.

All right, next her "bed" needed attention before the light was completely gone. There were six or seven sacks, the sort that were used for transporting wool. She lifted one to her nose and sniffed it gingerly. Surprisingly, other than smelling a bit musty, it was clean and held the rich smell of raw wool, which Anne had always loved. She spread three of the sacks out on the dirt floor, then tied the rest together at their corners, creating a sort of blanket. She stepped back and surveyed the place again. She was quite proud of herself, she decided. She would survive until Gibson came back or the soldiers found her.

Her ale-produced euphoria lasted only a short while, however, and when the last light died away and she realized it was time to extinguish the lantern and crawl under her makeshift covers, it took all her courage to do so.

She could feel the damp floor through the burlap

and, pulling her blanket over her, she lay there shivering.

"Tha will not get hysterical, Anne Heriot," she told herself out loud. "This will only be until tomorrow. Patrick will alert the troops. They will find you, maybe even early tomorrow." Then she thought of Patrick, hanging unconscious over the tree limb. What if he were dead? What then? But Gibson had promised to release her, and he'd have to come back, if only to get her to write out his demands.

Oh, God, why hadn't she listened to Jack? Why hadn't she waited a day or so, so that he would have been with her? Why hadn't she married him before coming home?

"Now don't be foolish, lass," she told herself. "Now that tha knows it were Tom Gibson, not Joseph, marrying Jack Belden wouldn't have made a bloody bit of difference!" Except that Jack would have insisted on escorting her to the mill. Gibson would never have risked a kidnapping with two men there to protect her.

How long would it take Jack to get to Yorkshire? And what would he think when he knew she was missing? Would he care? "Tha'rt being foolish again, lass. Of course he would care." But would he care because he needed her money or because he needed *her*?

She needed him. It was a sudden but sure revelation. Why had it taken her so long to see? She had been attracted to him the first moment she saw him, but she had fought that attraction, knowing it was pulling her away from safety, away from her world of debits and credits, where things could be made to add up, into a world where calculation was useless. Even when Jack had shown himself to be in sympathy with her, she had pushed him away, adding up, in her mental ledger, the advantages of marrying safely, of marrying someone she felt some easy affection for, not that maelstrom of distrust and desire that Jack Belden precipitated.

She had *had* to push Jack away, because somewhere, deep down, she wanted him close to her, inside of her, knowing her body and mind almost better than she did herself. How could she have allowed herself to admit that, given the circumstances of her marriage? She had always been in charge of her life, but with Jack Belden, the independent Anne Heriot was threatened.

But she wanted him, she finally admitted to herself. She needed him. And she suspected she was halfway to loving him. That was almost as frightening as being a prisoner in this cellar.

Love was so often described in terms of light and fire, but Anne realized it could also be thought of as a darkness, a place where there were no known landmarks. A place where one could so easily lose one's way, a place where black and white pages dissolved together. In darkness, things didn't add up. In darkness, one was blind and yet could see more than one had before.

She could see Jack Belden, could hear his voice and feel his hand gently touch her cheek. Please God, Tha will help me out of this, she prayed, and if Tha does, I will let myself learn what it is to love.

Chapter Twenty-four

Jack settled his affairs as quickly as he could and left London only two days after Anne. His ride was easier than at Christmas, of course, although the further north he rode, the more rain he encountered. Once again, he loved it, the freedom to move, the sense of having a mission. The dark mood that had fallen on him when Anne left lifted after half a day in the saddle.

He made good time, changing horses often, and reached Heriot Hall the day after Anne's disappearance. It was lunchtime, and he expected he would find Anne and Sarah still at the dining table. Instead he was ushered into the drawing room by a grim-faced Peters, where he found Sarah sitting with Patrick Gillen.

Sarah jumped up when she saw him. "Oh, Lord Aldborough, I am so glad you are here. I thought we had no hope of seeing you until tomorrow at the earliest!"

"I settled my affairs as quickly as I could, Miss Wheeler. I didn't want to leave Anne alone too long. Although I knew she was in good hands with you, Patrick."

Patrick lifted his head and Jack saw it was bandaged. "What happened, Patrick? And where is Anne?" he asked sharply.

"God help me, but I acted like a raw recruit and walked right into an ambush."

Patrick started to get up, but Sarah ordered him

down. "The doctor said you should still be in bed, Patrick."

"I can't stay there, not knowing where Miss Heriot is."

Jack felt as close to fainting as he ever had in his life. He took a seat next to Patrick. "What do you mean, Sergeant?"

"Patrick drove Anne to the mill yesterday," Sarah explained. "On the way home, they encountered a fallen tree across the road."

"I shouldn't have gotten down," said Patrick with a groan. "Although there wouldn't have been any way to get away from there without movin' the damn branches."

"There wasn't anything else you could have done, Patrick," Sarah reassured him.

"So you were hit from behind?"

"I never even heard him comin'. And when I came to, I was draped over the branches like a sack of potatoes and the carriage was empty."

"Was there any sign of violence?" Jack was surprised he could ask the necessary questions so calmly.

"It looked like she had fallen to her knees in the ditch and then climbed out. There were muddy prints leading up the hill, but I couldn't follow, sor. I was still too dizzy."

"I don't know how he even managed to drive himself home, Lord Aldborough," Sarah exclaimed. "He has a concussion from the blow."

"I knew I had to get back to alert the troops, Sarah. Enough time was lost as it was."

"Who do you think is behind this, Sergeant Gillen?"

"When we got to the mill, Joseph Trantor was just leavin'. He would have had plenty of time to get there and block the road . . ." Patrick's voice trailed off. "He was angry at Miss Heriot's visit and blamin' the fire on Ned Gibson, but I didn't see any signs of a horse and carriage, although I wasn't in any condition to do a full search," Patrick admitted.

"Could it have been Ned Gibson, then?"

"I've been thinkin' it could, though he never struck me as a violent man. But he's been on the run from the troopers for over a week now. He could have been skulkin' around town and seen us drive by. Maybe he thought he could kidnap Miss Heriot to get the troopers called off."

"But we have heard nothing, my lord," Sarah told Jack, having a hard time keeping her voice steady. Her hands were shaking, and Patrick reached across very naturally and clasped them in his. "There, there, Sarah," he said comfortingly.

Any other time, Jack would have been amused by the fact that a small romance had obviously been blooming and he'd never noticed, but he was too worried about Anne to dwell on it.

"I don't like the waitin', sor."

Jack was quiet for a minute. "I think the first thing to do is pay a visit to Trantor."

"I'll go with ye, sor."

"You can't, Patrick," protested Sarah.

"Miss Wheeler is right. And I need you here to wait for any communication that may come. Tell me how to get to the mill, and point me to the stables. I'll need a fresh horse."

"The stable lad can take care of you," said Patrick, after telling Jack the way to Shipton.

"Don't worry, Miss Wheeler, I am sure we'll have Anne home soon," Jack said reassuringly before he headed out.

Of course, it was easy to tell someone else not to worry, thought Jack as he trotted down the road to Shipton. It was easier to tell oneself that kidnappers had a vested interest in keeping their victims safe than it was to believe it.

When he reached the mill, he made his way to Trantor's office and walked in despite the protests of the clerk.

Trantor was absorbed in conversation with a man Jack guessed to be one of the foremen.

"Get rid of him, Trantor."

"And who t'hell art tha, sir?" Trantor demanded.

"Viscount Aldborough. Miss Anne Heriot's fiancé."

Trantor sank down in his chair, a puzzled look on his face. "Tha may go, Jacob," he said, dismissing the foreman. The man hurried out and Jack sat down in his place.

"I suppose congratulations are in order, my lord. May I wish tha happy."

"You may wish me to the devil for all I care," said Jack with an ironic smile. "But you will tell me where Miss Heriot is."

If the surprise on Trantor's face wasn't genuine, then the man made Kean look like an amateur, thought Jack, and his heart sank. If it wasn't Trantor, then it was this Ned Gibson, and where the hell would he have her?

"What do you mean, where is my cousin? I would assume she is at home. Why ever would you come here looking for her?"

"Miss Heriot's groom was attacked yesterday, and it appears she has been abducted."

"And tha thought *me* responsible?" Trantor was clearly shocked, at both the news and the accusation.

Jack sighed. "You do have a strong motive to wish Anne harm, Trantor. Once she is married to me, you have no chance of getting control of her fortune either by wedding her or . . ."

"Does tha think I would . . . what? . . . kill Anne Heriot to get her inheritance?" Trantor had gone pale from shock and then red with fury, and Jack knew both emotions were genuine.

"I am sorry, Trantor, but you did want to marry her."

"She never gave me a chance of asking her. But aye, tha'rt reet, I did. But not for her money! Though I won't deny I'd be happy to have it. I'd be a fool not to feel that way. No, I asked her because . . ." Trantor struggled with the words. "Because . . . I am reet fond of my cousin, Lord Aldborough. I always have been. But she set her sights higher, and I had to accept that."

Jack felt sorry for the man. Clearly he was sincere in his affection for Anne. And though he was harsh with his workers, it seemed he was soft as any other man where a woman was concerned.

Trantor stood up again. "My God, tha'rt wasting tha time with me when tha might be out looking for her!"

"So do you have any ideas where to start?"

"With Ned Gibson, that's where! Have tha had any messages?"

"Not yet," Jack admitted.

"Troops are on t'lookout for him now, but I'll send a message to the lieutenant to widen t'search. And I'll go down to Shipton to see his Nance."

"I'll go with you." The two men started toward the door. "And Trantor, I apologize for my suspicions of you."

" 'Tis not important now. What's important is finding Anne."

As they made their way through the narrow streets, Jack was very conscious of being watched. Nance Hutton's home was a small dwelling at the end of her lane.

Trantor pounded on the door, and a boy of about ten opened it. There was a mixture of surprise and fear on his face, Jack noticed, which confirmed all he had heard about Trantor as a master.

"Where is tha sister, Jimmy?" Trantor demanded.

"She'll be home any minute, Mr. Trantor." Jimmy hesitated. "Would tha like to coom in?"

"We'll wait outside," Trantor told him dismissively.

"Thank you for the hospitality, lad," Jack countered with a smile, and ducking his head, he went in.

It was a dark and cheerless place, but as his eyes adjusted, Jack could see Nance Hutton kept it spotless, despite the number of people living there. Three younger children were sitting on a cot in the corner, looking at him wide-eyed with curiosity and awe.

"Sit down here, sir," said Jimmy, pulling out two chairs from around the table.

They all sat silently for a moment and as the children got used to his presence, Jack was amused to see them start chewing the pieces of bread they had in their hands. They reminded him of young birds in a nest, and he gave them a smile.

Just as the silence was beginning to get uncomfortable, Nance opened the door and walked in. The two younger children jumped off the cot and ran to her, hugging her and clinging to her skirt.

"Such a welcome," she teased. "Does tha think I have soomthing special tonight?"

"We have visitors, Nance," said Jimmy with a warning glance.

Nance's face, which had been open and warm, closed down when she saw Joseph Trantor. "What does tha want, Trantor? Troops have been here three times this week. I'll tell tha what I told them: Ned isn't here."

Jack didn't doubt her; there was hardly room for those who were there. Clearly there was nowhere for a fugitive to hide.

"We didn't think you would be hiding Ned, Miss Hutton," Jack told her reassuringly. "We did hope, however, that you might know of some way to get a message to him."

"And just who art tha?" Nance asked angrily.

"Mind tha tongue, lass," said Joseph. "This is Lord Aldborough, Miss Heriot's fiancé."

A collective gasp went up from the children on the bed, and Jack grinned at them. "A very recent lord, I assure you. Before this spring I was plain Captain Belden."

"Why does tha want Ned, my lord?"

"Because he has kidnapped my cousin," Trantor

said angrily, "and by God, he'll hang for it if he's hurt a hair on her head!"

Even in the bad light, Jack could see Nance blanch. "What does tha *mean*?" she asked, her voice shaking.

"Miss Heriot came to investigate the fire at the mill yesterday, Miss Hutton," Jack told her calmly. "On her way home, her groom was attacked and she was taken."

"Aye, and another thing tha thinks to blame on Ned!" Nance said indignantly. "If tha troopers hurt a hair on *his* head, Joseph Trantor, I'll make tha suffer, I swear it. My Ned would never set fire to mill. Or kidnap Miss Heriot! Why would tha think that?"

"Don't get on tha high horse, Nance. He came for me first," Trantor told her with more humor than Jack would have given him credit for. "Ned might have taken her to get her to call off the troopers. Or perhaps just for revenge."

"Ned wouldn't harm anyone. And he isn't a vengeful person, not like that brother of his."

"Maybe his drunkard brother finally got to him, Nance," said Joseph. "Foolishness runs in the family."

"What reason would his brother have for revenge?" Jack asked curiously.

"He were put into jail twice by Mr. Heriot. His wife lost a babby, and he's done nowt but drink and rail against t'whole Heriot family since then," Nance replied, her dislike and disgust obvious.

"Could he be behind this?"

Nance was quiet for a minute, considering. "I don't know how. He's always so far gone in t'drink. He almost lives at t'pub."

"Jimmy . . ."

"Yes, Mr. Trantor," Jimmy said sullenly.

"Go over to Hart and Horn and see if Tom Gibson is there now."

Jimmy looked at Nance. "Go ahead, lad," she told him. "Miss Heriot's groom were attacked, tha said? I wouldn't have thought he'd tell lies about Ned. He seemed like a fair man."

"He hasn't blamed it on anyone. He was hit from behind."

"So tha has no proof at all!" Nance said indignantly.

"Who else would have a wish to hurt Miss Heriot?"

Nance was quiet. "I suppose under t'circumstances, Ned being sacked and all, it looks bad for him," she admitted reluctantly.

"Can you get a message to him?"

"I won't say yes, I won't say no," Nance answered stubbornly.

Jimmy was back in a few minutes. "Tom is sitting there, drunk as usual. Looks like he'll have to be carried out tonight, Nance."

"Then it doesn't look good for Ned, Miss Hutton," Jack told her firmly but kindly. "You would be doing him a favor if you got him to turn himself in."

"I won't promise anything, my lord."

"I understand. Come on, Trantor, let's leave the Huttons to their dinner."

After they stepped outside, Jack turned to Trantor. "What do you think?"

"I say it is that young firebrand," Trantor said stubbornly. "Nance loves him, so of course she can't see it."

"I am very thirsty all of a sudden. Why don't we wander over to the Hart and Horn and see this Tom Gibson for ourselves?"

It didn't take a genius to figure out which one he was, thought Jack, as they surveyed the pub. There was only one man who qualified as a habitual drunkard, and he was snoring facedown at one of the corner tables.

"Has he been here long?" Jack asked the barkeep.

"All afternoon, as usual. He wakes up late and then stumbles in here, looking like death warmed over. It takes an hour or so before tha can even talk to him . . .

and then another hour and he's off on his ranting, and then one more ale and he's out like tha sees him!"

"Would we get anything out of him now?"

The barkeep smiled. "T'Angel Gabriel couldn't wake him, sir!"

When they arrived back at the mill courtyard, Jack turned to Trantor. "Get in touch with the lieutenant, Joseph, and make sure the troops comb every inch around here. I am going back to Heriot Hall and pray that some word of Anne has arrived."

Anne slept fitfully that night due to the cold and damp and discomfort of the floor. Finally a thread of light appeared, and she lay there watching it grow wider, until the cellar became light.

Despite her grim circumstances and her exhaustion, she felt her spirits rise. "Sorrow may endure for the night, but joy cometh in the morning," she whispered. Perhaps "joy" was too strong a word, she told herself with dry humor, but at least a small ray of hope that Tom Gibson would come back, she would write her letter, and would be free by evening. Or, if she was very lucky, she would be found before Tom returned.

She walked around the cellar, trying to work the stiffness out and get warm. Then she pulled out a chair, sat down, and realized she was so hungry that she could have eaten all that was left of the bread and cheese. She forced herself to break off only a third of each, so that she would have "lunch" and "supper" left. Just in case Tom Gibson doesn't get back until evening, she told herself.

If it was hard to resist the food, it was even harder to resist the ale, for she was even thirstier than she was hungry. But she took only a few sips.

Once again, after eating, she felt strong and hopeful, and once again her euphoria faded as the reality of her circumstances was borne in on her.

"Tha must do something, lass. If tha were at home now, tha would be out riding or walking after breakfast. Well, tha can't ride, but tha can walk."

How many times around the cellar would equal a walk to the village and back? "Now there's a sum for tha, Anne Heriot."

It took her approximately thirty seconds to walk the cellar. "If it takes me twenty-five minutes to walk into Wetherby, then that's fifty in and back. That would be one hundred times around the cellar, lass."

The math was so simple even a ten-year-old could have done it, but it gave her the feeling that she was not completely helpless but had some control about what she did all day. Either she could sink into a self-pitying heap or she could start walking.

She walked as briskly as she could in such a small space, and while she walked, tried to imagine the road into Wetherby. "Now I'd be passing t'farm. And here's t'old yew tree." By concentrating all her mental energy, she managed to make the routine circles around the cellar bearable, and by the time she got to one hundred, she was feeling better.

While she was walking, the time seemed to pass quickly, but once she stopped and realized that a whole day stretched before her she wanted to crawl back under the burlap covers and cry.

"Tha will *not,*" she told herself. "Tha will do *something*!" She sat at the table and closed her eyes and tried to imagine the first page of her Euclid. "Tha will go through all t'theorems, lass, as though tha were back at school." And so she began, letting her mind rest in the sweet purity of parallel lines.

She deserved lunch, she decided, after all that exercise, physical and mental, so she pulled off the next third of bread and cheese. Her hunger subsided, but her thirst did not. It took every bit of willpower she had to keep herself from draining the last of the ale.

She felt a languorous tiredness coming over her. She

should be tired, of course, for she had gotten so little sleep. But if she napped, what would happen in the evening? Would she have an even more restless night?

"Tha will not be here tonight," she told herself as she stumbled over to the pile of sacks and fell instantly into a deep sleep.

Nance knew that Ned was still near town, for he had snuck back one night after the troopers had searched a second time. She sent Jimmy to the two places Ned had told her he'd use as a hideout, and late that night after the children had gone to bed, Nance heard a scratching at the back window.

"Is that you, Ned?" she whispered.

"Tha had better not be expecting anyone else, lass!" he whispered back, and half laughing, half sobbing, Nance opened the window and helped him in.

"Oh, Ned," she cried and threw herself into his arms.

"There, there, lass. What is it?"

"I had to see tha one more time before tha left."

"I told tha, I'm not leaving."

"Tha will have to now. Soomone has taken Miss Heriot, and they are sure it is tha, Ned."

"Taken Miss Heriot? What does tha mean? She's in London."

"She came home just a few days ago, after she heard about t'mill fire. She were there, asking questions, and on her way home, her groom was attacked and she was taken."

"Why, for Christ's sake, would anyone think I'd need more trouble tha I already have!"

"Mr. Trantor came here with Miss Heriot's fiancé. They thought tha might have taken her and be wanting a pardon and soom money to get away as ransom."

"Tha knows I'd never do anything like that, Nance. I never wanted of hurt t'woman, only to wake her up so she'd listen to us."

"I told them that, Ned. Coom into t'kitchen and I'll get tha soomthing to eat."

As Nance busied herself with leftovers and tea, Ned tried to make some sense of what she'd told him.

"So they think I did it because I set t'mill fire?"

"Aye."

"But I didn't set t'fire. And I've been trying to figure out who did. If they hadn't caught it in time, it would have destroyed more of t'mill, and more than t'children would have been out of jobs, Nance. Anyone who did that wasn't thinking clearly. And anyone thinking he could get away with taking Miss Heriot was either mad or stupid."

Nance turned to him at the same time as he stood up. "Could tha brother have been so foolish, Ned?" She was almost afraid to ask the question. Ned was disappointed in his brother, but he still loved him.

Ned gave a short, harsh laugh. "Tom could be that drunk, couldn't he, Nance? And think he was doing me a favor."

"But he were drinking at t'Hart and Horn when they came."

"He could have taken her somewhere safe and left her."

"Where? Tha've been using all t'safe places in town. And t'troopers are out in full force besides."

"Soomwhere outside of town." Ned thought for a few minutes. "I think I know where, Nance. Tom told me that they used to use t'old Witham cellar as a meeting place in days of General Ludd."

"Why, that's right up from scree," Nance's face lit up. "And t'path is right by where they attacked Miss Heriot's groom."

"I'm going to see Tom," declared Ned.

"Tha can't, Ned. What if soomone sees tha?"

"No one is going to turn me in, Nance."

"Be careful, Ned," Nance said, giving him a fierce hug.

"I will, lass."

The Hart and Horn was closed, and Ned knew his brother would have stumbled home. He snuck in the back door and crept upstairs to the bedroom.

His brother lay on his back, snoring loudly and filling the room with the stench of stale ale. His wife lay curled away from him, and Ned shook her shoulder gently to wake her.

She woke up and stared at him, sleepy and confused, until she realized who it was. "Ned, what art tha doing here?"

"I came to talk to Tom, but I didn't want to frighten tha."

"Well, tha already has," she told him tartly. She sat up against the bedstead. "There he is," she gestured, "and good luck to tha, waking him."

Ned walked around and shook his brother a few times. Tom only groaned and rolled away from him. Finally, Ned grabbed a pitcher of water from the washstand and poured it over his head.

"What? 'Tis too early to get up, lass," Tom mumbled.

" 'Tis Ned, and tha better get up, Tom, or I'll pour worse than water over tha!"

"Ned? What are tha doing here, lad?" Tom gave his brother a puzzled squint.

"I've coom to find out if tha'rt t'one who took Miss Heriot."

"Miss Heriot, Ned? Now why would I want to be troubled with t'bitch?" said Tom, giving his brother a sly glance.

"Tha did it, didn't tha! Goddamn it, Tom, why would tha do such a mad thing?" said Ned, grabbing his brother by the shoulders and shaking him.

"So she would take tha back. I did it for tha, Ned," Tom whined.

"Troops are back full force looking for me," Ned told him disgustedly. "Now where has tha got her?"

Tom shook his head as if to clear it. "Got her?"

"Coom on, Tom. Tha didn't just take her. Tha took her *soomwhere.*"

"Aye, I did," Tom mumbled, his forehead wrinkling in confusion.

"Was it t'old Witham root cellar?"

"That's it, Ned. T'old root cellar. They'll never find her there," he added proudly.

"Tha took her yesterday. Did tha just leave her there?"

"I left her there with food and drink. And I went back today." Tom rubbed his eyes. "Did I go back today? I can't remember."

Ned groaned.

" 'Tis t'drink, Ned," Sally interjected. "He starts drinking at Hart and Horn and forgets everything. But, Tom, how could tha have left her there in t'old dark cellar?" she asked, with growing panic as she realized what the consequences could be.

"I didn't mean to leave her there," he explained patiently. "She is going to write a note and Ned will get his job back and we'll get enough money to go to America."

"How does tha know she is still there, Tom?"

"I got a strong padlock and chain."

"Give me t'key."

"Now, Ned," Tom whined, "tha could get tha job back."

"I'll hang first and tha too, tha great drunken fool! Give me t'key."

Tom stumbled over to where his clothes lay in a heap on the floor and fumbled through his pockets. "Here it is, Ned."

Ned looked at his brother and his heart sank. Even if he freed Miss Heriot, Tom could hang for his actions, or at least be transported, if Miss Heriot was inclined to be merciful. Though why she should be, Ned didn't know.

"I'll go at first light, Tom. If tha left now, tha might be able to outrun troopers."

"I won't be run down like an animal," said Tom. "They can just coom to get me." As he spoke, he squared his shoulders, and Ned caught a glimpse of the old Tom, the brother he had been so proud of.

"Then tha'd better pray that Miss Heriot is all reet."

Chapter Twenty-five

Anne slept a good two hours, but awoke feeling less rested than when she had fallen asleep. She lay there, tired and growing more despondent as she realized it must be close to late afternoon and Tom Gibson had not returned. Maybe he was never coming back. Maybe he had never intended to let her go, but just to let her die here. Anne shuddered. It would take a long time to die of thirst and starvation. But surely someone would find her before then.

She should get up and exercise, she told herself. Walk around the cellar two hundred times. Go through Euclid again. Keep her hopes up. Divide up her remaining food so that she had a few bites for tomorrow . . .

Oh, God, but she couldn't bring herself to do it. What difference would it make if she walked or recited theorems? She was going to die here, slowly and alone, and there was not a thing she could do about it. She, the ever practical Anne Heriot, had no solution to this problem.

She huddled there and gave in to her despair. She would never see the sun again. She'd die clawing at the stones, maddened by thirst, like a trapped animal. Jack Belden would arrive in Yorkshire, only to find that his wife-to-be had disappeared. What would he feel? He would mourn the loss of her fortune, of course. She closed her eyes and pictured him hearing the news of her disappearance. He would be shocked, distraught, and angry.

He would be angry, lass, she told herself. It wouldn't matter why, and if he was angry, he'd try to find out who took her. He were a soldier, lass. A *guerrillero.* She pictured Jack in a motley uniform, riding through the mountains of Spain, searching for her. Tha'rt delirious, Anne Heriot. He doesn't have to comb t'mountains of Spain. He only has to ride t'Yorkshire moors.

He'd ride t'moor and he'd see t'tumbled-down house and he'd see where Tom Gibson had pulled at t'grass and he would shoot padlock off and climb down t'stairs and she would rush into his arms. She so wanted to be in his arms. To feel his strength, to let someone else carry the burdens.

She could feel the tears welling and the sobs rising. I won't cry, I can't cry. But her usual control had deserted her. The tears came, and she lay there and sobbed her heart out. "Please find me, Jack," she cried. "Please find me. I *want* to be tha wife. I want to have tha children. I want to love tha."

She did, she realized. She wanted to love him. Not just physically, although that was a strong part of it. She wanted to know him, to get to the heart of him and let him know her. He knew her strength and her independence, but he didn't know her need. She hadn't really known it herself, till now.

She had needed her father, she finally realized. All her life she had needed her father to put his arms around her and show her he loved her. She had known he loved her in theory, but, oh, theory was so cold next to what might have been reality. Her father had wanted to see only one part of her—her intelligence and her capability. But he'd never been able to see her need for love and affection. Perhaps because he'd shut off that part of himself. And so she had shut off her vulnerability, too.

"Please God, let Jack find me. And when he does, I promise Tha, I will give myself a chance to love."

* * *

When Patrick had stumbled into the drawing room, his head bloody, his eyes dazed, Sarah had gone into shock. Her first thought had been for him. She had gently wiped his face and bandaged his head. She was so intent on him that it took the strong grip of his hand and his agonized "I must go back for Miss Heriot" to make her realize Anne was in danger.

She was terribly ashamed. She had known and loved Anne for years, and yet her first thoughts had been for Patrick Gillen.

She was in love with him, but what he felt for her was unclear. He had never even sought out a conversation once they'd returned from London.

With the doctor's help, Sarah had persuaded Patrick to rest, and once Jack arrived, all was taken out of her hands. She had nothing to keep her busy but the everyday running of the house, and her worry over Anne's safety grew by the hour.

She stayed away from Patrick, making sure she wasn't at the stables when he was likely to be. Although she appeared her usual calm self, inside she was in turmoil. She was terrified that Anne was dead and half convinced it was her fault. She should have insisted on accompanying her to the mill! A kidnapper would have had a hard time dealing with two of them. And she should have been worried about Anne first, not Patrick.

By the afternoon of the second day, Sarah was sure she would go mad if she didn't get away, and after getting Jacob to saddle her horse, she rode the moor as though all the devils in hell were after her. When she returned, Gypsy and she were both exhausted, and there was Patrick in the stable yard, grooming his gelding.

"Let me help ye, Sarah," he offered. As she kicked her leg free, his strong hands went around her waist and lifted her down. It took him a minute to release her, and Sarah couldn't meet his eyes.

"It looks like ye gave Gypsy a workout," he said, running his hand over the mare's sweat-streaked side.

"I did walk her the last mile," Sarah replied defensively.

"I'm not blamin' ye," Patrick replied mildly. "I don't wonder ye wantin' to ride hard. God knows, I've been wantin' to myself." He added heavily, "I keep thinkin' it was all my fault."

"Oh, no, Patrick, you were attacked from behind," protested Sarah.

"That's no excuse. I should have stayed by the carriage a bit longer when I spotted that branch."

"But if I had insisted on going, the kidnapper might have thought twice about taking two women."

"Don't tell me ye've been worryin' at yerself, too! Ye've got no reason to, Sarah," he added, reaching out and running his hand gently over her hair.

His touch was so light but so caring that Sarah felt all her defenses crumble, and the tears she had been holding in for two days finally came. "Anne is like a sister to me, Patrick," she whispered. "I could not bear it if anything happened to her."

Patrick patted her shoulder awkwardly, resisting the impulse to pull her into his arms. "There, Sarah, we'll find her, I know we will." He hesitated. "Em, why don't ye come up and I'll fix ye a cup of tea? There is nothing a good cup of tea can't fix, me mother used to say," he added, smiling down at her.

Sarah wasn't sure it was wise, but she didn't want to go back to the house with a tearstained face, so she followed Patrick up the stairs. But it was hard to compose herself when all she could think about was her last visit, and when Patrick handed her a cup of tea and sat down next to her, she was so embarrassed by her memories that she stood up suddenly. "I should go," she said abruptly.

"I thought ye enjoyed our last cup of tea together," said Patrick softly.

Sarah could hear the hurt in his voice. "I did, Patrick. But I shouldn't be here with you."

"I thought we agreed last time that ye were old enough . . . I mean, independent enough, not to worry about what is proper," he said lightly, with a teasing glint in his eye.

"But I feel so guilty," Sarah whispered.

"Whatever in the world do ye have to be feelin' guilty about? I thought we decided that neither of us should be blamin' ourselves."

Sarah could hear the tenderness in his voice, and it undid her. "Oh, Patrick, all I worried about was you. I didn't even think of Anne. Maybe if I'd sent James for the troops right away . . ."

"Stop torturing yerself, *a stor*. A few minutes more or less wouldn't have made any difference." He enfolded her in his arms, and she rested her head on his shoulder with a little sigh.

"So ye were worried about me, *a stor*. And why is that?"

"What does *a stor* mean?" Sarah asked, lifting her head.

"What do ye think it means?" he teased.

"I would like it to mean 'my love,' " she confessed, ducking her head.

"Ye're close," Patrick told her with a smile. "And here I am sayin' it to a woman who hasn't said a word about love to me."

"You haven't given me a chance."

"Ye have yer chance now, Sarah Wheeler."

"I love you, Patrick. You are first in my heart, whether that is right or not."

"And ye are first in mine." Patrick sighed. "But how can I be askin' ye to marry me when ye're the granddaughter of a . . ."

"Don't even say it," Sarah told him with a little catch in her voice. "You can ask me very easily."

"Will ye be my wife, Sarah?"

"Oh, I will, Patrick, I will."

Patrick lifted her chin with his finger and kissed her. All the pent-up longing both had been holding in went into their kiss, which was long and deep and satisfying.

"I don't have much to offer ye, Sarah," Patrick said after they'd reluctantly and breathlessly pulled apart.

"You have enough, Patrick," she whispered. "You have yourself." And she lifted her face for another kiss.

By the time Ned got back to Nance's house, it was only a few hours before dawn. They spooned together on her bed, holding on to one another as though it was the last time. Which it might well be, if Ned was caught.

When the sky began to grow light, Ned pulled himself out of her arms. "I must go, lass," he whispered. Nance got up and flung her arms around him. "Why must tha take care of this, Ned? It were all tha brother's fault."

"Because Tom has done enough mischief already. I can't trust him to get Miss Heriot home safe."

"I love tha, Ned. Coom back to me."

"I will, Nance. I will."

Ned had to take the road out of town, and he was thankful for the ditches on either side, for at any sign of troopers, he could hide. But he was lucky and reached the crossroads safely. He climbed the scar as quickly as he could. He was about two miles from the old Witham place, and that meant at least half an hour of being visible on the moor, for the path ran parallel to the road over more than a mile. He was greatly relieved when the track turned off onto the moor itself.

He hadn't been up there for years, and he actually went right past the little valley. It was only when he'd gone another fifteen minutes without seeing it that he turned around and went back, walking very slowly now, keeping an eye out for the almost invisible path that led down to the ruined home.

He shook his head in disbelief when he saw the tumbled-down house. If it weren't for the place where Tom had pulled the grass away, it would have been impossible to tell the dwelling even had a cellar. If Tom had forgotten to come back, if Nance hadn't sent for him . . . Ned didn't even want to think about it.

He pulled the key out of his pocket, and as he fumbled with the padlock, he called down, " 'Tis Ned Gibson, Miss Heriot, coom to free tha. Don't be afraid."

He pulled the door open and went down the stairs slowly. At the bottom, he waited a moment for his eyes to adjust. There was a little more light than he expected, which allowed him to see the old table and chairs. The cellar smelled of dank earth and faintly of human waste. He looked around and saw Miss Heriot sitting against the wall on a makeshift bed of wool sacks, staring at him, her eyes wide with fear.

Ned didn't move. "I am not here to hurt tha, Miss Heriot. I am here to bring tha home," he said reassuringly.

"What of your brother?" Anne whispered. "He was supposed to come yesterday and have me write a note."

"Aye, he told me, after I shook him a little to jog his memory," Ned told her with sad irony. "He is a drunkard, Tom is, and he couldn't even remember whether he'd been back or not."

"So I might have lain here, forgotten." Ned saw her shudder and pull the sacks around her shoulders.

"Troops are searching for tha, Miss Heriot, and tha groom and fiancé. I am sure they would have found tha."

Ned wasn't sure at all, for Tom had picked a place that few people knew about. Even if the troops or Lord Aldborough had ridden by here, the cellar was too well hidden unless you knew what you were looking for.

Anne felt her whole body begin to tremble with relief. Ned Gibson wasn't going to harm her, she was sure of that. And Jack was out there somewhere, looking for her. She would have been found, sooner or later. She pulled the burlap sacks around her again to stop the shivering, and then Ned was kneeling in front of her, pulling off his coat.

"Here, put this around tha, Miss Heriot." He pulled the sacks away gently and helped her slip into the coat.

"What happened to tha wrists?" he asked when he saw the rough bandages she had fashioned.

"The rope rubbed them raw."

"T'rope?"

"Your brother tied my hands and dragged me over the moor," she said flatly.

Ned sighed. "I don't know what to say, miss. He did it for me, tha knows. To convince tha to give me my job back. Not that I am excusing him, mind tha."

Anne struggled to her feet, and he reached out his arm to support her.

"I can walk, Mr. Gibson."

But just walking over to the table made her head spin and her legs start to tremble again. She sank down on one of the chairs.

Ned looked at the crusts of bread that she had carefully divided up. "Tha must eat soomthing first." He shook the bottle of ale. "There is a little left. I am sorry, I never thought to bring anything with me, I was in such a hurry to get to tha."

Anne struggled to chew the bread, but as hungry as she had been yesterday, now she had lost her appetite. The few swallows of ale were welcome, but they only made her frantic for more.

Ned watched her hands shake as she put down the bottle.

"Does tha think tha can make it home, Miss Heriot? 'Tis at least six miles from here to Heriot Hall across t'moor."

Anne gave him a wan smile. "I don't think I can, Ned."

"Then I'll be off and coom back for tha in a few hours. Can tha wait?"

"I can. What is it like outside?"

" 'Tis cloudy and looks like rain, miss, so tha had better stay in cellar. But I can prop t'door open for light and air."

Anne gave him such a grateful look that Ned realized how terrifying the cellar must have been.

"Art sure tha are all reet?"

"Yes, Ned, I am fine, just a little weak and cold, and your coat helps with the cold."

As he turned to go, Anne called out to him. "Be careful of the troops, Ned."

"I haven't seen any this morning, miss. I'll be safe."

The light from the propped-up door was so welcome that Anne was tempted to drag herself up the stairs and outside. But it would be foolish to get herself wet, especially since she was just warming up in Ned's coat. So she turned her chair to face the stairs, and pulling another over, put her legs up. She could enjoy the light, because she only had a few hours of waiting and then she'd be free. She felt too weak to exercise and geometry couldn't satisfy her, so she finally closed her eyes and, starting at the beginning, tried to remember every one of her encounters with Jack Belden, praying that when she opened them, he would be there.

Ned was a mile from the house when the troopers saw him. He had known that the last mile and a half, when he had to come down off the moor, would be dangerous, and when he heard the hooves and the jingling of bridles, he ran down the road, hoping he could reach the field ahead and hide behind one of the stone walls.

He felt the bullet slam into him almost at the same time he heard the order to "Stop and surrender." He kept on running, but of course it was no use. He was surrounded in moments.

"He's hit, Lieutenant."

"Good shot, Corporal." The soldiers holding Ned parted as their officer walked through.

"Ned Gibson, you are under arrest for kidnapping and attempted murder."

"He's bleeding bad, sir."

"Miss Heriot. I have to get back to her," Ned whispered and then crumpled into a heap in front of them.

"We are only a mile from Heriot Hall, Sergeant. Take him there, and I'll take the rest of the men and continue our search. He can't have hidden her far from here."

Jack had spent a restless night, frustrated by his inability to act and anxiously awaiting the morning so he could be doing something, anything.

He got up early and after a quick breakfast went off to the stables to find Patrick, who was already up and brushing the horses.

"How is the gelding, Sergeant Gillen? I rode him very hard."

"He's recovering, sor. But if ye're riding today, ye should take Samson. He's fresh and eager for the exercise."

"I'll be riding," said Jack, "but where, is the question. I don't even know where to begin. It would be easier if Anne had been kidnapped by the French instead of by one Yorkshire radical! At least then I'd know the territory."

"I've been thinking, sor. I've done some questioning on me own, asked some of the maids and footmen if they know of any old barns or such like where Gibson might be keeping her."

"Did you have any luck?"

"No, sir, no place the troopers haven't already searched."

"Give me one of those brushes, Sergeant. I need to do something, or I'll go mad."

The two men had just finished with the last horse when they heard the troopers ride up the drive.

"They've got someone, sor," said Patrick, as they ran around the side of the house. "It looks like Ned Gibson, and it looks like he's bleedin' like a stuck pig."

The sergeant in charge of the troops was just dismounting when Jack reached him.

"Have you found her?" Jack tried to keep his voice even, but all the strain and worry of the past two days showed in it.

"No, sir. Are you Miss Heriot's cousin?"

Patrick snorted. "This is Miss Heriot's fiancé, Lord Aldborough, Sergeant."

"I beg yor pardon, my lord. I was told Mr. Trantor was here."

"He was yesterday, but he went home for the night. Is that Ned Gibson?" Jack asked, pointing to the limp body that two troopers were holding between them. "Did you get any information out of him before you shot him?" Jack added angrily.

The sergeant flushed with embarrassment. "He was running from us, and one of the men got overenthusiastic, I'm afraid. But he's still alive."

"But not likely to be much longer if we don't stop the bleeding. Bring him into the house," Jack ordered.

He had them put Ned upstairs in one of the smaller bedrooms and sent James into the village for the doctor.

"Get me some water," he barked to one of the maids.

"Yes, my lord. Right away, my lord."

Jack wanted to shake Ned awake and scream, "What have you done with her, you bastard?" but instead he gently pulled off his vest and shirt. "I need some cloths," he said sharply.

"Here they are," said Sarah, who had come in without his realizing it. "Patrick told me what happened."

"Thank you, Miss Wheeler."

Jack pressed the cloths against Ned's shoulder and soon they were soaked with blood. "More linen," he said, less sharply and Sarah handed him another folded cloth. It took three makeshift towels to slow the bleeding, and then Jack was able to inspect the wound.

"It looks like the bullet went right through," Jack muttered, "He'll live to hang, unless an infection sets in."

A quarter of an hour later, the doctor confirmed Jack's diagnosis. "You did a good job, my lord," he told Jack. "If he'd lost any more blood, we might have lost him."

"When will he regain consciousness?" Jack asked anxiously. "He's the only one who can lead us to Miss Heriot."

"So you think Ned is your kidnapper?" the doctor asked thoughtfully.

"Who else?"

"It just seems odd he should be caught so close to the house. Why would he be heading into trouble rather than away from it?"

"To make his demands?"

"It's possible. But I've known Ned a while. He's a good lad. I don't see him doing something like this. Someone needs to sit with him. Are you willing, Miss Wheeler?"

"Of course, Doctor."

"I'll sit with him." Both Patrick and Jack spoke at once, and the doctor chuckled. "As long as someone is here in case the shoulder starts to bleed again. He'll likely get feverish tonight, but I'll check on him tomorrow morning."

Ned lay still for an hour or so and then started to toss and turn. Sarah was up immediately, her hand to his forehead. "He is getting warm," she said, confirming the doctor's prediction, and dipping a clean cloth in the basin, she wiped Ned's face gently.

It was another two hours before he opened his eyes. Jack thought he'd never waited so long for anything.

"Water," Ned whispered, and Sarah looked at Patrick. "I'll get ye some, lad." When he returned with a pitcher and cup, Sarah had him set it on the table.

"Lift him up, Patrick. Gently now, so he doesn't start bleeding again."

Sarah poured a sip at a time into Ned's mouth and then motioned to Patrick, who lowered him onto the pillows.

Ned closed his eyes. "Ye can't be sleepin' yet, boyo," Patrick told him. "Where is Miss Heriot?"

"Yes, Miss Heriot," Jack said sharply.

Ned frowned and shook his head as if to clear it, then groaned as the movement jarred his shoulder. "T'troopers . . ."

"Yes, boyo, t'troopers got ye. But ye're safe now, so where did ye hide her?"

"I was coming to tell tha where she is," he whispered.

Jack started to move impatiently toward Ned, but Patrick lifted a hand to stop him. "And where is she?" he asked quietly.

"T'old cellar. Up on t'moor."

"What old cellar?" Jack whispered fiercely.

"Up on t'moor," Ned repeated.

"Is she locked in, lad?" Patrick asked.

"She were, but I opened t'door."

Patrick looked over at Jack, a puzzled look on his face. "But *where* on the moor, lad?"

"T'old Witham place," Ned murmured, and then closing his eyes, lost consciousness again.

"Wake him up, Patrick," Jack demanded.

"I don't think he can tell us anything more right now, my lord," said Sarah. "He's unconscious again. We'll have to wait."

"We can't wait. Patrick, you question all the stable and yard staff, and I'll handle the house servants. Someone must have heard of this Witham place."

A half hour later they met in the morning room, "Nothing," said Jack with a grimace.

"Nothing outside either, sor. But there's one person we haven't tried. Ben Rudd. The old shepherd."

"Saddle the horses, Patrick."

They were lucky Ben was at his hut, having just come in for a cup of tea and some bread and cheese.

"What is tha doing up here, Patrick?" he asked.

"Ye know about Miss Heriot, Ben?"

"That she got herself an earl? Aye, I heard that, Patrick."

"Only a viscount, Mr. Rudd," Jack told him dryly.

"Coom in, then, my lord, and let me get a good look at tha."

"We don't have time, Ben," said Patrick. "Ye haven't heard?"

"I've been up on moor all week, lad."

"Ned Gibson kidnapped my fiancé, Mr. Rudd. He's been keeping her in the cellar of the old Witham place. We were hoping you would know where that is."

"No, I'll not believe it of t'lad!"

"The old Witham place. Do you know where it is?" Jack asked impatiently.

" 'Tis up on t'moor. 'Twere used by General Ludd's troops. If tha rides up t'track at t'beginning of t'road, then tha must turn off on a smaller path west. Soomwhere off that path tha'll see a little valley. T'house is there, in that hollow of t'moor."

"Can you get us to the road, Patrick?"

"Yes, sor."

"Thank you, Mr. Rudd," Jack said, shaking his hand warmly.

"But Ned would never do soomthing like that," Ben muttered as the two men rode off.

They rode past the track once before Jack finally

spotted it, and when they reached the old house at last, he said, "My God, I can see why the troopers never found this place. If the door were closed, you'd never even think it had a cellar."

He dismounted quickly and, peering down the stairs, called Anne's name.

Chapter Twenty-six

Anne had tried to guess how long it would take Ned to get to the hall and then come back for her. An hour or more to the hall. Half an hour to tell the news and get the horses. But then only half an hour later or so back to the cellar. She decided to give him three hours, just to be safe. Having survived forty-eight hours, surely she could make it through another three.

She dozed in the chair, dreaming of Jack, but when she awoke, the sun was going down and she was still alone. She fought the panic that rose. What if Ned had been caught, or even killed, by the troopers? But she was free, she told herself, and no matter how weak she was, she could surely make it across the moor.

Maybe she should try to walk around the cellar again. She made it fifty times before she collapsed in the chair. Surely it was three hours by now?

Tha will not let thaself get hysterical, lass, she told herself sternly. Tha will stay calm, and if soomone doesn't coom soon, tha will walk out of here thaself.

She burrowed deeper into Ned's coat and tried to conjure up Jack's face again. Ned would get to Heriot Hall. Jack would be there. He would ride out to find her. He would fold her in his arms and hold her safe against his heart. "Oh, God," she said with a little sob, "I so want to be held there."

She was so tired and frightened and dizzy from lack of food and drink that she sank into a kind of reverie, and when she heard Jack's voice calling to her, she thought it was only a dream. But the third time she heard her name and someone lifting the door wide open, flooding the cellar with light, she realized she wasn't dreaming the rescue and stood up on trembling legs as Jack stepped down into the room.

Jack stood there for a moment looking at her. She was wrapped in an old wool coat, her hair in tangles, looking up at him with wide eyes as though she couldn't quite believe he'd come. Then they moved together, and he was holding her just as she'd wished, so close to his heart that she could hear its rapid beating.

"Thank God, you're safe," he whispered.

"Tha *did* come," Anne murmured.

"Of course, I came, sweetheart." He felt her shoulders begin to shake. "Are you all right, Anne? He didn't hurt you?"

She pulled herself out of his arms and looked at him with tear-wet eyes. "You called me 'sweetheart.' "

Jack began to stammer an apology. "I'm sorry, it was just that you looked so frightened . . ."

"But I am so glad you did."

Jack had no time to say anything, for Patrick was coming down.

"Mother of God! I hate to think what it was like here in the dark!" he exclaimed.

"Not very pleasant," Anne told him in a dry, tight little voice, trying to regain her equilibrium.

Patrick swore under his breath. "I'll hang Ned Gibson meself for ye, Miss Heriot."

Anne's eyes opened wide. "But Patrick, wasn't it Ned who told you where I was?"

"Yes, but he was only on his way to make his demands when the troopers caught him."

"Oh, no, we must get back, Jack. He likely saved my life. It was his brother who took me. Ned came out of hiding and risked himself to let me go. He would have taken me with him, but I felt too weak to walk."

"So it was Tom Gibson all along. I thought of him after questioning Joseph, but he seemed too much a drunkard."

"He was sober enough to get me here," said Anne. "He was going to come back with more food and have me write a ransom note."

"And instead he was lying dead drunk in the Hart and Horn. I was a fool not to question him further," groaned Jack. "You might have been home yesterday."

"It is all right, Jack, now that you've found me."

Jack looked around the cellar, taking in the pile of wool sacks, the tin chamber pot, and the last crumbs of bread. "How did you stand it?" he asked her quietly.

Anne looked at him and laughed. "It *was* awful, but I made myself exercise. I recited theorems . . . I thought of . . ." No, she could not admit that she had replayed every meeting with Jack.

Patrick laughed. "Ye are something, Miss Heriot. The Frogs could not have broken ye."

"Patrick's right, my dear. You would have made a splendid *guerrillero.* But come, let's get you home." He took her hand and helped her up the stairs.

Patrick led the horses over, and Jack mounted behind his saddle. Then Patrick helped Anne up in front of Jack.

"We'll go slowly, sweetheart," he promised, and she settled herself against him with a little sigh.

By the time the slow procession reached Heriot Hall, Anne had fallen asleep against Jack's chest. He handed her down carefully into Patrick's arms, and then, dismounting, ran up to open the front door.

Sarah, who had been watching out the window forever—or so it seemed to her—was in the hall to meet him.

"Show Patrick up to Anne's room, Sarah. I am going to get something for her to eat and drink."

By the time Patrick got her upstairs, Anne was awake, and although somewhat disoriented from her ordeal, she smiled weakly up at Sarah as Patrick laid her on the bed.

"Are you all right, Anne?" Sarah asked her anxiously.

"I am fine," she whispered. "Jack came for me, you know."

"I know, dear." Sarah couldn't help but be amused at the childlike pride in Anne's voice. She was sure Anne would be her own independent self by morning, but a little vulnerability toward her rescuer would not hurt the relationship, Sarah was sure.

When Jack came in carrying a tray with a pitcher of barley water and some slices of bread and butter, Anne pulled herself up against the headboard and reached out for the cup with shaking hands. "Drink it slowly," Jack warned her. But she couldn't; she was so thirsty, she gulped it down and held the cup for more.

Then she took a slice of bread and dunked it into her drink to soften it. She ate it slowly and with great appreciation. When she looked down and saw the crumbs floating in the cup, she gave a soft laugh. "I remember telling you, Sarah, that once I married a duke or an earl, I wouldn't be able to dunk my bread or muffins."

Sarah smiled and nodded. "I remember."

"You're only marrying a viscount, sweetheart, so you can dunk all you want!" Jack told her.

"Thank you, Jack. Thank you for finding me," she added softly.

"If it hadn't been for Ned Gibson and Ben, I am not sure I would have," he admitted.

"How is Ned?" Anne asked.

"Sleeping," Sarah told her. "He is running a slight fever, but that was to be expected, the doctor told us."

"He risked his life for me, and he had no reason to

risk anything for a Heriot," Anne said with a catch in her voice.

"Don't think about that now," said Jack. "You need to rest."

"And I want a bath," she declared, her voice sounding more like herself since Jack had found her.

"Then I will leave you to your bath and your rest," said Jack, planting a kiss on her forehead. "Come, Patrick, we need to make sure that the troops find Tom Gibson before he attempts to escape."

After her maid had helped her wash and rinse her hair, Anne dismissed her and leaned her head back against the rim of the tub, letting the lavender-scented water dissolve her stiffness, tension, and fear. When the water finally began to cool, she pulled herself out and, wrapping a towel around her, went to stand in front of the pier glass in the corner of her bedroom.

Her face was pink from the bath. As she stood there, gazing at herself, she wondered how Jack saw her. She let the towel fall; soon he would have the right to see all of her, she realized. What would it be like to have a man get to know her that intimately?

Of course, he did know some intimate parts of her already, she thought, blushing furiously as she picked up the towel, dried herself off and pulled her flannel nightrail over her head.

She realized that with all the thought she had given to finding a husband, she hadn't spent much time thinking about the physical intimacy that would be involved once she had one. She knew how children were conceived, but her "wifely duties" had been merely one of the practical details she had considered back in September.

But duty had nothing to do with the reality of it, she realized. At least not where Jack Belden was concerned. Pleasure, on the other hand, very much would, she suspected, and she crawled under the covers and fell asleep with a smile on her face.

* * *

After sending the troopers into Shipton, Jack left Patrick with Sarah. "I am going to sit by Anne tonight," he told them. "I don't want her waking up alone and frightened. That cellar was enough to give a brave man nightmares."

When he got to Anne's bedroom, she was fast asleep, and he settled himself into the small armchair next to her bed. He had intended to stay awake, but after only an hour his head was nodding. The worry of the past few days had exhausted him, and he fell asleep despite the discomfort.

Anne's cry a few hours later woke him immediately, however. She was tossing and turning, and he could tell she was in the throes of a bad dream. Leaning over, he shook her gently. "It's all right, Anne. You're safe," he whispered.

"Oh, Jack," she whimpered, reaching for his hand. "I prayed and prayed that you would come for me . . ."

His heart melted at the naked vulnerability in her voice, and he sat down next to her on the bed and put his arm around her shoulder. "There, there," he whispered, stroking her hair. "I did come." But, oh, God, how close he had been to losing her, he thought with a shudder.

He dropped a kiss on the top of her head, and her arms tightened around him.

"I *want* to be your wife, Jack."

"I know," he murmured.

"No, I mean I want to love you. I *do* love you," Anne confessed, burying her head in his shoulder.

Jack thought he had heard her correctly, but he wanted to hear it again. "What did you say, Anne?"

Anne lifted her head and gave him a smile. "I think I love you, Jack Belden."

"And I *know* I love you, Anne Heriot. So I would say our marriage will be much more than we could have expected it to be," he told her lightly, so touched by what she was telling him that he was afraid to speak more seriously.

"Do you really?"

"Do you think I call every woman 'sweetheart'?" he asked her with a tender smile.

"You might have called many a woman that, for all I know," she said with a spark of her old tart humor.

"I may have been called the Jack of Hearts, but I have never stolen nor kept a one," he assured her. He leaned down and captured her mouth, which she surrendered eagerly.

"You should go back to sleep," he whispered after they finally pulled away from one another.

"I am not that tired, Jack," she told him shyly, putting her hand on his chest. He clasped it in his.

"Truly, Anne, I should go back to my chair. I don't know if I can trust myself . . ."

"But I trust you, Jack." And she did. This man loved her. She knew it, not just because he had told her in words. She could feel it in his kisses, in the warmth of his hand holding hers.

"You shouldn't have said that," he told her with a low laugh, and he slipped his hand beneath her nightrail to caress her breast.

"You are so beautiful," he whispered.

"How do you know?" she teased. "You've never seen me."

"But I like what I have seen very much," he told her.

Anne reached up and pulling his loosened cravat off, opened his shirt. "You have seen more than I have," she whispered, and she explored his chest with her fingers, tracing the hair that ran down to his waist.

"You are playing with fire," he warned her.

"Take your shirt off, Jack, and light the lamp."

"So you want to inspect the goods, Miss Heriot," he teased her.

"My father taught me always to do that, my lord."

Jack lit the lamp and unbuttoned his shirt.

His shoulders and chest were broad, but tapered down to a slim waist. Anne drank in the sight of the black hair against brown skin and ran her hand down his chest again, this time going all the way to the waist-band of his trousers, where her fingers, quite on their own, busied themselves with opening his buttons.

"I must see all of you," she teased.

"It is your turn," said Jack, and pushing her hand away gently, he unbuttoned the nightrail and slipped it off. He buried his face between her breasts and then suckled one. Anne gave a sigh of pleasure and pressed herself against him.

Jack pulled away. "We have to stop" he said softly.

"No, we don't, not unless you want to. I want you to love me."

"I *do* love you."

"I mean with your body."

"You won't regret it?"

"Not unless you disappoint me," Anne said with a teasing grin.

"Oh, I will try very hard not to disappoint you," he promised, as he stood up and took off his boots and breeches and smallclothes, leaving them in a heap on the floor.

He stood there bathed in the lamplight, and Anne thought she had never seen anything more lovely than his tall, slender body. She reached out her hand and he took it, interlacing their fingers.

"Come, Jack," she whispered, pulling him down next to her.

At first it didn't seem that anything could be more pleasurable than his skin against hers and the feeling of pressure against her belly from his manhood. But when he plunged his tongue deep into her mouth, she realized their kisses gave them the intimacy that their skin so desired. Yet it still wasn't enough. Not enough. When his hand reached down and found her, she was warm and wet.

"Now feel me," he whispered and, guiding her

hand, placed it on the silky-soft yet rock-hard shaft. She ran her fingers gently down it and felt him shudder.

She wanted him inside her. Then maybe they would be close enough. So she pulled herself up until he was against her. "This will hurt the first time," he told her. And it did, the first time. But once he had broken through, the feeling of him filling her was enough to make up for any pain.

The second time it didn't hurt at all. She lost herself in the rocking motion of their bodies moving naturally together and the darkness of the place he drove her to, up and up, only so she could fall back down into his arms, crying out her release.

The next morning Jack decided he would reward the Heriot rooster with an extra handful of corn, for had it not been for the bird's early-morning serenade, he might well have been found asleep in Anne's bed with his arms around her. They would be married soon, it was true, but he didn't want the servants gossiping. He slipped out of the bed carefully, picked his clothes up off the floor, and made his way quietly to his own room.

When Anne awoke a few hours later and reached out for Jack, she gave a little sigh of disappointment, but she was also thankful for his thoughtfulness.

She felt wonderfully rested and absolutely ravenous. She dressed quickly, and when she got to the breakfast table, she found Sarah sitting over a cup of coffee. She gave another little sigh, for she had expected Jack to be there.

Sarah smiled at her. "He's gone to Shipton with Patrick, Anne. They want to see if the troopers caught Tom Gibson."

Anne gave a little shiver.

"I hope the man hangs for what he did to you," Sarah said with a hardness very unlike her. "Come, you must be starving."

Anne filled her plate and sat down. She didn't think she had ever enjoyed a breakfast so much. The fragrance of ham and sausage filled her nostrils. The sight of butter melting in the crevices of her muffin delighted her. And a whole potful of tea seemed like a miracle. She didn't have to measure anything out, and she could drink as much as she liked.

Perhaps it was the aftereffects of the night before or the food or both, but she had never felt so satisfied or so relaxed. The fear and tension were gone. She was safe at home. She was loved. And she loved. Oh, how she loved Jack Belden!

She sat back and gave another little sigh, this time one of utter contentment. "I don't wish Tom Gibson to hang, Sarah," she said seriously.

"But he must be punished," Sarah protested.

"Oh, I agree. But if he hangs, his family will be punished along with him. And he had some justification."

"He had none, Anne! You've never harmed him."

"My father did," Anne declared quietly. "He used the Combination Acts to take away what should be everyone's right."

"Machine breaking is not a right."

"But machine breaking didn't send him to jail, Sarah. He was only guilty of meeting with other workers."

"Plenty of men have gone to jail and not come out murderers."

"Tom Gibson is no murderer. Oh, he's a vengeful, angry man. But he's mainly a drunkard. He never intended to kill me."

"But you might have died, Anne, had it not been for Ned."

"Yes, but only because Tom had drunk himself into a stupor. It would only have been murder by omission, not commission," she added with a touch of humor.

"I don't see how you can joke about it!"

"I am alive, I have just feasted on ambrosia, and I

am marrying Jack Belden," Anne replied with a euphoric smile. "How could I hate anyone this morning?"

Sarah looked down to hide a smile. She had her suspicions about where Lord Aldborough had spent the night. She was sure it was not folded up in a small, uncomfortable chair.

"If Tom Gibson were transported, he would be punished enough. I would see that his family went with him, if they wished, and had a way to support themselves, either here or there. It would be his choice, whether he stopped drinking or not. His fate would be in his own hands, not in the hands of the Heriot family anymore."

"You are far more generous than I would ever be, Anne."

"I can afford to be, Sarah, for look at all I have."

Anne made sure to visit Ned later that morning. His fever had broken, and he was sitting up in a chair, gazing out the window.

"Are you sure you should be out of bed, Ned?"

"Miss Heriot! They did find tha."

"Only thanks to you and Ben Rudd." Anne sat down on the window seat opposite him.

Ned cleared his throat and asked the question that had been torturing him all morning. "Have t'troopers found Tom?"

"I don't know. Jack—Lord Aldborough—and Patrick have ridden over to find out."

"I am reet sorry for what Tom did to tha," Ned told her, nodding at Anne's lightly bandaged wrists.

"I am fully recovered, Ned. I wanted to tell you that I will press charges against your brother."

Ned looked agonized. "Tha has to, I understand that," he whispered.

"He *did* kidnap me, and I might well have died up there. But I will make sure he is only transported. I am hoping if his family chooses to go with him, he may take responsibility for himself and them again."

Ned's face was transformed. "I can't thank you enough, miss."

"And I can't thank you, Ned. You saved my life. I can't reward that by taking your brother's. Although he will be lost to you in a way," she added.

"He's been lost to me in t'drink for all these years anyway."

"I want you to take over as overseer of the carding shed," Anne told him, taking refuge from embarrassment in a brisk, businesslike tone.

"There is no carding shed, Miss Heriot," he reminded her with an ironic smile.

"But there will be, and it will have a new, safer carding machine. And the children's hours will be cut."

Anne could see Ned struggling with both gratitude and concern. "Without their wages being affected, Ned."

"Thank tha, Miss Heriot," he said with an openhearted smile.

"And after a few years, I am hoping to make you a foreman."

Ned gave her a look of disbelief. "I don't think Mr. Trantor will agree to that, Miss Heriot."

"Mr. Trantor works for me and will agree to whatever I say."

Ned laughed. "Tha sounds just like tha father!"

Anne blushed. "My father and I have some things to answer for."

"Tha father was a fair man, as owners go, Miss Heriot. 'Twas Trantor that caused some of the problems."

"Things will change, Ned, I promise you that," Anne told him as she stood up.

"Nance and I can get married," he whispered joyfully.

"Yes, and she can do all the whistling she wants about it!"

They both laughed, and then Anne placed her hand gently on Ned's shoulder. "I hope we will have many years of working together, Ned. Thank you again," she said softly as she left.

"Thank *tha,* Miss Heriot," Ned called after her. Then putting his face in his hands, he let the tears fall, washing away the terrible guilt he had felt at saving Anne Heriot's life at the expense of his brother's.

When Patrick and Jack returned, the two women were waiting.

"Tom Gibson met the troopers like a man, I must give him that," Jack told them. "He's in Shipton jail and shall be arraigned at the fall assizes."

"I want him spared, Jack. Will you do everything you can to have his sentence reduced to transportation?"

Jack protested and then agreed. "You are an amazing woman, Anne Heriot," he told her, his eyes warm with approval, and with something else that made her wish they were alone.

"No, just a very happy woman, Jack."

Patrick cleared his throat. "Lord Aldborough, sor . . ."

"Oh, yes, I forgot. We brought Miss Hutton back with us."

Anne smiled. "That was kind of you, Jack. Sarah, will you take her up to Ned?"

"I will." After a quick glance between them, she and Patrick left Anne and Jack alone.

"Are you sure you want to spare Gibson, Anne?"

"I am. Ned Gibson saved my life. I can't take his brother's. And I feel my father was partly responsible for all of this." She hesitated. "I am making Ned the overseer of the sorting shed. I hope you approve, Jack."

"The mills are yours, Anne," he said with a quizzical grin.

"I know I had it written into the marriage settlement. But I was hoping we might act as partners in everything. I would like to help you in your work also," she added hesitantly.

"I am honored to be your partner, Anne. We won't be able to change the British factory system, but perhaps we can make some small dents in it." He came over and enfolded her in his arms. "You fit just where I imagined you would. Just under my heart," he murmured, and she looked up at him and smiled.

"You have my heart, Jack. Is one enough for you?"

He laughed and then dropped a kiss on her lips. "We are one heart, now, Anne Heriot."

Epilogue

The wedding was to be held the third week of June, for Jack and Anne couldn't bear to wait any longer.

"I would have been married weeks ago, but we wanted our friends and family with us," Anne told Elspeth when she and Val arrived the day before the ceremony. "And I think we were lucky to get tha, lass," she added, only half joking. Elspeth had managed to get through six months of pregnancy without showing much, thanks to her height, but she now looked very pregnant indeed.

Elspeth smiled. "Actually, you were, Anne. Val doesn't want me going further than the garden, much less twenty miles away! But the baby isn't due for a month, and I told him I would come by myself if I had to. I wouldn't miss your wedding for the world."

"Especially since I am marrying the man you preferred," Anne responded with a teasing smile.

"Especially because you're marrying Jack," Elspeth agreed.

Jack's parents had arrived the day before. Anne had been very nervous about meeting them, but they were so obviously pleased with her that she relaxed almost immediately. Jack's mother was a striking woman, her dark hair and skin proclaiming her Spanish heritage, but her blue eyes clearly from her English father. She had all of Jack's charm, and none of his melancholy.

His grandmother sent her regrets, since she no

longer traveled. "But I expect you to bring your wife to visit me before the summer is over, *querido*," she wrote to her grandson.

So the wedding was small, just as Anne had wished, with their family, friends, and a few of the closest neighbors. Joseph was there, of course, looking even more reserved. And Ned Gibson and his new bride, Nance, were also at the church.

Anne had considered having Joseph give her away, but she decided she could not ask him to do something that would so obviously be painful. He may have been a harsh man of business, but he did care for her. She had considered Lord Faringdon, but in the end had asked Patrick, for it seemed fitting that anyone who took the place of her father should be a man like him. As fond as she was of Charles Faringdon, she was still just a plain lass from Yorkshire, and Patrick had become as much her friend as her employee.

As Anne walked down the aisle of the little church, Jack's face lit up. If anyone there still thought this was a marriage of convenience, he had only to look at the groom to know that this was a union based on love and nothing else.

"You looked splendid walking Anne down the aisle, Sergeant Gillen," Mrs. Gordon told him at the wedding breakfast. "And your new suit makes you look every inch the estate manager. Anne was very wise to promote you."

"Then ye didn't see my knees shakin'?" joked Patrick.

"It was good practice for September, Sergeant," Major Gordon teased him.

Patrick turned and gave Sarah a look that made her blush. "I'm not nervous about that a'tall, sor. 'Tis Sarah who'll be walkin' down the aisle and me patiently waitin' for her," he added with a grin. "Of course, I don't feel so patient now. I'd go right back to the church and marry her today if I could." Patrick reached out and captured Sarah's hand. "But we agreed it was better to wait until Lord and Lady Aldborough get back from their honeymoon."

"I hope the weather holds for them," said Mrs. Gordon.

"Even if it rains every day, the house is small and cozy. And I am sure they will find ways to keep themselves warm," Major Gordon replied with a gleam in his eye. "We always did, Peggy."

"It was lovely of you to lend them your house in Scotland," Sarah interjected.

"Scotland is a romantic place for a honeymoon, and our little stone house holds only good memories," said Mrs. Gordon.

Anne had moved through the morning in a daze. Only odd things stood out: Patrick's white-gloved hand covering hers as he took her arm, the heady scent of the roses in her bouquet, and the burning look in Jack's eyes as he turned to her to say his vows.

The wedding breakfast was lovely, but Anne could hardly eat anything. She smiled and chatted and cut the cake, but everything felt somehow unreal. The only thing real was Jack, and he was as busy as she was, fulfilling their obligations as host and hostess.

It wasn't until they had waved the last guests goodbye and Jack was finally at her side that Anne began to realize that they were truly husband and wife.

"I hope Elspeth doesn't find the ride home too uncomfortable," worried Anne as they turned back to the house.

"I am surprised Val didn't bring the midwife with them," Jack said with a laugh.

"She will have had her baby by the time we get back."

Jack leaned down and nuzzled Anne's neck. "And perhaps by the time we return we will have started one of our own."

They were to leave for Scotland early the next morning, and suddenly Anne was very nervous. The whole afternoon stretched ahead of them—their first day as husband and wife—and they had nothing to do until evening.

But she did have one thing to do, she remembered. "We haven't exchanged our own presents, Jack," she told him. "Go into the morning room and I will be right down."

"Mine is upstairs also, Anne," he said with a mischievous smile as he followed her up the stairs. "In our room. Why don't we meet there?"

Anne blushed.

Jack was standing by the window when she entered, carrying a flat rectangular parcel, wrapped in brown paper.

"Here, Anne," he said, handing her a little box wrapped in rose tissue. " 'Tis merely a token," he warned her.

"And this is for you, Jack."

Jack couldn't imagine what it was. Perhaps some sort of document. "Is this our marriage contract, Anne?" he asked teasingly.

"Just open it."

He ripped the paper while Anne watched his face. When he realized what he was holding in his hands, his smile faded, and Anne wondered if she had made a mistake. Oh, no, lass, tha has wounded his pride instead of pleasing him.

He looked at her, his face unreadable. "How did you know?"

"Helen told me what you'd done . . . I'm sorry, I shouldn't have, I see that now. You wanted to give me something that was truly from you and now I've spoiled it . . ."

"I spent hours looking at him as a child," Jack murmured.

"You look just like him."

"Yes, and I needed to know that a man need not

look like a Gainsborough to be worthy of admiration." Jack put the painting down and took her in his arms. "I would have to be a great fool not to appreciate your gift, sweetheart. You haven't spoiled anything. But how did you ever find it?"

"I got Mr. Smythe to search for it. The dealer had already taken it out of its frame, but we can have another made."

"It is a lovely gift, Anne. Now, open yours."

In her anxiety, Anne had forgotten the small box. It was obviously jewelry, and she half expected something like a bracelet to match her garnet necklace, or perhaps an heirloom piece from the family that his father and mother had brought with them.

It was neither. Inside the box was a small, delicately filigreed silver cube.

"It's a charm," Jack told her. "You can wear it on a bracelet or necklace."

Anne took it out. "It is lovely," she told him. It *was* lovely, but it was an odd sort of gift. She held it in her palm and then realized there was something within it. When she shook it, something rattled around inside. She looked at Jack, a puzzled expression on her face.

"It's a charm inside a charm," he told her. "From the Christmas pudding."

"You saved it all this time," Anne marveled.

"Well, I slipped it in my pocket at the time. I didn't have a hope of winning you, but I hung on to it anyway," he confessed with a shamefaced grin. "I found it a month ago and it seemed like something I could give you that would mean something . . ."

"Oh, it does, Jack," Anne whispered, lifting her face to his.

It rained two weeks out of their three in Scotland, but by the time the sun came out, beckoning them to long tramps on the moors and boating on the small loch, they were almost disappointed. After three days of activity, Anne looked over at Jack at breakfast and said wistfully, "I suppose we must go for a walk today."

Jack looked out the window. "It *is* a shame to waste the sun."

" 'Oh, western wind, when wilt thou blow . . .' " she quoted with a teasing glance at her husband.

"So you have learned to like poetry, Miss Practicality?"

"No," she answered seriously. "I have learned to love my husband. I have learned that love has nothing to do with debits and credits. And I would never have known that but for you."

"Then, to quote another poet, sweetheart, let's let that 'busy old fool' shine all it wants. We will go back to bed and pretend it is raining." Jack took his wife by the hand and led her up the stairs to the small bedroom, where they proceeded to prove to one another that they were each the other's debtor.